• NIGHTINGALE SONGS BOOK ONE •

UNDER THE LAVENDER MOON

by

CHRISTINA MAI FONG

OAK TREE PRESS

An Imprint of Acorn Publishing

This is a work of fiction. References to real people, events, establishments, organizations, or locales are intended only to provide a sense of authenticity and are used fictitiously. All other characters and all incidents and dialogue are drawn from the author's imagination and are not to be construed as real.

To my grandma, Alice Hsueh Mai Lee.

May I live up to your name in everything I do.

And to my grandpa, Theodore Yu Hsi Lee.

Your lives tell the story of the American dream

and the Asian American experience.

Without you, there would be no me.

✦　✦　✦

♦   ♦   ♦

UNDER
THE
LAVENDER
MOON

♦   ♦   ♦

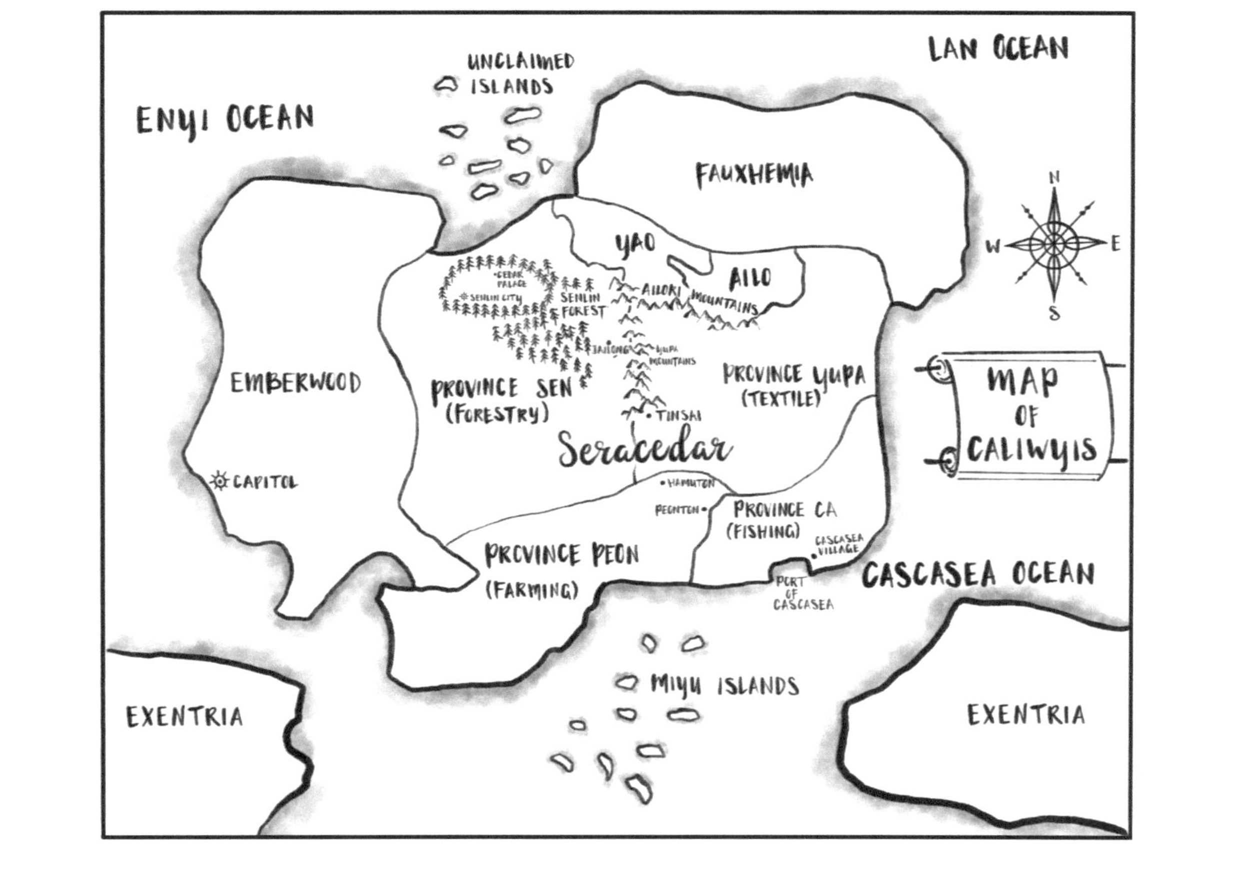

MAP OF CALIWYIS
LAN OCEAN
ENYI OCEAN
CASCASEA OCEAN
UNCLAIMED ISLANDS
FAUXHEMIA
YAO
AILO
AILOKI MOUNTAINS
CEDAR PALACE
SENLIN CITY
SENLIN FOREST
JAILONG
YUPA MOUNTAINS
PROVINCE SEN (FORESTRY)
PROVINCE YUPA (TEXTILE)
TINSAI
Seracedar
EMBERWOOD
CAPITOL
HAMMTON
PEGNTON
PROVINCE CA (FISHING)
CASCASEA VILLAGE
PORT OF CASCASEA
PROVINCE PEON (FARMING)
MIYU ISLANDS
EXENTRIA
EXENTRIA
N
E
S
W

CHAPTER 1

I hurried along the beach trail on my way home. A spasm pulled at the back of my leg. I winced. Five miles to and from the harbor every day. Would I ever get used to it? At least my eight-month pregnant sister-in-law wasn't making the trek herself. Thank Old Grandfather Heaven I'd finally convinced her to let me take over her job at the sea market.

A commotion of voices drew my attention down to the shore. Dozens of village girls and their mamas were gathered on the beach. At the sight of them, a shiver coursed through my body.

Your voice is powerful, and that makes it dangerous, Rilla.

My mama's warning echoed in my head. It must be that time of year. The palace scouts were probably in the village. But why hadn't I seen any notices of their arrival?

I continued down the path toward the crowd on the main shore. Someone there should be able to tell me what was going on.

The group of young ladies lounged on soft towels in the sand, taking cover under pastel parasols. They wore black knitted bathing suits that came over their thighs but clung tight to their bodies, flaunting their curvaceous figures. Behind them, their mamas stood baking in the late afternoon heat. The dedicated mamas wore ankle-length, black and white kipa, the formal close-fitting dress. The closed collar fastened around their necks must be stifling. I couldn't imagine wearing one in this heat. Yet the mamas dabbed the sweat from their sunburned faces and made no move to shield themselves. Instead, they readjusted the parasols to ensure the shade fully covered their precious daughters' delicate moon-pale skin.

The mamas' excited chatter carried like the clucks and squawks of squabbling hens.

"If the scouts see my daughter's magic, she is guaranteed to secure a spot in the showcase," one mama said. With one foot, she nudged her daughter's shoulder. "Show these aunties what you can do, dear."

The slender girl rolled her narrow, tawny eyes and let out a longsuffering sigh, but she rose on her knees and sat back on her heels. She leaned forward and stroked one finger through the sand. The shapes she outlined slowly lifted from the ground. Vibrant color poured from her hands into her artwork until painted flutterflies rose off the sand, drew breath, and soared into the sky.

Another mama smirked. "What an adorable tin-chai. Might be enough to get you through the palace gates, but certainly not into the emperor's harem. The key to becoming one of the emperor's beloved faela is seduction."

She yanked her daughter by the arm and forced the tall, full-figured girl to stand. I recognized her. I hadn't seen Galai Cresta since we both turned sixteen a few months ago and were no longer permitted to attend the village school.

Galai covered her plump chest, but her mother swatted her hands away. "Stop that. You need to show off your figure."

My mama, if she were still alive, would never parade my assets in front of the entire village. I cringed, imagining how mortified Galai must feel.

Her mama slid the straps of Galai's top so they fell loosely off her rounded shoulders. "Rehearse your water dance for these aunties, and remember to smile."

She pushed Galai toward the surf. With a reluctant groan, Galai tied up her chestnut brown hair into a bun. Then she dove into the water and twirled across the surface of the sea, her toes pointed in perfect parallel lines. Her curvy body shifted into water and fused with the waves as she danced and flipped like a dofei fish.

I waited until Galai came out of the surf. She saw me, so I waved. Hesitating, she looked at her mama, who was busy talking to the other women, before she approached me.

"Are the palace scouts coming?" I asked.

"I can't talk for long," she said. "But rumor has it the tryouts for the Faela Showcase start tomorrow."

"Tomorrow? But the palace usually posts a notice a week ahead."

"This year the scouts decided to arrive unannounced, but one of the village aunties heard from her cousin, who is a Supervisor Madam at the palace."

I had to make sure I was far away from the main shore when the tryouts took place.

"You should try out this year," Galai said. "Sixteen is the favorable age for being selected as a trinket. Everyone says you've got the most beautiful big eyes. I would die for your double eyelids. And I wish I had your petite frame. You've got curves, but you aren't fat like me."

"You aren't fat," I said. "You just have a taller, curvaceous figure. Besides, you have a tin-chai. I don't. The scouts rarely choose girls without tin-chai."

"The emperor has koong faela in his harem," Galai said. "He even has non-Shyan faela from distant kingdoms. Besides, all the girls who don't win the showcase stay on as serving trifles, and they get a monthly allowance of at least five hundred Seran. That's more money than my mama and baba make in a year."

I played with the ends of my long, black hair. I had no interest in anything the emperor had to offer. Not if it meant I had to leave home and give up my dream of becoming a healer. "I don't think palace life is for me. I'd miss my family too much."

Galai squirmed, looking behind at her mother. "Honestly, I would, too." She lowered her voice. "Don't tell anyone I said this, but I've always wished I could marry for love. Make no mistake, His Majesty is handsome and rich, and I'm sure I'll be able to fall in love with him. But what if he doesn't like me? What if I become a serving trifle and never know what it's like to be kissed? Or worse, what if I become a faela, and His Majesty never visits my bedchamber?"

I shifted my feet in the sand. "How can that be? If the emperor chooses you to enter his harem, it means he likes you. He wouldn't simply forget you."

Wouldn't he?

"I'm being selfish by having these thoughts." Galai brushed at her swimsuit. "It would be an honor to even be selected as a competing trinket. Whether I become a serving trifle or an elite faela, I'll bring wealth and honor to my family and fulfill my filial duty to my parents. That's all that matters."

Irica Tiders, my neighbor, came up behind Galai. Irica flipped her light, brown hair over her bony, pale shoulder. "Why are you wasting your time talking to her?"

I suppressed a groan. Irica was my nightmare and constant torment. Why did she hate me?

Irica's sharp eyes seemed to pierce into my skin. She sneered. "My mama and baba said that even though you're the prettiest girl in the village, you'll always be worthless as a koong without an ounce of magic in your blood."

How I wanted to wipe that smugness off Irica's face. If only I could sing one refrain. Prove I wasn't a koong.

But once again, Mama's words warned me: *Your voice is powerful, and that makes it dangerous.*

Irica wouldn't do anything to me now, but once her mama was out of sight, she'd bring some other girls to find me. Last time, they'd held me down and sheared my hair.

Irica grabbed Galai's arm. "Come on. Watch my performance. I'm going to dazzle the scouts."

Galai sent me an apologetic look, but she'd never dare stand up to Irica.

Irica sang. My hands rose to protect my eardrums.

"Today I dream of glory and fame,
For tomorrow all will exalt my name."

It was Irica's rendition of the Faela Anthem, *Exalted One*. The sea danced along to the rhythmic ballad. Jet streams of water leaped and arced in a grand display. Irica stopped singing, and the waves crashed. Applause and shouts of awe broke out among the mamas and girls watching.

Before she had the chance to sing another refrain, I scurried through the crowd. I fought the flames of anger and jealousy that rose in my chest. Jealousy. How could I be jealous of someone as vindictive as Irica? Yet I was. She had the freedom to use her tin-chai without worrying about the repercussions.

Meanwhile, I was forced to keep quiet and stay unseen. Mama had always warned me against using my tin-chai. I knew one of her reasons was to make sure the palace scouts didn't choose me for the showcase, but Mama said even after I turned eighteen and was no longer eligible to compete, it was too dangerous to reveal my gift. Girls could never become healers or doctors. Folks would brand me as an outcast.

"Forget this foolish dream," Mama had said. "You may want to help people, but they won't appreciate it. You'll only receive criticism. The only way to live a safe life is to do what is expected of you. That is to marry a nice village boy. But no man will want you if your ambitions are greater than his."

Yet no matter what she said, I was determined to become a healer. I didn't care if I was scorned. Not when I could do so much good with my tin-chai. If a man couldn't accept that, then I would never marry at all.

I continued along the familiar pebble-strewn trail. On either side of the path, clusters of purple wildflowers pushed out of the ground. The path took me to the whitewashed cliffs, high above the shore, where I usually went to clear my head and heart.

In the fading light of dusk, fireflies flickered like garlands of lanterns winding through the heavens. A herd of flying seahorses rose from the waves. Their luminous bodies gleamed like meteors. They galloped a short distance across the sea, then dove down, disappearing once more. I closed my eyes and listened to the soft serenade of waves caressing the shore below. Drops of sea foam danced on my skin, and salty spray wafted into my nose.

Other than a snorting sihai, its glossy gray body sunbathing on the rocks below, I was alone. Breathing in the fresh air eased the tightness in my chest.

A high-pitched caw drew my attention. My gaze fell upon a white-winged seatern hiding behind a patch of grass. Her wings unfolded and flapped, but she couldn't take flight. She spotted me and warbled. *Kee-yah. Kee-yah.*

"Hello there. I won't hurt you." I reached into my pocket for a handful of sunflower seeds left over from lunch and sprinkled them onto the sand. The bird hobbled out of hiding and ate as though starved. Part of her right wing was shredded, and infection had set in, exposing patches of ruptured skin. The poor thing would never fly again.

Unless I healed the bird. I had secretly healed a few animals before despite my brother's warning against singing in public. As long as I remained of eligible age for the showcase, it was a risk to use my tin-chai. One never knew who was watching, especially today with the scouts in Cascasea Village.

But nobody ever came up here. Tryouts weren't until tomorrow, and the scouts would be focused on the main shore where all the girls gathered. They had no reason to come to the most isolated part of the beach.

The bird cried out again. I couldn't look the other way.

Besides, it was infuriating to be forced to hide my gift when I could be healing the dying and the sick. Infuriating that I had to conceal who I was while Irica showed off her tin-chai and was praised for it despite not helping anyone but herself.

Without touching the bird, I drew upon my spiritual energy, my wyis, letting it filter through my soul channel and croon low in my throat.

> *"Although I no longer a child may be,*
> *The song of your zither still enters my dreams;*
> *Soft moonbeams navigating shadowed seas*
> *Play a timeless refrain of your memory."*

The seatern's wings swept open as the bones reset. Down feathers, soft and white, grew back and covered the bare skin in a fine coat of fuzz. The layer of gray flight feathers emerged and spread. The bird's dull, watery eyes sharpened and cleared. An animated *kip* escaped from her throat, and with a burst of renewed vigor, she ascended into the heavens.

A peal of laughter broke the stillness, the noise as sudden as a crack of thunder on a cloudless day. My heart pounded, the rhythm pulsing against my throat.

Hands trembling, I crept low toward the cliff's overhang and looked below, hoping and praying I wouldn't see what I most feared.

Two heads bobbed on the surface of the billowing swell. At first, I thought the heads were detached from their bodies, but then limbs and torsos—translucent and fluid—ascended from the ocean. The bodies of two middle-aged women, one blonde and the other a redhead, solidified. Their skin was covered in a shimmering silver sheen of water, which morphed into bright blue and yellow silk kipa dresses that fit snug against them. The cedar tree emblem of the palace was emblazoned on the back of their dresses.

Scouts from the palace.

CHAPTER 2

My heart thudded against my chest. What were the scouts doing here? They were supposed to be in town preparing for the tryouts.

The scouts waded toward the cliffs and climbed the rocks below me. From their vantage point, they would be able to see me, but for now, their gazes remained locked on the sunset. I was too afraid to move.

"There's a lot of talent here in Cascasea Village," the blonde said. "I like our new strategy. I get a better sense of what the girls are like when they don't know they're being watched. We might even discover a girl with a hidden tin-chai if we happen upon her unawares."

"I agree, but if you do find one that way, she might not have registered for tryouts," the redhead said. "Remember to make sure her birth date contains no inauspicious fours. We cannot make the mistake of bringing curses back to the palace. I hope that dancer doesn't have a four in her birth date. She was stunning. "

The blonde made a dismissive snort. "Nothing special, if you ask me. She's got more blubber than an yiwhal. The singer has much more promise. She made the water dance. Now *that's* talent."

"That girl? She's all skin and bones, not to mention, she sounds like a wailing water wanpo. She'll likely end up as a serving trifle, scrubbing a faela's chamber pot."

The blonde sniffed. "Well, it's not up to us anyway. Madam Yasmina makes the final decision." She turned to the stack of rocks. "Madam, would you rather represent a chubby dancer or a confident, poised singer who can make water dance?"

I jolted at the sight of a third woman. Her gray dress camouflaged her against the rocks. I could have sworn a snorting sihai had been sitting where she now lay. She stretched her lazy body, lifting her torso to sit up. "Shh. Both of you are making such a ruckus. A girl was singing the most beautiful song I've ever heard, and you interrupted her." Her gaze lifted toward me. I ducked. "I believe it came from up there. Do you see anyone? Having a lovely voice means nothing if she doesn't have the looks to match."

I pulled the hood of my cloak over my head.

The redhead pointed. "Look, Madam Yasmina. That must be her." She waved. "You there, can you hear me? Lift away your cloak and show yourself."

I pretended not to hear and stood.

"Stay right where you are. By the command of His Royal Majesty, you are hereby—"

I bolted, almost stumbling in my haste.

"Stop!"

I propelled myself down the hill away from them.

"After her. She's wearing a blue cloak."

Their shouts mingled with the roar of the waves. I dared not look back. I tore off the cloak and flung it into the sand. I sprinted to the main shore, my breaths heaving in my chest. The girls and their mothers were still there. The black blouse and white skirt I wore blended in among the kipa the mamas wore, but the scouts could still detect my age if they looked at faces.

I slowed to a saunter and lowered my head, mingling with the crowd. Footsteps and shouts sounded behind me. I risked a peek at the scouts. The blonde and the redhead were here, but I didn't see the third woman who had been lounging on the rocks.

The blonde scout turned to the redhead. "Where did she go?"

Their blue and yellow kipa dresses stood out, especially with the cedar crest stamped upon them. Perfect.

I approached a village girl practicing her twirling with her mama's coaching.

"Look. Are those the scouts?" I pointed to the approaching women.

The girl's mama saw them. Her eyes widened. She murmured to another mother and daughter pair. "They're here."

Whispers spread. Eager mothers and daughters vying for attention enveloped the scouts. I slowly retreated, and when I was sure no one could see me, I ran.

I returned home, still shaken. Darkness bathed my brother and sister-in-law's room. He wasn't back from work, and she was probably resting. A decade older than me, they were my second set of parents, and I was in for a lecture.

I hadn't realized the scouts would be spying on us. Perhaps it had been foolish to heal that bird, but I didn't regret it. No use thinking about what I'd already done. But I needed to make sure the scouts didn't catch me again.

If the scouts had been hiding today, then they might do the same tomorrow. I could conceal my tin-chai, but what if they were also looking for koong girls? The village aunties always gossiped about how it was a pity I had the looks but no magic. If the scouts saw me, they might think I was pretty enough to take to the palace anyway.

Cedar Palace, the emperor's residence, was based in the capitol, Senlin City. It was so far from home, at least a three-week journey. I didn't want to leave. I wanted to stay with my family, in the same house where I was born, where it was safe and familiar and comfortable.

I studied my childhood home. The four sections of our cozy house encircled the courtyard on each side of the quadrangle. My brother and sister-in-law's quarters lay on the east side, and my own bright bedroom was opposite theirs on the west side. The sign of our family surname—written in the ancient Shyan characters—hung above our front door. Beyond the entryway, the stone bench sat in the center of our courtyard. Lion sculptures and bright coral peonies surrounded it. When my parents were alive, we sat there to stargaze during the warm summer nights and listened to Mama play folk tunes on her zither. If I left, I'd never see any of this again.

No, I would make sure the scouts found me thoroughly disgusting if we met again.

I set to work and boiled onions and garlic with a special fermented thousand-year-old bean paste. It was called thousand-year-old paste for a reason. The whole kitchen smelled like something behind the walls had decayed and molded. I dipped the hem of the dress I planned to wear to work tomorrow into the nasty concoction.

I mixed clay, water, and red paint in a bowl. I took this into my room and used the hardening cement to create tiny globules. I applied this to my face, plastering my skin with fake boils and bulging red nodules.

Nia, my sister-in-law, wobbled into my room, round belly first. My future niece or nephew would be popping out any day now. "What have you done to the kitchen? I'm burning three candles in my room just to tolerate the smell. How am I to make supper?"

"I'll make it when I'm done here. Sorry if it's causing you to feel nauseated."

She saw what I'd done to my face and folded her arms across her chest. "All right, explain."

"The palace scouts are in the village, and they heard me sing."

"Oh no." Nia plopped onto the edge of my bed. The bedsprings groaned under her weight.

"Don't worry," I said quickly. "I managed to outrun them, and they didn't see my face. I don't think they saw me heal the bird either. They just heard me. I'm taking extra precautions to make myself look ugly when I go to work tomorrow."

"You're not leaving this house until tryouts are over and the scouts have left the village. I'll tell Auntie An that I'll return to work until then." She struggled to stand, but her ripe belly impeded her movements.

"No. You can't be trekking up and down those beach cliffs. What if the baby decides to come early?"

"Both of us will stay home then. I'm sure Auntie An won't mind."

"Auntie An is too kind to say anything. She has no one else to help her." Auntie An had been my parents' closest friend when they were still alive, and she had no children of her own. Her fiancé had been killed years ago in Terran's war against the Miyu, and she had never been able to forget him. She'd never had the desire to marry if not for love. She was getting older, and if she didn't have her sea market booth to support her financially and us to help her run the business, she'd be living in poverty. There was no place in this kingdom for an aging, unmarried woman.

"I promised to work until you're able to return. I won't break my word." I looked into the mirror. "Do you think this is enough to keep the scouts away from me?"

Nia pinched her nose. "Hmm. Smell's an overkill in my opinion." She fanned the air with one hand and studied me a second time. "I hate to say it, but no amount of dirt will hide your beautiful brown eyes, among other things."

Her look acknowledged my ample chest. She reached for something in the closet. "I can't do anything about your eyes, but I think I can solve the other problem." She handed me a long strip of cotton cloth. "You need to bind your breasts. The flatter, the better."

She opened the back of my dress and wound the strip around me, tightening the bindings until they constricted my airflow. The material chafed my skin. I inhaled, and my ribcage felt on the verge of shattering. A sharp pain gathered in my chest.

"It's too tight."

Nia rebuttoned my dress. "Don't whine. You chose to sing where anyone could hear you, and this is the consequence. Your brother will want to talk to you about this."

Footsteps echoed in the courtyard outside my room and stopped outside the door. I heard my brother say, "You sang in public?"

Nia opened the sliding door to let him in. "It gets worse. The scouts heard her."

Rell regarded me and scrunched his brow. "What do you have on your face?"

I smoothed out my dress. "It's a disguise. The scouts didn't get a good look at me, but I want to be sure they overlook me in case we cross paths again. I didn't know this year they started spying on girls before tryouts."

"This is serious," Rell said. "If they discover your gift, they'll take you."

"I know. I'll be more careful next time."

"If you really understood, you wouldn't have opened your mouth at all."

I was taken aback by Rell's sharp tone. He rarely lost his temper. But this went deeper than anger. This was fear.

Nia's gentle gray eyes met Rell's, and they exchanged a knowing look.

"I'll go clean the kitchen and make supper," she said. "The two of you should talk."

I followed Rell to the main house. As we always did in the evening, following the commandments in the Analects of Heaven, we approached the mantel to burn incense and pay respects to the emperor and our parents.

Emperor Terran's massive portrait, mounted in a solid oak frame and gilded with gold leaf trimming, hung on the wall. Three summers ago, Terran had gifted it to all of his subjects for the celebration of his fortieth birthday. All subjects were required to display the current emperor's image in our homes.

Though he was a little past his prime, he had aged well. Despite some extra weight around his waistline, he still had chiseled features, a strong jawline, and deep, brooding eyes. He maintained a full head of hair with no sign of balding. His dark hair, kept long to signify wealth and power, was tied in a topknot that didn't hide the few strands of silver, the only sign Wise Grandmother Time spared no one.

I understood why many of the girls wished to become his concubine despite his age and knowing they'd have to compete with other women for his affection. If his policies hadn't been the reason my parents were dead, I might find him attractive. Handsome even. If one had to be bound to an older man, Emperor Terran was a better option than a decrepit man with no teeth.

But if I had any desire to marry into royalty, I would rather marry a prince closer to my age. I wondered if Terran's sons took after him. The older princes must be of marriageable age. Did it bother them that their new stepmothers were younger than them? I never paid much attention to the latest gossip regarding the princes and had lost count of how many were still alive. It seemed every few months brought news of either a new prince's birth or a prince's tragic demise, killed in a hunting accident, perhaps, or by sickness.

My attention turned to the two modest frames that hung on either side of Terran's portrait. My father, Baba, was on the left. He looked like an older version of Rell. His straight, black hair was cut above his ears, styled in short spikes. His grin swept wide across his face, and his deep, dark brown eyes—the part of him I'd inherited—twinkled with humor. Right by his side was Mama with her tawny eyes and long, honey locks. She was unsmiling, as serious in the portrait as she had been in reality.

I reached for an incense stick, lit it, and raised it above my head. I knelt by their portraits and bowed my head to honor their memory. Cinnamon and frankincense drifted from the end of the burning stick, forming a wave of smoke that rose to the ceiling. I set the stick in the censer that lay before Mama and Baba's portraits. Rell did the same. Then we knelt on the floor, sitting back on our heels, and watched the incense burn.

Rell glowered and pointed at the emperor's portrait. "If the palace scouts catch you, you will be forced to serve him as a slave or a faela. We'll never see each other again. Do you want that to be your fate?"

"Of course not." I looked upon Mama and Baba's faces, and a rush of emotion caused tears to rim my eyes. "I dislike Terran as much as you do."

"Then how could you be so foolish to use your tin-chai where anyone could see?" Rell slammed a hand down on the wooden floor. "Didn't you pay any attention to Mama's warnings? She told you revealing your tin-chai is dangerous."

"That's only because she feared the villagers would disapprove of my ambition to become a healer, and no one would ever want to marry me."

"No, it's also because she knew if the palace discovered your gift, you could be forced to compete in the showcase," Rell said.

"I get it," I said, feeling a surge of exasperation. "I made a mistake today. Won't happen again. I won't use my tin-chai until I'm no longer eligible for the showcase."

Rell glared at me. "Are you naïve enough to believe age will stop the palace from taking you?"

"What do you mean?" I frowned. "The law states that when a girl reaches eighteen years she no longer meets the requirements of the showcase and is free to marry the man she chooses."

"Emperor Terran considers himself above the law. That would never stop him if he desired you and your tin-chai," my brother said. "That's why Mama was so insistent for you to hide it. She told me once that she would prefer death than life in the palace."

"Mama must have been exaggerating. How could she know about the palace when she was never there?"

Rell swept a hand through his hair. "You don't understand. She was there. Mama was a showcase trinket."

My mouth fell open. "Mama was a trinket?"

Why hadn't she ever told me? And how had she escaped? I thought all competing trinkets were never permitted to leave whether they won or lost the showcase.

"She competed when Emperor Yikan was still on the throne," Rell said.

The current emperor's father.

"Mama saw Emperor Yikan use his tin-chai to turn his older faela, trifles, and trinkets into terracotta statues if they refused his advances."

I knew Yikan had been a terrible and abusive man. He had cared more about bedding women than running the kingdom's four provinces. He had ruined the economy, and many had died under his rule.

"None of the girls wanted to become Yikan's faela, knowing of his abuse. They were forced to the palace anyway. Mama tried to run away. She was caught and imprisoned, but a princess helped her escape by hiding her in the compost bin. She was so afraid the palace would find her that she never returned to her family. Instead, she came here, the village furthest away from the capital, and she took on a new identity."

I stared at Mama's portrait. What other secrets had she taken to her grave? I didn't even know if she had a tin-chai. I'd asked my brother once, but Mama had never told him either. Perhaps she would have told us everything if she hadn't been killed.

"Why didn't she ever talk about it?" I asked.

"You were still so young when she was alive. The only reason I know is because Baba and Mama caught me eavesdropping, and I was old enough that they had to explain everything to me."

I returned my gaze to Terran's portrait. A golden headdress, rectangular and decorated with twelve strands of jade beads, crowned his head. His right hand held a long staff, the Sacred Cedar Scepter. Carved in its head was the emblem of Seracedar, a cedar tree extending its branches as though offering prayers to Old Grandfather Heaven. The Sacred Cedar Scepter symbolized that Terran possessed the Will of Heaven, and the scepter's power had amplified his tin-chai, granting him the ability to command numerous natural elements. He could summon fire and lightning, bend the earth and trees to his will, even control the wind and water.

Terran's tin-chai was another reason women found him desirable. Though it frightened me to imagine what he could do with such powers if he were as corrupt as his father.

"Mama was in the palace during Yikan's reign," I said. "But Old Grandfather Heaven interfered by removing Yikan from power and granting Terran the Will of Heaven. Surely Terran treats the showcase trinkets and his faela better than Yikan did."

Witnesses said the moment Terran touched the scepter, his tin-chai had amplified, and Yikan died from a heart attack.

"I thought to spare you from knowing the full extent of Terran's oppression and what Mama witnessed. I wanted to preserve your childhood and make you feel safe. I wanted you to continue believing you could be a healer without crushing your dream, at least for a little while. But I can't protect you from reality anymore."

"I know our family hates Terran because his politics were responsible for killing Mama and Baba, but what makes you think I will still be in danger of being taken to the palace after I turn eighteen? Why can't I be free to be a healer and use my tin-chai? Terran is the one who set the age requirement for the showcase. He wouldn't break his own rules. At least in that way, he isn't like his father."

"No. He's worse," Rell said.

"No one could be worse than Yikan." At least that's what I'd learned in school. "Even Terran apologized for his father's wrongs. He vowed to restore prosperity to Seracedar and to treat all his subjects with respect. Besides, why would Old Grandfather Heaven have given him the Will of Heaven if he wasn't sincere?"

Rell's glare could have burned a hole through Terran's portrait. "Terran may have started his reign determined to right his father's wrongs, but he never put those promises into action."

"What about when he expanded our kingdom to bring more resources to Seracedar?"

Terran had conquered the kingdoms of the rock-dwelling Ailo and shapeshifting spirit creatures called Yao, two nations that produced gold and precious gemstones in their mountains. They provided tribute to Terran, and in return, our kingdom's army protected them from invaders.

Rell made a sound of disgust. "Terran forced the Yao and Ailo to give him all their assets. They've been left with nothing. The only threat to them was us. They pay tribute to Terran so our army won't slaughter their people anymore."

I had never felt so ignorant. My fists clenched. "Then why did the newspapers say all three kingdoms have benefited, and the economy is growing stronger?"

"If you believe everything you're told without question, perhaps I have coddled you too much." Rell rubbed his temples as though it hurt him to think. "Did the palace come to our aid after the tidal wave devastated the harbor? It has been seven years, and Terran has yet to offer the finances needed to rebuild the port."

"Then where is all the money going?"

"Financing all of Terran's ridiculous wars, of course," Rell said. "If he truly cared about his people, he would not have sent our men to be slaughtered by the Miyu."

I could not disagree with him on that point. Our men didn't stand a chance against the Miyu, creatures who were half fish and half woman. They had powerful hallucinogenic magic and were said to be demigoddesses, descendants of the sea goddess Mi, but unable to have sons. Sailors and fishermen told tales of how the Miyu women trapped men and used them to breed.

But Baba had told me that the Miyu never attacked a ship or seduced a man unless they were threatened first.

"Terran should have surrendered long ago instead of hiring those vulgar pirates." Rell's gaze lingered on Mama and Baba's pictures again, and a sadness that I knew all too well filled his face. Even Wise Grandmother Time had no power over grief.

Mercenary pirates had offered Terran their services to hunt the Miyu, but they had also plundered fishing villages. The pirates who killed my parents had never been found.

"There are also talks of that rebel group called the Zhynites stirring up trouble again," Rell said. "Rumor is they are trying to convince the Embers to help them overthrow Terran. Though I'm sympathetic to their cause, I'm afraid another war would only devastate the kingdom further."

My brother closed his eyes. A crease formed between his brows, and he lowered his head. I knew he was talking to our parents, saying a prayer, as he often did when something troubled him.

When he looked at me again, his eyes had a glassy sheen. "I must make you understand. You and others like you, those with powerful tin-chai, must not fall into Terran's hands. He could use your gift as a weapon to further his political agenda and conquer the world. Your tin-chai would heal all of our soldiers and create an invincible army to crush the opposing side."

A tin-chai used as a political weapon? The thought was so horrifying, I would never have even dreamt it. "Terran wouldn't be that evil, would he?"

"All I know is what Mama told me. When she was imprisoned, another girl was charged with murdering a prince. Her tin-chai allowed her to liquefy people with her stare. Terran promised to set her free if she helped him kill his enemies, but Terran's fiancée, the current Empress Limera, begged him not to use the girl as a weapon. Terran agreed. But a day later, Terran came for the girl. He blinded her, then gifted her to a powerful nobleman in exchange for his allegiance."

My stomach twisted into knots. No wonder Mama lived in such fear. If Terran had committed such evil back then, he was sure to have crossed more lines since. What other terrible deeds might he have executed behind the palace walls? And what if he did find out about my tin-chai? I didn't want to become his puppet.

"I know it is your dream to become a healer," Rell said. "But right now, you must think of your safety first. Then maybe one day you'll be in a position to help with no risk to yourself. Sometimes we need to lose a battle to win the war."

Lose a battle to win the war.

Baba had always repeated the adage, though I wasn't fond of it.

He believed evil people would receive justice one day, but we could do nothing for now except stay alive.

"One day, things will get better," he always said.

But how could a war be won if soldiers refused to fight? And why couldn't "one day" be now? Rell's warning did scare me, but I couldn't just hide from the palace my whole life.

"I know you're worried the scouts will find me," I said. "But I can't let them stop me from fulfilling my promises. Auntie An has no family to help her. She only has us."

Rell hesitated another moment, then sighed. I had won this point at least. "If it wasn't for Auntie An's sake, I wouldn't allow you to go. Just promise me. No matter what, do not use your tin-chai again. Stay unseen and unheard. It is the only way to survive."

CHAPTER 3

On my way out of the house the next morning, I glared at Terran's portrait hanging over the mantel. I wished I could warn the other girls against trying out for the showcase and tell them what Mama had seen Terran do.

Yet Rell had warned me against interfering in anyone else's affairs and to look out for myself first. I understood his point. Those girls were intent on becoming showcase trinkets. They might think I was competing with them and tell the scouts what I was saying about Emperor Terran. I didn't want to be punished for trying to help them. I already had enough to worry about with hiding my tin-chai and keeping out of the scouts' sight.

Would I really never be able to freely use my tin-chai without fearing the palace would capture me? Why had Old Grandfather Heaven given me this gift if it was safer to bury it away?

I still remembered that wonderful feeling of healing a lullapiper's crushed wing the first time I'd discovered my tin-chai. My family members all had varying reactions.

Mama's stern expression had pinned me down. "You are to pretend to be a koong, do you understand, Rilla?"

"Atta girl." Baba slapped his thigh and chuckled. He saw Mama's glower and sobered. "I mean of course, you must be careful. But you have been blessed with a powerful tin-chai. You must draw your wyis from a different dominant channel than most of us Shyan."

"Rilla's a healer, like me." Rell's bright eyes mirrored Baba's excitement. "Our dominant channel is *ha,* the soul channel. But her tin-chai is even stronger than mine. I can detect a patient's illness with a single glance and know what medicine to prescribe, but Rilla can heal them instantly."

"What are channels?" I had asked, still too young to understand.

Rell explained. "There are four channels only Shyan can use to derive the energy that controls our individual tin-chai. *Dai, ha, ji,* and *kai.* Body, soul, mind, and heart. Most Shyan use *dai,* the body channel, so common tin-chai have to do with manipulating the natural elements in the physical world."

"For example, I use *dai* to manipulate the water element for my tin-chai," Baba said. "This is how I'm able to stay deep in the ocean for hours without coming up for air. Other men use *dai* to hurl boulders or uproot trees. I had a distant cousin whose dominant channel was *ji,* which gave him the tin-chai to talk to animals. Also, your grandfather used *kai,* the most atypical dominant channel. He was an emotional man, and his body temperature changed depending on his mood, which then affected everyone in the same room as him."

"I also read about some Shyan who can draw energy from multiple channels to enhance their tin-chai," Rell said. "Let's say a man uses *dai* to summon lightning bolts. Add *ji* to that, and he can control where the lightning strikes, even if it's five hundred miles away. If he can use *dai, ji, ha,* and *kai,* he can potentially create natural disasters that wipe out entire villages."

"Imagine if our little Rilla could use multiple channels," Baba said. "Her tin-chai is already special. I wonder what other hidden layers her tin-chai might have."

"Enough, both of you," Mama said, throwing an exasperated look at Baba and Rell. She turned to me. "What your baba and brother mean to say is there are terrible people who may harm you because of what you can do. Your voice is powerful, and that makes it dangerous. You must keep your mouth shut."

I'd taken Mama's warning to heart. Whenever I had to sing for the school choir, I'd been able to control and inhibit my tin-chai. But what Baba and my brother said made me wonder. What if my tin-chai possessed other layers? Undiscovered powers? I might be able to heal incurable diseases. Or use my singing to control the elements.

But I'd never know. Because I didn't have the freedom to practice my tin-chai without the fear of being caught.

I sighed. No use thinking about undiscovered powers now. I had to get to work. I checked my disguise in the mirror one more time. I looked and smelled hideous. Perfect. There was no way the scouts would want me as a showcase trinket now.

It has been said that the sea goddess, Mi, once traveled to the horizon to seduce Old Grandfather Heaven. As punishment, Wise Grandmother Time imprisoned Mi at the bottom of the ocean, her breaths regulating the ebb and flow of the tide. But Mi's mood swings were unpredictable. On most days, she drew in steady breaths, but when upset, her roars resounded in earsplitting crashes against the shore, drowning everything in her path.

I looked up at the three moons. The Lavender Moon—seen only during the Spring Equinox—pressed its round face against the sky. The White Moon bared its crescent smile above the Lavender Moon, and half of the Turquoise Moon sat in the shape of a mushroom top to the right.

Once I saw the moons were far apart, I breathed easier. We

couldn't afford a second mega eclipse. Seven winters ago, the moons had aligned. The resulting tidal wave devastated the port. My family was lucky not to have been there at the time. Others weren't as fortunate.

I walked along the harbor and closed my eyes. I could still picture the bustling center it once was. When I was a child, hundreds of fishing dinghies had been lined in rows on the pier. Back then, I'd hear whistles and foghorns sounding in the distance. Boats passed each other, some returning to port, others setting off to sea.

The market had smelled of fish and the sea, salty and pungent, comforting and familiar like my baba whenever he returned home from one of his deep-sea dives. From one direction, the scent of fresh-baked beechnut bread and blue moon cheese sandwiches would drift to my nose. In the opposite direction, grilled shrimp and roasted black coral skewers were basted in fermented chili sauce and cooked over flaming pits.

Merchants sold their wares and pitched their sales. Golden egg-laying chickens roamed free on the streets. Cages with lucky crickets and fire-spitting songbirds hung on wires overhead. Reams of fine starlight-spun silk and fabrics lined the tables for women to touch, and above the food carts, bright red lanterns aligned to become a dancing kaigon.

The bellowing toy hawker would try to catch my attention. "Miss, you want to buy a lucky maocat? It waves its paw. No magic involved. A new craft from Emberwood."

Colorful knickknacks and toys lined his cart, but the lucky maocat figurine had been my favorite. I found it amazing someone could invent such a delightful toy without the use of magic. It raised its paw and waved back and forth as if saying hello.

I could never linger. The shoppers shoved and pushed against each other, competing to be the first to access the choicest produce and freshest cuts of meat. They would press against my eight-year-old, four-foot frame, urging me forward and forcing me to find holes to fit my body through before they crushed me. I would dodge and dart through waves of people, ducking under sweaty armpits, jumping over wheels of food carts, sidestepping fishmongers and peddlers haggling with customers.

I blinked and returned to the present. In a moment, all of it was gone. Fishermen and merchants, women and children, all pulled into the sea, never to surface again. Scraps of wood, dead animals, and glass shards had washed up on the shore days later, adding to the debris.

Now only three shabby skiffs, tied with frayed ropes, remained docked to wooden posts. They nodded to and fro, lost souls letting the waves decide which way to push their hulls. The peddling booths were few and far between. Haggard women in rags set up shop with their meager merchandise. Browned from sun exposure, their skin was as thick and tough as hide, and their faces were scored with lines of worry. Gone were the succulent smells of roasted eel and shrimp slathered in sauces. The only familiar odor was stale fish, lingering like a ghost. Nothing had changed to fix the calamity in the last seven years. My brother was right. This was further evidence of Terran's failure to make things better for the common folk.

Some of the women stared at me and frowned. One of them pinched her nose and stepped back as I walked past her. My repulsive disguise was working.

I arrived at Auntie An's peddling booth and smelled salt and the sea. Dozens of ribbed seashells, some cone-shaped, others spiraled, lined the booth. An urn filled with seawater sat in the center of the shells.

"Rilla, is that you?" Auntie An flashed a warm smile. Her tanned face was shiny and coated in sweat and wizened laugh lines. Dimples dotted her plump cheeks.

I bowed low in a respectful greeting. "Good morning, Auntie."

"I almost didn't recognize you. You look and smell quite . . ." She paused, and her mouth quirked up. "Interesting."

"Taking extra precautions. I don't want the scouts to notice me."

"Ah, I see." She nodded in understanding.

I slapped my forehead. "I'm sorry, Auntie. I hope I don't scare off the shoppers."

"Don't worry. I think the customers will be too focused on our merchandise to care about your appearance anyway." A hovering goldfeng flew toward her, buzzing loudly. Its tiny black and gold striped body lingered above her head. She winced and shielded her face. "Bothersome creatures. Watch that they do not sting you. I know the poisonous ones are rare, but I almost died from a sting when I was a child."

"Just ignore it. Hopefully it will go away."

"Yes, and we have far too much work today to worry about goldfengs." Auntie An's teeth glinted as she beamed and gestured to the booth. "Look what treasures the sea delivered today. Aren't they beautiful?"

The ocean bestowed gifts upon Auntie An whenever she stepped into the water. She sold everything the sea gave her, from pure sea salt, to seafood, to pearls.

Today she had seashells.

"Seashells bring good luck," she said. "Charms for young women who want good marriages."

Or to become a faela. The words died on the tip of my tongue.

"Now," she said, "I'll handle the haggling and let you manage the transactions."

She set to work, calling to the passersby. "Seashells for sale! Get your lucky shells, and say a prayer. Old Grandfather Heaven will surely grant your wishes."

Shoppers swarmed the booth, and I collected their money. The hovering goldfeng landed on one of the Seran coins. I swatted it away. Annoying pest.

A thirty-year-old spinster grabbed several shells—a white ribbed clam shell, a dusky yellow cone, and a burnt orange ear-shaped shell. The woman extended her hands and lifted her red-rimmed gaze heavenward. "Please let this be the year I marry. I don't want to die destitute and alone. No husband, no children, no honor."

She dropped to her knees, prostrating her entire length on the ground. The hovering goldfeng flew around her head, but she ignored it. She rose and then bent down again, repeating the motions until the skin on her forehead peeled and bled. When she finished her prayers, she approached the urn of seawater. The woman poured the water over her shells and pocketed the damp shells in her bodice for safekeeping.

A group of thirteen-year-old girls gathered behind her, surveying the variety of shells several times before making a selection.

One girl bent forward in supplication. "Mama says I'm the family's beauty and our only hope. I know it's my duty to love and serve my family. Help me become a faela to His Excellency, Emperor Terran, so I may bring prosperity and honor to my family."

"My baba says he must marry me off or sell me if a scout doesn't discover me by my sixteenth birthday," her companion said. She sprinkled seawater over her shell and chanted the prayers we learned in school. "Grant me the courage to make sacrifices though my unruly heart may sometimes wander. Give me the humility to submit to those in positions of higher authority, especially to His Honorable Majesty, Emperor Terran."

Hearing their petitions didn't shock me. Duty and filial piety were the most important of life's virtues.

Even if it meant sacrificing one's own happiness.

The seashells were a popular commodity, and by early afternoon, we'd earned quite a profit.

Auntie An turned to me. "Well, Rilla, we can close shop early today. There probably won't be many more customers." Her gaze lifted to the cloudy sky. "These days, the slightest chance of rain is enough to scare folks away from the harbor."

She winced and bent to massage her ankle.

"Are you all right?" I asked.

"I think so. There's a spasm I can't seem to get rid of. I suppose this is what happens with age."

"If you need any medicine, come by to see Rell." I waved goodbye.

I was exhausted. Time to go home.

I crossed the rickety bridge that weaved across the strait leading from the sea market to the beach. The water was smooth and clear, a glass floor encasing the red rocks forming the base of the bridge. I skimmed my fingers along the salty foam. The path descended, forcing me to pick up my pace. I ambled along the shore.

Ten feet away, a mound of sand moved. I froze.

To my ever-growing horror, the sand dune shook, revealing a shielded guitle. But the guitle's black shell shimmered and elongated. Within seconds, the shape of a woman took form. The woman from yesterday, the one who the other scouts had addressed as Madam. She had her head tucked between her shoulders, but she slowly straightened and stood.

She looked at me. "I was at the sea market today. I heard you talking to that older woman and thought I recognized your voice. I'm sure you're the girl I heard singing yesterday."

Not many Shyan had a tin-chai allowing them to transform into multiple animals. She must have been in the form of that snorting sihai yesterday. No wonder I hadn't seen her sitting on the rocks at first.

I was too petrified to answer or move. She studied my raggedy dress and dirty face, and she scrunched her brow in disgust. "Disappointing. You are certainly nothing to look at, but I understand the language of animals. A seatern thanked you for saving her wings. Do you have a healing tin-chai?"

The sky darkened. The sun had gone into hiding, and black clouds closed in. I shook my head and stammered. "N-no. You must be mistaken."

"Do not lie, child. I rarely make a mistake. You cannot deny that you were the girl singing yesterday."

"Yes, that was me. I can carry a tune, but I do not have a healing tin-chai. I'm a koong. I knew how to mend the seatern's wing because my brother is a doctor."

She smirked. "Well, if that is the case, we shall see."

Two stray drops of water fell onto my face.

"Rilla!" Behind me, a voice shouted.

I turned around. Auntie An limped toward me. "Rilla, call your brother. I think I—"

She broke off with a sharp cry and collapsed into the sand.

"Auntie!"

I sprinted toward her. The bindings around my chest loosened in my hurry. I reached Auntie An. "What's wrong?"

She motioned to her ankle and through labored breaths said, "I-it feels like it's on fire. I think I was stung."

The rain fell steadily now. I brushed away damp hair from my eyes, then touched Auntie An's ankle, but even the delicate brush caused her to cry out in pain.

"I'm sorry, Auntie. I need to have a look."

I folded back her skirts and stockings. Her skin was colder than the ocean in mid-winter. Immediately, I located the problem. Her swollen ankle had a laceration in the shape of a V. "A hovering goldfeng sting."

And it was the poisonous kind. Rare, but deadly if the proper medicine wasn't administered right away.

The shadow of a figure crossed my path. The madam stared down at us. "Does she need a doctor?"

If she had any intention of summoning a doctor, she would already have done so. She watched Auntie An and me as though she wanted to see the drama play out.

"Or perhaps you can help her." The woman's smile grew wider.

This was her doing. She'd transformed into a poisonous hovering goldfeng. Stung Auntie An to force my hand.

Auntie An jerked forward, pulling away from me. Her tongue and throat had swelled to twice their normal size. She convulsed like a fish writhing on dry land. Then her eyes closed, and she stopped moving.

I placed my hands above her, not touching, but close enough. This was the first time I attempted to feel a person's wyis, or spiritual energy. Rell had told me the wyis of a healthy person was supposed to thrum with a steady beat, like the drumline of a bass. But the vibrations of Auntie An's wyis pulsated beneath my palms like a flickering candle in the wind.

Dismay twisted my stomach. I was out of options. I needed to use my tin-chai. I had only ever practiced healing on myself a few times when I'd caught a cold and when I'd broken my arm. My tin-chai hadn't worked on me. But I had healed animals. It had to be similar to people. Still, what if I did something wrong? Worse, if I saved Auntie An, I'd most certainly be taken to the palace.

But I had to try *something*. I couldn't let her die.

I focused on my own wyis, channeling it through my soul as I'd done before when healing birds and small animals.

"The lady of the sea lost her one true love
Beneath the stormy, billowing swell.
She pled with the waters for his return
'til the sea surrendered a silver shell."

A tiny stir thrummed beneath my palms, and Auntie An's breathing steadied. Her wyis pounded in a fixed rhythm once more.

I leaped back in shock. Auntie An still lay before me, but she looked different. In my desperation to save her life, I'd applied much more of my wyis than I should have.

The laugh lines and wrinkles around her eyes and mouth were gone, the skin now taut and unblemished. Her thinning, silver hair had grown out, the damaged follicles replaced with voluminous amber waves. The drooping folds under her belly retreated to reveal a trim waistline, and her once tight dress now draped her body like a sack. She looked no older than Nia's twenty-five years.

Her eyes fluttered open, and she stared at me in confusion. "What . . . what happened, Rilla?"

"Auntie?" I hesitated. Could she sense the change? "A-are you all right?"

"I've never felt better. For some reason, I feel like I could run miles." She sat up, and the sleeves of her dress threatened to slide down her shoulders. She clutched the fabric to her chest. "What in the world?" She caught her reflection in a puddle of rain and gasped. "Rilla Marseas, what have you done?"

The madam cleared her throat. I looked up. She stared at me with elated eyes. "Well, well. Not as homely looking as I thought, and your tin-chai is as rare as an endangered sea leopard."

Lifting my hands to my face, I felt a rush of nausea come over me. The boils and welts had dissolved in the rain.

"Rilla Marseas," the woman said. "Now that I know your name, do not think you can get away. Return to your home, and inform your family that I will be visiting shortly. Do not attempt to escape, or I will throw your entire family in prison."

She sauntered away without another word.

Fainting, flushing faela. I'd saved a life as I'd always wanted, and that had cost me my dreams.

CHAPTER 4

My family sat for what would be my last meal in this house. I smelled the spice-scented candles Nia placed in the center of the table. Even if I was still imprisoned in Cedar Palace forty years from now, I'd never forget the fragrance.

I'd already told Rell and Nia what happened and that the madam was coming for me. The three of us stared at our plates in silence. Rell stabbed his food with his chopsticks.

"I couldn't let her die," I said. "I'd never forgive myself."

"No, you did the right thing." Spikes of his short, ruffled black hair jutted up from his head. It looked as wild as his destroyed dinner. "I blame myself for not telling you about Mama's experience earlier. You would have been more careful, and this never would have happened."

My eyes stung from trying to hold back the tears. Still, I tried to remain positive.

"At least Auntie An has a chance at a fresh start," I said. "With no family here to hold her back, she can travel the world."

She could smuggle across the border to Emberwood Kingdom, where the women were rumored to dress like men and allowed to attend school past the age of sixteen and even become doctors and healers. Or perhaps she could live among the artists in Fauxhemia Kingdom and become a painter or musician unburdened by censorship laws.

"Maybe she'll finally even allow herself to fall in love again," I added.

So many possibilities lay before her now. How I envied her. Living in Emberwood or Fauxhemia would be a dream come true. So much freedom.

"Yes, you've blessed her at the cost of your own life," Rell said. "But I won't let them take you away. They'll have to kill me first."

Nia's eyes widened, and she took a sharp breath.

"Stop scaring your wife," I said.

Nia blinked, brushing at the tears on her cheeks. "This is my fault. I shouldn't have let you set foot outside the house until after showcase tryouts."

"Please stop blaming yourselves," I said. "When the scouts come for me, I will go with them. I won't let you sacrifice your own safety to protect me."

"No," Rell said. "You—"

"I'm sixteen now, not six. This is my decision."

I pushed away my uneaten plate of food. The spiciness of the curry I usually loved fell flat on my tongue. The contents of my stomach threatened to push their way out. An irritated gurgle sounded in my lower abdomen.

Rell's attention turned to the window. I followed his gaze. A dozen palace soldiers and several scouts entered through our front gate. At the head was the madam from the beach. She navigated the courtyard, her body seeming to float as though she were moving in water. A chill started in my gut and sent tremors into my fingertips.

Rell motioned to Nia. "Go wait in the kitchen."

"But—"

"Rell is right," I told her. "You're pregnant, and they're dangerous."

A tear slid down Nia's cheek, but she reluctantly rose from her seat and made her exit.

The inevitable knock announced our visitor's arrival. I stood and walked to the door. With clammy hands, I pulled the cold door handle. The door slid open with a rickety creak. Dread clamped down on my shoulders. I lifted my gaze to our visitors.

The middle-aged woman from the beach had tidied herself up. Her hair parted into eight braids flaring out like tentacles. She stretched her arms, and the appendages bent and twisted. Though she hadn't fully transformed into an eight-legged seazhi, it didn't stop her from imitating one. She must have been using only a part of her tin-chai as a warning. If she'd been able to turn into a poisonous hovering goldfeng, she would also possess the deadly toxins of a seazhi. She was letting us know she had the power to kill us if we did not do as she pleased.

Rell made no show of fear. Scrutinizing her, he propped himself against the door and barred her entry. However, she looked comfortable enough standing outside.

"Miss Rilla Marseas." She stared at me with bulging amber eyes. "Well, my little guppy, now that I see you out of the rain, I can happily confirm you are a beauty. My name is Madam Yasmina Flopsy. I am a Supervisor Madam at the palace, and these are my subordinate scouts." She gestured to the two women I'd seen with her yesterday. "They have been scouring this village in search of talented girls like you, and they have given me a list of candidates to consider. I have the final say in choosing three girls to bring to the palace, whom I will represent."

She beamed and held her head proudly. I could tell she took pride in her position as Supervisor Madam.

"While my subordinates have done a superb job in recommending candidates, those girls pale in comparison to you. When I first heard your singing, I knew I needed to bring you to the palace. I have come to extend a royal invitation. In the name of His Royal Highness, the Honorable Emperor Terran, you are summoned to compete in the Annual Faela Showcase. This invitation is mandatory. If you attempt to escape or show an unwillingness to participate, you will be executed."

The candor the madam displayed was disturbing.

Madam Yasmina lifted her arms in a fluid movement. She smoothed her hands across her hair. The plaits flattened and relaxed against the base of her neck.

She cast a glance to the guards and the scouts standing behind her. "I need to have a private word with Rilla and her family, if you please." At their dismissal, they bowed and went to stand by the front gate.

She pushed her way past Rell and entered the house. She took note of the mantel and Emperor Terran's portrait hanging above it. Looking pleased, she waited for no invitation and sat on one of the wooden chairs by the dining table. It was jarring to see her seated where I had just been eating. I couldn't believe this was real.

Rell and I remained standing.

Madam Yasmina returned her attention to me. "I've never seen anyone with a tin-chai like yours, my dear, so I'm willing to forgive you for trying to hide from me. I'm confident that with my guidance, you'll outshine not only this year's competition, but all the faela in the palace. If you become an elite faela, I'll be immensely rewarded, and your family will be well taken care of for a lifetime. It's in all our best interests to cooperate with one another. As of now, I haven't told my subordinates about your healing tin-chai, and after tactfully interviewing the other candidates in the village who have grown up with you, it seems you have kept your tin-chai a secret from them as well. This is to your benefit. I believe it is best for us to continue pretending you are a koong until the showcase finale."

"What is your reasoning behind this?" Rell asked. "I never wished for my sister to be taken to the palace, but now that you've discovered her, there's no point in staying hidden."

The madam bristled at his admission, but Rell continued, unafraid. "The other girls have always flaunted their tin-chai, and they bullied my sister because they believed themselves to be superior. I don't want them to continue tormenting Rilla at the palace."

"Set your mind at ease, Doctor," the madam said. "I shall make sure the other girls do not touch your sister. It's more dangerous for her if they *should* know. The other girls will be jealous and try to sabotage her. The safest course of action is letting everyone believe she's a koong. Then during the finale, when she finally plays her hidden trump card, she shall emerge as the dark horse. The judges will surely choose her to become one of this year's five new faela, and I know the emperor will raise her status to that of an elite faela."

To be an elite faela was the highest tier in the harem. Elite faela were given incredible wealth, and their families were paid a million Seran annually, enough to live as aristocrats.

"Prospective faela are called trinkets, and you will be one of about thirty trinkets competing," Madam Yasmina said, telling me what I already knew. "The showcase is divided into three rounds."

That I hadn't known.

"In the preliminary round, the trinkets will perform a tea ceremony."

The tea ceremony was a long-practiced cultural ritual, first developed by the Lotuses and Crocuses. The ritual was a spiritual experience, one that brought peace and enlightenment, and all girls were required to learn it before becoming a bride.

The madam continued. "Based on the judges' evaluation of the trinket's performance, she is matched with a faela for the second round, called a *trinketship.* The trinket will shadow the faela for six weeks to learn how to please the emperor as his concubine, and if the trinket does not win the showcase, she will become a permanent serving trifle to the same faela who mentored her."

"How do the judges decide which faela to pair with a trinket?" I asked.

What a nightmare it would be to get matched with a cruel faela. Especially if a trinket lost the showcase and became that faela's permanent serving trifle.

"You'll submit your top three mentor choices when we arrive at the palace," Yasmina said. "If you do well in the preliminary round, there is a higher chance you'll be paired with a faela on your list. But if you perform poorly, the judges choose for you."

Madam Yasmina made a face. "You do not want that to happen. If the judges don't believe you have a chance of winning, they'll pair you with a low-tiered forgotten faela."

I worried my bottom lip. "What is the goal of the trinketship?"

"At the end of the trinketship, the faela give the trinket a grade which will be taken into consideration amongst the judges going into the finale."

"And what is expected in the finale?"

"Each trinket prepares a performance for the emperor. This is when the trinket finally reveals her tin-chai, if she has one, to His Majesty in order to impress him. Five trinkets will be chosen as showcase winners and receive the title of faela, but the emperor will choose only one as his favorite to become an elite faela."

The madam beamed. "I believe your tin-chai shall mesmerize His Majesty. Any other questions?"

Before I could answer, Rell acted as my mouthpiece. "If Rilla is not chosen to become a faela, will she be able to come home instead of becoming a faela's permanent trifle?"

"Under no circumstance are any of the girls allowed to leave the palace. It is protocol for—"

"I wish for my sister to return home where she belongs. If you won't allow her to come home, then I decline your invitation."

What was Rell doing? All that talk of losing the battle to win the war, but here he was, speaking with such risky candor.

Madam Yasmina narrowed her eyes, and her face turned a deep shade of red, so dark it was almost black. "Do you now? We'll see about that, Doctor Marseas."

She stood, walked to the door, and shouted into the courtyard. "Guards, come!"

Footsteps sounded. The two scouts from yesterday led a troop of palace guards. They filled our courtyard.

"This family refuses to participate in the showcase," Yasmina said. "They must be taught a lesson for their ingratitude. You know what to do."

The blonde scout waved a hand. "Destroy the property."

The guards forced their way into the back and side houses. Glass shattered and porcelain broke as they ransacked every room.

The red-haired scout emerged from my room. She held my mother's zither and lute. I cried out and reached for them, helpless to stop her. A guard lifted his sword and sliced through both instruments in midair.

Pieces tumbled to the ground. Strings snapped and wood splintered, the sound like bones popping out of their sockets.

"Seize the doctor," Yasmina ordered.

Two guards moved toward Rell. He tried to evade them, but three other guards surrounded him. They overtook him and forced his arms behind his back. One guard punched him in the stomach. He keeled over, his breath rushing out in a pained wheeze.

"No!" I shouted and reached for the guard's arms, but he shoved me aside.

The guards took turns beating my brother until blood spilled from his mouth and nostrils.

Nia ran out from the kitchen, took in the sight, and screamed. Another guard reached for her, but I launched forward, placing myself over Nia and her belly. "Please, don't hurt them! I'll go with you."

Madam Yasmina put up a hand, commanding the guards to stop. "It is your brother who should apologize. I should have him thrown in prison."

I knelt in front of the madam and bowed my head to the ground. "I beg of you, Madam. I a-apologize on my brother's behalf. Please don't punish my family. I'm sure my brother did not mean to overstep his bounds. He has always been overprotective of me. I'm honored to participate in the Faela Showcase."

The words tasted bitter on my tongue. But I'd do anything to keep my family safe, even if I was locked up in the palace my whole life.

Madam Yasmina smoothed her hands on the front of her dress and recollected her composure. "Since you've shown some humility, I'll spare your family for now. I'm determined—you *shall* become a faela. I stake my life on it, and Madam Yasmina Flopsy never fails."

The guards let go of Rell and shoved him away. He managed to hobble toward Nia, and she ran to hug him. She trembled in his arms, and he murmured soothing words into her ear.

There was still no guarantee for their safety. "I have one request, if I may, Madam. My sister-in-law is about to give birth. I want my family left in peace when I go with you to the palace."

"As long as you're a good girl and do what you are told, there's no need to worry. I'll give you ten minutes to collect your things. We leave tonight."

CHAPTER 5

From outside my bedroom, Madam Yasmina watched me pack. "You do not need to bring much. The palace will provide everything."

I stuffed three dresses into a knapsack. Nia tried to help, but broke into sobs and sank down on my bed. My brother sat in silence, holding a cloth to his bloodied face. I grabbed my greatest possession. A glass globe Baba bought for Mama. Within the globe was a small ship built from tiny glass beads. I had fashioned the globe into a pendant. I placed it around my neck. The clasp was loose and sometimes undid itself, but I wasn't leaving without it.

"Come along," Madam Yasmina said.

I followed her outside and heard Rell and Nia behind me. No one else was there.

"Where is everyone?" I asked.

"The guards and my subordinates are already on their way back to the palace. Cascasea Village was our last stop to discover new talents. I'll be escorting you and the other two girls selected from your village to Senlin City and the imperial palace."

Senlin City, the capital of Seracedar Empire. I'd never been there, but Baba had often taken trips to the capital to sell seafood. Before, I had wanted to visit Senlin and other distant places, but this wasn't how I'd envisioned my first time outside Cascasea Village.

A two-wheeled, canopied palanquin was parked in front of my house. Two horizontal bamboo poles protruded from the front. Four horsemen carried the palanquin. They had altered their bodies to become man-horse hybrids, their lower halves taking on the form of stallions. They bore the weight of the poles on their shoulders. Their muscles rippled, bare backs glistening under the sun. I'd never seen that tin-chai before. In any other situation, I'd have found them more impressive.

Curlicue carvings covered the palanquin's gold-plated exterior. The carvings depicted contorted figures, positioned in questionable postures, faces writhing with the pain of desire.

Embarrassed to be staring, I averted my gaze.

"I'll let you say your goodbyes," Madam Yasmina said. "Do not take too long."

Nia hugged me as close as her full belly allowed. "I'll miss you so much, my sweet girl. I—oh!" She choked, and fresh tears poured down her face.

It made me more miserable to realize I wouldn't be there to witness the birth of my niece or nephew.

She whispered into my ear. "No matter what, remember you must never give up hope. We love you."

I faced my brother. My eyes were hot and watery. A tightness formed in my throat and shot pain into the nerves of my teeth.

Rell embraced me. His arms tightened around my shoulders, and his gruff voice struggled not to break. "I'm so sorry. I swore to Mama and Baba that I'd always protect you, but I couldn't keep that promise. I've . . . I've failed you."

"No," I said. "You did your best. Never doubt that, Rell. You're the best big brother a girl could ask for."

I bit the sides of my mouth, trying to let the physical pain stifle the emotional heartache. Still, I choked on the dry air that clogged my throat. My breath hitched, and I blinked back tears. I couldn't let Madam Yasmina see me. She might accuse me of being rebellious and ungrateful.

I stood back from my brother and brushed away the tears with the back of my hand. I took a deep breath and then turned away from my family. Nia's broken sobs echoed behind me. Every thought told my feet to disobey orders and run back to the safety of my home. Instead, I forced my heavy legs to trudge toward the carriage.

Scarlet silk curtains covered the sides of the palanquin, shielding the interior from outsiders. When I climbed aboard, I saw two other village girls. They were petting a furry animal with a puffy tail. A shuroo. I knew the two girls all too well—Galai and Irica.

Dreams did come true for some girls.

Irica scowled. "How did *you* get selected? You weren't at the tryouts."

Galai didn't seem pleased to see me either. "I thought you didn't want to compete."

"I didn't try out," I said. "Madam Yasmina caught me—"

Yasmina kicked my foot. "I caught a vision of her beauty. She's the prettiest in the village despite being a koong." The madam sent me a warning glance, reminding me that I was to continue hiding my tin-chai.

"Didn't you say you told her that the emperor has koong faela?" Irica said to Galai. "You gave her the idea. She probably put herself right in the scouts' line of sight after talking to you."

Galai's look of betrayal meant she probably hadn't thought I'd actually be selected. I guess I couldn't count on her to be my friend at the palace. For Irica and Galai, the competition between us started now.

"That's enough, girls." Yasmina took the shuroo into her arms and stroked its head. "We have a long journey ahead of us, and I do not want to hear you quarreling."

The horsemen clopped their hooves, and the carriage sped off. I tugged back the curtains and allowed myself one last glimpse at everything and everyone I loved. I didn't stop waving goodbye until Rell and Nia shrank to two fuzzy dots, and then they disappeared from view, along with my dreams and aspirations to be a healer.

I was on my own. Forced into a future I didn't want for myself.

This had to be a bad dream. Soon I'd wake in my bed and hear Nia call me for breakfast. Everything would be all right again.

I pinched myself again and again until my skin reddened. *Wake up, wake up.* But it was no use. I couldn't awaken from this nightmare.

Maybe something would stop the carriage and make us turn around. Maybe the showcase would be canceled this year, or Old Grandfather Heaven would realize he made a mistake in allowing Yasmina to see my tin-chai, and he would cause lightning to strike and kill her.

We had three weeks before we reached Senlin, and until then, I'd pray for a miracle.

Homesickness morphed into annoyance when two nutcracker teeth jutted out of Madam Yasmina's upper lip, mimicking the shuroo as she spoke to it. "Chit cha chatta chit cha."

The creature sat atop her head like a hat, angling its face down to be kissed. The madam made another loud squeaking noise and fed him an acorn. The shuroo jumped down to her shoulder and into her bosom, where she cuddled him in the tight circle of her arms. I didn't doubt she enjoyed the shuroo's company more than that of her own species.

Although the seat cushions were made of luxurious velvet, I was impatient and uncomfortable. I shifted several times before leaning against the soft headrest, and I tried not to bang the back of my head against it.

I repeated Mama's words, trying to allow them to dissolve my building rage. *Keep your mouth shut.*

I didn't want to be imprisoned for disrespecting the madam before I even reached the palace, so I couldn't do anything to express my annoyance. Couldn't frown. Couldn't sigh. Couldn't cringe, even when Galai asked how Madam Yasmina had enjoyed her stay in Cascasea, and the madam revealed she and her team of scouts found several early bloomers in the village.

"The emperor loves juveniles," she said. "We found an entire nest in Cascasea who are a little too underdeveloped this year, but when they reach puberty and start their bleeding, we shall come to collect."

I suppressed the urge to gag.

Madam Yasmina continued talking to her pet, though the critter was on the verge of naptime and close to becoming as annoyed with his mistress as I was. At least he could show his displeasure by biting her finger off.

Irica and Galai tried to earn Madam Yasmina's favor by petting her shuroo and mimicking her squeaking noises.

Maybe the shuroo would bite them, too.

The three-week journey might as well have been ten years.

We passed through the agricultural towns of Province Peon, north of Province Ca where Cascasea was based. I was surprised to see that all the fields were dry and brown.

"The newspapers reported that the drought in Peon was over," I said. "But I don't see anything growing here. Is there going to be a food shortage after all?"

"His Majesty has reassured us that we are not to fear a famine," Yasmina said. "His word is not to be doubted."

Her stern tone told me not to ask any more questions. But we drove past miles of farmland, and the scarce crops all looked withered and sickly. If the newspapers in my province had covered up the true devastations of Peon's drought, had they also lied to other provinces about the tidal wave's havoc upon the Port of Cascasea?

It took a week to travel across Province Peon. We took rest breaks in small towns and stayed at inns run by local farmers who were excited to see us and the palace carriage, probably because Madam Yasmina left a hefty sum of Seran for their hospitality.

During the second week, we crossed the border from Province Peon into Province Yupa, taking us through the valley in the shadow of the Yupa Mountains. We passed factories and workshops, dome-shaped buildings that looked like truffles sprouting from the ground.

Each small town in Yupa had a monastery, usually occupied by brother Crocus monks, but in Jailong Village, Madam Yasmina announced we would stay the night at an abbey of sister Lotus monks.

From the holy shrine, where worshipers burned incense and honored their ancestors, a smoky amberwood scent pervaded the air and filled Jailong Abbey's stone dome. Another line of devout disciples presented offerings to Old Grandfather Heaven, hoping to receive blessings for matrimony, fertility, and prosperity.

I had often burned incense at the monastery in Cascasea Village and offered prayers to Old Grandfather Heaven, but I watched the worshipers today with a newfound cynicism for these rituals. I'd asked for my dreams to come true, for the freedom to become a healer, and for protection over me so no one would discover my tin-chai, but Old Grandfather Heaven had ignored all of my prayers.

Still, I offered one last silent plea for Old Grandfather Heaven to intervene and allow me to return home. If he didn't stop me from entering Senlin City and Cedar Palace, I didn't think I could ever have faith in Old Grandfather Heaven again.

No holy Lotuses were about in the abbey, only a handful of Lotuses-in-training.

"Where are the Lotuses today?" Madam Yasmina asked the holy sister who showed us to our room.

The holy sister bowed her head and replied, "All Lotuses and Crocuses in this region have taken a solitary retreat to meditate and pray."

"Is that so?" Yasmina said. "Any idea when they will reemerge into society?"

"They have promised to remain secluded until the earthquakes that continue to plague us stop."

Galai gasped. "Earthquakes? Do they occur frequently?"

"Province Yupa has always had occasional tremors, but the earthquakes have become longer and more violent of late, especially in Yupa Valley. Many buildings have toppled and killed residents."

"What if one should strike while we're here?" Galai asked. I had the same question.

"Don't be worried," Irica told her. "If it were truly dangerous, I'm sure His Majesty would have told the residents to evacuate until the buildings can be rebuilt to be safer."

"I agree," Madam Yasmina said, making Irica beam as though she'd won a prize. "Besides, we won't be in this high-risk region for long. The odds of an earthquake hitting us tonight are extremely low."

That night, I heard Galai's restless movements in her cot. The anxiety of a potential earthquake scared me as much as it did her.

But the next morning, after a breakfast of rice porridge and salted soybeans, we were off again without experiencing the slightest tremor. Thank Old Grandfather Heaven.

After another week of travel through Province Yupa and staying at other monasteries and small town inns along the way, we crossed into Province Sen. Only one day remained until we reached Senlin City. Although I was far from excited to enter the palace, I was still relieved that the journey was almost over.

The foliage swept past the window, a brush spreading a fan of watercolors on a blank canvas. We were now deep in the Senlin Forest. The trees were full and lush, flowers dusted the ground, and the spicy-sweet essence of purple lilacs drifted into the carriage.

Irica and Galai kept their conversation between themselves. They'd ignored me throughout the ride, and this showed no signs of changing. And I had no desire to talk to Madam Yasmina. To pass the time, I mentally recited the lesson I used to memorize as a child.

"As noble as bamboo growing straight and strong,
Relentless as the river continues coursing along,
Ambitious as mountains stretching to greater heights,
This defines a gentleman—honorable and upright.

"As delicate as cherry blossoms floating in the breeze,
Harmonious as the lute always tuned to please,
Demure as the White Moon girdled still in the sky,
This defines a maiden who will soon be a wife."

I felt for the chain around my neck until my fingers brushed against the glass globe pendant. It brought me some comfort and strength, a part of Mama and Baba I carried with me. I was glad I had brought it with me, and even more thankful I'd managed to save it from the pirates who robbed and killed them.

The pirates. The thought of them sent anger slicing through my chest. I closed my eyes, steadying my breaths, and tried to calm myself. But the images of that day still haunted me. I drifted into restless sleep, their taunting faces plaguing my dreams.

I saw myself seven years earlier, watching the waves from my spot on the cliffs. Gray clouds loomed over the tossing sea.

Baba's ship drifted in on the tide. I jumped up, eager to run down to meet them when they docked at the port. But before I could move, I sensed something strange. Why was Baba's ship heading toward the beach instead of the harbor?

I squinted. A dozen watery forms held the sides of the ship. Their bodies solidified when they came up on the beach. They were dressed in black from head to toe.

Pirates.

I propelled my tiny body forward as fast as I could toward the shore. The ship washed up on the shore. My feet sank into the wet sand, and I took cover behind a tall column of red rocks. The violent surf broke against the sea stack, salty spray drenching my shivering body. I held on, unmoved, fear rooting my feet deeper into the pebbled strand.

The pirates threw Baba onto the sand. Another held a knife to Mama's throat and ordered her off the ship.

A pirate drove his foot into Baba's chest. His glinting sword slashed Baba's throat. A second pirate pulled his arm back, and thrust a blade into Mama's stomach. Blood gushed out, and she slunk forward. I bit back a scream, terror racing through me. An animal-like whimper sounded, and in a daze, I realized it had come from me. Tears mingled with the sea. My thudding heart sent vibrations through my entire body.

Baba's killer waved his bloodstained sword through the air. "Take all you can. Hurry. We've still got the whole village to rob."

The pirates went onboard to pilfer Baba's hard-earned treasures. I ran toward my parents and fell hard on my knees. I was too afraid to move, but I couldn't leave them there like that, without dignity.

Mama's chest stirred. She still breathed. A bit of hope blossomed in my own pulse. If Mama was still alive, then maybe Baba was, too. Maybe I could still save them.

I opened my mouth, but Mama grabbed my arm before I could let out one note.

"Keep . . . mouth . . . shut."

"But . . ."

"No . . . the pirates . . . will hear . . ."

"I don't care." Tears mingled with snot, dripping and oozing into my mouth and onto Mama's face.

"Well, hello." A pirate's laughing voice caused a shriek to pitch halfway out of my lungs. "And who is this pretty young maiden?" He ran a finger down my cheek.

"Don't . . . touch her." Mama gasped. She rolled onto her side and threw herself over me. Blood splashed on the sand and my face.

The pirates howled, and one pushed her aside. Another seized my arm. He kicked Mama in the stomach, delivering one final blow. Her head drooped. It was too late. Not even my tin-chai would save her now. I shrieked, pure agony causing my body to writhe.

I glared at the pirate captain and screamed. "You monsters. You'll pay for this."

"Oh? How do you plan on making me pay?" His gaze skimmed my body up and down. I didn't like the way he looked at me. It made me want to run away, but I couldn't. I had to avenge my parents.

"You're a little young for my taste, but I'm sure I can teach you a pleasurable kind of payback."

More laughter.

"The law will punish you," I shouted.

The captain grinned. "Emperor Terran is the law, fair maiden. If he wants us to slay those pesky shapeshifting Miyu, he'll let us take all the pearls and riches his subjects can offer. We're worth more to him than this entire village combined."

How could the emperor not make them pay? I thought Old Grandfather Heaven required our ruler to uphold the law.

But the pirates had to pay. If Terran wouldn't punish them, someone had to.

I wanted them to hurt. I wanted them to *die*.

"I'll make you pay!" I screamed.

Every ounce of frustration and anger within me roared. I sang complete gibberish at the top of my lungs. A red haze blocked my eyes. Then red faded to black.

CHAPTER 6

◆ ◆ ◆ ◆ ◆ ◆ ◆ ◆ ◆ ◆

I opened my eyes. Tears flowed down the side of my face, trickling into my ear. A bit of drool pooled from the corner of my mouth onto the cushioned seat. I brushed it away, cleaning myself up as best I could.

I remembered I was far from home and would never see my family again. Tightness returned to my ribcage. My temples pulsed in an incessant beat, the steady ache drilling at my brain.

"Oh, this is incredible! I've never seen so many people."

I groaned. Irica's screeching only made my searing headache worse.

I felt around my neck, but the weight of my pendant was missing. I searched the floor and located it rolling at Irica's feet. The clasp must have unhooked.

I reached for it.

Irica saw me and made a sound of disgust. She pushed my necklace away with her foot. "Why would you bring cheap, broken trash to the palace?"

I clutched the pendant, cushioning it to my chest. I couldn't lose my last connection to home.

I fixed my eyes on the window. Senlin, the capital of Seracedar, stared back at me. The city was a main trading hub of the world, where people from all corners of Caliwyis met.

Built around the border of Cedar Palace, the imperial city was contained within Senlin Forest, every edifice created out of hollowed trees. Climbing vines and gnarled boughs formed stairways and crossing bridges, pillars and balusters. Roads were paved with enchanted foliage that supported the weight of moving carriages and carts. The bustle of activity here reminded me of what the Cascasea Port used to be. It seemed Senlin City hadn't been touched by any trace of the natural disasters plaguing the other provinces.

Red lanterns decorated streetposts, and the flag of Seracedar hung outside each business. The main road was filled with horse and horsemen-drawn carriages. Oxen and oxenmen weaved their way through the busy streets, pulling carts filled with everything from silks to stacks of fodder to piles of cabbage. We passed inns and taverns, restaurants, tea shops, winemakers, seamstresses, and pawn stores.

Traffic accumulated, and our carriage slowed to a crawl. Through the open window, I heard people of all shapes and sizes and colors speaking several dialects and accents at once. Tall, tan-skinned men spoke with soft, sing-song lilts. I'd never heard that accent before.

Men and women with bright, neon hair stood out among the crowd. Their unique style looked like the description my baba had told me of the Exentriks. They spoke a harsher-sounding language with pointed tones, almost like they were arguing.

I also heard people speak in the common Shyan language, but with guttural inflections. Judging by their shorter stature, I'd guess they were from Ailo, one of the empire's tribute kingdoms.

Two men covered in tattoos made their way across the street. I heard their lazy drawl and thought of the toy vendor I used to know at the Cascasea seamarket who shared the same accent. They were Embers from Emberwood, Shyan like us, but we called them *Zhei Shyan*. Traitors.

Our relationship with Emberwood had always been tense. Finally, a decade ago, they had shut their borders. All trading between our nations had stopped.

"If these Embers are allowed so near to the palace, it must be a sign that our relations with Emberwood are improving," I said to Madam Yasmina.

She clicked her tongue and scowled. "Don't pretend to know about political matters, and most certainly do not speak of those *Zhei* when we're in the palace."

Maybe I was wrong then. Perhaps the men were smugglers or mercenaries.

Our carriage halted long enough for me to observe a fortuneteller at his booth. He shook his oracle sticks and let one fall on the table to decide his patron's fate. The man reminded me of the fortuneteller I'd visited outside the Cascasea monastery. He'd told me that I had a bright future and would grow up to be an exceptional healer. Now I knew he was nothing but a con.

Neighboring the fortuneteller, a street vendor stood at his food cart, roasting skewers and panfrying meat dumplings. The smell of sweet fermented chili and spices stirred my longing for home and childhood.

Our carriage sped off again.

We took a side alley away from the main street. A sweet, resinous scent whirled through the air. Stillness descended. The paved roads softened to muddy trails, the moisture from the trees seeping into the soil. No longer could I hear the clip-clop of horsemen's steps. The dirt was red and damp. Streaks of clay splashed the sides of the roadways. In the distance, a wall of redwood trees stood like sentinels, so tall they climbed into the clouds, and still, I couldn't see the tips. High in the trees, rectangular openings had been hollowed out from the trunks. The windows of watchtowers, by the look of it. Stationed in the towers were the tiny figures of border patrol guards overlooking the city and beyond. From their viewpoint, they'd be able to see if invaders from another kingdom, such as Emberwood, were about to initiate an attack.

Etched lower on the trees was a pattern of two heavenly creatures, the kaigon, the emperor's symbol, and the hongni, the empress's icon. The kaigon's scaly face looked like clouds strewn together, and its slender body curved in a serpentine shape. To the left, its talon-like claws held the top of the Sacred Cedar Scepter, and on the right, the hongni bird's wings embraced the scepter's staff.

Straight ahead of us was a wide redwood tree. Its trunk was carved through to the other side, exposing an open gateway. A two-way road crossed through it.

Our carriage edged closer to the guards patrolling the gate.

"Girls, we approach your new home, Cedar Palace," Madam Yasmina said. "Once we are on the other side, those in the palace will be your new family. You would do well to forget your past. This is your future."

New home. New family. I didn't want them. I wanted *my* home and family. The weight of her words finally sunk in. No longer did this feel like just a nightmare. This was my reality, and nothing was going to stop it from happening. Even as the guards let our carriage through, I waited for someone to chase after us and say there had been a mistake, the showcase was cancelled, or the emperor was dead, and we could go home.

But no lightning struck. No voice roared down from Heaven to stop us. No one was going to save me.

We passed through the gate. No turning back. My childhood was dead. So were my dreams. I'd never become a healer now.

CHAPTER 7

Behind the redwood gateway, we headed through tunnels made within hollowed out Sequoia trees. After driving through several channels, we drove into a large courtyard. It was a huge, open quadrangle, similar in structure to my home in Cascasea, but it could fit my house ten times over. A sharper minty smell replaced the redwood scent. The trees lining the courtyard lit up with colored floating lanterns. Each tree had a doorway with a signpost hanging above, and each sign had a number carved in it.

Pebbles decorated the ground in a perfect pattern of raked lines. Shadowed corridors bridged the trees together, and paths wound from the courtyard into the surrounding gardens and the rest of the forest. Servants moved with hurried steps.

"This is the Elite House," Madam Yasmina said. "His Majesty's most treasured faela live here. Only serving trifles and androgies are allowed inside. No palace guards."

It made sense. Androgies usually had powerful tin-chai, so they could protect the faela. But since they were castrated males, there would be no way for them to take a faela as a lover. Or even if they did, they couldn't impregnate her.

"The Central House lies behind, where middle-tiered faela

reside," Yasmina said. "Beyond that, the Dark Court houses the lowest-tiered, forgotten faela. The middle and forgotten faela are not as tightly guarded as they used to be. Empress Limera's orders, and His Majesty can never refuse her."

She made a disapproving face. "Her Majesty also removed the androgies from guarding the trinkets, so the responsibility has fallen on us madams. We enforce your curfew and take shifts watching you."

A rather odd demand. What was the empress's reasoning behind this? If the faela and trinkets used to be treated like captives during the reign of Emperor Yikan, perhaps Empress Limera was encouraging Terran to change the rules. Maybe the empress was sympathetic and fought for the faela and trinkets to have more freedom to leave their chambers and explore other parts of the palace grounds.

A chilling breeze blew through the window. I thought I saw a melting snowbank, but before I could take another glance, we took a sharp turn through the hollowed trunk of an overturned redwood tree. At the other end, a picture of gold and crimson greeted us in a second courtyard. This was even larger than the Elite House. Autumn leaves covered the ground, and across the court, a gnarled cedar stood.

"The Royal House, where His Majesty and Empress Limera keep residence and conduct official business," Yasmina said. "We will cross Moon Lovers' Pond, where the emperor enjoys taking walks."

We crossed a curved bridge. Below was a lily pond. Golden leaves floated on the water like gilded ships reflecting the sunset. Swans drifted under the bridge, their arched necks seemingly bowed in prayer.

Though the palace was to be my prison, I had to admit it was magnificent in design. Not even in my imagination would I have been able to create such a whimsical place, so bizarre yet alluring.

Our carriage followed the water. On the banks of the stream, a few treehouses were dispersed, spread far from one another. Some had golden doors while others had silver, white, or red. I speculated that aristocrats, princes, and servants inhabited these trees, and the color of the door depended on the resident's societal status.

We came to a lake so clear that it looked like diamonds were floating in the water. Archways made of silver birch joined the banks together, meeting at a pagoda that seemed suspended in the center of the still water.

"Silver Tears Lake," Madam Yasmina said. "Serving trifles wash clothes here, and you trinkets will also be able to explore these banks during your trinketship."

To our right, I noticed a scattering of cherry trees. Their delicate blossoms flew down like pink flutterflies.

"That's so pretty," Galai said. "Will we be able to explore that grove?"

"No." Madam Yasmina's tone was short. "That is forbidden territory. You must never wander beyond that border of cherry trees. Understand?"

Juniper trees now grew thick and tall all around us, hiding wherever we were headed next. The palanquin stopped before the trees, and they parted, allowing us to continue on our way before they returned to their original position, once more hiding the view from outsiders.

I didn't see a Shyan controlling the trees. This was a form of magic I hadn't seen before. How did it work? The magic had to be from a Shyan with a tree-bending tin-chai, but how could the Shyan control his magic without being present?

On the other side of the juniper trees, the carriage came to a halt.

"This is our stop," Madam Yasmina said. "Apple Barrel Court, where you and all the other trinkets will stay."

"Why is it called the Apple Barrel Court?" Galai asked. "Are there apple trees here?"

"Oh no." Madam Yasmina laughed. "It's called the Apple Barrel because the judges select which of you shall be faela as one chooses the best apples from a barrel at the market."

I moved to get out of the carriage, but Irica pushed me aside. "Out of my way, koong."

She stepped out first, and Galai followed.

Then I took a step down, allowing one of the horsemen to offer me a hand. My legs were numb from sitting so long.

Madam Yasmina gestured up to a wooden bungalow that stood on top of a willow tree. "This is Treehouse 37, the cabin you girls shall be sharing."

I looked around and saw similar cabins in other trees. Tree branches of weeping willows had been woven together in tight, intricate lattices to form the infrastructure of the buildings from the walls to the rooftops. The cabins seemed modeled after birds' nests perched high in the treetops.

We climbed a ladder to access the doorway.

In the interior of the cabin were two rooms—a washing room, and a bedchamber. The washing room contained a single pulley faucet and a washbowl, and the chamber pot was placed to the side. In the bedchamber, three beds fit side by side. A dresser, a mirror, and a wardrobe sat at the front of the beds, and the three of us were meant to share the space. Terran's portrait hung on the wall to the side of the dresser, and an incense burner sat on the dresser.

I let Irica and Galai pick their beds before I took the one that remained. The horsemen carried our luggage into the cabin. Their tails had disappeared, and their hind legs had straightened, returning the men to Shyan form.

"Before I leave you to rest, we must address one more important matter," Yasmina said. "The preliminary test is next week. For your homework tonight, you must list your top three mentoring faela picks for the trinketship, so I can turn in the forms to the judges."

Irica pulled a piece of paper from her dress and showed it to Madam Yasmina. "I already have an idea who my top three shall be since I've been researching the elite faela. What do you think, Madam?"

"These are all decent choices," Yasmina said. "But I have one suggestion. I've no doubt you'll become an elite faela, but even then, you'll have to outshine the other women to maintain His Majesty's attention. There is only one woman who His Majesty returns to after the allure of his newest faela fades. The empress herself. The madams usually do not suggest her as a mentor to their girls because she can seem aloof, but I believe she may be the best instructor of all. If she agrees to be your mentor, you'll be able to learn all her secrets."

Empress Limera. I didn't know much about her, other than that she was the emperor's official wife and queen of the harem. I did recall my brother say my mama witnessed Limera beg Terran not to use the captive girl as a weapon.

Irica worried her bottom lip. "I don't know. Does the empress have a similar tin-chai to mine? And what if she doesn't like me? She seems to have so much influence over His Majesty. You said the emperor always listens to her."

"Isn't that an advantage? If she likes you, she'll put in a good word to His Majesty. She is the best at navigating palace politics, and this is key to ensuring you maintain high rank among the faela after you win the showcase. You don't need to share a similar tin-chai with your mentor as long as she is adept at teaching you how to imbed yourself in the emperor's head and heart. Learn how she is able to get His Majesty to cater to her every whim, and one day, you'll also be able to get him to give you whatever you desire."

Irica nodded. "All right, if you recommend her, then the empress will be my top choice, and Lady Poisi and Lady Ogaw are my second and third choice. Lady Poisi has had seven sons, and Lady Ogaw is said to have the most conjugal visits from His Majesty.”

“You cannot go wrong with those choices.” Yasmina handed Irica a blank document, ink, and a writing brush.

Irica beamed and skipped to her bed. She flounced belly-side down and set to work writing the faela names on her form.

“What about me?” Galai asked.

“In your case, I’d suggest you select a faela who shares a similar tin-chai to you since it’s your dancing, not your beauty or personality, that is your strength.” Yasmina handed her a record log, and as Galai flipped through the pages, I caught a glimpse of the faelas’ pictures listed with their names, ranks, and tin-chai.

“You mean you aren’t going to help me choose?”

“I already gave you the faela record log,” Yasmina said. “Put in the work for yourself.”

“But—”

“Now I know why you are overweight. You are lazy and make no effort to achieve your goals. At least Irica did her research before asking for my advice.”

Galai pouted but returned to reading the faelas’ profiles in the record log.

Now Yasmina turned to me.

“I haven’t done any research,” I told her.

“Quite all right, my kitten. I gave much thought to your list and will submit it to the judges for you.”

Without any input from me? If I cared at all about the showcase, I’d be offended.

“Your top three picks are Ladies Dreama, Kinsah, and Elin.”

Those names meant nothing to me. I looked to Galai’s faela record log. Perhaps I could borrow it and find out a little bit about them.

Yasmina must have noted my concern. “You must trust me.

These three faela have mentored in past showcases. They are elite faela who exhibit grace and class, and they take the trinketship seriously."

I supposed I had no choice. I hoped the faela who Yasmina had picked were not abusive.

"Now I shall leave you ladies to rest for the evening," Yasmina said. "Tomorrow, you will meet the other trinkets and get fitted for your new day gowns and formal kipa."

CHAPTER 8

Early the next morning, we had breakfast in the dining hall two treehouses down from us. Then Madam Yasmina led us into the courtyard at the center of all the treehouses. Apple Barrel Court was smaller than Elite House, but still wide and spacious, with a single tree in the center. The knotted trunk spread as wide as the Cascasea schoolyard, and dangling boughs curled down to form hammocks, making comfortable niches for trinkets to perch. Stone benches, rooted to the ground, served as seats around the tree, probably for the consideration of those who feared heights. The warm, dense air smelled of varied perfumes fused together in one nauseating odor.

At least thirty girls were scattered about the courtyard. Most girls hadn't taken the tactic of hiding their tin-chai. They were already hard at work practicing for the showcase finale, perhaps eager to brag and scare the competition by openly demonstrating their tin-chai. One girl grew flowers from any surface she touched. Another turned water into intricately designed ice sculptures. So many different talents. I had to admit I was impressed, despite fearing what aggression might emerge from the competition.

Their haughty airs and jealous scrutiny floated in the atmosphere like poisonous gas, invisible to the eye but meant to kill. This place was a battlefield of women who would sabotage each other to climb to the top. For the first time, I appreciated Madam Yasmina's decision to keep my tin-chai a secret.

Some girls practiced song and dance routines. A couple of dancers leapt through the air, toes as pointed as dried bamboo stalks. A few others warmed their vocal chords, singing arpeggios in changing octaves.

A quieter bunch gathered on benches, sewing tiny flutterflies onto delicate silk pillowcases. Perhaps they believed if they couldn't sing or dance, then at least they could show off their domestic skills. Less ambitious girls dozed on the tree boughs, while a few chatted with each other and batted their eyelashes with worldly innocence.

I assumed the girls who weren't demonstrating their magical tin-chai must be koong. Or at least pretending to be, like me.

Would I make any new friends, or would they all turn out to be bullies like Irica? Worse, what if I made a friend only for them to abandon or betray me? My heart still hurt, remembering how Galai and I used to be friends. I'd stood up for Galai when Irica taunted her weight, but the next day, Galai had become part of Irica's group of friends. That same group had sheared my hair, and Galai hadn't done anything to stop them.

Madam Yasmina and the other madams stood in the center of the courtyard. They clapped their hands, calling our attention.

"Ladies," Yasmina said. "Please stand in a single line facing us."

Standing among the others, I placed my longer locks over my face and shied away, wishing I could hide. As long as none of the trinkets noticed me, I'd give them no reason to be jealous, and I wouldn't be subjected to any bullying.

Through my bangs, I noticed a girl staring at me. Her honey-brown hair was cut above her shoulders. She appeared more confident than other girls. She dressed in an unconventional style. Black stockings puffed out from her legs, giving the illusion of a skirt, before they tapered at the ankles. A white blouse was tucked in at the waist. Over this, she sported a smart red blazer with shiny black buttons. She wore the stockings like pants, which bordered on inappropriate.

She grinned and waved. I looked around, but no one else was watching her. She was looking at me, but she couldn't be waving at me. We were strangers. I didn't want to wave back and look foolish if she was greeting someone behind me.

I averted my gaze but secretly admired her for wearing whatever she wanted and not giving a cod's crud about what the scouts thought. If we were anywhere but here, I might have tried to befriend her.

Madam Yasmina stood before us and centered herself among the other dozen madams. Behind the madams stood about twenty subordinate scouts. I recognized the blonde and redhead who had been with Yasmina.

One of the Supervisor Madams stepped forward and cleared her throat. "Welcome, trinkets. I am Madam Gomi. I and these eleven other women standing before you are Cedar Palace's Supervisor Madams. Behind us are the subordinate scouts, who will now be in charge of your hair, makeup, and costume design, and they will tidy up after you so that you can focus on your training. We Supervisor Madams shall take on the responsibility of training you this week in preparation for the preliminary test. You will learn proper palace etiquette, such as how to walk gracefully and serve tea properly. Until the start of the trinketship, you may not leave the Apple Barrel, and you must not break curfew.

"Your performance in the preliminary round will decide which faela you shadow during your six-week trinketship. During your trinketship, your mentor will decide your schedule, and you will have more freedom to navigate other areas of the palace and familiarize yourself with your new home. However, you must never wander past the border of cherry trees. Your mentoring faela will provide weekly progress reports to be turned in to your madam to ensure you are learning how to become a dedicated faela to our blessed emperor. May he live one thousand years, and a thousand more."

"May he live one thousand years, and a thousand more," we echoed in unison. Though my real sentiments played in my head: *Drop dead.*

The first item of business was to meet the seamstress in Treehouse 35. While we waited, the madams gave us permission to speak to one another if we kept our voices to a lady-like whisper. I sat on a round stone away from the crowd and listened to the madams call out the first batch of names. These girls entered the seamstress scouts' workstation, five at a time.

The girl wearing the red blazer approached me. Her amber eyes shone with unabashed fearlessness. "May I?" With a toss of her unbound hair, she gestured to the empty space next to me.

I nodded once.

She crawled onto the rock and brought her knees up so she could rest her chin on them. Then she cocked her head sideways to regard me. "I'm Radiana, Radi for short. What's your name?"

"Rilla."

I looked away, expecting the conversation to end.

"I'm from Jailong Village. Judging by your high cheekbones and black hair, I'll take a guess that you're from"—she folded her brow, focusing on me, and then waggled a finger—" Cascasea Village, am I right? You have a beach glow about you. So . . . what do you think we should do to get out of this depraved pit of agony?"

My gaze darted from her, to the scouts and madams, then back to her. Was she testing my reaction? Trying to get me in trouble?

Radi laughed. "Don't look so worried. I'm not searching for a reason to tattle on you. I just decided to start a conversation with the only other girl besides me who looks like she doesn't want to be here."

I bit my lower lip and stared at my feet.

"Terran's tentacles. It's a challenge getting you to talk, eh? Good thing I like shy folks. Gives me the chance to talk more."

I couldn't help cracking a smile. "I'm not shy. I'm cautious."

"Do you usually speak so softly? I can hardly hear you."

"I don't want anyone to hear us."

"Hear us? Ha. What do we have to say that they don't already know? If not for the money and power, nobody would have those pretentious smiles pasted to their faces." She lifted her index finger, pointing and shaking it at the girls around us. "These phonies wouldn't be clawing at each other to climb *into* Terran's bed, but to *escape* it. I can't be the only one who thinks becoming his faela would be worse than death by a thousand cuts."

My jaw dropped, shocked she would dare voice something so brazen. I had these thoughts, too, but I wasn't courageous enough to say them aloud. My gaze shifted from side to side. Had anyone heard her? Some girls paused to look at us, but after a moment, they returned to what they had been doing.

"You're quite bold."

Her mouth arced wide across her face. "Speaking my mind is the one thing I'd never change about myself, though everyone else seems to think it's a flaw."

Radi's snarky attitude was refreshing in this land of silly, submissive conformists.

Time passed quickly now that I had someone to talk to, though Radi did most of the talking. I still didn't trust her enough to reveal much about myself, but I liked listening.

When the madams finally called our names, the courtyard was almost empty. We were in the last group to see the seamstress. Most girls had returned to their rooms.

"Come on, girls." Madam Gomi beckoned to us. She beamed at Radi as though she were a huge, glittering gem. "Oh my, out of this year's thirty-three trinkets, I believe my Radiana possesses the finest features. His Majesty will surely reward me for discovering her." She flashed Madam Yasmina a smirk.

Madam Yasmina whispered into my ear. "Do not get too close to Radi. I'm certain she has a powerful tin-chai, like you, and Madam Gomi has also instructed her to hide it. I shall not let Madam Gomi win. I bet against three other Supervisor Madams that you will become an *elite* faela. Twenty thousand Seran. Win this wager for me, and I promise to give your family ten percent of my profits from this bet and from what the emperor rewards me."

Her words made my stomach clench and my fists curl.

As the seamstress scout took my measurements, a trumpet sounded in the courtyard. A man's voice called out, "Announcing the empress's impending arrival. Assemble yourselves to greet Her Majesty."

Empress Limera. Was she here to welcome us?

"Oh no." Madam Yasmina jumped out of her chair. She pushed me toward the door. "We shall finish this later. Go into the courtyard. When Her Majesty arrives, do nothing to attract her attention, and try not to sweat or she shall smell fear on your skin. Her tin-chai allows her to smell your emotions. The last thing we want is for her to figure out that you are hiding your tin-chai."

CHAPTER 9

✦ ✦ ✦ ✦ ✦ ✦ ✦ ✦ ✦ ✦

Trinkets and madams scurried out into the courtyard to greet Empress Limera in a flurry of commotion. At the madams' instructions, thirty-three trinkets stood in a straight line with our backs upright, chests thrust forward, and shoulders back.

A woman approached. Empress Limera. Her lavender silk robe was decorated with golden hongni birds, an icon only the empress was allowed to wear. On silent feet, she glided across the path, but her posture and head remained corpse-still. Her ice-blonde hair was piled high into a pleated twist, held in place by a gold hairpin with strands of jade pendants. Another hair adornment was woven through her hair, covered in clusters of purple-tipped garden phlox with real flutterflies seated on the flowers. The poor flutterflies were fused onto the ornament to keep them from flying away. Only their black and orange dotted wings remained free to flap back and forth with the faela queen's every movement.

Several coats of colorless makeup plastered her face, giving her the pallor of a ghost, though her lips were heavy with rouge. I couldn't tell her precise age through all the makeup, but she was at least in her mid-forties.

She didn't look anything like I'd imagined. After what my brother had told me, I thought she'd have kind features and a pleasant smile. But the empress looked at us like we were insects she wished to crush beneath the soles of her shoes.

The royal trumpet sounded again, and the herald cried out, "The Honorable Empress Limera has arrived. Bow to Her Majesty."

We bowed low. The empress stepped toward us, and a bouquet of jasmine and coconut flooded my nose. I clenched my teeth to stop from coughing.

She scanned us, and a slight pucker appeared at the corners of her eyes.

"Stand straight, and lift your heads, trinkets." Her voice, though low and even, carried a darkness that rumbled like distant thunder. "Madams, I have come to evaluate the crop you have chosen this year."

She stood at one end of the line and cast an assessing glance at the first girl. "You have the teeth of a horse." She moved on to the second girl. "Such small-slitted eyes. I cannot tell if you are asleep or awake." Then the third girl. "Suck in your stomach. You must have the appetite of three heavy-set men. Either that or you are pregnant."

The empress studied this girl for a second longer, and a fleeting sneer passed over her. She moved down the row, continuing her criticism of each trinket.

She came to Galai, and the empress rolled her eyes. "What are the scouts thinking? Another fat girl."

Galai's cheeks went red, and she settled her gaze on the ground.

Next to Galai, Irica cleared her throat and stepped forward. "My lady, I do not mean to interrupt, but I wish to tell you that you are my top choice as mentor for the trinketship. I admire your elegance and sharp mind."

Empress Limera maintained her cold demeanor. "Do you now?" She considered Irica for a moment. "Despite your insincerity, I still love a flatterer. Let us hope the judges deem you worthy enough to become my apprentice."

Irica beamed.

I was next. I swallowed hard. The empress's glance carried up and down my figure in close scrutiny. A displeased glower settled upon her face.

I had a feeling she was trying to detect my weakness, and she'd take great joy in magnifying my slightest shortcoming. A trickle of sweat slid down my back, causing an involuntary shiver.

"You have a pretty face. I will give you that. Tell me, trinket, do you have a tin-chai?"

I never would have believed I'd agree with Madam Yasmina on anything until now. If the empress ever discovered my power, what would she do to me?

"N-no, my lady," I whispered.

"Ugh. I can smell your timidity. You are sweating as though I asked you to make a speech in front of thousands. Quiet and boring as a common moonrabbit. My husband will soon tire of you. The highest status a koong trinket will ever achieve is a forgotten faela."

Her words stung more than I thought they would. *Timid, quiet, boring.*

The empress moved on where Radi stood. My new friend, calm and unafraid, met the empress's gaze straight on. I admired her boldness, but I feared for her.

Limera scowled at Radi. "I do not like your expression nor approve of your unusual fashion sense. You look far too self-assured, as though you believe you are superior to everyone here, including myself."

"This is the face I was born with," Radi said. "If others take offense at my natural look or how I choose to dress, that's out of my control. I also can't help if my confidence makes someone else feel uncomfortable or inferior."

Limera jerked back her hand and hit Radi across the cheek so hard that Radi fell to the ground. The other girls, myself included, jumped back and cried out in surprise. Radi held the side of her face. Blood trickled from a cut above her lip.

"Insolent girl, how dare you speak to me in that manner." Limera assessed her hand. The long painted black tip of her index fingernail had chipped. She whined. "Look what you did. I just had this done."

Radi picked herself up, still looking undaunted.

"Apologize to Her Majesty at once," Madam Gomi told her.

Radi stuck out her chin with defiance, but I nudged her in the side, urging her to obey before she got herself into more trouble. She gritted her teeth and bowed to Limera. "I apologize if you disliked what I said, *my lady*. My words were not intentionally directed toward you."

Limera's gaze dropped to the blood on Radi's chin and lingered there. "I shall accept your apology this once since you only arrived to the palace and have yet to receive training, but I smell your rebellious spirit. If the madams do not succeed in taming your wildness before the preliminaries, then I will disqualify you from the rest of the showcase."

"Rest assured, my lady," Madam Gomi said. "Radiana has great potential. I promise she will be transformed by the time I am through with her training."

"We shall see. Make sure the trinkets change into their traditional white robes. I do not want to see any other bizarre outfits." Limera stalked away without looking at the rest of the girls.

When she was out of sight, Madam Gomi grabbed Radi by the arm. "Radiana, let's speak in private."

I didn't see Radi for the rest of the afternoon, but during the supper hour, she sat alone in the dining hall, wearing the white robes we had all been given. A bandage covered the cut on her lip.

I took my supper box and went to sit with her.

"Radi, are you all right?"

She gave me a puzzled look. "Yes, of course. I'm not going to die from such a small scratch."

"No. I meant did Madam Gomi punish you?"

She shook her head. "She just lectured. I pretended to listen. Gomi thinks I'll instigate trouble. Now, I'm tempted. Maybe I'll sneak out to find the empress and paint a moustache on her as she sleeps."

"What if someone hears you? The empress isn't someone to cross. Not even in jest."

"She doesn't scare me. What's she going to do? Disqualify me from the showcase and make me serve as a trifle? We all become faela or trifles one way or another."

"But if you are disqualified, she may have worse plans in store for you. What if there are harsher punishments than being sentenced to become a serving trifle?"

"Like a beheading?" Radi shrugged. "If I'm dead, at least I won't have to suffer the emperor's unwanted affections or be ordered about by a faela."

I frowned. "Don't say that. If you get punished, don't you care that it might affect your loved ones? It's better if you do what the madams tell us from now on."

She said nothing for a moment, and I thought I'd finally talked some sense into her.

Then she said, "If I die, there's no one left to care."

Radi had no family left? Now I didn't know what to say.

"I don't care if they kill me for it, but I want them to know they will never be able to control me. If I must remain imprisoned here, then I'll make sure they know I won't play by their rules."

There was a dangerous glimmer in those wide, blue eyes of hers. The streak of a rebel.

"Let's do something tonight to break the rules," she said.

"I don't want to get into trouble."

"We won't, I promise. We'll break curfew and sneak out of the Apple Barrel to swim at the lake."

"What lake?" I didn't know why I was asking. I had no plans to go with her.

"Silver Tears Lake between the Apple Barrel and the Dark Palace. We drove past it on our way here. It'll be deserted after curfew."

"But the madams will be keeping watch after curfew. And what about the guards?"

"I'll take care of them."

I didn't answer. Just because she could afford to be reckless didn't mean I could put my family at risk.

"Come on, please? It'll be our secret way of telling Terran to hurl his cursed soul into the eighteen levels of the underworld. Besides, you're from Cascasea Village. If you grew up by the beach, I'm sure you're longing for a swim."

A swim did sound nice. I was homesick for the ocean.

"Consider it an initiation of our friendship," she added.

Friendship. I did long to have a friend, an ally. One who would not let jealousy come between us.

"If you can make sure the guards and madams won't be a problem, then I suppose I'll go with you."

She beamed. "Done."

I couldn't believe I'd agreed. What had I gotten myself into?

CHAPTER 10

✦ ✦ ✦ ✦ ✦ ✦ ✦ ✦ ✦ ✦ ✦

Back in the cabin I shared with Galai and Irica, Madam Yasmina had us prepare for bed.

We burned three sticks of incense, one to honor Old Grandfather Heaven and his will through the Sacred Cedar Scepter, a second for Emperor Terran, and the third to pay respects to our ancestors.

The familiar amberwood scent permeated the air. I bowed, then, along with Irica and Galai, chanted the words we knew so well.

"Old Grandfather Heaven, grant me the courage to make sacrifices though my unruly heart may sometimes wander. Give me the humility to submit to those in a position of higher authority, especially to His Honorable Majesty, Emperor Terran."

I watched the burning sticks shrivel and curl into themselves, and I added my own prayer. *Old Grandfather Heaven, please don't let Radi and me get caught tonight.*

The lights went out at exactly nine o'clock. Hands trembling, I slipped under the covers, closed my eyes, and pretended to sleep. I listened for signs of my roommates drifting into deeper slumber and forced myself to take deep breaths to relax, but it did no good. The mere thought of sneaking out caused a nervous gag to rise into my throat, which I fought to suppress.

But I couldn't back out now.

With hushed movements, I climbed out of bed. Under my sleeping gown, I already had dressed in my white day robes, prepared for the night's adventure. I pulled off the gown and slipped it under the covers, and then I added pillows to create the shape of a sleeping form.

Irica rolled over in the bed next to mine. I froze. She sat up, eyes wide open, and looked straight at me.

"Today I dream of glory and fame,
For tomorrow all will exalt my name."

She belted the tune, closed her eyes, and plopped onto her pillow again. Fresh snores erupted from her throat. They mingled with Galai's heavy wheezes.

I bolted for the door before Irica took another swing at my eardrums. The door parted at my touch. The vines remained recoiled until I stepped outside, and then they merged back into place.

Outside, the Lavender Moon shone bright, and the stars seemed to dance, free wanderers in that large expanse of sky. How I envied them. A hint of cherry blossom perfume drifted in the air, but it was a saccharine smell, synthetic, mimicking the freshness I associated with cherry trees. It came from the extensive gardens beyond the Apple Barrel. Forbidden territory. That scent was thick and heavy like the air in a room with no windows.

What caused it?

Someone tapped my shoulder.

I jumped. But it was only Radi. Her face was bright with amusement. "Jittery, are we?"

My stomach was a jumbled mess and gurgled with anxiety. I spoke in a hushed whisper, still mindful that someone might hear us. "I didn't ask you earlier, but how are we going to swim in the lake? We don't have bathing suits."

I hoped that would deter her.

But she shrugged and kept her tone low. "Don't need them. We're swimming naked."

I stared at her, mouth agape. "N-no."

My head rotated in frantic wobbles. Radi had to be joking.

But her dead-pan look said she was serious. "Don't tell me you never went skinny-dipping. You lived by the ocean."

"Mama and Baba never allowed it. They thought it was too dangerous."

"And of course, you never disobeyed Mama and Baba." Radi's eyebrows arched. "Where's your sense of adventure?"

"In my adventures, I remain fully clothed."

Impatience crinkled Radi's eyes. "We can't go swimming with our clothes on. The madams will see that our clothes are wet in the morning."

"Must we go to the lake? We're already outside our cabins. We've broken curfew. Let's go back inside."

"Friendship initiation, remember? Unless you don't want to be my friend."

"Fine," I grumbled. I hated that plying me with guilt always worked.

"Besides," she said. "I want to show you something, and the lake is the best spot for it."

"Are you sure no one will be there?"

"It's too late for the royals, and I already asked about the guards. Most are stationed closer to Terran's quarters. The few guards patrolling the lake don't take their job seriously. They're too busy having fun in the forbidden parts of the palace gardens."

I scrunched my brow. "Having fun doing what?"

"Probably drinking and playing cards."

"How did you manage to find all of this out?"

"Used my portion of boar stew to bribe a young androgy who serves us at the dining hall. They might feed us well, but those poor boys are starved. Anyway, the boy said the guards don't make their first rounds at the lake until they're done carousing, well past midnight. We have plenty of time."

"What about—"

"Madam Yasmina is on guard duty. I mixed sleeping serum into her drink. Told Gomi I was having insomnia, and she gave me something called valelily tea."

I knew the ingredient. Valelily tea was a diluted sleeping serum derived from valelily oil extract. Valelilies smelled of alcohol, and the extract was so potent, it needed to be kept in small, airtight vials, away from heat. Valelily oil had many special properties. If mixed with fire, it had the power to dissolve metal while still remaining non-toxic to living organisms. If taken at a high enough dose, it could make someone forget all his memories between ingesting the drug and waking from a deep sleep.

I had to admit it. Radi was resourceful. But far too daring for her own good. Still, I wished I could be more fearless like her.

"We're just going swimming. Only the fireflies will bear witness."

She took my arm, dragging me with her.

We walked through the grove of juniper trees. On the other side, we reached the shore of Silver Tears Lake. Hard to believe it was just yesterday that our carriage had driven past the lake before entering Apple Barrel Court. Then, the beauty of the lake had barely registered. All I'd been able to feel was the dread of entering a prison. But now, I took in the wondrous view. For a moment, all my fears fled. Tonight, the sight of the lake felt like freedom. Silver birch trees grew all around the banks and connected with each other in archways across the sky. It was easy to imagine we were in a secret place in the woods, far away from the palace, where we could forget about our captivity.

Radi shed her clothes and waded into the waters. I took my time. I still couldn't completely shake off the anxiety of getting caught. I unfastened my buttons and looked around to make sure no one was watching.

But Radi was right. No one wandered about the palace at this time of night. With the chirping crickets the only sound surrounding us, I pulled up my blouse before I could change my mind, tossed my clothes on the bank, and waded into the water. The melody of the water's movement remained the purest song I'd ever have the pleasure of hearing. The sand, silver between my toes, tickled like maocat kisses. A faint hint of honeysuckle floated over from the bushes that grew on the side of the lake. In this moment, at least I could pretend I still had a future.

A night howli bird *whooed* as Radi dunked herself under the water. When she came up for air, she grinned. "Aren't you glad I talked you into this?"

I dived deeper into the pool. Tonight, the Lavender Moon reigned as Queen of the Sky. Even the crescent of the constant White Moon paled in comparison to her. She cast a glowing lilac spotlight upon us as though encouraging our spontaneous adventure in the name of freedom. The cool air was refreshing on my face, and I let my head fall back to absorb the water into my hair. The soft silkiness seeped into my pores, and the swaying waves caressed my skin, replenishing my spirit. My wyis circulated through my entire body. Only one word could sum up this experience.

Divine.

We treaded water, our feet kicking out in soundless strokes. Neither of us spoke, but it was a comfortable silence. We cherished this liberating experience, this fleeting moment.

I floated on my back and gazed at the sky, taking pleasure in the weightless sensation. Between the tree branches, the stars played like candlelight on the back of a silver spoon. They danced again, waltzing and twirling to the strains of a distant lullaby.

"Radi, look." I pointed up. "The stars are swaying. I've never seen anything like it."

"I've always wished I could go to the sea and watch the stars from the shore. What was it like to live there?"

"Amazing. My family used to lay in the sand during the evening and spin stories about the constellations."

Distant memories played in my mind. I still remembered a story Baba told us about a man turned into a eucafrog on the Miyu Islands who managed to outsmart the Miyu with his wit and charm to escape from getting eaten.

Radi spoke, drawing me out of my thoughts. "I wish I could visit your village and see the beach for myself."

"I wish I could be there, too." An unbearable wave of home-sickness caused a knot in my throat, and my voice hitched.

Radi sighed, sorrow and longing weighing down her words. "I used to watch the stars with my older brother all the time. He'd take me on camping trips to the top of the mountains, overlooking the city."

"You have an older brother?"

"Had."

I'd forgotten. She had no family left. "Oh, Radi. I'm sorry."

"So am I. Tyne was ten years my senior. He raised me after my parents died."

Grief filled her long exhale. Slight tremors broke through her speech. "Five years ago, he was taken into Terran's army to suppress the skirmishes on the border of Yao Kingdom. Thought he could earn enough money to marry his sweetheart. He was assigned to spy on two of the Yao's chief leaders. One a daowolf shifter and the other a kaigon shifter. They must have discovered him. All that was left of my brother for his comrades to find were his bones and spectacles mingled in animal excrement."

She took a shuddering breath. "My would-have-been sister-in-law killed herself, and I lived in an orphanage run by sister Lotus monks until the scouts discovered me. Imagine what those pious Lotuses thought of my wildness. At least they were kind. I would much rather have remained with them than be stuck here."

Knowing our family circumstances were so similar caused a stinging ache to rise in my chest. How could it be that I was lucky to have had my brother and Nia raise me but Radi suffered the tragedy of losing her entire family?

"What about your family?" she asked. "Are they still alive?"

"My brother and sister-in-law are. They should have had their baby by now."

I wondered if it was a boy or girl. I couldn't believe I'd never see my niece or nephew. Heat rimmed my eyes. Tears threatened to spill.

"What about your parents?" Radi asked.

"They were killed by pirates right in front of me."

Radi gasped. "And you survived? I've heard the pirates are merciless."

"I don't remember what happened. I blacked out."

I had woken up in my bed. The chief magistrate said I was lucky. When he found me, all he saw was a pile of bones the pirates left behind, souvenirs of their victims. The chief magistrate believed the pirates had come to find a burial ground for their trophies, which were too burdensome to carry on their small ships. My parents had been there at the wrong time. The pirates had gotten what they wanted, so they left me alone.

"I don't know why they didn't take me to sell as a slave," I said. "I guess Old Grandfather Heaven was watching out for me."

Although, I didn't know why he'd saved me then, only to let the palace take me now.

"I've always blamed Terran for letting the pirates pillage our villages in exchange for their mercenary services. And now I might have to join his harem."

"I'm sorry," Radi said. She treaded water, swaying as though dancing. "I didn't mean to turn this night into a gloomy one. Let's talk about something else. I want to show you something. Look up."

My gaze shot to the sky. The stars played in a light show.

"I can make the stars dance with my body's movement. That's part of my tin-chai."

"Wait, I thought Madam Gomi wanted you to keep that a secret."

A rain of gold dust sprinkled through the trees and into the water.

"I also turn starlight into gold."

"Radi, why are you telling me this? You could get into trouble."

"I told you, I don't live by anyone's rules but my own. I'm telling you as a sign of my friendship. I trust you. You're not going to blab."

"I'm honored. Whatever happens, I swear on the most excruciating pain of death to be your faithful friend for as long as the three moons rule the Caliwyis night sky."

She snorted. "You are *so* dramatic. But since I showed you mine, you have to show me yours. I'm curious what amazing tin-chai Madam Yasmina won't allow you to reveal."

I hesitated. I believed I could trust Radi, and I wanted to show her that our friendship was important to me. But I was still scared. She might not intentionally reveal it, but she did like to talk. What if she accidentally said something between us about my tin-chai, and a madam heard in passing? We could get in trouble.

Before I could reply, the bushes rustled. We both froze. The stars did, too.

Then all was quiet again. Most likely, it was only a moonrabbit, but Radi wasn't taking chances. She waded out and dried herself. "I'm going to walk around and keep watch. Take your time. I sense you miss the water."

She tiptoed off, and I dunked my head once more. I floated on the water and hummed an old lullaby, making sure to keep my tin-chai out of my words. It felt good to sing a few notes after I'd been forced to stifle my voice all these weeks. As much as I didn't want the night to end, I had to get out soon. I sighed.

A splash sounded behind me.

Someone, or something, swam toward me.

CHAPTER 11

The hairs on my neck stood straight up. Although my brain told me to swim to safety, I remained rooted to the spot.

In the middle of the pool, a boy—no, *boy* was too young a description—surfaced. He was at least nineteen or twenty, yet his mischievous grin still came across as boyish. He was looking right at me.

He shook his wet hair, golden locks illuminated by the moonlight. His hair fell in rebellious waves, shorter than what was traditional for men in the court, though not like the shaved head of an androgy either.

His hair flopped on his forehead, giving him a raffish appearance. Water droplets sparkled in rows of tiny mirrors on his tanned skin. I found myself unable to stop staring at his beautiful form. Upon his chiseled chest, a tattoo of a flaming torch burned bright gold embers in the dark of night. The emblem of Emberwood.

What was one of the kingdom's enemies doing here in the palace?

He looked me up and down, then paused, his grin growing wider. My senses finally kicked in, and I got my legs to move. With swift movements, he glided to my side, blocking me from leaving. "What a pleasant surprise. Are you a goddess from the White Moon who has come to spirit me away?" Then he shook his head, laughter in his eyes. "No, I'll bet you're a faela's trifle who heard the eighth prince likes to bathe here at night, so you decided to try and seduce him. Sorry to disappoint. I'm no prince, just a mere slave like you. However, if you wish it, I'll take you on an adventure equally as exciting."

"I'm not a trifle."

To my everlasting shock, he moved closer as though to steal a kiss.

I splashed him. "Keep your hands to yourself."

He lifted his hands in a gesture of surrender and dipped his head as though to apologize.

I dashed out of the water, picked up my clothes, and ran. When I was sure he wasn't following, I fumbled with my buttons and dressed with haste, then went to search for Radi. Through the grove of silver birch trees, I caught sight of a burst of white. A trinket's robe.

But Radi wasn't alone.

Another young man stood facing her. This one was dark-haired, and his fierce scowl indicated he lacked the humor of the man back at the lake. His garments, a long layered silk robe with loose wide sleeves and a cross collar, revealed he was someone important, perhaps the son of an aristocrat. The outermost layer was a dark purple overcoat, embroidered with elaborate circular designs.

His hair was of similar length to the man at the lake, styled far shorter than the older generation of aristocrats who made a point never to cut their hair to set them apart from the commoners. Also unconventional was his lack of a headdress.

He straightened the sash that tied his ensemble and maintained a clear, stern gaze on Radi. "It is past the trinkets' curfew, and you are not allowed to leave the Apple Barrel before the start of your trinketship. There are grave consequences for breaking the rules. Are you alone?"

The young man didn't know I was here. I could still run back to the Apple Barrel. But I couldn't let Radi fend for herself. I wasn't only worried that he would alert the madams. What if he meant to do her harm?

I stepped forward and placed myself in front of Radi. "I'm with her."

His eyes widened at the sight of me.

He held himself with dignity, and his menacing eyes narrowed. "Why are you out here?"

I ventured a glance at Radi. Why wasn't she speaking? Her mouth had fallen open, and she tilted her head to the side, like a painting hung askew on the wall. Her inner garment wasn't buttoned all the way. She flaunted a liberal amount of skin, but though she was as pink as cherry blossoms, she made no motion to cover herself. I took her outer robe, draped it over her shoulders, and tied the sash for the sake of her decency.

The man tracked my movements.

"We . . . umm . . ." Radi's gaze remained on the man's face. She was redder than elderberry jam.

"Blistering ballasts, will you speak up? I have no patience for comatose moonrabbits."

"We only wished to swim in the lake." I folded my hands and bent my head low in a show of humility. "Please excuse us this once. I promise we won't do it again."

"I cannot make exceptions for anyone who breaks palace rules. You will receive ten lashes each when the madams hear about this."

Radi placed a hand on my shoulder and pushed me behind her. Finally finding her voice, she said, "It was my idea. I forced my friend into it. If you must report this, please leave her out of it."

"No," I said. "I went along with you."

Radi ignored me. "Your Highness, I've heard of your kindness and charity. Please spare my friend. She tried to stop me, but I didn't listen."

Your Highness?

The young man blinked at us. "I must say, I have not met one trinket or faela who would display such loyalty for another rivaling Father Emperor's attention."

Father Emperor? Fainting faela, he was Terran's son. A prince.

No way would he spare us.

He looked at me. "I am most impressed that you decided to stand by your friend. You could have left her to take the fall on her own." He turned. "Nevertheless, you were a fool for staying. Dangers abound that will crush your spirit until you wish you were dead."

He marched away, leaving Radi and me standing in awe, our mouths dangling open.

"I can't believe he let us go," I said.

But Radi, still mesmerized, didn't reply. A dreamy expression clouded her gaze.

"Terran's twisted torso. That was Prince Carrick, the eighth prince." Radi was close to squealing like the silly girls she usually ridiculed. I swore her eyes had taken the shape of hearts.

Gripping her shoulder, I shook her. "Get a hold of yourself."

"How can I, when I spoke to Prince Carrick?"

"What's so special about him?"

"What's so *special*?" She glared at me like I was a dunderhead. "He's only the most powerful prince in court. He can summon lightning and thunder at the bat of an eye. He visited my village once to discuss how to help the children orphaned from the wars. Our chief magistrate attests to Carrick's character. The scepter will bestow the Will of Heaven upon him for sure. Unlike the other royals, Carrick cares for the citizens."

"Do you think there's a chance he'll change his mind and report us after all?"

"Oh no. He's far too nice."

I flexed my brow in disbelief. "Your village's chief magistrate may know him, but you don't."

"I'm just saying, he looks nice."

I shook my head, amazed to hear these words from my usually jaded friend. I never thought Radi could become smitten so easily.

"Prince Carrick's pretty boy face does not guarantee our safety."

"He's not a pretty boy, he's a *handsome* prince. And he was impressed by our loyalty. Tonight is the best night of my life."

She grinned, entirely convinced of our safety. I hoped she was right.

CHAPTER 12

Madam Yasmina stood close to the window of her treehouse. We sat cross-legged on the floor of her sitting room. For the past five days, we'd been training with her to prepare for the preliminary test.

"I have unfortunate news," Yasmina said. "The judges have decided to conduct the preliminary test in private with each individual trinket. In fact, some of the trinkets are already testing today. I'm not sure what the new requirements will be."

I could barely concentrate on her words. Her outfit distracted me. Instead of transforming into a flutterfly, she had taken to pretending to be one. She dressed in a pastel rainbow kipa, so bright it hurt to look at her. Her eyelids and cheeks were painted in a kaleidoscope of color, and flutterflies kept flying through the window to land upon her head and shoulders. They were probably attracted to her colors or the scent of her pungent perfume that exaggerated the sweetness of midnight peonies. I usually enjoyed the subtle fragrance of peonies, but I wanted to sneeze.

"Today?" Galai said, her eyes widening. "I thought the test was two days from now, and we'd all be watching each other."

Irica frowned. "Why are the rules changing? And why are there new requirements? We've been practicing the tea ceremony all week."

"Let me clarify," Yasmina said. "A tea ceremony will still be part of the test. However, His Majesty has charged Androgy Haming with the preliminaries this year. The androgy is a top royal advisor, but he's also a slithering serpent. He loves creating chaos and changing the rules last minute to keep us on our toes. I guarantee he'll put a scheming twist to the tea ceremony. You may be required to entertain your guest with a song or dance routine or answer questions about the kingdom's history or politics. There's no way of knowing what it is."

She sighed. "However, I do know you three aren't scheduled to test until the day after tomorrow. All I can do is train you to perform the tea ceremony perfectly, but the rest is up to you. Rilla, I would like to focus on you first."

I knelt on a circular mat and sat on my ankles, then lit the fire to heat the water. I pulled back my sleeves, trying to demonstrate grace and delicacy. A burning smell filled my nose. A flash of orange caught my attention to my smoldering sleeve.

"Fainting faela!" I jolted and hit my fiery sleeve against the ground. I knocked over the bowl containing powdered tea, spilling it all over the floor.

All the flutterflies on Madam Yasmina scattered.

"Rilla!" Madam Yasmina cried, but she helped me extinguish the flame.

Galai and Irica burst into laughter. Madam Yasmina glared at them. "Shush, both of you." She turned to me. "Try again."

She placed a new bowl with the tea powder in front of me. This time I managed to boil the water and clean the utensils without lighting anything on fire.

Then I inhaled a whiff of Yasmina's perfume. I sneezed.

Madam Yasmina sighed. "Let's pretend you did not mimic a snorting sihai and move on. Your guest may ask you personal questions to understand more about your background. Let's practice."

I scooped the powdered tea into another bowl. It smelled clean and sweet, a grassy perfume that reminded me of summer nights.

"Rilla, tell me about your childhood home and your parents," Madam Yasmina said.

I added boiling water to it, whisking the ingredients together to make the thick tea, before answering the question.

"I grew up in Cascasea Vill—"

"No," Madam Yasmina said. "You took too long to answer. Your job is to answer while you prepare the tea, without faltering. Flawless grace. Again."

I repeated the procedure, taking the tea and whisking it with the hot water. "I grew up in Cascasea Village. My parents were deep sea fishermen, and I have an older brother who is a doctor."

I passed the bowl to Madam Yasmina. She turned it three times before sipping.

"Good, but you can do better with more practice. Your movements need to be more graceful. Think of a flutterfly's wings, not the blundering of a lumbering ungbeetle."

She had me practice three more times before she allowed me to stand. My knees wobbled. I'd lost all feeling in my legs.

"You might be asked about politics and inter-kingdom relations," Madam Yasmina said. "If so, you'll probably be asked about the Miyu, given that you lived in the closest village to the Cascasea Islands. So tell me, what do you think about the skirmishes near the Cascasea Islands, and how should we deal with them?"

"First of all, they are called the Miyu Islands," I said. "They belong to the Miyu, not us. I believe the Miyu are misunderstood. They are only trying to protect themselves. Leave them alone, and they will leave us alone."

"No, no, horrible answer." Madam Yasmina clicked her tongue. "You cannot disagree with the emperor's policies, nor do we care to hear your true opinion. When in doubt, always say you agree with whatever the emperor believes."

Galai and Irica giggled behind their pretty silk folding fans and whispered to each other. Madam Yasmina spun around to face them. She addressed the girls in a calm voice, but her words were sharp. "Ladies, I told you to stop laughing. You aren't without faults either."

Irica pouted. "Why are you giving Rilla all the attention? How are we to know our faults if you've barely given us any training?"

Madam Yasmina's smile was radiant, though danger lurked behind the thick layers of magenta lipstick coating her mouth. "You are correct, child. I should give you an honest opinion of your faults. Galai, you are a fat caterpillar. You need more exercise. Irica, your singing makes me want to return to my cocoon and not emerge for my entire life cycle. If not for your pretty faces, I would never have agreed with my subordinates to bring either of you here."

The two girls gaped, too shocked to make a rebuttal. Madam Yasmina turned to me again. "Rilla, my beautiful flutterfly. Why don't you go practice your folk dance while I instruct these less colorful humoths?"

I exited the treehouse but didn't wander far. After circling the courtyard several times, I sat upon a stone next to the large tree. On the other side of the trunk, a woman spoke. She sounded furious.

"I cannot believe Androgy Haming changed the rules. One of my trinkets already had her preliminary test. I asked her what the test entails, but she was charmed to remain silent until all the girls have tested."

The woman on the other side of the tree must be a madam.

"Two of my girls never came back," a second madam said.

The trunk was wide enough to obscure their view of me, so they must not know I was here.

"What do you mean?" the first madam asked. "Did Androgy Haming disqualify them?"

"I asked, but he wouldn't say," the other madam said. "It's strange. Even if they had been disqualified, it would be our job to set them up as serving trifles. But Androgy Haming said those girls were no longer my business. He told me not to ask any more questions."

They walked away, and I couldn't hear them anymore.

I frowned. If those trinkets weren't to be trifles, then where had the androgy taken them?

The sound of footsteps drew me out of my thoughts.

A young boy, eyes wide and rattled, sprinted across the courtyard. He held a basket containing several scrolls, and in his hurry, one of the manuscripts flew out behind him. It fell to the ground, the parchment rolling out to reveal small scripted brushstrokes.

The boy didn't notice his missing scroll and continued down the lane, past the boundary of the Apple Barrel Palace. It would take but a few seconds to deliver the scroll back to him, so I picked it up and chased after him.

Cherry trees grew on both sides, scattering pink blossoms with the slightest rustling of wind. Maybe this was forbidden territory, but it was beautiful.

I caught up to the boy and called out. "Excuse me. You dropped this."

He turned around and took the scroll from me. "Oh, thank you. I would have been scolded by my training master if I lost it."

I took note of his light blue uniform. He must be an androgy.

The boy looked at my uniform. "Trinkets are not allowed here. You should return to the Apple Barrel before someone catches you."

He hurried away, and I turned back. A breeze blew through the trees. The same sickening sweet perfume I'd smelled the night I snuck out with Radi came through the cherry trees. What was the source?

I hiked down the lane. Voices sounded, and I saw Prince Carrick headed my way. I couldn't let him catch me here, especially when he'd already let me go once.

I took cover behind a bush.

Prince Carrick walked past me. His attention was on the trees. "Give me the signal when you secure the area."

Who was he addressing?

He continued down the trail and then vanished into the air. I blinked. Were my eyes playing tricks on me? Where had he gone?

Curiosity overcame my fear of being caught. I tip-toed through the trees, approaching the spot where he had been standing.

No one was there. Instead, I saw a one-tiered pagoda, its foundation built upon the ground. The gazebo pillars were made of white birch trees, twisted and monstrous. Tube-shaped, red trumpet vines climbed four tree trunks, the vibrant color a sharp contrast against the faded greens and whites. Branches stretched down from the treetops, twining together to form the arches of the roof. At the top of the roof was a circular dome made of flowering vines with bursts of red and yellow star-shaped flowers. All corners of the roof curved upward, pointing to sharp peaks at the ends.

I crept toward it, compelled to get a closer look. This pagoda was beautiful and unlike any other I'd seen. Gazebos were usually open on all sides, but this one had bars, formed by roots that sprung from the ground. A large birdcage. A white curtain fell between the red pillars on all sides, veiling what the bars did not conceal.

I stopped in front of it and looked around. Dozens of similar birdcages stood, scattered throughout the forest floor. I scanned the other cages. They were all similar in structure, but each was built from a different type of wood—elm, pine, cherry, maple, mahogany, oak, and hickory.

Two birdcages neighbored the one where I stood, but unlike the other birdcages, these were only half constructed, and the curtains had not been hung up. The white fabric covered the bottom of the cages like a pile of discarded dresses. I moved closer to get a better look. The cages were empty. My gaze fell upon two metal plaques laid out on the dirt.

Etched into the first plaque were these words:

Emperor Terran's Prized Novelty #389
Dominant Channel: Ha
Touch Cleanses Body of Toxins

And on the second plaque:

Emperor Terran's Prized Novelty #390
Dominant Channel: Ha
Tears Act as Temporary Relief for Physical Pain

These sounded like healing tin-chai. What did this all mean? What were novelties?

A shrill rustle echoed behind me. I jumped and stifled a shriek. No one was there. Just the wind blowing at the curtains of the veiled birdcage I'd first seen.

A muddled shape of something moved inside. My heart thudded in my ears, and I swallowed my fear. Step by step, I tiptoed back toward the cage and squinted, searching for some clue as to what it could contain. A monster kept caged, its grotesqueness only unveiled for the palace to marvel upon rare occasions? Or perhaps a trained pet for the emperor's entertainment?

The odor was stagnant here, overpowering. The fragrance of cherry blossoms mingled with sweat and body fluids. I sniffed. The smells came from the cages.

An unnatural silence filled the air. Not one bird chirped. It was as though every bird and critter had fled the scene.

On the cage before me, the sun glinted on the metal plaque nailed to the bottom of the bars. It read:

Emperor Terran's Prized Novelty #388
Dominant Channel: Dai
Controls the Weather with Song

The wind blew the curtain up, shifting it so a sunbeam shone through, and I caught a glimpse of a silhouette. I covered my mouth. Not a monster or an animal. A woman.

"She is the emperor's pet novelty." The low baritone came from out of nowhere. I jumped, stifling a shriek.

A man emerged from the shadows. My gaze darted to his face.

Prince Carrick.

CHAPTER 13

I assessed the prince with caution. Would he call me out again for treading into forbidden territory? Then I realized what he'd called the woman.

"A novelty?" My jaw slackened, and I turned to Carrick, waiting for further explanation.

But the prince remained silent. He stepped closer to the edge of the pagoda. From his pocket, he extracted a triangular-shaped coin, a two-piece Seran, and inserted it into a small slot on the base of the structure.

The curtain parted as though revealing some elaborate theater stage. A woman sat on a lavish bed, which barely fit in the tight space. Beside the bed were two bowls—one filled with food, the other with water. A porcelain pot was set next to the bowls. Brown and yellow stains smeared its sides.

I estimated the cage's diameter to be no greater than eight feet, while the height doubled that. I couldn't imagine a pet godog living in that tight space, much less a woman or man.

Both the woman and the bed were embellished in dark emerald green silk. A green headdress covered the woman's hair, and a silk scarf veiled the bottom half of her face. Only her clear gray-green eyes remained exposed. Sad, soulful eyes that lit up at the sight of the prince before they faded to emptiness once more.

Instead of greeting us as I thought she would, she sang a chilling melody. The music burrowed into my core, stealing every last ray of warmth from my body. I couldn't stop shivering.

"Oh, blossoms of June, sweet blossoms of June,
How the love of our youth e'er did bloom,
'til the fading light of that autumn noon.
And then, oh, those sweet blossoms of June
Died under the light of the Lavender Moon."

The lyrics carried a heavy weight of loneliness that sat on my shoulders and refused to budge.

The notes flowed out of her, and a crash of thunder raged overhead. Raindrops pelted the trees, but the water bounced off the air around me as though an invisible force field surrounded my body. Prince Carrick also remained dry.

The last note died away, and the rain stopped. The prince stood and slipped a basket covered in white cloth through the cage bars.

"Fresh peaches. I know they are your favorite."

The woman kneeled on the ground, close to one of the red beams, edging against the bars as far as her prison would allow. She reached through the forested barrier and took the gift but set it aside and clasped the prince's hands in her own. A smothered sound died in her throat.

A single tear slid from the corner of her eye. Prince Carrick reached through the bars and wiped it away. "You mustn't worry about me," Carrick said.

The woman tilted her brows, a question forming in her eyes. She looked beyond his shoulders, her gaze reaching toward the trees. She waved to someone there. I followed her line of sight, searching up and down. There was only empty air.

Perhaps she greeted the ghosts of a previous life.

"Yes, my friend sends his regards and hopes to visit you soon," the prince said. After a lingering second, he pulled away from the woman. His feet dug into the dirt as though it burdened him to move an inch. "I must go before Androgy Solar discovers I am not studying my lessons. You know how fussy he gets when he thinks I'm being lazy."

His body moved away from the cage as his head remained facing the woman. She waved and blew a kiss, and the curtains closed, concealing her face from the world once more.

The prince paused before circling around. He regarded me with the same sad gray-green eyes as the woman. He resembled her.

"She's your mother," I said. My eyes widened at the realization. I grabbed hold of a tree to support my wobbly legs.

"Yes," he said. "Meet Faela Lady Cirisa."

"Why couldn't she say anything to you?"

"She is not allowed to talk. She can only use her tin-chai to entertain her guest. Father Emperor personally designed these cages, infusing his tin-chai into the trees so they move even without his presence. The branches and vines are charmed to whip novelties for speaking or for disobeying their guest's commands."

"What is she doing here? And how is she a novelty if she's a faela?"

His lips tugged up in a humorless smile. "Don't tell me you were naïve enough to believe all the faela live in luxury. No woman is safe."

He brushed past me, and I thought he would leave without saying another word until he tipped his head and said, "Come. You should return before your madam misses you. I will walk you back."

I couldn't grasp what I'd just seen. This had to be a nightmare. No woman was safe, Carrick had said. But how was it that even a faela could be subjected to such a cruel punishment? I had believed all faela lived in comfort as long as they remained submissive to the emperor.

But if this wasn't the case, what use was there in trying to win the showcase?

My mouth opened at least seven times on the verge of asking a question when Prince Carrick said, "Scorching nutshells, will you stop imitating a fish? Either speak up, or shut up."

"There are so many cages. How many hold faela?"

"You tell me. Father Emperor has over one hundred wives, and the number grows every year. What happens to all the women? Not only the faela he grows tired of, but also trifles who possess tin-chai he finds useful or entertaining end up here."

I gawked. "Faela he tires of? Trifles? They *all* end up in cages?"

"Not all," he relented. "Some faela waste away in their cold, lonely palaces. The lucky ones win the emperor's favor if they are able to bear him sons, but even they may end up in a cage if they're not careful of palace politics. Most trinkets who become trifles die untouched virgins unless Father Emperor or a prince or aristocrat finds one who catches their fancy."

I waited for him to continue, but he paused to pluck a cherry blossom from the tree and held it out to me. I accepted the gift and inhaled its sweet fragrance.

"Father Emperor is a mercurial man. There was no reason he should have been displeased with my mother. She was beautiful, talented, kind, and she bore him a son. One day she was singing, trying to bring the sun out for him. Maybe he was tired of her, but in a moment, he complained she burned him on purpose, and he cast her into prison."

I hadn't needed further evidence of Terran's despicable character, but here it was. He would cage a woman for her entire lifetime simply because he desired it.

"I begged him to let her go," Prince Carrick said. "He compromised for my sake, turning her into a novelty instead of executing her. Not all faela are lucky to be kept as novelties who purely entertain him and the aristocrats. Usually, he needs to find their tin-chai useful."

I was almost too afraid to ask. "If not for entertainment, what purpose does a novelty's tin-chai serve him?"

"Father Emperor believes in keeping novelties with powerful tin-chai. You know there are numerous types of tin-chai, some rarer than others. Everything from shooting electricity from one's eyes to bringing a withered flower back to life. He keeps them in cages for future use, whether to become his weapons against enemies or as a means of accumulating resources during trying times."

I thought of the two empty birdcages and the two trinkets who had been taken after their preliminary test today. Could it be that they were intended to become the emperor's newest novelties? Maybe they had revealed their tin-chai during the test.

If so, then none of us was safe. I could not reveal my tin-chai at any cost. I had to warn Radi. If the emperor got a hold of her, he would have enough gold to do whatever he wished. Start another war. And he could force me to keep him young.

"When the curtains are open, novelties are forbidden to speak a word and are whipped if they do," Carrick said. "But most of the time, the curtains are closed, and novelties live in solitary confinement. No one is allowed into their cage except the trifle who cleans up after them."

I shuddered. "Why doesn't anyone outside the palace know about these cages?"

Prince Carrick snorted as though the answer should be obvious. "If they taught this to you at school, none of you would be begging to come to Cedar Palace, not even for the chance of having all the money and power in the world. That would damage Father Emperor's pride."

I looked away. "It's not always for the money and power."

The prince paused to assess me. "If not, then why are you here?"

"My madam threatened to kill my family if I didn't comply."

"Then she must believe Father Emperor will be taken with you. The madams are known for making bets on their trinkets. What is your tin-chai?"

I hesitated. True, he hadn't turned Radi and me in, but he was still a prince whose father was the one person I didn't want knowing my tin-chai.

"I don't have a magical tin-chai," I said. "I'm a koong who can sing well, and Madam Yasmina said music is the way to your father's heart."

"I see." Carrick's face was unreadable. I couldn't tell if he believed me, but he didn't question me further.

"Is there any way to forfeit the showcase without endangering my family?" I asked, my voice small.

"No, and by no means should you attempt to run away. Father Emperor has given Empress Limera free reign to punish all attempted runaways and trinkets who appear unenthusiastic about the showcase. Mother Empress is not one to be crossed."

I thought of the way the empress had assessed all the trinkets to look for our faults. I was sure I'd prefer death to whatever torture she had designed for her victims.

"And your mother? Is there a way to set her free?"

"One way," he said, the corners of his mouth slanting up in a resolved glower. "I will claim the Sacred Cedar Scepter and prove I have the Will of Heaven to take the throne from my father. Then I shall free everyone."

CHAPTER 14

When I told Radi about the cages, she paced the room, pulling her hands through her hair. "This changes everything. I'd thought obeying the madams was the only way to survive. But there's no guarantee we'll be any safer whether or not we do become faela."

"But what can we do?" I said. "It's too dangerous to run away."

"I can't sit here and let Terran lock me in a cage."

"We can't be impulsive either. Prince Carrick said—"

"Who cares what Carrick said?"

I stepped back at Radi's outburst.

"Terran's tentacles, Rilla. It's always 'my mama said,' 'my brother said,' 'Carrick said.'" She mimicked my voice in a whiny falsetto. "Don't you *ever* form your own opinions?"

My breath hitched as though she'd punched me in the gut.

I stopped myself from biting back and managed to keep my tone even. "This *is* my opinion. If we're caught running away—"

"We'll have to make sure we aren't caught then."

"So we become fugitives and hide for the rest of our lives?" I shook my head. "You might not have a family to worry about, but I do. I won't have Terran threatening them to get to me."

Radi stopped pacing and scowled at me. "If you don't want to come with me, that's your choice, but I won't leave my fate up to them. Terran will lock me in a cage and use my tin-chai to replenish the palace gold reserves. Then he'll have the means to conquer all the kingdoms of Caliwyis."

"All I'm asking is for you not to be rash. We'll come up with a plan. One that will keep us safe and doesn't involve breaking the rules."

"Don't you see? There is no solution but to break the rules and take a risk. I suppose I shouldn't have expected you to understand. After all, you're such a rule follower, you haven't even told me what your tin-chai is."

I hadn't meant to keep it from her. "My tin-chai—"

"I no longer want to know. But if Madam Yasmina has made you keep it a secret, you must be special, and chances are Terran will want you, too. Will you continue living the rest of your life knowing there's a possibility you'll end up in a cage? Knowing he will use your tin-chai for his benefit, which might harm the rest of the world?"

I trembled at the thought. No, I didn't want to live the rest of my life in fear, nor did I want the emperor and empress to use my voice to attain eternal youth.

"Following the rules is the best option to keep myself and my family out of danger," I said. "If I can find a way to stop Madam Yasmina from revealing my tin-chai, I might be able to become a trifle, unseen and unheard. Even if I'm trapped in the palace my whole life, at least my family will be safe."

She stood and glanced away, stone-faced. "You know, there's nothing I detest more than when someone proves to be a coward."

Coward. The word dug into me, stabbing deep into an old, unhealed wound—that I'd always allow fear to keep me hidden in the shadows.

She walked away. "Do whatever you want."

The following afternoon, Madam Yasmina ended another tea ceremony lesson and lounged on the settee. I stood and stretched my arms, rolling my head from side to side. Something between my shoulder blades cracked. The sound reverberated through the silent room.

Madam Yasmina hissed. Her hair—plaited in a single tail running down her back—puffed out, doubling from its normal thickness like the fur of an angry maocat. "Stop behaving like a godog puppy unable to sit still."

I forced myself to take a deep, calming breath. "Yes ma'am."

"Perhaps you should take a short reprieve while I help the other girls. But when you return, I expect your performance to improve."

I wandered to Treehouse 38 to find Radi. I hoped she was no longer mad at me.

One of her roommates, Vy, sat in front of the mirror.

She played with strips of eyelid glue, but she stopped when she spied me watching. She rolled her eyes. "What do you want?"

"Sorry to bother you. I'm looking for Radi."

"Well, you can see she's not here. Haven't seen her all day."

"Do you know where she is?"

She gave a longsuffering sigh. "How should I know?"

She swished her hair over her shoulders with an air of self-importance and returned her attention to her eyes, now pinching her eyelid back to apply the glue.

"Thank you," I said. She ignored me, too busy trying to achieve the double lids she coveted.

I checked the dining hall next. Though our meals were limited, maybe Radi had decided to sneak a midday snack. But she wasn't there.

I ambled around the rest of the Apple Barrel searching for her. She wasn't with the seamstress scouts either.

A sense of worry settled in the pit of my stomach. I knew she hadn't taken her test yet. She was scheduled for tomorrow. What if she had run away?

I turned toward Treehouse 30, the beauty parlor. It was highly unlikely Radi would have gone for a pedicure or to style her hair, but I had to check anyway.

Radi emerged from the doorway. A gushing breath rushed out of my lungs.

She saw me and waved. "Rilla, there you are. I was looking all over for you."

I rushed toward her and hugged her.

"Does this mean I don't have to apologize for my poor behavior to you yesterday?" she asked. "I'm really sorry. You were right. I was being impulsive."

"I'm sorry, too. I didn't mean to keep my tin-chai from you."

She shook her head. "I don't need to know it right now. We have something more important to think about. We need to come up with a strategy to make sure the emperor never learns our tin-chai."

We sat on one of the tree boughs in the center of the courtyard. Not many girls were outside today. Most were in their rooms or with their madams, probably either practicing for the test or keeping their charmed lips sealed regarding the details of their test performance.

"You made a good point during our argument," Radi said. "If we become trifles, we can keep our distance from Terran. But we still have a major problem. How do we stop the madams from revealing our tin-chai in the finale? Once our tin-chai are revealed, we will either become novelties or faela."

"I've thought a lot about that, but I still don't have an answer," I said.

Radi sighed. "Well, I suppose there's no use thinking that far yet. Let's get through this preliminary test without betraying ourselves. Then at least we'll move on to the trinketship and have six weeks to think about how to continue keeping our tin-chai a secret."

She was right. If we accidentally revealed our tin-chai tomorrow, the game would be over. No matter what was in store for the test, I wasn't going to let anyone trick me into using my voice again.

CHAPTER 15

"Girls, wake up." Madam Yasmina's shrill voice reverberated in my ears. I rubbed the sleep from my eyes and sat up.

Irica and Galai stirred in their beds.

Madam Yasmina pulled my arms and dragged me to my feet. "Hurry, girls. Your test begins at the start of the next hour."

The other girls and I quickly dressed. Madam Yasmina had already prepared porridge for our breakfast since we didn't have time to go to the dining hall, but after two spoonfuls, I pushed the bowl aside. I was too nervous to keep anything down.

Then I trudged behind Galai and Irica as we made our way to the courtyard. I wiped my clammy hands on my dress. What was this Androgy Haming like? Madam Yasmina had called him a slithering serpent. For someone who could change the rules of the long-standing tea ceremony test, he had to be a powerful influence in the palace.

A group of men gathered around the wide, knotted tree of Apple Barrel Court. But three leaders stood up front. I recognized the man in the middle. The emperor. He was a replica of the picture displayed on the chimney mantel back at home. The same deep, dark eyes. Silver streaks interspersed on a still-full head of black hair, arranged in a dignified topknot. He held himself straight-backed and confident, head lifted high.

I'd hoped his portrait was a gratuitous rendition, and I'd find him much uglier and obnoxious up close. Seeing him in person only confirmed he was handsome. He looked like the kind of man I'd once imagined as the hero of the adventure stories I'd read, not the vindictive demon trying to kill the hero and rape the village maidens.

A hunchbacked androgy stood next to Terran. Postured like the hull of a capsized boat, his gaze remained parallel to the ground. Was he Androgy Haming?

Then there was the third man on the other side of Terran. This man was dressed in deep amber garments as rich as the emperor's own robes. Who was he?

A bevy of the emperor's followers surrounded them. The pretentious aristocrats—ranging from the emperor's own royal relations to noblemen and army officers—stood behind their almighty leader.

Several bodyguards dressed in black encompassed the group in an outer semicircle. It was impossible to guess what they thought or felt under their masks.

Six other trinkets approached the tree. They must be the girls who were also testing today. Radi was among them. I didn't have time to exchange greetings with her. A trumpet blared.

"Trinkets, bow to His Majesty."

We fell to our knees. A choir of echoes resounded in the air. "Long live His Majesty, Emperor Terran. May he live a thousand years and one thousand more."

Terran stepped before us. "Please, lift your heads. I want to gaze upon your lovely faces."

A wide grin spread across his face. Terran's extravagant garments glittered under the sun. The outline of a flaming kaigon was sewn onto the center of his robe. "As I have told the other trinkets who have already tested the past two days, you are a striking bunch. I am eager to choose my new faela from the fairest and most charming among you."

I wanted to gag. Couldn't anyone else see he was no god? Did they fear Old Grandfather Heaven? The power of the Sacred Cedar Scepter?

Wait... where *was* the scepter? I thought the emperor was supposed to carry it with him.

Terran gestured to his left. "May I introduce you to General Boti Penweather. He is one of the showcase judges."

The man dressed in extravagant robes bowed his head. Not even the flowing cut of the fabric could hide the general's corpulence. He kept tugging his robe closed and retying the sash around his waist, a futile effort. The blubber of his belly continued to dislodge the sash, the layers of fat spreading out like pleats of a folding fan.

Terran continued, indicating the man to his right. "This is Androgy Haming, my advisor, who in a moment shall be providing you with more instruction on your test."

The androgy inclined his head in greeting. His face was emotionless.

"Now I shall leave you in Androgy Haming's capable hands," Terran said. "May the best of you be allowed to win over my affection."

He took his leave. The other aristocrats and bodyguards followed. Only Androgy Haming and General Penweather remained.

General Penweather stepped forward. He smoothed over what was left of his thinning hair, which he had slicked back into a mini bun, then cleared his throat. "Trinkets, I have a few other matters to address before Androgy Haming calls the first contestant into the test room. In the past, some faela have been known to stray from the teachings of the Analects of Heaven. During your trinketship, if you know your mentoring faela is committing sins against her husband

and ruler, it is your responsibility to report her to your madam, or you will be considered her accomplice by association. If your mentor's secret sins are discovered, you and your birth family, along with the faela and her birth family, shall be executed accordingly."

How many faela had been caught conspiring against the emperor or taking on lovers for the palace to enforce this rule of the trinkets? It seemed unfair to punish us for their crimes.

"Likewise, madams are not infallible," the general continued. "Although it is not illegal to make bets on a trinket, a madam cannot tamper with showcase proceedings to favor a trinket she has bet on, nor can she indulge in spirits or engage in any form of unseemly behavior as the Analects of Heaven instruct of older women. We encourage trinkets to come forward if your madam is breaking proper conduct. We take these crimes seriously, and if found guilty, the madam will be promptly executed. However, you must have sufficient proof. You cannot accuse a madam simply based on your dislike for her strict training."

Impartiality? Madam Yasmina did favor me above the others. If I could get her in trouble for it, maybe she wouldn't be able to reveal my tin-chai. But how could I get evidence?

"And that was the last order of business," General Penweather said. "Androgy Haming, you may proceed."

Haming moved toward us. His footsteps were effortless, like he was gliding through air. He unrolled a scroll, his gaze drifted across the paper, and then he lifted his emotionless face.

"The test will proceed at Treehouse 26. First up, Miss Radiana Ying from Jailong Village. Follow me."

I exchanged glances with Radi as she passed me, and I mouthed to her. "Good luck."

She smiled back at me and then proceeded to follow the androgy down the lane.

I closed my eyes for a second, saying a quick prayer for Radi.

The rest of us sat on the bench. No one spoke. I felt the nervous energy, and my stomach lurched. Thank goodness I hadn't finished that porridge earlier.

When Androgy Haming returned, Radi was not with him. A tightness formed in my chest. What if she had been taken for her tin-chai? I wished I could ask where she was.

I waited and watched as, one by one, each girl went with Androgy Haming. Whenever he returned to retrieve the next trinket in line, the previous girl did not return with him. I relaxed a bit. Certainly not all of them would have failed, which meant they must have just been sent back to the madams.

Finally, I was the only one left.

Androgy Haming came out and looked at me. "Miss Rilla Marseas, you're the last one."

I followed him through the rows of treehouses in the Apple Barrel until we came to Treehouse 26. Androgy Haming's footsteps were light on the polished veneer of the wooden floorboards, but my heels clicked as I walked inside. Haming paused behind me and shut the door. The sound echoed. I shivered and looked around. We were in a spacious chamber with high-vaulted ceilings. I couldn't tell how many floors this house had, but there had to be more than one. On this level, there were no windows to the outside world, but candles made up for the lack of light.

I spotted a second door behind me that led to a staircase going up to a second floor. And higher on the back wall, one floor up, there was a darkened window looking down over the room. I couldn't see what lay behind it. Perhaps another room?

A low, round wooden table was centered in this room, and all the utensils necessary for a tea ceremony were laid out on the table. I had expected my guest to be seated there already, but no one was in the room other than the androgy and me. Was Androgy Haming going to be my guest?

Haming held his hands behind his back as he regarded me. "Your guest, Androgy Unther, shall be here in a minute. You will perform the tea ceremony, but this is not your true test." A shadowed smile curved on Haming's lips. "Androgy Unther believes his job is to interview your intelligence on the kingdom's foreign polices to make sure your opinions are aligned with His Majesty. But the truth is I have found evidence that he is a traitor to the kingdom, and Emperor Terran wants him dead."

My heartbeat skittered. Surely he wasn't about to ask me to commit murder.

Haming smirked. "His Majesty must be assured that his potential faela will be loyal to him and do whatever he commands. Your instruction is to poison your guest's tea without revealing any emotion."

He grabbed my hand, placed a paper pouch in my palm, and closed my fingers around it. I felt a powdery substance through the thin paper. This could not be happening. How could I kill someone?

"What if I cannot complete this task?" I asked. "Will I be disqualified and assigned to be a trifle?"

"Perhaps," he said. "But perhaps there are worse fates for being disloyal to His Majesty's desires."

A threat. I thought of the birdcages, and my stomach lurched.

"I will be observing you from upstairs," he said. "Once you poison your guest's tea, you must mask all your emotions and watch him die. You must not interfere or ease his suffering. If you reveal even one tear, you will lose points, and you may not be paired with the faela mentor you wanted for your trinketship."

Who cared about the trinketship? I didn't want to kill a man, even if he was a stranger. It went against everything I believed in as a healer. But if I didn't pass this test, I could be punished. Become a caged novelty.

"You have a minute before your guest enters the room. Put the poison in the tea powder before his arrival. I hope for your sake you do not fail." Androgy Haming walked to the back door and ascended the stairs.

CHAPTER 16

I stared at the pouch of poison in my palm. Haming was watching. I had to do it.

I rushed to the table and located the dish of elderberry tea powder. My hands shook. Taking the paper packet, I ripped it open and poured the contents into the tea. I mixed it with a pestle, and then I ran back to where I'd been standing. My heart hammered in my chest, the beat pounding in my ears.

A knock sounded on the front door. A short man entered. He was bald but had a pointed white beard, giving him the wise look of a sage. He reminded me of a village grandpa, like one of my brother's patients who always gave my family a crate of golden citrus whenever my brother treated him.

I was about to kill an old, defenseless man. I steeled my emotions. Haming could not see me break down.

I bowed. "Androgy Unther. Welcome."

Androgy Unther returned the bow. "Good morning, Miss Marseas. Androgy Haming has instructed me to interview you as you perform the tea ceremony." He had a friendly tone.

He walked to the table. I swallowed a gulp of air. My whole body shook, but I maintained a straight-backed posture and approached the table.

I kneeled on the woven mat and pulled back my sleeves in preparation to steep the tea. I boiled the water and cleaned the utensils, then scooped the elderberry tea powder into a bowl. Was it my imagination, or could I smell the poison?

I poured some hot water over it and whisked the mixture in a clockwise motion. What was I going to do? My hand shook, and some of the water splashed onto the table.

"There's no need to be nervous," Unther said. "Just be honest, and I am sure you'll do fine."

He smiled. A genuine smile that reached his eyes. I could not kill this man. There had to be a way out of this.

What if I used my tin-chai? But how? Haming was watching.

"Let's begin with a simple question," Unther said. "Where is your hometown?"

I took a deep breath for courage before answering. Still, my voice shook.

"I'm from Cascasea Village."

I pulled back my sleeve, then lifted the teapot high and poured a steady stream into his cup. The moisture from the steam condensed on my chin, and the fresh, lemony fragrance of elderberry tea cut through the air.

He lifted the cup to his lips and took a long sip. I stopped myself from flinching.

"Tell me about your family."

I tilted my gaze downward to appear demure, just as Madam Yasmina had instructed. "My brother is a doctor. My parents passed away when I was young, so my brother raised me."

Androgy Unther coughed and rubbed at his neck. "Excuse me, my throat is a bit dry." He emptied the contents of his teacup.

I fought the urge to knock the cup from his hands.

He continued, though there was a hoarseness to his voice. "Tell me about your education. Were you trained in music and dance?"

The question sparked an idea. This was an opportunity. Perhaps I could save him after all.

"Like most girls, I received formal education until my sixteenth birthday," I said. "And I did receive musical training. In fact, allow me to sing you a song."

Before he could approve or disapprove, I cleared my throat and sang off key.

"Although I no longer a child may be,
The song of your zither still enters my dreams."

I felt my power reach into the androgy.

He covered his ears and winced, interrupting me. "Enough, Miss Marseas. I do not need to hear any more."

Had I exerted enough of my *wyis*? At least I knew I hadn't overdone it this time. He still looked his age. The last thing I wanted was to turn him twenty years younger like Auntie An.

"Let us continue with the tea ceremony," he said. "Music is not a requirement today."

He no longer coughed as he spoke. A good sign.

I feigned embarrassment, sitting down and looking away. "Yes, I'm sorry. My mother always said I was tone deaf, but that never stopped my enjoyment of singing."

"I am sure you are talented in other ways," Androgy Unther said. "But let's move on. One final question. I must ask you about your views on current politics. Since you grew up near the Cascasean Islands, you must have an opinion regarding the Miyu skirmishes. What do you think should be done to stop them from killing our men?"

I smiled. Madam Yasmina had prepared me for this question. "I believe in the emperor. He knows what is best for our kingdom."

Unther stood. "Thank you. That concludes the test. Wait here. Androgy Haming will come with your results."

His footsteps echoed through the empty room as he went upstairs to find Haming.

What would Haming do? I had to keep calm. Unther might not be dead, but I had done as instructed.

Voices came from behind me. Haming and Unther walked down the stairs. The two androgies bowed to one another. Haming kept his eye on Unther until the older androgy took his exit through the back door.

Then Haming turned toward me. His expression was unreadable, expressionless. "That man should be dead. Can you tell me why he is not?"

Though my heart was pounding, a strange sense of composure came over me. I looked directly into his eyes and shrugged. "I did as you instructed. You must have seen me from upstairs. I put the poison into the tea powder."

"True," he conceded, still revealing nothing. There was a calculative gleam in his eyes. He assessed me, but I refused to look away. "Why did you sing?"

"Androgy Unther asked if I was trained in music and dance," I said. "I thought a short performance might help me earn more points."

A crescent moon smile formed across his face, giving him a sinister appearance. "The other day, I watched two girls break. Even though they poisoned the tea, they ended up using their tin-chai to save their judge's life. When I informed His Majesty, he took great interest in them."

The empty novelty cages. Those poor girls. My stomach squeezed. I swallowed, my throat tight. "I don't know what you're implying."

He paused a long moment, still studying me. His thin lips widened into a grin. "I've seen three reactions during this test. Some girls were ruthless. They had no problem poisoning their judge as long as they passed the test. Other girls forced themselves to put the poison in the tea, only to start sobbing when their judge started choking. Just so you know, neither of these groups was disqualified."

I remained silent. What was his intention in telling me this?

"Then there were the two I told you about. But they were fools. Only fools get caught."

My heart thudded faster. "I did what you asked and nothing more. I don't know why the poison didn't take effect."

His smile disappeared. "Perhaps you're right. I cannot find fault with what you did." He made a gesture of dismissal with his hand. "You are excused."

"Th-that's it?" I said.

"What else would there be?" His tone was cold and bored. "This is the last day of testing. No one needs to be charmed into keeping their silence anymore."

"What about my results?"

"Wait outside, and you shall be informed shortly."

I had never met anyone so cryptic, so indecipherable. He definitely suspected I had saved Androgy Unther, but he couldn't prove it. As long as he had no proof I had a healing tin-chai, I was safe. At least until the finale.

I trekked back to the Apple Barrel Courtyard. The other trinkets who had tested before me today all sat under the tree. Radi was there as well. I exhaled a relieved sigh. She stood when she saw me.

I rushed toward her and grabbed her elbow. "What happened during your test? Did you get your results yet?"

"Not yet," she whispered. "Androgy Haming said I was to kill my judge."

"I was told the same. What did you do?"

"First of all, you won't believe who my judge was," she said. "General Penweather."

My eyes widened. "But this morning, it seemed he was close to the emperor."

"He wasn't in any danger," Radi said. "None of our judges were. The test was to see if we were willing to kill for the emperor."

"How do you know?"

She smiled. "I eavesdropped after I poured tea on Penweather's lap."

"You what?" I poked at my ears to see if I had heard correctly.

"I'd have had no problem killing the general. He was already leering at my chest when I walked into the room. But then he made an untoward advance. Groped my thigh. I lost my temper. Dumped scalding hot water right on him. You should have seen his face."

"I can't believe how fearless you are," I said. "Aren't you scared they'll punish you?"

She waved me off. "Don't worry. I made it look like an accident, and I never revealed my tin-chai. That alone will keep them curious, so I won't be disqualified yet."

She had a point. As long as we continued hiding our tin-chai for the duration of the showcase, we wouldn't end up in a novelty cage.

"Androgy Haming came out to stop the test," she continued. "He dismissed me, but I lingered to eavesdrop. That's how I learned he had an antidote, and the judges were never in real danger. He admonished the general. Said Penweather wasn't supposed to touch the emperor's property. Penweather said he couldn't help it, and the emperor wouldn't mind. They're disgusting beasts."

Radi's test experience sounded more stressful than mine.

"So what happened during your test?" Radi asked.

A handclap sounded, earning our attention. Yasmina, Gomi, and two other madams approached. My story would have to wait.

"Ladies, your results are here," Madam Gomi said. "Listen for your names."

The madams took turns reading off the names of the girls and their assigned faela mentors.

"Radiana," Madam Gomi said. "You are assigned to follow Lady Soo of the Central House."

A faela from the Central House? Madam Gomi must be disappointed. Both Radi and I had been expected to shadow elite faela. I'd bet pouring tea on the general had contributed to this decision, but at least it did lower Radi's chances of winning the showcase.

Now I waited for my fate.

"Rilla," Madam Yasmina called. Her face drooped with disappointment. "You have been paired with Lady Arlyn of the Dark Court."

Radi and I exchanged glances. Dark Court. The lowest-tiered of the concubines lived there. My chances of winning were next to nothing. I was probably ranked as the trinket least likely to emerge as a faela. Androgy Haming was responsible for placing me in the Dark Court. But why? He had to know that if I wouldn't kill for the emperor, then I didn't want to win the showcase either. By placing me with a low-tiered faela, he was only helping me.

But why would Haming help me? I was probably overthinking. He was the emperor's servant. Placing me in the Dark Court was probably just a consequence of his frustration that he couldn't prove I'd saved Androgy Unther's life.

In any case, Radi and I were one step closer to losing the showcase. Now we needed to figure out a plan to remain serving trifles. How could we stop the madams from revealing our tin-chai?

"All trinkets report to your madams," Madam Gomi said. "You'll be introduced to your mentors this afternoon."

Radi whispered to me. "Good luck. Look for me at the lake every afternoon. If we get the chance, we'll meet there."

"Good luck to you, too," I said.

Madam Gomi took Radi by the arm and guided her away. "Let's go."

Radi looked at me one last time and then followed Gomi.

I turned to face Madam Yasmina. She strode toward me and sighed. "I'm so disappointed in you. Lady Arlyn won't teach you anything. The judges likely expect you to fail the showcase and continue to act as Lady Arlyn's trifle. Her old trifle passed away not long ago."

"What do you know about Lady Arlyn?" I asked.

"Only that she has an unstable personality," Madam Yasmina replied.

What if she was worse than Limera? I hadn't considered that before. I pictured a bitter, scorned woman who took her frustration out on her trifles, slapping and whipping them into submission.

Chills crawled along my skin. I brushed at my arms.

Madam Yasmina clicked her tongue. "I believe you are due for an unpleasant six weeks."

CHAPTER 17

A perpetual fog encased the gray birches that formed the Dark Court, keeping it in an enchanted nocturnal state. The conifers in the surrounding forest formed tall walls, blocking out all traces of light. Their woody oils bathed the forest with a resinous incense, cold and viscous. Branches strained and twisted, withered faces that stretched their necks in desperation for a chance to see the sun.

Long corridors and bridges made of thick vines joined the treehouses together. The pathways zig-zagged throughout the shaded canopy, farther than one could see. One faela occupied each treehouse, although the houses might as well have been vacant. Not a peep came from inside any of the trees, nor did any light shine through the veiled windows.

Anxiety scrunched my gut into a wad of nerves. I'd changed into a simple blue frock with a white apron covering the front. I wiped my clammy hands on the apron and followed Madam Yasmina around a curved sycamore, its trunk as thick as ten husky men standing side by side. A shaded green door was built into the bark, and on the door, the number 4444 was carved. Treehouse 4444. All the treehouses in the Dark Court contained the number four, but to have four of them?

The madam knocked once. No answer.

She scratched her scalp, and a quizzical frown settled in her brow. "Strange. She should be expecting us." She knocked again. "Lady Arlyn, this is Madam Yasmina with the trinket who has been assigned to shadow you."

Silence. The madam tugged on the doorknob, and it twisted with ease. She shrugged. "I suppose we should go in and wait. It wouldn't hurt to give you a quick walk around."

The treehouse had multiple stories. On the ground floor, a small bed was stashed in the corner, two blankets neatly folded at the foot of it. A closet was situated adjacent, where a washstand and a porcelain pot peeped out from behind the door.

"If Lady Arlyn requires you to stay late, you'll sleep here," Madam Yasmina said. "Otherwise, you shall return to the Apple Barrel."

She took me up the winding staircase, the bannisters made of creeping plants, and the steps created from beds of compacted leaves. I was surprised I hadn't yet acquired a splinter, nor had I come across a single thorn.

The second floor split into a kitchen and a dining area. The kitchen had a counter and a sink, stacks of dirty dishes piled in it.

Yasmina wrinkled her nose. "I know Lady Arlyn has been without a trifle for a month, but one would expect her to live with a little more civility."

"There is no stove or food stocked here," I said. "Where will I be preparing meals?"

"The kitchen staff prepares all the meals. You'll retrieve cooked meals for yourself and Lady Arlyn from Treehouse 4389, which is the division of the imperial kitchen that serves the Dark Court."

A low-rise, round wooden table was positioned in the center of the dining room. Two bamboo sitting mats lay on the floor on either side.

A white plate was set on the table. A pair of ivory chopsticks had been thrown haphazardly upon it, one stick crisscrossing the other.

On the plate sat a stale piece of a beechnut bun filled with rancid meat. The outline of a single bite mark was the only indication it had at one time been fresh food, but now an ungbeetle crawled over it. Alongside the plate stood an open container of puffed silkworm cocoon crackers and a glass of spoiled shuroo milk that smelled like vomit, which a flurry of ravenous flies attacked.

Madam Yasmina frowned. "I wonder if Lady Arlyn is all right. Where is she?"

I ascended the next flight of stairs. Terran's portrait hung on the wall. A steady *tick-tock, tick-tock* brought my gaze to a wooden clock next to the portrait. The minute hand swung to the twelve. The bells chimed, and a frantic bird figurine burst out of its hidey-hole.

Cuckoo-koo-koo. Cuckoo-koo-koo. Cuckoo-koo-koo.

The bird repeated its bizarre cluck ten times.

On the third-floor landing, I smelled a noxious whiff of paint—musty, metallic, and vaporous. A woman sat at a workbench. She drew long, delicate brush strokes on her canvas, the beginning of what looked to become mountains and a waterfall.

The woman's disheveled hair and rumpled robe indicated she hadn't changed her outfit for some time. A sour note wafted off her body. Artist's tools, paints, and brushes filled the shelves. Canvases were stacked everywhere, against the shelves and the walls, even burying the bed in the corner. The sheets were thrown to the floor like cluttered piles of autumn leaves.

"Oh, Lady Arlyn, there you are." Madam Yasmina bowed. "I thought you knew we were coming."

Lady Arlyn didn't bother to look up. She dipped her brush into the black ink beside her. "I did. I left the door unlocked." Her voice was cool and distracted.

Madam Yasmina and I waited for her to say something further, but we might as well have been painted flowers.

"I'll leave the trinket with you, my lady. Please remember to write up a weekly progress report detailing your lessons."

Lady Arlyn waved her off. "Mmm-hmm."

Yasmina walked away, and Lady Arlyn continued to paint, lost in her work. I waited in silence, taking the time to observe her. Despite her unkempt appearance, Lady Arlyn was a striking woman. I guessed her to be about my brother's age. Her hair was darker than an onyx stone, her eyes upturned and a fierce midnight blue, and her skin was bronzed like a field of wheat during harvest.

Lady Arlyn placed her brush into a jar of water and swished it around until the solution became gray and murky. I stood, silent and still, and listened to the seconds tick by on the clock. The silence grew more awkward, yet after a quarter of an hour passed, she still didn't acknowledge me.

I cleared my throat. The small noise caused her to turn and look at me. She made a startled movement and blinked. Confusion clouded her features. "Oh, I forgot about you. Wait, what time is it?"

I paused, surprised by the question and by how high her voice had become, so unlike her tone to Madam Yasmina. She sounded like a five-year-old girl trapped in a grown woman's body.

She spun around and searched for the clock. "I didn't realize it was so late." She smoothed her hands over her hair. "What is your name again?"

"Rilla, my lady."

"Well, Rilla, you may be a trinket now, but as you've been assigned to me, you are not expected to win. Nevertheless, we are obligated to complete the assigned lessons. I'm afraid I have nothing much to teach you, though. I have not seen His Majesty since my wedding night."

I nodded, not knowing what to say.

"My rules are simple. We shall have our lessons in the morning.

Then you will take on the tasks of my trifle. Clean house, wash clothes, fetch meals, and prepare the table. When you are finished with chores, you are free to do as you please. I'm usually busy painting. Do not disturb me when I am creating my art. Understood?"

"Yes, my lady."

How perplexing. I had imagined her to be a cruel mistress, yet she allowed me more freedom than I'd had since arriving here.

"Good. We shall begin lessons tomorrow. Use the rest of your time today to wash the dishes and retrieve my supper, and then you are excused."

I dipped my head and curtsied before making my way downstairs.

CHAPTER 18

The next morning after breakfast, I started my first lesson under Lady Arlyn's tutelage.

Lady Arlyn sat on her mat across the table from me. "Madam Yasmina left me an agenda of what I am to teach you. This week's lesson is on seduction."

She cleared her throat and straightened her posture. "Body language and eye contact are key." She leaned forward and focused her gaze on mine. She batted her lashes and sent me a coy smile. Her hand touched my elbow, and she drew a finger up my arm.

I swallowed. Was she really a forgotten faela? For a woman who the emperor hadn't touched in years, she seemed quite experienced.

"Now you try," she said.

I fluttered my eyes and tilted my head at an angle like she had, but my eye ticked.

"Try again. Don't bat your eyes if it doesn't come naturally to you. Look at me like I'm the first boy you were smitten with."

"I'm not sure I can."

She gave me a knowing look. "You must pretend. Part of this lesson is convincing the person in front of you that they are the center of your world, even if you are not in love with them. You must make

His Majesty believe he is all you want, and there is no other. If you cannot do that, you'll live a lonely existence or be punished with a worse fate."

Her eyes glazed over, haunted.

"My lady, are you all right?"

She blinked. "Yes, never better. I forget. You don't need to perfect these lessons since you are expected to lose." She scribbled onto my progress report. "We're done for today."

"That's it?"

"I documented the completion of today's lesson. The judges and your madam cannot accuse me of negligence. I wish to paint, and there is a basket of clothes downstairs I need you to wash. Let me know when supper is ready tonight."

She gestured, dismissing me.

I went downstairs and found the hamper. It was light in my hands. The few pieces of clothing didn't even come up halfway in the basket. A washing board had been placed by the washstand. I grabbed the washing board and placed it on top of the laundry basket, then walked to Silver Tears Lake.

Several dozen trifles and a few trinkets waded knee-deep in the water, scrubbing stains from clothing.

Among them was Radi. I smiled at the sight of her. Now I'd have a friend to chat with while doing my chores.

"Radi, how's your first day with Lady Soo?" I asked.

She looked up. A cut crossed her cheek.

"Fainting faela, what happened?"

"Lady Soo is a nightmare," Radi said. "Demanding and bitter about her lot in life. She's already treating me like her permanent trifle, not a showcase trinket. She pushed me for speaking out of turn, and I crashed into the edge of the table."

Behind her, clothes heaped high, overflowing out of the basket.

"This is ridiculous." Radi wrung water out of the robe she held. "Some of this is clean. She just piled it on because she didn't like the way I walk. I can't believe I'm saying this, but she might be worse than the empress."

Her sleeves were folded up, exposing her upper arms. They were covered in fresh bruises.

I winced. "She did that, too? Come with me. Let's go somewhere more private."

"I can't. If I don't finish this mountain of laundry before her afternoon tea time, she's threatened to whip me."

I lowered my voice. "But I can heal that cut and those bruises. We just need to be sure no one sees me use my tin-chai."

Radi stopped wringing the robe and gaped at me. "You have a healing tin-chai?"

"I meant to tell you sooner but didn't get the chance. I can heal any ailment when I sing. Even old age."

"Then I definitely can't let you use your tin-chai on me," she said. "Don't you know how dangerous that would be? Lady Soo will find it strange if my bruises suddenly disappear, and I don't want her or anyone else discovering what you can do. The emperor will use you to attain eternal youth."

I frowned. She was right, but I hated not being able to help her. "What will you do? If you lose the showcase, you'll remain Lady Soo's trifle indefinitely."

"Nothing's indefinite. Maybe I can request to serve another faela. Let's just figure out a way to stop the madams from revealing our tin-chai. I've been thinking. We need to get the madams in trouble. Then they'll be executed."

"Executed?" I almost dropped the washboard. "Surely we can find a solution without getting anyone killed."

"As long as they're alive, they remain a threat. I'm willing to do whatever works. That's the only way to survive."

I balked at the idea of getting someone else killed, even to save myself. That would go against my entire moral code as a healer.

"What if we accuse them of breaking the code of sobriety?" Radi said.

I scrubbed clothes against the washboard. "We can't prove that. They wouldn't be foolish enough to leave behind evidence."

Radi threw a washed robe into the basket. "Stop trying to play by the rules. We need to play dirty and frame the madams. They'd do the same if they were in our place. If we're not willing to sacrifice them, then it'll be our lives at stake." Radi stood and hauled up the basket. "I need to go. My time is almost up, and I still need to hang all this to dry. I don't know if I can meet with you for awhile. Lady Soo wants me to do the wash first thing in the morning, before the other trifles do the laundry and pollute the lake water."

She rolled her eyes and marched away.

I watched her leave. She sounded miserable and not like herself. I was worried.

I sighed. Though we'd been placed with lower-tiered faela, our situations hadn't changed for the better. Radi was stuck with an abusive faela, and we still had our madams to worry about. I couldn't possibly frame Yasmina. I wasn't clever enough. What if the judges saw through my lie? Besides, Yasmina would probably sense my scheme before I could implement it.

I touched the pendant around my neck. The clasp unhooked itself, and the pendant fell into my hand. I felt its weight in my palm. Frustration continued to pile up inside my chest. Everything in my life was broken. I wanted to shout out my rage and retaliate. Instead of healing, I wished my voice could be used as a weapon. If only *this* could be a hidden layer to my tin-chai. I'd kill anyone who threatened my loved ones.

I gasped. Where had those disturbing thoughts come from? I shook my head. A doctor's job was to heal, not kill. And music should not be used as a weapon. Radi's talk of breaking rules and all the palace's darkness must be getting to me. I couldn't let it. I'd find a way to stop Yasmina from revealing my tin-chai without lying or cheating. But I could never let the palace consume me into its darkness, or I'd be surrendering the last part of myself that believed I could still be a healing light.

CHAPTER 19

* * * * * * * * * * *

I returned to the Dark Court, still perturbed by my dark thoughts.

I didn't notice the man standing in front of Treehouse 4444 until I collided into him. A small yelp emerged from the back of my throat. Strong arms grabbed me before I fell.

"Rilla."

I took a step back. "Prince Carrick?"

Why was he here?

I remembered palace protocol and curtsied to him. "Your Highness."

"Drop the honorifics. Carrick will do." His pleasant tenor tickled my ears. "I heard you are shadowing Lady Arlyn during your trinketship. I was hoping I would chance upon you."

A blush heated my cheeks. He had come here for *me*?

"You are doing well, I assume." A dimple formed in his cheek but faded.

"Yes. Thank you for asking."

Except for Yasmina threatening my family.

"What's wrong?" he asked.

"I miss my family. I hope they're all right."

"Yes. It's a pity trinkets and trifles are forbidden to correspond with their loved ones. If you would like, I will send my servant to see if they are well."

"You would do that? My village is far."

He shrugged. "It is, but I can spare a servant for the job."

"Thank you, Your Highness."

He gave me a sullen look. "Once again, stop Your Highnessing me. Leave the subservient nonsense for my Father Emperor."

His hand curled into a fist, and he worried his bottom lip with his teeth. He studied me as though expecting a response.

"Thank you, Carrick," I said.

He looked to the sky, his calculating expression seeming to gauge the time of day. His movements were brusque. "I . . . uhm . . . would you care to walk with me?"

"I should return to prepare Lady Arlyn's supper."

"It is early yet. Lady Arlyn won't miss you for another hour or two."

"Oh, I suppose I could—"

"Let's go then."

He took the basket from me and set it on the ground outside the treehouse door. He grabbed my hand and steered me away. My gaze wandered to where his warm, bronzed hand clasped mine. It was flattering to receive a boy's attention. Especially one who happened to be a prince. I'd never been this close to any of the boys in Cascasea due to Rell and Nia's overprotective nature.

My breaths grew shallow and shorter. Whether from our hurried pace or from my heightened emotions, I couldn't be sure. We walked along an unfamiliar route, past the cherry trees, and into a grove of oaks on the border of forbidden territory.

"I thought you told me not to trespass into forbidden territory," I said.

Carrick stopped abruptly, and I almost crashed into him. He let go of my hand, and I felt the loss. "You are under my protection today."

He looked into the trees and tugged his ear.

"Did you just signal someone?" I searched the trees and surrounding area but didn't see anyone there.

"Yes, I signaled my androgy and bodyguard, who are hiding in the trees to alert me if danger approaches. But they won't bother us. As far as you're concerned, we're alone."

"Alone," I repeated. "And walking into forbidden territory? Just what are your intentions, sir?" I kept my tone light, meaning it as a joke, but I did wonder where he was taking me. Had I been foolish to trust him so easily?

No, I decided. If he'd meant to do anything untoward, he would have made a move already. Aside from his servants in the trees, who probably wouldn't stand against their master, no one was around. Even if someone were here, I doubted anyone would stop a prince from doing as he pleased.

Carrick's jaw twitched, a sign of amusement. "Perhaps I used this walk as an excuse, and I plan on luring you to a private place so I can seduce you."

I folded my arms and thrust my chin up. "Really? Go ahead and try. I'm not so easily charmed even if you do have pretty eyes and an air of mystery."

He laughed. "Blistering ballasts, Rilla. I thought you were shy. But dare I say, it sounds like you're attempting to flirt with me."

"And what if I am?" The words slipped out before I could think. I wasn't sure what drove my boldness. But this banter was . . . exciting.

"Then you're treading in dangerous waters." He put a hand on my shoulder, drawing me closer.

I stifled a gasp. "What are you doing?"

"You should know, I can't control myself when a pretty girl flirts with me, so I expect you to follow through."

I used both hands to push him away. "Stop. I didn't mean for it to go this far. We barely know each other."

He loosened his grip and let out a bark of mocking laughter. "Did you think I was being serious? Blistering ballasts, your naïveté is refreshing. I'd bet my crown you've never even been kissed before."

I trembled, shocked that he could toy with my emotions so easily. I sniffed. "I think I shall return to Lady Arlyn."

"Oh, come now. Did I frighten you? I was just teasing. Rest assured, innocents like you have no appeal to me. If I wanted female companionship, I would find an older woman who has experience in pleasuring a man."

My cheeks burned. I hated that his attempt to embarrass me had worked. My hands played with the loose strands of my hair. I wished I could hide. My first attempt at flirting with a boy, and I'd been rejected. What had gotten into me? Flirting with a prince. I was a trinket, with the possibility of becoming his stepmother.

He held out his hand. "What do you say? Let's continue our walk, shall we?"

Ignoring his hand, I curtsied low to Carrick and stayed there longer than was customary, leaving my gaze directed at his shoes. "What business do you have, Your Most Eminent Highness, to demean yourself by inviting a lowly trinket such as myself to walk with you?"

"You're back to Your Highnessing me? I see. I did not mean to injure your feelings. My intention in seeking you out today was with the hope that we could be friends. I find you interesting, and I like the loyalty you showed your friend that night at the lake. I only establish friendships with those who have proved themselves capable of loyalty."

He said this as though I should be flattered that he'd found me worthy of his friendship.

"That's why I invited you to walk with me," he said. "I have no ill intentions. Friends do seek each other out for company, do they not?"

I still didn't budge. "Yes, that is what friends do. But I wasn't clear that you were *asking* me to be your friend."

His gaze fell to the ground. "Oh, I assumed . . . I didn't consider that maybe you don't wish to be my friend."

If he had flashed me a charming smile, I would not have forgiven him. If he had apologized with sweet words, I would have walked away without a backward glance. But it was the hesitancy in his voice, the hint of vulnerability he revealed that pulled me back into his gravity.

"Of course, we can be friends. But you still haven't said why you want me to go with you into forbidden territory."

"Yes, I was getting to that part, but our conversation was side-tracked," he said. "I came to find you not only to establish our friendship, but to tell you I intend to keep you safe now that we are friends. The palace guards who patrol this area are loyal to me, and my treehouse is right across from the Dark Court. Treehouse 8 if you need to find me. You shall have my protection if you stay within the Spring Gardens and the Dark Court.

"As for our walk, I wish to give you a tour of the palace grounds and show you where you should not venture. There are those who may hurt you or take advantage of you regardless of your trinket status. My servants will follow and protect us today, but in the future, do not wander alone where I tell you not to go. I cannot guarantee your safety if I'm not with you."

I followed Carrick's long-legged stride. We hiked to the edge of the path, where the grove of cherry blossoms ended. The colors shifted from jade and emerald greens to yellow and mustard browns. A satisfying crunch of autumn leaves sounded beneath my feet, and the incense of musky earth and smoky timber drifted to my nose. A flurry of golden flakes floated with the breeze like childhood memories. Watching in wonder, I let one fall into my hand.

Carrick indicated the dirt road, half buried under bundles of dusky-hued mounds. "This is the Autumn Courtyard. Farther down the path is the Royal House, where Father Emperor and Mother Empress reside."

I remembered this from my first day here when the carriage had taken us through the palace grounds.

Royal guards marched on the path toward us. I jumped and leaned toward the foliage, but Carrick placed a hand on my shoulder. "They can't see us. My androgy has a shield tin-chai."

The guards passed, looking through us as though we were part of the air. Carrick gestured for me to follow him. We reached a clearing where purple lilacs and orange poppies were again in full bloom. They flooded the area with their vibrancy.

"In between each seasonal garden," Carrick said, "are transitional gardens where some of the princes live with their servants in separate, smaller residences scattered throughout the forest. Some novelty cages are also placed in the transitional gardens. Like the Dark Court, these parts experience the seasons in real time."

We continued on, and a forested area lay to my right. A sudden chill prickled my skin, summoning goosebumps. Shadows obscured whatever lay hidden within the forest. All I sensed was darkness. The smell of pine—sharp and strong—filled my nose, but there was also something else . . . something base and sour like decaying flesh mingled with rotten fruit. A strange yowl echoed through the misted gloom, sounding like a mad godog.

Carrick's voice lowered. "We must not linger here. We shall take the longer path around the woods. If you should ever find yourself in the Winter Woods, you might as well be dead."

"What's within the Winter Woods?"

He took hold of my shoulders, driving me away. "This is where Mother Empress punishes the disobedient trifles and trinkets and the faela accused of infidelity. I believe she convinced Father Emperor to reduce the security around the courts because she hoped some women would take lovers and others would be tempted to wander into forbidden territory or try to escape. There is nothing she enjoys more than catching rulebreakers in the act and punishing them. Beyond the Winter Woods is the Summer Fields, a place of entertainment for noblemen."

I had questions, but there came a howl, which sounded more like a man than an animal. Then came a whistle, the imitation of a bird's warning call. This rang closer, directly above us in the trees.

Carrick looked above him and whispered. "Right now? I suppose it cannot be helped."

"What is going on?" I asked.

"My servants have informed me that Father Emperor has summoned his sons, elite faela, and officials to court for an announcement. I need to go, or I shall be missed. Come, I'll walk you back to the Dark Court."

As I turned to follow, my gaze caught a golden glimmer of sunshine in a field of peach trees.

Spring Gardens, Autumn Court, Winter Woods. Carrick had shown me all the seasonal gardens except for one.

What lay in that peach grove? Part of me feared the answer.

What if the Summer Fields was the most terrifying of all the gardens?

CHAPTER 20

After returning to the Dark Court, I headed into Treehouse 4444. I continued up the stairs to Lady Arlyn's room to tell her I'd retrieve our supper and have the table set soon.

I reached the top step and crossed the threshold. The faela's startled voice yelled out. "Wait. Do not come up!"

An unclothed Lady Arlyn, surrounded by paper and paints, stood in the middle of the room. My eyes widened.

Earlier, the canvases were hidden from view, but now, they faced forward. Vibrant colors brightened the room. Colorful landscape paintings of flower fields, apple orchards, and the sunset over the ocean.

I took a sharp breath at the sight of such beauty. The metallic smell of drying paint filled my nose. There was also a hint of sandalwood mixed with lavender.

Lady Arlyn scrambled and grabbed a brown canvas tarp. She threw it over the easel holding her current work in progress and then flipped several canvases around so the painted sides faced the wall again.

"These are exquisite, my lady. Why do you wish to hide them?"

Bright color flooded her cheeks. She paused in her endeavor to wrap another piece of art in a white oilcloth. "Do—do you think so?"

"Yes. Only one with no eyes would not see how talented you are."

A small smile lit up her face. "Thank you. You weren't supposed to see them, though."

"Why not?"

"I never share my paintings. They are private."

A tinge of pain broke into her voice. Her eyes were hollow, her voice hushed and hurt, like a lost little girl wondering what she'd done wrong. "I wasn't good enough for my father. He only cared that I had the beauty to become a faela, and I suppose he was right. I wasn't good enough for the emperor, either. He discarded me after the first night."

She must have been about my age when she arrived here. If my guess was correct about her being my brother's age now, it meant she'd been imprisoned in the palace for over a decade. Thanks to Terran and her father, she was wasting her life away. Her paintings should be shared with the world, not buried in the closet.

"My lady, your paintings are beautiful, and you should never believe otherwise."

"Some good it did me." Her lips flickered into a momentary smile. "Thank you for trying to offer me comfort."

I returned the smile. No longer distracted by the paintings, I became aware that she was still naked. A jagged scar lay on her neck, and tiny burns dotted her forearms. Candle wax burns. I'd helped my brother care for a patient with emotional wounds who had taken out her inner pain by burning herself with candle wax every night. Had Lady Arlyn done the same to herself?

I retrieved her robe from the bed and handed it to her.

"Oh, I forgot I am not dressed," she said, unperturbed. Did she always paint while naked? Lady Arlyn was proving to be a peculiar woman.

She draped the robe around her shoulders and tied it closed. My gaze drifted to the easel with the piece she had been working on when I had walked in. The tarp she'd thrown over it had slipped. I approached and straightened it.

"May I see what you're working on? I'm sure it must be beautiful."

I wouldn't have uncovered it without permission, but she must have misread my intent. With a gasp, she jumped and pushed me away.

"No, you cannot see that one." She glowered and blocked the canvas with a shielded stance. "You should not be prying into my private affairs. You will do well to remember you are training under me. We're not friends."

I reeled from her sudden change of mood. "Of course, my lady, I apologize."

"In the future, do not return so early. I like to paint in private until sunset."

It was well after sunset now. In fact, complete darkness filled the window pane. Even so, I inclined my head in deference to her. "It won't happen again, my lady."

"That will be all for tonight."

I bowed and made my exit. But as I closed the door behind me, she threw the canvas I had wanted to view onto the floor. With a scream, she trampled upon it. Her angry screams echoed as I descended the stairs, and then those screams broke into sobs.

The next morning, Lady Arlyn didn't show up for breakfast or my lesson. I went to check on her and called her name through the door.

"Go away," she called back. "I have a headache and need rest."

"I'll go fetch medicine from the apothecary," I said.

"Whatever you do, just leave me alone."

I sighed. Without completing the lessons, I wouldn't have a

progress report for Madam Yasmina. I hoped I wouldn't get in trouble.

Whether or not Lady Arlyn was feigning her illness, I still felt obligated to fetch medicine for her. She had no one else.

I walked away from the Dark Court. Carrick came down the path opposite from me. He didn't see me and hurried down the lane. I took a breath, intending to call out a hello, but I caught sight of a flash of silver high in the trees. A hooded figure jumped from bough to bough, following the prince.

Who was he? What if he intended harm upon Carrick? I followed them, past the Dark Court and beyond the cherry trees. Into forbidden territory again. What if the trail took me to one of the seasonal gardens Carrick had cautioned me to stay away from?

Yet I had to warn Carrick.

The trail led to a brighter path. On the ground, a discarded peach lay at my feet. A breeze rustled the leaves, conjuring a ghastly whiff of sweat and vomit mixed with a hint of sweet peaches.

Carrick was too far away to hear me. If I called out to him, the man in the trees might attack. That man vaulted through the branches, his movements soundless. He must be trained in martial arts. Was he a spy? An assassin?

Carrick's body blurred. I blinked, thinking it a trick of the eye. But he was no longer in front of me. The man in the trees was nowhere in sight either.

I remembered Carrick's androgy had a shield tin-chai. I was such a fool. The man in the trees must be Carrick's bodyguard.

If the androgy had hidden both of them, danger approached.

Footsteps sounded down the lane, and a loud voice said, "There is nothing further to discuss."

That voice belonged to Emperor Terran.

CHAPTER 21

I took cover behind the trees. My heart pounded.

A group of men emerged from the forest and approached. General Penweather, the despicable judge who had interviewed Radi, was at the forefront. Behind him, Androgy Haming walked with Emperor Terran. Two soldiers trailed them.

I bit my lip, quelling a sound of fear. The men came into full view, standing so close to where I hid, I could touch their cloaks.

Penweather stood closest to me. His stench, sour and musky, made my eyes water. "His Majesty requires rest now, Androgy Haming. Let us continue this discussion later."

"But, Your Majesty, I was appointed your chief advisor. It is my duty to tell you when a decision of this magnitude will affect your political standing. The Zhynites continue preaching that Old Grandfather Heaven is displeased and has taken the scepter away from you."

The revelation jolted me. Could it be? Was Old Grandfather Heaven finally answering my prayers? My heart sped faster, not from fear this time, but from a glimpse of hope.

"The imperial army is stronger than those superstitious fools," Terran said. "March through all the villages and have the soldiers disperse any public gathering. Kill anyone who refuses to comply."

Haming remained unmoved. "But, Your Majesty, there are also whispers that the empress has stolen the scepter."

Empress Limera? My heart tumbled again.

Penweather gave a snotty laugh. "Ridiculous. A sovereign empress is unheard of. Old Grandfather Heaven would never grant a woman the Will of Heaven. Besides, if her tin-chai had been amplified, she would have already made it well known to everyone."

"You know as well as I that the divinity of the scepter remains somewhat a mystery. Not all who hold the scepter will be granted the powers that come with the Will of Heaven." The androgy passed a glance at Terran. "And even those who once had the Will of Heaven can have his tin-chai taken away."

Terran snapped his head back and glared at the androgy. "Are you questioning if I maintain the Will of Heaven?"

"I am not, but the rest of the kingdom will." Haming's brazen manner shocked me. How could an androgy speak to the emperor this way? Yet, Haming seemed unmoved and unafraid.

"Insolent half-man!" Terran roared. He pivoted to face the soldiers. One of the men emitted a pained high-pitched screech. His body erupted into flames. Vines whipped down and wrapped around the other soldier. They pulled, ripping the man's limbs from his body. His horrified screams diminished into sudden silence. Blood spattered onto Androgy Haming, but even this did not faze him.

"Is that proof enough for you? You may be a favorite of the empress's, but remember, she is not the divine ruler. I am. Question me again, and your next job will be as a clay statue decorating my garden."

Androgy Haming bowed. "Yes, Your Majesty. I apologize for upsetting you." As soon as he made his exit, Terran's knees wobbled beneath him. Penweather reached to catch him.

"Your Majesty, let me summon the doctor," Penweather said.

"No, I only need some rest. I cannot risk—"

"Shh!" Penweather froze. "Someone else is here." He looked around. "Who is there?"

I was as good as dead.

But to my surprise, Penweather didn't come toward me. He moved to the tallest peach tree on the far left of me. "Show yourself." The general unsheathed his sword. "This is your last chance."

A rustle came from the highest branches. Then footsteps padded on the ground. Someone ran.

"Stop!" Penweather gave chase.

They were distracted. Now was my chance to get away. I fled in the opposite direction.

A root curled up from the ground. I tripped. Another shoot slithered around my body. It bound me, arms tight against my sides, and raised me into the air. A shriek ripped from my throat.

Emperor Terran stood before me. Hadn't he followed Penweather?

Terran clutched his chest. His breath sounded winded. "Are you one of the empress's trifles?"

"No, Your Majesty. I'm a trinket."

The vines tightened around me so painfully I couldn't breathe. "A quick check with the madams will tell me if you speak the truth. I will give you one more chance to confess."

"I swear I am only a trinket."

My bindings loosened slightly, but Terran's dark glare said I was nowhere close to being out of danger. "You are trespassing on forbidden territory. Do you know what happens to girls who break my rules? I send them to be broken until they learn to never rebel again."

My teeth clicked together. "I did not mean to, Your Majesty. I'm shadowing Lady Arlyn at the Dark Court. I was going to the apothecary but made a wrong turn."

"A trinket at the Dark Court?" He grinned, and it amazed me how much Carrick physically resembled him. "That must mean you did not do well in the preliminary round." He came closer, his gaze looking my body up and down. "You are lovely. Would be a pity to disqualify you from the showcase." He reached for my face, skimming his fingers across my cheek. His touch brought a lurch of revulsion into my throat. "No, I would not want to ruin such perfection. Just like a lotus flower. I wonder, is the rest of your body as soft and white? If so, then I long to be the painter brushing your skin with a tinge of blush."

He leaned in, his face coming within an inch of mine. He nipped my earlobe, and I cried out.

"Delicious. How I love hearing the noises my pets make at my touch." Terran sneered, reminding me of a mountain maocat toying with a moonrabbit before devouring it. "I want to see how you compare with the other trinkets in the showcase finale. Then I will decide whether you should decorate my garden or my bed or simply be stowed away."

The branches released me. I crumpled to the ground and gasped for air.

He strode through the peach grove. Footsteps lightened into padded echoes and disappeared into the Summer Fields.

"Rilla, what the blistering ballasts are you doing here?" A whispered bark made me jump. But I relaxed slightly when Carrick emerged from the trees. "Are you all right?"

I didn't answer. My stomach churned. All I wanted was to wash Terran's touch away from my skin. I rubbed at my earlobe and cheek until my skin turned raw.

"Stop that." He grabbed my hand. "You'll hurt yourself. This is why I told you not to wander. Thank the ancestors Father Emperor did not do worse to you. He must not have had the energy."

"Were you hiding here all along?" I asked.

"Yes, I was spying on them. I didn't know you were here until I sent my bodyguard as a decoy to distract Penweather, and you started running. What are you doing here, anyway?"

"I saw someone following you and thought he meant you harm. I didn't realize until too late that he was your bodyguard."

Carrick gaped. "You endangered yourself to warn me? Why?"

"We're friends. As your friend, it's my job to protect you."

"You, protect me?" He shook his head, incredulous. "Come. You look so pale. I'll take you to my house to recover."

As I followed him, my nerves settled. "Do you think the empress really has the scepter?"

"I don't know, but I believe it is no longer in my father's possession. After the Zhynites instigated a coup, my father stopped carrying the scepter. I thought he was simply being cautious."

"How can your father still use his tin-chai at all? I thought he could only use those powers if he possessed the scepter."

Carrick looked at me. "Did you see Father Emperor's reaction after killing that guard? I believe without the scepter to renew his power, using his tin-chai causes him great pain." He curled his fists, his expression resolved. "I have to find out if Mother Empress does have the scepter. It would be just like her to hold it over Father Emperor simply for his attention. If I can find the scepter, I only need to touch it, and I know I'll receive the divine blessing. Then Father Emperor will lose his tin-chai forever."

His determination made me feel something I had locked away long ago. Hope.

I had wondered why Old Grandfather Heaven would bestow the Will of Heaven on a monster like Terran. Perhaps Terran was only the means by which someone worthy of the scepter could be born, so that one day Old Grandfather Heaven could grant Prince Carrick the Will of Heaven.

Carrick had to win. For the first time since my parents' death, I found my faith in something, in *someone*, restored.

CHAPTER 22

I continued bumping into Carrick outside the Dark Court every afternoon on my way back from washing clothes at the lake. He'd invite me to sit with him on a stone bench to chat about my day, almost as though he planned to meet with me. I wondered why he always passed the Dark Court at the same time until he mentioned that he visited his mother in the Spring Gardens everyday, and the Dark Court was on the way. After five straight days of meeting this way, I ran late on the sixth day. I thought for sure Carrick would not linger, but I found him waiting for me.

Did I dare hope he might actually enjoy my company and conversation as much as I appreciated his? Whenever I was with him, I was almost able to forget that we were in the palace, and I was a showcase trinket.

But our time together was never enough. And when I returned to Lady Arlyn's treehouse, I could no longer ignore reality.

A full week had passed since I'd caught Lady Arlyn painting in the nude, and I hadn't once seen her emerge from her room. Every time I tried to talk to her through the door, she said she wanted to rest. She wouldn't take her medicine or eat her meals.

I worried, not only for her, but because we hadn't done any

trinketship training. Without completing any of my lessons, would Madam Yasmina punish me?

Then one morning, Lady Arlyn was waiting for me in the sitting room.

"Good morning, my lady. Would you like some breakfast?"

"No, I'm not hungry," she said. "I realize we have not completed your lessons, and your progress report is due this afternoon. We should get to work and do as much as we can."

"I'm glad you're feeling better."

She nodded. "I must apologize for this week. I am prone to bouts of melancholy, which worsened after my old trifle passed away."

Melancholy. That might explain the candle wax burns on her arms that I'd seen the other day.

"Please know that if you are feeling lonely, I'm here for you," I said. "You can talk to me as little or as much as you'd like."

She smiled, the first real smile I'd seen. "Thank you. That is very kind. We should start your lessons."

Arlyn stood and stepped to the center of the room. "Dancing is another tool for seduction."

She sang a song and swayed from side to side, undulating and shimmying her legs and hips. Her movements were sinuous and smooth. Mesmerizing. How could she be a forgotten faela when she knew how to entice a man?

I followed her movements. In my head, I added my own instruments to Arlyn's voice and imagined a zither playing. I held to the beat, circling the room with Arlyn.

"You are quite good at keeping to the rhythm," Arlyn said. "Have you taken dance lessons before?"

"No," I said. "But I do like music. Where did you learn to dance?"

"My best friend, Bree." She whispered the name like a sacred chant. "My half-siblings used to enjoy tormenting me. My father was a Shyan diplomat, and my mother a seer in the Fauxhemian court. After she died, my father took me back to Seracedar, and I was raised with his other full-blooded Shyan children. Whenever my siblings were exceptionally cruel, I would find Bree. We would run off and braid flower necklaces and talk about our dreams."

The corners of her mouth tilted up at the memories. "I wanted to explore the world and draw fields of flowers and sunsets, and all she wanted was to dance." Her smile disappeared. "All of our dreams are dead now. She is dead, too."

Tears fell down her cheeks. "Bree and I were brought to the palace together. We were selected to be faela in the showcase finale." Her voice lowered to a hush. "We made a pact to die together before the ceremony joining us to His Majesty."

Lady Arlyn's grief lay in the tortured lines of her face. "She took a hair pin, and . . . and . . . I tried to do the same." She swallowed and, lowering the high neckline of her robe, pointed to her neck. A jagged red line ran across her collarbone to the tip of her shoulder.

So this was how she'd acquired the scar.

"I was too much of a coward to cut deeply enough. I was a fool who still believed in hope. Now I know Bree was the fortunate one, for I am left in this desolate place, isolated and forgotten."

She cleared her throat and looked to the floor. "Excuse me. I'm going back to my room."

I watched her rush up the stairs.

Poor Lady Arlyn. How many other women had the emperor crushed? Was there to be no end?

I looked at the half-filled progress report she'd left behind. Madam Yasmina would be livid, but I no longer cared. I grabbed the slip of paper and headed back to the Apple Barrel.

When I entered Treehouse 37, Irica and Galai were not present, but Madam Yasmina greeted me. "Well? How was your first week?"

I handed her my progress report.

She frowned as she read it. "As I thought, Lady Arlyn is doing the bare minimum. That mad woman is useless. No wonder His Majesty discarded her after one night."

My fists curled. Madam Yasmina was despicable.

Yasmina pointed a finger in my face. "You dare look at me with such defiance? I warn you. Don't try to challenge me, or you'll regret it. I heard your brother and his wife had a baby boy."

A boy? I had a nephew.

"Wouldn't it be tragic if they were required to give their baby to the palace to become an androgy?"

I bit my tongue, fighting the urge to lash out at her.

She ripped my report into shreds and stormed away.

This was another reminder that unless I found a way to get Yasmina in trouble, I'd have no choice but to reveal my tin-chai in the finale.

I returned to the Dark Court to complete the rest of my chores for Lady Arlyn. On my way, I passed Silver Tears Lake, where several trifles were busy washing laundry.

Among them was Radi. My gloomy mood brightened somewhat to see my friend. She hadn't been at the lake all week, but I remembered Lady Soo required her to wash the laundry earlier in the morning.

"Radi."

She turned. Half of her face was swollen, and a black circle marked her eye.

I gasped. "Did Lady Soo do that?"

Tears rimmed her eyes, but it was anger I saw in her face.

"I don't have much time," she said. "I slipped away while Lady Soo is having her massage, but I hoped to find you. I wanted to tell you that I'm making a run for it. I can't stay here anymore. You can't dissuade me this time."

I stayed silent for a second. Before the preliminaries, I would have tried to coax her out of it, but this time, I wished I could join her. If only Yasmina could no longer use my family to threaten me.

"Do you have a plan?" I asked.

"I used some gold I made from starlight to bribe a young androgy in exchange for his uniform. I'm going to impersonate him and leave the palace through the front gates."

Daring but sensible. Young androgies appeared effeminate enough for Radi to pass as one, and they were also sent into the city on errands.

"I'm asking you once more, do you want to come with me? I can find another androgy uniform."

"I can't take the chance. Today, Madam Yasmina threatened my family again. I'm sorry."

"Don't be sorry. We all must choose our own path."

Tears clouded my vision. "I'll miss you."

"I'll miss you, too. Good luck with Madam Yasmina. I hope one day you'll be able to escape, too. Remember what I said. You can't play by their rules. It's impossible to keep your hands clean if you wish to survive." She hugged me, squeezing tight. "I must go, or Lady Soo will hit me again."

"Good luck, my friend."

I watched her leave. "And goodbye," I whispered. Would I ever see her again? We'd only met recently, but she had turned into my best friend.

Please protect Radi, Old Grandfather Heaven.

Though all my other prayers had gone unanswered, I hoped this request would be met.

Several weeks passed. Lady Arlyn proved to have volatile mood swings. It was hard to tell which mornings we would have lessons.

Sometimes Lady Arlyn was waiting for me when I arrived, but most days, she remained locked in her room.

On the mornings we did have lessons, she taught me more dances, and sometimes we would sit and chat over tea. She'd talk about what it was like to grow up in Fauxhemia and about all the Fauxhemian artists who had inspired her through their paintings, sculptures, architecture, and storytelling. She told me Fauxhemians bled different colors of blood—diamond, amethyst, sapphire, and emerald. Blood magic enabled them to communicate with deities and the dead, to see past events and visions of the future, and to read the thoughts and intentions of other people.

"Faux-bloods, they're called," she said. "My mother was an emerald-blood, the rarest of all blood castes. She could manipulate a person's emotions and in so doing, control their actions. My father swore this was how she seduced him."

"Can you do the same?" I asked.

"I am not a true faux-blood as I am half Shyan. My blood is as red as yours. But I do have a heightened sense of emotion. I can feel when others are afraid, angry, or happy. I experience their pain, sorrow, and joy as if it were my own. But I cannot manipulate emotions like my mother could."

What a terrible curse, to experience another's pain as if it were your own. No wonder Lady Arlyn took solace alone and in her art. I would find such overstimulation unbearable.

I enjoyed our conversations together, and though most of the time we talked of matters that had nothing to do with showcase lessons, time passed quickly.

Madam Yasmina still checked my progress reports, but she said nothing further about my uncompleted lessons. She was confident in my tin-chai and finale performance.

One afternoon, I was back at the Apple Barrel for a physical examination. The imperial doctor would check each trinket's wyis to ensure we had no diseases and that our maidenhead was still intact.

What punishment would a trinket face if she was found to be no longer a virgin? Execution? Or worse? I thought of the novelty cages and shuddered.

Galai and I had already changed into our examination gowns and waited on our beds, but Irica and Madam Yasmina were not here yet.

I hadn't spoken to Galai or Irica much. Neither slept in Treehouse 37 most nights. No surprise. Galai was shadowing an elite faela, and Irica was with the empress. Because of their busy schedules, it was easier for them to stay with their faela.

"I wonder where Irica and Madam Yasmina are," I said.

"Irica's probably complaining again. She has her monthly bleeding and doesn't want to be examined today." Galai rocked back and forth, looking nauseated.

"Are you all right?"

"I'm worried about the exam. Do you think it will hurt when the doctor examines our maidenhead?

"I can imagine it might be a little invasive," I said. "But it should be quick."

"That's not helpful," Galai said. She wrapped her arms around her chest and shuddered.

Despite knowing she didn't think of me as a friend anymore, I still felt sorry for her. Perhaps I could help ease her mind. "Don't think about it right now. How is your trinketship?"

"Well enough. One night, His Majesty came to dine with Lady Ulah. I was able to help serve him, and we performed a dance together for him."

Galai's experience was so different from mine. Not that I envied her.

"Irica told me she's learning a lot from Empress Limera and can't imagine having a better mentor," Galai said. "But I think she's lying. I saw bruises on Irica's arms. She claims she fell, but I think the empress abuses her. Serves her right. She thought she was better than everyone else for getting the empress as her mentor."

Madam Yasmina entered the treehouse.

Irica followed, groaning. Her hands rubbed her abdomen. "I want to curl up and die."

"Don't be so dramatic," Yasmina said. "I already told you the doctor will test your maidenhead through your wyis."

Galai gasped. "There's an alternative method? Why can't we all be tested that way?"

"Because there are ways to tamper with the reading," Yasmina said. "If it were the standard test, trinkets with a past to hide would be tempted to cheat."

"What if Irica's test comes back with a false negative?"

Irica glared at Galai. "Are you accusing me?"

"Girls, no fighting." Yasmina sighed. "We only make an exception for girls on their bleeding. Doctor Cherrywood's tin-chai is strong in his ability to evaluate the body through one's wyis. He is rarely wrong."

A man with spectacles and a black robe entered the treehouse.

"Ah, Doctor Cherrywood," Yasmina said. "You are right on time."

The doctor gave a curt nod. He took a thin metal probe and laid it on the table. Then he took a cotton swab and dipped it into a vial of liquid. Jorlang juice. Its acidic properties helped to sterilize medical devices.

The doctor cleaned the probe, and Galai stared at it. She gulped. Her face turned green.

"Who am I to examine first?"

"If Galai doesn't want to go first, I will," I said.

Madam Yasmina pulled a curtain up for privacy, separating me from her and the other girls.

Doctor Cherrywood placed his hand over my wrist, taking my pulse. He studied my face, looking into my eyes. He squinted in thought.

"You have a strong wyis, young lady," he said. "Stronger than many men I've examined."

A thought occurred to me. Would he be able to identify my tin-chai? My pulse raced, and he sensed my nerves.

"You have no need to be stressed," he said. "I will make this as comfortable as possible."

No, I decided. Madam Yasmina would have said something if the doctor could determine my tin-chai. I took deep breaths, waiting for him to finish.

Irica's voice carried through the curtain. "Did you hear? Lady Soo's mentee was caught trying to escape."

I gasped. Radi.

"She dressed as an androgy and tried to pass through the front gate," Irica continued. "If Androgy Haming hadn't been there to catch her, she may have succeeded."

Doctor Cherrywood cleared his throat. "Now I will check your maidenhead. You may have some discomfort, but it will be quick."

The pinching and prodding was uncomfortable, but it wasn't enough to distract me from my inner thoughts. What would happen to Radi?

"You are all done," Doctor Cherrywood said. "Everything looks in order, and you are the healthiest trinket I have yet examined." He called through the curtain. "Who is next?"

I pulled on my regular day gown.

Madam Yasmina approached. "You heard what happened to your friend. Let this be a lesson not to follow her example."

"Will she be executed?"

"That shall depend on her tin-chai," Yasmina said. "Perhaps His Majesty will find some use for her."

My stomach squeezed and churned. There had to be some way to rescue Radi before the emperor used her to replenish the palace reserves. Before she was imprisoned as a novelty. I would ask Prince Carrick if he could help.

I wouldn't rest until I found a way to set Radi free.

CHAPTER 23

When I entered Treehouse 4444 that evening to bring Lady Arlyn's supper, the faela sat at the dining table. A decanter of wine sat before her. Drops of wine marked the table. Arlyn's eyes glazed over in stupor. Had she been drinking all day?

She hiccupped. "Oh, you're here. Let's have a lesson. I'll teach you how to serve wine to His Majesty. You can learn by serving me."

I didn't have time or energy for this right now. Not when I'd just learned my best friend had been caught running away.

"I said, come here." Lady Arlyn slammed down the jug of wine, and some of it sloshed out onto the table.

Guess I had no choice.

I took my place on the mat across the table from Lady Arlyn and sat back on my ankles.

A hiccup emerged from her throat and turned into a burp. "Tonight marks the anniversary of my entrance into His Majesty's harem. Pour me another cup, and let's celebrate."

I did as she asked. Arlyn grabbed the cup and tossed its contents down her throat.

"It is also the anniversary of my best friend's death, which the empress was so kind to remind me when she visited this afternoon."

"Empress Limera called on you?"

Arlyn was just one of many forgotten faela. Why would the empress waste her time visiting Arlyn?

"Her Majesty comes every year to make sure I recall what happens to rebellious girls who try to evade their duty. I was the first faela she was charged with punishing. Makes me special." She laughed. "She also told me Lady Soo's trinket mentee was caught attempting to escape."

I cast my gaze downward. "That girl is my friend."

"Oh? Then you need a drink, too." Arlyn poured me a cup. The wine overflowed, spilling down the table and onto my lap.

"What do you think will happen to my friend?" I asked.

"Let us hope she doesn't become a bauble."

"What are baubles?" The unfamiliar term brought to mind the novelties. Goosebumps rose on my arms.

"What are baubles?" Arlyn's laugh turned into another hiccup. "You will wish you never asked. There are two kinds of baubles. Limera's baubles are girls she keeps in cages to torture. For your friend's sake, it would be better if she were Limera's bauble than the emperor's bauble."

She shoved her wine cup at me. With trembling hands, I refilled it.

"I told you my friend took her life, but I was unable to take mine. I didn't tell you what happened to me the day after. His Majesty said attempted suicide was less of a crime than trying to evade marital duties. Instead of imprisoning me, he made me spend a night watching his baubles as a warning. The empress was charged with keeping me there. He said rebellious girls needed to have their spirits broken. Those noblemen went into the bauble cages and—and—"

Her voice broke, leaving the sentence unfinished, but I knew what she was unable to say.

I almost dropped the jug of wine.

Lady Arlyn's words became more slurred, and her movements slackened. "The empress said I should feel lucky. Did I take joy in watching them suffer, knowing it could have been me? And I hated myself because I *was* glad. Better them than me. Oh, deities! I can still see them. Chained and lying in their own blood and vomit."

Her face contorted, stretched in a silent scream.

"Lady Arlyn." I shook her shoulders. What nightmares she must be reliving.

Her breathing remained heavy, and through dilated pupils, her gaze refocused on me. "Oh, Rilla, it's only you. What was I saying?" She blinked slowly. "Ah, yes. Bauble cages. Never, ever," she waggled her index finger, and her entire body swayed with the motion, "*ever* try to run away, or you may end up like them."

She pitched forward, her head hitting the table. Her eyes closed, and her breathing slowly steadied.

Winter Woods. When Carrick had shown me the seasonal gardens, he had also mentioned Limera punished her victims in the Winter Woods. Radi could be there. Maybe I could free her before she faced a worse punishment. Before she became the emperor's bauble.

I needed to hurry. I had to retrace the path Carrick and I followed to the Winter Woods.

I rushed away from the Dark Court.

Behind me, someone called my name. It sounded like Carrick. I couldn't tell him what I was doing. He would only try to stop me. I pretended not to hear and ran faster, hoping he was too far to give chase. I didn't hear him come after me, so I risked a look behind my shoulder. There was no sign of him. Good. I didn't want to have to lie about where I was going.

I continued on, creeping through the Dark Court and into the

Spring Gardens, then tiptoed through the corridors across the Autumn Courtyard. Two night guards approached. I hid behind a pillar and waited for them to pass. Their lanterns glowed dimmer until only the lights of the Lavender and White Moons shone above me again. I crossed the bridge over the pond, and once at the junction, I veered left.

Deeper into the dark forest I walked until I came to where the woods grew thicker, pine trees scattered on all sides. The air became bitter, and white frosted puffs formed in front of my face each time I breathed.

The forest now lay in eternal winter. Despite the cold fingers of fear gripping my shoulders and trying to hold me back, I forced one foot in front of the other, determined to continue.

I marveled at the way the snow seemed to stretch its fingers, leaving behind an endless sea of white on all it touched. I'd once thought the Dark Court cold, but here, even the trees were immortalized in their frozen state. They formed pockets in the blankets of snow layering the earth, reminding me of the fish placed in ice tubs for preservation at the sea market.

The sight was beautiful and terrible, alluring and repulsive, a daydream and a nightmare.

The fresh, crisp scent of pine and snow melted away into something more noxious, making me gag. Ammonia, sweat, and decaying waste. I held my nose and trudged on.

In the near distance, bird cages scattered both sides of the path. A naked woman covered in red welts lay dead in her prison. Frost covered her brows and unseeing eyes, still open, frozen in death.

CHAPTER 24

I surveyed the other cages. A red birthmark in the shape of a four marked one woman's shoulder blade. Had she been thrown in a cage simply for possessing a mark believed to be cursed?

The cages all held dead or dying women. They had been beaten, their bodies bruised and cut. One cage contained nothing but black ash. Fragments of terra cotta clay, figurines of petrified women, littered the floors of other cages, but the broken pieces and moss that grew on the wooden cage bars indicated they had been killed long ago and left forgotten. They hadn't even been given the decency of a burial. Angry tears burned my eyes.

A chilling scream broke through the frozen silence of the forest. The piercing cries of desperation echoed in my ears. "I promise I'll do whatever you want if you spare us."

Some poor woman was being tortured.

A whip cracked. "There is no forgiveness or mercy for those who have sinned against His Majesty. Sneaking around the palace to see your lover is disgraceful."

A hint of jasmine and coconut wafted through the air, cutting the rot and death. That was Empress Limera's perfume. I remembered it from when she had come to assess the trinkets.

"True love is not a sin. It is the emperor who forced me to leave my fiancé."

"You had no business becoming engaged with a man, a palace soldier nonetheless, when you were still of eligible age to be His Majesty's faela. You and your lover deserve worse than death."

"Punish me, then. Leave him alone."

"It is too late. He was beheaded this morning."

"No!" Broken sobs reverberated through the forest. "We committed no wrong. It is you and your lecherous husband who deserve worse than death. May both of you be cursed in your next four afterlives."

Another series of lashes sounded, and Empress Limera's shouts rose above the young woman's screams. "You continue to deny your infidelity, and now you shout blasphemies at your sovereigns? I promise by the time I am finished, you will wish I had left you a way to take your own life. Oh, how I shall enjoy hearing you beg me to stop."

Footsteps sounded, quickly growing closer. I jolted up and hid behind the trees. Empress Limera emerged from the path, appearing so quickly, she could have been a specter summoned from the depths of the underworld. Three women followed her close behind—two older middle-aged women dressed in trifle uniforms and the third in trinket robes.

Irica. My childhood tormentor carried herself with dignity, mimicking the empress's haughty demeanor, but her pale face and wide eyes reflected terror.

I held my breath until they walked past me. I felt for my necklace, trying to let the pendant calm me.

I came out of hiding and headed in the direction where the empress had come.

I recognized the tortured girl. She was one of the other trinkets.

She was a little older than I, between eighteen and twenty years old. The girl lay on her side, her back covered in blood and shredded skin. There was still a roundness to her belly, but she bled so much, I was afraid she had already suffered a miscarriage.

Not only had she suffered physical torture, her hair, a woman's pride and beauty, had been shaven from her head, the mark of an adulteress. Not one strand had been spared; even her eyebrows were stolen from her. Only a fine layer of black fuzz remained to cover her naked head.

She appeared so small and fragile, so helpless.

I needed to smuggle her out of the palace. But first, I had to heal her. So I sang the words of a new song.

"Crimson autumn returns and leaves fade to dust.
The weeping trees shed broken, crinkled hearts.
Stripped bare, they raise their arms to Heaven,
Awaiting rebirth to discover who they are."

Her body began to heal, and her hair grew out several inches until it reached her shoulders. But before I could sing another verse, she turned toward me. "Shut your mouth."

She glared, anger clouding her features. "Are you under her employ? Limera must have sent you to repair my wounds, so when my body rips open again, it will be fresh torture."

"No, I'm here to help you escape."

"Is it not enough to physically abuse me? Must she emotionally torment me as well?" She touched her hair and let out a bitter laugh. "Thank you for this. A pity I shall have to wait until the next life to get my revenge."

She pulled at her hair. It stretched and grew until the long, black curls extended all the way to the ground. The mass of hair formed several coils and wrapped around her neck, squeezing tight. Her neck snapped, and her limp body fell to the ground, her eyes still wide open.

I sank to my knees and stared in disbelief at her lifeless body and the bump of her unborn child. All I had wanted was to help her. But I'd made things worse. Just like that, she was gone.

Footsteps came behind me. I ran and took cover, but the clasp around my neck snapped. My necklace fell to the ground. Too late to reach for it. The empress approached.

I prayed she wouldn't see it.

Trailing behind were Limera's two trifles and Irica, who carried a metal bar.

The empress saw the dead woman and scowled. "How did this happen? I heard someone singing."

Irica's gaze searched around and caught onto my necklace. "Your Majesty, excuse me, but I recognize this." She pointed to my necklace. "It belongs to my fellow trinket. She must have had something to do with this."

Irica looked around. Empress Limera snatched up my necklace and sniffed the air. "Yes, I can smell her fear."

Limera marched to my hiding spot. Her gaze fell upon me. She threw my necklace at my feet. Seizing me by the arm, she pulled me to face her. "You have one chance to tell me the truth. What did you do to this adulteress?"

CHAPTER 25

✦ ✦ ✦ ✦ ✦ ✦ ✦ ✦ ✦ ✦

The empress glowered. "Did your singing have something to do with this adulteress's death?"

Behind her, Irica copied the empress's displeased expression. "Rilla, you're such a liar. You must have pretended to be a koong—"

The empress turned and slapped her. "Did I say you could speak?"

Irica stumbled back. "No, my lady. I apologize."

"I did not help her," I said. "She killed herself. I was lost and scared. I usually sing when I'm frightened. She was already hanging when I stumbled across her."

"You are still lying. I made sure she was powerless to kill herself. Unless someone was able to grow out her hair, she would not have been able to use her tin-chai. So I ask again, what *did* you do?"

Beads of sweat formed on my brow. "I did not do anything."

Her eyes narrowed at my slight stammer.

"Lift your head." She took my chin in one hand and angled my head. She closed her eyes and brought her nose to my face, inhaling my scent as though I were a flavorful delicacy. A slow smile spread across her face. "Well, well, I believe those are tears on your cheeks, not yet dry. Don't you know empathy and love are weaknesses? They betray you, my dear. Fear did not summon those tears. Pity did. You watched her die."

She let her manicured index finger tap my cheek. The sharp tip of her nail grazed my skin and then dug deep, piercing my flesh, and I cried out. She slapped me. A slow burn spread across my cheek. I held the side of my face in my hand, stunned.

"I remember your face now," Limera said. "You were with the rebellious trinket. What a fool she was to try to run away."

"Radi," I said. "What have you done to her? Is she here?"

Limera laughed. "She is not here. Not yet. You are lucky, my dear, for your punishment today is nowhere as severe as what I have planned for her." She beckoned her trifles. They grabbed my arms and forced me to kneel in front of the empress.

Her long fingernails traced over my throat. "My husband has a weakness for singers, and you have the sweetest voice I have ever heard." She snapped her fingers at Irica. "You there. Be useful for once and fetch some jorlang juice from the apothecary. Tell them to make it three times as potent. Show them my seal, and there should be no questions. If they refuse, give me their names. I will punish them later."

Irica cast me a malicious beam. "Gladly, my lady." She curtsied, dropped the metal bar she held, and ran off.

Jorlang juice? Drinking the acidic juice at three times its normal strength would destroy my vocal cords permanently. I'd never sing or talk again.

My whole body quaked. "Please, don't do this. You can't take away my voice." I struggled against the trifles and almost broke away, but they tackled me to the ground. "No, please. I promise to do anything." What purpose would I have to live if I had my tin-chai taken away from me?

A man called out, breaking through my pleas. "Mother Empress,

I was passing through on my way to the Summer Fields and heard a commotion. Is everything all right?"

The trifles held my face to the ground so I couldn't see who it was, but I recognized Prince Carrick's voice. He must have followed me.

"It is nothing, Number Eight," Limera said. "I was about to teach this trinket a lesson. She has been most disrespectful, interfering with my punishment of an adulteress."

"Then I'm sorry to disturb you. She must be deserving of your punishment, especially for a trinket as lowly as she. Who is she to believe she could challenge one as beautiful and talented as you?"

"I know you are only flattering me to get on my good side, Number Eight. I've always liked you, though. A pity what happened to your mother, but her sentence was justified. You should not visit her. She does not deserve it."

That must have been meant to get a rise out of Carrick. But he replied without missing a beat. "Yes, I am sure Father Emperor had his reasons. However, she is my mother, and I do not dare defy the Analects of Heaven by dishonoring my parents lest I become cursed in my next life."

Limera paused. "Hmm. Did you say you were on your way to the Summer Fields? I have never known you to frequent that part of the palace like your dear brother Nelan."

"True, I don't often frequent the Summer Fields or overindulge in such pleasures like my dear brother Nelan does. I have far more important matters to keep me busy, but it doesn't mean I don't like to appease my desires once in a while. I am a man, after all."

"Yes, I suppose all of you princes take after your father," she said. "Go on your way then, Number Eight."

He cleared his throat. "I cannot leave knowing you are upset. What has this trinket done? Perhaps I can assist in her punishment."

"You are showing more concern for this trinket than I would

expect," Limera said. "Do you, in fact, know her? Perhaps you have already been taken by her beauty. She is the prettiest of the trinkets and is proving to be rebellious and prideful because of it. I would not be surprised if she has tried to entice you."

"That is certainly not the case," Carrick said. "I don't know her. In fact, I haven't paid attention to this year's trinkets at all."

"Are you sure? Take a look at her face before you answer so quickly."

The trifles let me up and pushed me around to face Carrick. He scrunched his face as though he had eaten an ungbeetle. "You call her a beauty? Her entire face is swollen, and her hair looks like an unsightly mess of cobwebs."

He sounded so believable. I couldn't stop the tightening in my chest. My face did feel swollen from when the empress slapped me, and I had been tossed into the dirt.

How humiliating to be caught looking like this in front of Carrick. A tell-tale blush rose into my already burning cheeks.

Carrick laughed. "Mother Empress, if she is the prettiest, the other trinkets must be revolting. This girl's ears are too large, and she has a pouch here." He motioned around his waist area.

I sucked in my stomach, suddenly self-conscious about my weight when I'd never thought much about it.

Limera's lips formed a pout. She sniffed the air. "Number Eight, I smell anxiety in your sweat. I have a suspicion you are lying. Has she already seduced you?"

"I respectfully ask that you not accuse me of such an abomination, Mother Empress," Carrick said. "I would never betray Father Emperor."

His gaze flashed to my face, and for a moment, his mask of composure slipped. Only a second passed before his stoic expression returned, but it was enough for Limera's suspicion to grow.

"I still do not believe you. Satisfy my doubt, and I will allow her to keep her voice." She grabbed the metal bar Irica had been carrying earlier. "I had this branding iron personally designed. It leaves behind a special mark." She waved a hand to her trifles. "Tie her up. We shall let Number Eight take over."

The two women dragged me to an oak tree and tied me against it with a rope. They bound my arms behind me.

I squirmed as Limera approached. Slowly, she used her finger to trace the number four on my cheek. "Brand the trinket's face with the cursed mark of four, and I will consider this punishment enough for her misbehavior today."

Carrick's hands shook, and for the first time, his real emotions threatened to betray his usual confident persona.

"I don't believe in curses or superstitions," I said, more for his sake than mine. He needed to do this, or he would get into trouble, too. "I've never cared for the attention my beauty attracted anyway."

"You say that now, my dear, but beauty is all a woman has to offer," Limera said. "Each time you look in the mirror, you will realize you shall never be beautiful again. You will regret you ever pitied another woman when you are the one who should be pitied."

She held the branding iron out to Carrick. He hesitated for a moment before taking it. The empress took a step back, and her trifles stood behind her. They waited for Carrick to move. He remained frozen.

Limera's grin widened. "I believe I smell more anxiety on you, Number Eight. In fact," she made a show of sniffing the air, waving her hand in front of her nose, "are you harboring true, romantic feelings for this trinket? His Majesty will be quite disappointed. He has always favored you."

"I have committed no wrong, Mother Empress," Carrick said. "This trinket means nothing to me. I hesitate because I am figuring out how to get the iron hot." He raised his gaze upward and closed his eyes.

The wind crashed through the trees, and a sudden flash of lightning brightened the sky. Electric sparks struck a bush and lit it on fire. Carrick placed the iron rod into the fire, and when he pulled it away, the tip glowed a bright orange. He approached, and a tremor of fear shook through me. He stared into my eyes and positioned the branding iron forward until it stopped mere inches from my face. The heat emanating from the metal made me queasy. Drops of sweat trickled down my spine.

But he stopped, standing so still, it was as if some enchantment had befallen him. He wouldn't be able to close the final distance. He didn't want to hurt me. But if he did not finish this, Limera would punish us both.

I couldn't let him get in trouble. So I clenched my teeth, braced myself, and shoved my head forward into the fire of the branding iron.

CHAPTER 26

Heat blistered my skin. I screamed. The smell of burning flesh, so foul I tasted it, filled the air. The contact lasted barely two seconds, but my face felt like it had been lit on fire. Tears poured down my cheeks. My vision blurred.

I barely registered the shocked look on Carrick's face. The iron slipped from his fingers. A sizzled hiss sounded where it hit the snow.

Limera's glistening red lips curled into an arc. "Well done, Number Eight."

The trifles untied me. Limp and exhausted, I fell into a boneless heap. I couldn't feel anything except my burning face.

The empress laughed, the pleased sound echoing through the woods. "My, my, you certainly *are* hideous now, aren't you? Well, I would have preferred to take away your voice, but a deal is a deal." She snapped her fingers at her trifles. "Go tell that dim-witted trinket she no longer needs to fetch jorlang juice." She flicked her wrist at Carrick, beckoning him. "Number Eight, you may accompany me back to my suite."

Carrick took one last look at me before following Limera and her trifles, leaving me crumpled on the forest floor. I let myself feel the pain. The salt from my tears added to the burn on my cheek. I didn't know how long I stayed there before I forced myself up.

I sat and saw my discarded necklace on the ground a few feet away. I picked it up and cushioned it in the palm of my hand, holding it so tightly that I felt the links of the chain dig into my skin. I stared into the forest. Dozens of cages lay scattered on the snowy banks. The shadowed outlines of bodies occupied those cages.

Was Radi among them?

The young woman who had hanged herself still lay in the cage in front of me, her hair remained strung around her broken neck.

I had always believed suicide was the coward's way out of life's trials, but looking at this woman now, I had no right to judge. Perhaps we were all better off dead instead of clinging to some fragment of hope for change.

How would I be after decades trapped here? Years from now, would I be able to hold onto hope? If I became a bauble like this woman, would I, like her, give up and surrender to madness?

I must have fallen asleep because, when next I opened my eyes, the sun was high in the sky. I remained curled under a tree, and the bauble cages were as grotesque and ominous during the day as they had been at night.

How had I spent the entire night in the Winter Woods without freezing to death? Though it was a little chilly, it wasn't unbearable. A warm blanket had been wrapped around me, and before me lay the embers of a dying fire.

My face still throbbed but wasn't as painful as I thought it would be. I raised a hand and touched my cheek. A sticky substance covered the burn. It gave off a menthol smell. Carob bark, used to reduce pain and swelling. The same person who had given me a blanket must have applied ointment to my burn. Maybe Carrick had returned. But if he had, why hadn't he awakened me?

No time to wonder now. It was already late morning. I needed to leave in case the empress returned.

I stood, folded the blanket, and headed to the Dark Court. Yasmina probably thought I had spent the night there when I didn't return to the Apple Barrel.

Arlyn still lay asleep at the dining table. I closed the door, and the sound woke her. She opened her eyes and came to full alertness. Her gaze flew to my face. "Child, what happened? Who did this to you?"

I must've looked a mess if I'd managed to scare her out of her still-drunken state.

"No need to answer. I already know who," Lady Arlyn said. "The empress is known for her methods of torture. What happened?"

"I was looking for my friend. The one who ran away. The empress caught me."

Lady Arlyn gasped. "Why would you endanger yourself? It is unfortunate what happened to your friend, but you should never have put yourself at risk. I would say it is a blessing your face is ruined. However, the judges are superstitious. You may become a bauble simply for wearing the curse of four."

My stomach lurched.

"I have a solution," Arlyn said. "It would be a pity to lose you as my trifle. I've taken a liking to you."

I headed upstairs to her chambers, and the smell of paint hit me once more. Canvases, paintbrushes, and paint-stained containers littered the cluttered room. Today, all the paintings were covered and hidden away from view. What a shame. I would have loved to admire her work.

I stepped over a stack of boards and nearly knocked over two glass jars half-filled with murky water.

"Remind me to remind you to clean those later," Lady Arlyn said, with an absent-minded gesture of her hand. She led me to her desk and waved to the chair. "Sit and do not move."

She took a small bottle from the top drawer. A minty smell wafted through the air when she opened it.

"Linthin extract," I said.

She poured some out onto a clean handkerchief. "Is that what it's called? All I know is it helps replenish the skin and lighten burn scars. Enlin, my old trifle, always used it on me."

Lady Arlyn dabbed the handkerchief against my face. The sting made me wince. But my attention diverted away from the pain as Lady Arlyn's movements caused her sleeves to fall back from her forearms, exposing the candle wax burns. The sight of the marks on Lady Arlyn made my eyes brim with tears. I blinked them away before she could see.

"If you apply it everyday, the scar will fade, though I doubt it will ever completely disappear. In the meantime, you cannot go about the palace looking like this."

From the drawer, she withdrew a rectangular container separated into small squared compartments, each holding a different color of paint.

"I make my own paints from flowers and herbs," she said, taking up a brush. "I imagine if I had a different life and became a mother, I would have so much fun with my children." A wistful, longing expression settled in her features. "I would paint pictures on their faces. Flutterflies, hearts, colorful animals, and rainbows."

Her eyes glistened. She shook her head. "No use thinking of what will never be. At least I have you."

She dipped the brush into water and red paint, then drew the outline of a heart around the hideous number four. She filled the heart with color until the mark was no longer visible. Then she added curlicues and bright-colored flowers upward to the corner of my eyebrow. She dipped another brush into a shiny silver paint, then dotted my face with an ending flourish, so the entire design sparkled and glittered.

"There," she said. "The paint should last for a while without washing away. When it does, I will draw it on again. There are no rules against painting one's face, so the judges should allow it for the finale."

The finale was in three weeks. What would Yasmina say when she saw me? Would she accuse me of sabotaging myself? Maybe I could avoid her and the Apple Barrel until the finale. If I sent notice saying Lady Arlyn wished me to stay at the Dark Court, Yasmina couldn't deny the request since most of the trinkets already stayed with their mentors.

"Thankfully, the empress is forbidden to attend and cannot interfere," Arlyn said.

It took me a second to refocus on Arlyn's words. "Empress Limera isn't allowed at the finale? Why not?"

"A few showcases ago, the empress attacked a trinket who had the emperor smitten. Ever since, His Majesty banned her. But he would never do anything further to remove her power. She possesses a great deal of influence over him."

Lady Arlyn paused in thought. "I do recall hearing the empress was kind once. Hard to believe now. I suppose this is what being in a position of power is like, always worried someone will take your place." She patted my shoulder. "This is why it's better to remain my permanent trifle, safe and sound from the dangerous drama of the elite faela. Do not stray into Limera's territory or try to save your friend. It isn't worth it."

She busied herself with washing her brushes. I studied my face in the mirror. I couldn't see the scar any longer, only a heart. It gave me hope. As long as I was alive, there would always be hope.

I was determined to remain Arlyn's trifle, so the emperor would never use my tin-chai for his selfish purposes, but I also had to rescue Radi.

Radi had been right. I could no longer play fair. This was a twisted chess game, and I could only win if I changed the rules.

CHAPTER 27

Every afternoon of the following week, I waited at the border of the Dark Court and the Spring Gardens, hoping Prince Carrick would come to visit—but he didn't.

This continued for a week before I finally crossed into the Spring Gardens and went to Lady Cirisa's cage. I brought a basket of strawberries that I'd smuggled from the kitchen that morning when I'd prepared Lady Arlyn's breakfast. Not only would it be nice to see Lady Cirisa, but I hoped I would come upon Prince Carrick. There was no way he wouldn't visit his mother.

I approached his mother's cage and saw him, proving I was correct. Carrick's gaze sharpened. "What are you doing here?"

"I came to see you since you're avoiding me."

A hooded figure dressed in a green and brown cloak stood behind Carrick. He had been so silent and camouflaged into the background that I hadn't noticed him from the start. A sword was strapped to his waist, and he carried a bow and a quiver of arrows on his back. A black mask concealed his face, but his eyes shone between two narrow slits.

A strange but pleasant flicker of heat formed in my chest. His eyes glowed gold and amber, warm and welcoming. Somehow familiar. Why did it feel like we'd met before?

I addressed him. "You must be Prince Carrick's bodyguard. I've seen you running through the trees. What's your name?"

Carrick stopped him from responding. "Blistering ballasts, keep an eye out, will you? With Androgy Solar away, I need you on high alert. I would prefer if my idiot brothers did not succeed in their plots to kill me."

Carrick's bodyguard bowed. His agile form sprang into the trees to scan the area.

"Your androgy is away?" That meant we had no shield.

Carrick tossed me a pointed glare. "For the next few weeks."

I replayed what he had told his bodyguard. "Did you say your brothers are trying to kill you?"

"Don't worry. My bodyguard won't let anything happen." He pointed to my face, muttering so low I almost didn't hear him. "You covered the scar."

"Yes, Lady Arlyn was kind enough to paint over it so no one would give me trouble."

"I wanted to come find you, but I—" He cleared his throat, an uncomfortable blush rising into his cheeks. "I . . . I did not want . . . I'm sor . . . Why did you move into the branding iron?"

"That's why you've been avoiding me?"

"I was trying to figure out a way to not brand you," he said. "Now your face is ruined."

"There was no way out of it. You have nothing to be sorry for. We both would have been punished if you hadn't been able to follow through. If you had moved before I did, I still wouldn't have blamed you." I smiled. "Besides, I consider it a battle scar, and the design Lady Arlyn painted is whimsical, don't you think?"

"I told you not to venture into the empress's territory. I thought you would have learned your lesson after my father caught you."

"I was looking for my friend."

"Yes, I heard she was caught. It was why I went to find you at the Dark Court, to see if you were all right. But apparently all your sense fled when you went to the Winter Woods, thinking you could save her."

"If she's among the baubles, I need to help her. Empress Limera told me that Radi isn't a bauble yet, but she's in the empress's hands."

He shook his head and sighed. "I admired your loyalty from the first day we met, but you are going to get yourself killed. Since you are being so stubborn, I'll try to find out where Mother Empress is holding her. But that is all I'm going to do. I will not risk inciting Father Emperor's or Mother Empress's wrath by interfering."

"Thank you."

"Consider it a sympathy gift for burning your face." He held out his hand, revealing a similar vial to the one Lady Arlyn had. "Here. It will reduce the scarring."

"Linthin extract?" I guessed.

He raised one eyebrow. "How did you know?"

"I studied herbal remedies under the tutelage of my brother, who is a doctor. Also, Lady Arlyn gave some to me."

He pulled his hand back. "Then I suppose you don't need—"

I grabbed his hand and took the vial. "Thank you." The warmth of his skin brushed against mine. I looked down to where our hands touched. He did the same. I withdrew quickly. A flicker of heat rose into my cheeks.

I turned away, suddenly embarrassed to meet his gaze. Instead, I inserted a Seran into Lady Cirisa's cage. When the curtains parted, I presented the basket of strawberries to her.

"She likes peaches," Carrick said, attempting to sound surly.

At least this broke the awkwardness.

I aimed a cool look at him. "I'm betting she could use some variety in her life."

Lady Cirisa reached through the bars and swatted her son's shoulder in reprimand. She shot me a thankful look and took the strawberries.

Carrick crossed his arms. "Humph." He sat and watched his mother eat the berries. I paid him no attention and talked to Lady Cirisa.

"The cherry blossoms are in full bloom." I painted her a picture of what lay a mere fifty feet behind her cage, which she'd never witness for herself. "They fall like wispy, pink paper confetti, celebrating the pinnacle of spring."

"Scorching nutshells. How long are you going to bore my mother with your endless babbling?" Carrick interrupted. He put in another Seran to extend our time with Lady Cirisa. "I would like some time with her, too."

His mother sent him another scalding glare.

"All right. Your turn," I said. "I'll give you some privacy."

I perched against a cherry tree and crossed my arms to watch mother and son. Carrick said something to her, and his mother's eyes brightened. Though birds were uncommon around here, a sparrow flew into the clearing and settled on a branch to sing a joyful tune.

But the song took a hasty end. The bird cried an alarm and scurried away.

A glint caught my eye. A tiny silver tip pointed out of the tree, aimed for Prince Carrick's chest.

"Watch out!" I darted forward, placing myself in front of him. A flash of black jumped from out of nowhere and shoved me hard to the ground. Carrick landed next to me along with someone else, but I didn't have time to register who as a sharp pain entered the side of my shoulder. A piercing scream—*mine*—filled the air.

CHAPTER 28

✦ ✦ ✦ ✦ ✦ ✦ ✦ ✦ ✦ ✦

Carrick's bodyguard lifted me and cushioned my head into his shoulder. His arms were strong but gentle. He carried me through the cherry tree orchard.

The pain was overwhelming. I bit my lip to keep from crying out. My vision filled with darkness. I must have passed out because the next thing I knew, I woke, face down on a bed. I turned my head to the side and saw the bodyguard's masked face next to me.

The agony once again overcame my senses. I couldn't stop the whimper that escaped my throat.

The bodyguard spoke. A beautiful baritone that felt as safe and warm as a cozy fireplace on a winter's night. His voice sounded familiar, too.

"You'll be fine, I promise. Try not to move, and the pain will be over."

A gentle caress skidded across my bare skin, but the pleasant sensation ended there. A jolting sting tore through my shoulder. I cried out.

"I'm sorry for that." The bodyguard sounded ragged as though he were hurting more than I was. "This balm will soothe the pain."

In a matter of seconds, an icy prickle replaced the sting.

"If you had not pushed Rilla out of the way, the arrow would have pierced her heart," Carrick said. "This has Nelan's foul stench all over it. I swear I shall kill the blistering bastard. Did you see him shoot?"

"He hired a man this time. Rest assured, I'll find the assassin."

The bodyguard had saved my life. I wished I had the energy to thank him, but my entire body felt too heavy to move, as though I were sinking in a pool of molasses.

"Almost done." The bodyguard's voice now held a silvery quality, calm and steady. Warm, gentle hands moved over my shoulder and bandaged me.

"Are you sure she will be all right? Maybe we should take her to the doctor."

"It will work, trust me. You know it'll arouse suspicion if a prince brings a trinket to the doctor. You cannot attract attention to yourself again, especially given your recent encounter with Empress Limera and knowing how much Prince Nelan wants to trap you."

The medicine on my shoulder took effect, and all the energy drained from my body. Swarms of black blotches drew me in and out of consciousness. Carrick and his bodyguard still spoke, but their words were distorted and distant, as if I held a seashell to my ear and listened to the echo of waves rushing over the shore.

When I awoke, I lay against velvet pillows. A thick, steel-gray duvet covered me. Next to the bed stood an antique writing desk with a bureau of drawers on top, the entire ensemble painted off-white. A familiar scent came off my body.

Menthol. Carob bark, again?

The bodyguard, not Carrick, was responsible for tending to my burn and covering me with a blanket that night in the Winter Woods.

Carrick came into my field of vision. "You're awake." He exhaled in relief.

I scanned the room. "Where is he?"

"Who?"

"Your bodyguard."

"Oh, him. He's out taking care of important matters for me." He glared at me. "What do you think you are doing, taking an arrow for me?"

"Someone tried to kill you. Did you catch him?" I sat up in the bed and winced at the motion.

"It's being taken care of." He eased me back.

I finally allowed myself to relax and take in my surroundings. The room was lavish, part of a larger open space, similar to Lady Arlyn's residence. However, Carrick's house was built within a hollowed-out maple tree. Three-pronged leaves of ashen silver functioned as wallpaper, pasted in straight lines from floor to ceiling. The décor, from the curtains to the embellished carvings on the bedpost, had a masculine color scheme, thunderstorm gray.

The dim lighting cast a dreamy atmosphere. Incense burned, permeating the air with a heady scent of cinnamon and sandalwood that reminded me of Nia's candles back home. A pang of home-sickness settled in the hollow cave of my chest.

Until I remembered I was in Carrick's room.

Those feelings of homesickness fled, and my pulse beat faster for a different reason. I looked at the pillows and blankets that fell around me like the layers of a lacy gown tossed away in haste.

I was in Carrick's bed.

He stared at the side of my face so intently I felt self-conscious. Though the face paint hid the scar, I couldn't help but wonder if he found me unattractive now, knowing the cursed mark of four tainted my skin.

I reached for my hair, bringing a lock of it to try and cover the mark, but Carrick brushed my hand away and swept back my hair. "Don't be ashamed of your battle scar. Isn't that what you called it? Wear it proudly."

He touched my cheek, tracing the design Lady Arlyn had drawn. The warmth of his hand sent delicious shivers through my body. "Some of the paint is fading from where you landed in the dirt. Let me help you touch it up. I have the perfect paint for the job."

"You like to paint?"

"You seem surprised. Do I not seem like the artistic type? Or do you perceive me a cold-hearted soul with no emotions, incapable of creative expression?"

"That isn't what I—" I broke off as a smile played at his lips, exposing a single dimple.

He was already handsome, but if he smiled more often, he'd be so devastating, I would likely forget how to talk in his presence.

"The paint Lady Arlyn has used won't last more than two weeks before washing away. I have squidflower ink from Fauxhemia Kingdom. It's expensive and hard to procure, but it shall keep for at least two months without fading if you do not scrub it hard with soap." He took a brush and palette from the bottom drawer of his desk, then sat on the side of the bed and set to work, stroking the brush with meticulous movements along my skin. Gooseflesh raised on my arms at the sensations.

I had to distract myself before I made a fool of myself pining after him. "At least with this horrible mark, even after the showcase I'll be ugly enough to avoid unwanted attention. Your father only seemed to like me for my face." I cringed at the memory of Terran's disgusting touch.

The brushstrokes stopped. "Stop talking. You're making me mess up the design. And that is far from the truth. I've told you before, even trifles need to remain wary, and you are a pretty girl with or without the scar. Do not think you're safe from my father."

He thought me pretty? My heart danced. *Stop being such a giddy fool.*

We had no chance to be together. Our paths may have crossed for the moment, but we were meant to veer in opposite directions. Even if I managed not to become Terran's faela, I'd only be a trifle. And *he* was a prince, who I hoped one day would become emperor. He would probably marry a princess or a dignitary's daughter from a foreign kingdom. He might even have his own harem of faela, if not out of his own desire, then for political reasons.

No, I couldn't spin fantastical stories about an impossible future.

He painted in silence until he finished. He took a step back and assessed his work. "I deserve high praise. It's almost as perfect as what Lady Arlyn can do. Tell your lady to borrow squidflower ink from me when it begins to fade again. You should remain here until I confirm with my bodyguard that no one is spying on us. Then I will escort you back to the Dark Court."

My eyes widened at the reminder. "Do you know who would try to kill you?"

"Only all my brothers." He let out a self-deprecating laugh and stormed to the window. His fingers drummed against the windowpane in an absentminded rhythm. "Nelan, Number Eleven, is the worst. He is the most jealous of me. I suspect he was behind this attempt."

"What?" I jerked, and my shoulder protested at the sudden movement. "Ow!"

He swung his gaze from the window and scowled at me. "Stop moving so much."

"Why are your brothers trying to kill you? What is wrong with them?"

"Is it surprising? We share one father." He looked away, and his resigned sigh sounded tragic and jaded all at once. "But there is only one crown."

Carrick retreated from the window and went to the writing desk, where he slumped his weight into the cushioned chair like a drunken sailor at a tavern. "Would you find me detestable if I told you I happen to be one of Father Emperor's favorite sons?"

The question caught me off guard. It took a moment before I found a response.

"I would never find you detestable. But I cannot see how your father would favor a son so unlike himself."

He sent me a wry smile. "Perhaps you do not know me well enough then. I have more in common with him than you know. I am the eighth prince and the oldest of the surviving princes. Not only is eight considered a lucky number according to the old superstitions, but Father Emperor was also the eighth son of my grandfather."

"Well, if that is your only commonality, you don't have to worry."

He hesitated a moment before saying, "He always says I am the son who reminds him most of himself. He says I'm cold and cunning, that he knows I'd betray those who have been loyal to me if it serves my purpose." A shadow crossed Carrick's features. "But if that should ever be true, if I should truly become like him, may Old Grandfather Heaven strike me dead."

"No, do not think such a thought. If you were anything like him, you would have branded me without hesitation."

He made no comment but tapped his fingers against the desktop aggressively, like a dofei fish battering the side of a ship. "Currently, I am among nineteen princes still alive, four of whom are viable contenders for the throne, while the others are barely out of the cradle. The number of my brothers is never constant. New princes are born. Others are killed in what seem like accidents. But we all silently acknowledge these accidents are murders. My hands are not clean, either."

Carrick scooted his chair closer to the bedside and idly straightened the covers. "Father Emperor takes pleasure in watching us fight to win his stamp of approval. Any prince who shows the least bit of kindness is the first to die. The ones who manage to stay alive share our father's cruel spirit. I can perhaps say the same for myself, since I have survived this far."

No anger lay behind his words, only regret and acceptance for something he could never change. So this was Carrick's world, always on the watch, never feeling safe from his own family. I couldn't imagine being taught to hate my brother.

I ignored the stabbing pain in my shoulder and embraced him. "I'm so sorry."

He seemed surprised by my show of emotion, but he patted my back in return. His motions were clumsy and awkward. "Why? I'm still alive."

"Please make sure you continue to stay alive."

Carrick pulled away. "I intend to. Don't you worry. I'm fully capable of remaining one step ahead of all my idiot brothers."

"Do you have any sisters?" So far, I'd heard no mention of princesses, nor had I seen a princess in the palace.

"Midwives are encouraged to kill the girls, unless Father Emperor decides otherwise."

My chest tightened. "And the mothers never try to save their daughters?"

Carrick's breath puffed out with a snort. "If a faela is stupid enough to interfere, then she is probably either dead or locked in a cage. I have heard of a few cases when a faela paid an androgy or bodyguard to give the girl up for adoption by a common family."

That made sense in a sick, twisted way. Many faela would do anything to raise their status in Terran's eyes, even give up their own flesh and blood. But some might believe their child would enjoy a better life outside the palace.

"How horrible," I said.

Carrick's eyes were dark and determined. "It is. That's why I shall do anything to become emperor one day. I will find the Sacred Cedar Scepter and prove I am worthy of it, and then I shall have the power to overturn all of Father Emperor's dirty laws."

If the other princes all took after their father, and if one of them got their hands on the scepter and managed to attain the Will of Heaven . . . Old Grandfather Heaven help us all.

When Carrick was assured we were safe from any prying eyes, he accompanied me back to the Dark Court and made easy conversation. On occasion, our arms brushed together, sending silly, but lovely tingles down my spine.

"Rilla," Carrick said, regarding me. "I've been meaning to ask. How has Lady Arlyn been treating you? Be honest with me."

"Well, Lady Arlyn hasn't abused me . . ."

"But?"

"She's hard to understand. She's moody."

A fleeting smile passed his face. "Be patient with her, Rilla. She is a good woman, just a little peculiar. Artists often are, especially Fauxhemians." Carrick's lips set into a grim line. He peered into the distance, lost in thought. "Lady Arlyn has witnessed some unpleasant events in her lifetime. She was already a sensitive soul, but such haunting images have affected her mental state. Continuing to live such a lonely existence only worsens her condition."

"You seem to know her quite well."

"Her old trifle, Enlin, used to serve my mother. The woman often spoke to me about Lady Arlyn and revealed some of the faela's secrets. About a year ago, before Enlin passed away, I helped her cover up an affair the lady had with one of my brothers. The ass threatened to tell Father Emperor that Lady Arlyn was a lunatic, which would have landed her in a bauble cage."

"What did you do to stop him?"

He kicked at the ground and brought up a cloud of dust. "I did what my father would have done. I eliminated the threat."

He looked up for a brief moment. His eyes were shaded and filled with self-loathing.

"Carrick," I started, but he shook his head.

"We're close enough to the Dark Court. I trust you can find your way back. I shall take my leave now."

I watched him march away. Any attempt to force him to open up would've pushed him further away.

I stepped into the confines of the Dark Court and returned to Treehouse 4444.

CHAPTER 29

I slept outside Treehouse 4444, propped against the door. My shoulder was still sore, but bearable. Thankfully, the balm had worked wonders, or I would've been in such pain sleeping there.

I had nowhere else to go. Lady Arlyn was having another mood swing and had locked me out, and I planned on avoiding Yasmina and the Apple Barrel until the finale. Yasmina already expected my progress reports to be incomplete and had stopped asking for them anyway. As long as I was a good girl and performed in the finale, she wouldn't care where I stayed.

The Lavender Moon's purplish tint had begun to fade to black. A sign that spring was drawing to an end. The Summer Solstice would soon begin.

Meanwhile, the White Moon kept her face veiled behind the clouds tonight, far away and inaccessible, like a good friend turning her back with sudden coldness.

Half of the Turquoise Moon appeared. Her dark side blended into the starless sky, and her narrow, slivered smile cast a sinister sapphire light upon the shadowed cherry orchard. I searched for the constellations of old, the stories my family used to tell me by the campfire, but the stars refused to come out. They hid behind a sea of thick clouds.

If I was right about Carrick's bodyguard being my secret guardian, then he would come tonight, too. I blinked the drowsiness away from my eyes. I was determined to wait for him.

Just when I was about to give in to the longing to keep my eyes closed, a glint of silver caught my eye. A sword. The bodyguard approached. His dark cloak blended into the forest, but I recognized his eyes behind the mask. They glowed bright and fiery, a hearth restoring warmth to the weary.

I gasped as he formed a flame in his hand and used it to light a campfire. He looked up.

"Why are you being so nice to me?" I asked. "Is it because Carrick asked you to?"

He shook his head and then bowed deeply, his hands lifted in an exaggerated, gallant gesture as though telling me it was simply the gentlemanly thing to do.

"I never thanked you for saving my life."

He stood straight as a soldier and cocked his head in a salute.

"Why aren't you talking to me? We're alone. Besides, I don't think there's a rule against a bodyguard speaking to a trinket. Is there?"

A horrifying thought occurred, making me jerk upright from my sitting position. "Did Terran have your tongue cut out?"

He shook his head.

"Oh, good." I breathed out in relief. "Did someone command you not to talk to me?"

He didn't answer, but instead, he placed the blanket in my hands. He signaled he needed to go.

I caught the edge of his cloak before he could walk away. His gaze fell to where I held the fabric in my fingers. "Please don't go. I won't pry if you don't wish to answer. I'd like . . . it would be nice to have a friend tonight."

He hesitated but then gave in. His movements were soundless, graceful. Not one blade of grass rustled when he dropped down and sat cross-legged beside me.

There was something reassuring about the bodyguard. I couldn't explain it, but I felt I could tell him all of my burdens. He felt like home. He gazed at the sky, which made me look up as well. The stars had finally chosen to emerge.

"Thank you. If it's all right, could you listen to me talk for a bit? I don't want to sleep."

He dipped his head and tossed one hand out with his palm facing the sky, motioning for me to go ahead.

"I've been so worried about my friend, Radi. The empress said she's punishing Radi for trying to escape, and I'm so afraid . . . afraid . . ."

He stretched his hand toward my shoulder, but he wavered and retracted at the last moment. Instead, he found a handkerchief in his pocket and handed it to me.

I took it. "It's just . . . I have no idea how to save her. It seems impossible without getting caught."

He used a stone to etch into the earth. For a minute, I listened to the rock scraping against dirt. The warm glow of the fire illuminated the words he wrote.

I will help you.

My gaze returned from the ground back to his face. "Thank you . . ." I trailed off, not knowing how to address him. "What is your name?"

He paused before writing another word. *Friend.*

"Friend? That's what you want me to call you?"

His intent stare said he expected some kind of answer.

"Oh, yes, we're definitely friends now. But won't you tell me your real name?"

He shook his head, but in his eyes was a glint of mischief as though he were saying, "*Not yet.*"

I sighed. "I suppose I'll have to call you Friend, then."

He held his gaze on me, and I couldn't look away. He overflowed with a light that poured from his soul into mine. It filled me with what I didn't realize I'd been missing until now. It was as though I'd been hungry for so long, I'd forgotten what it felt like to be full.

He emanated with realness, with sanity, and with hope. As long as his light remained in this world, I'd never be lost and alone.

"What's your secret?" I whispered. "Why can't you talk to me?"

A familiar deep voice broke behind us. "Because he is loyal to me."

CHAPTER 30

The sudden interruption made us jump. I almost knocked my head into Friend's chin. He stood, sheltering me until he saw Carrick emerge from behind the trees.

"Leave us." Carrick's voice rang clear in the night. At first, I thought Carrick addressed me, but Friend bowed and dismissed himself. His gaze lingered on me before he left.

The fire outlined Carrick's brooding silhouette. I stood, and he stepped closer. The bottom of his robe brushed against my legs and crowded my space. Knowing he was trying to intimidate me, I stopped myself from taking two steps back and dug my feet firmly into the ground.

The need to defend my new friend overcame my fear of angering Carrick. "Why do you forbid him to talk?"

"Because I own him," Carrick said. Shadows played on the ground, looking like long monstrous claws. Carrick twisted away from me in a brusque movement. He spat into the fire. "I allowed him to become the warrior he is today. If I had not taken him to become my bodyguard, he would be an androgy now."

A sting of disappointment filled me to hear him speak this way. I had never expected him to sound like his father.

"That . . . that shouldn't matter."

"It matters to him. He knows he is forbidden to talk in the presence of his master's woman."

My eyes grew wide. *His master's woman?* I poked at my ears. Had I misheard? "What did you say?"

"You belong to me. I know I told you that I'm only interested in women who are experienced in pleasuring men, but your failure to win the showcase seems inevitable. You have no tin-chai, and now you have that scar on your face. I like you well enough, so I decided once you become Arlyn's trifle, I'm willing to teach you how to please me. That's how much I've come to like you. I believe you shall be a quick learner."

Words failed me. He sounded as though I should be pleased by his announcement. The dormant volcano inside of me boiled over. I finally found my voice, which now quaked from anger rather than from intimidation.

"I do *not* belong to you."

His shock at my response was apparent. "I had thought you'd be honored—"

"You *assumed* I'd be honored to become a prince's . . . a prince's mistress?"

"Our relationship would be deeper than that. I can't promise marriage since you will be a mere trifle, but I would never cast you aside."

"I thought you were better than that. I thought you were different from your father. But if this is what you believe, you are exactly like him."

At the mention of his father, Carrick's face turned ashen. He clenched his fists and sneered. "Your value is less than the emperor's harlot. He owns you, and when his rule is over, someone else will own you. Better it be me than someone who would turn you into a common whore. Is that what you want?"

My eyes clouded with tears, but I refused to give him the satisfaction of seeing me so affected by him. I fought to maintain composure. My fingers dug into the hem of my robe. "What I want is for you to know *this*. You and your brothers and your father all believe you can own someone. You take away our choices, control our lives. In that sense, maybe it's true, you do own us. But I'll never allow you or anyone else to own my soul or take control of my spirit."

I turned away but only managed to take a few steps when Carrick hugged me from behind. His body shook with emotion.

"Please don't go. I'm sorry. You know I don't wish to be like my father." He sounded like a little boy who needed affirmation. He allowed me to pull away and face him. His soulful, tortured eyes met mine.

"All I want is to undo the immoral laws my predecessors have instated," he said. "But I've grown up in chaos. In my world, we are required to either kill or be killed. I have so much blood on my hands, you have no idea. Sometimes I forget love and kindness still exist. But you, Rilla, make me remember."

His words softened my heart. I forgot I was angry.

"I need you in my life to help me remember that I'm not my father. That I can be better than him. I didn't mean to call you those things. As for my bodyguard, I regard him as my most trusted friend. I confess I was jealous when I saw him with you. I don't wish to lose you to him."

"Just because I've become friends with your bodyguard doesn't mean you'll lose me."

"I saw the way you looked at him. So intensely. Like you needed him, like you might be falling in love with him. I want you to look at me like that."

Had I looked at Friend that way? If I had, it was just because his presence lifted my mood.

"Being friends with him doesn't mean I'm in love with him," I said. "I'm grateful to him for saving my life and for building a campfire so I wouldn't freeze to death that night in the Winter Woods."

Carrick's features relaxed. "What about your feelings toward me? Do you feel only gratitude toward me as well? Or dare I hope you feel something more?"

"Carrick, I—"

"Wait, don't answer. Not until you know my true feelings for you. Since that night I saw you by the lake, I haven't been able to stop thinking about you. It's as though your presence exudes a light that chases away my shadows. You make me forget who I am and all the sins I've committed. Without you, I'm afraid I might lose my soul completely and become like him. Like my father. I know I've been an ass to you tonight. I shouldn't have assumed you'd be my mistress. I promise I won't make you do anything against your wishes. Even if you don't return my affection, I'd be devastated if I no longer had you as my friend. Please don't abandon me. I . . . I need you."

And with those words, I knew I could never give up on him. No one had ever needed me before.

"You aren't your father, Carrick, and I'm sorry I said so. Maybe you were forced to kill, but I know you're nothing like him. I'll continue to repeat this until you believe it. You'll never become like him."

"Does this mean I haven't lost you?" Hope shone in his features. "You won't leave me, even if one day you learn of all the terrible things I've done?"

"Never." I wrapped my arms around him and lay my head on his shoulder. He needed me. He wanted me. This had to be love.

"And . . . and I do like you." I whispered the confession. My heart had never beat so quickly.

Carrick pulled me away and gazed into my eyes. "Do you mean that?"

I nodded. "I still won't become your mistress, but—"

That sentence went unfinished because suddenly, his lips were on mine. A fleeting thought occurred that this was my first kiss. Then all thoughts disappeared, erased by Carrick's intensity and passion, as though he sought to possess me. But I didn't want him to stop. He smelled of summer storms and dark, unexplored forests. Tasted like spicy peppers and tea.

He altered the kiss into something deeper. His tongue forced my lips open. I broke away and pushed him off me.

He looked at me in surprise and took a step back. His hands smoothed across his face. "I apologize. I got carried away. Did I scare you? I didn't mean to."

I shook my head and smiled. "It's just that you have so much experience, and this was my first kiss. I'm not ready for more. At least not yet."

He reached with tentative movements and grasped my hands. "I meant what I said earlier. I swear I won't do anything you do not wish to do. If I ever push you beyond what you are comfortable with, you must tell me so. I shall stop. Promise you'll stay with me."

"No matter what, I'll always be here for you, Carrick." I raised his hand to my lips and kissed it. "I promise."

CHAPTER 31

Carrick told me I was to stay at his treehouse for the night. He insisted that I take the bed. I wasn't sure where he slept, but in the morning, he was there to wake me with a kiss on my forehead. After a lovely breakfast of porridge and elderberry jam on toast, he escorted me back to the Dark Court. I waved goodbye and turned to go inside. I couldn't stop beaming. I'd finally had my first kiss.

But when I entered Treehouse 4444, sobs echoed from Arlyn's chambers. I hurried upstairs. Arlyn sat hunched over next to her easel.

"My lady, are you all right?"

She looked up and rushed over, throwing her arms around me, so tightly I could smell the lavender perfume through her clothes. "Oh Rilla, where have you been? I need you."

Her entire body shook from distress. She faltered, and I steadied her before she could collapse.

"Come and sit here." I guided her back to the chair and poured a cup of tea, but she refused to drink.

"I don't know what to do. I wished for something impossible, and now I shall die."

I fanned her flushed face. "I fail to see how wishing for things could lead to your imminent death. A wish for something isn't a crime."

"Oh, but the wish has come true, and *that* is a crime."

I stiffened. "What do you mean, my lady?"

"At first, I only wished to use him as a subject to paint. But then I grew lonely, and one thing led to another, and then, *oh.*" She choked on a dry sob. "Why did I allow passion to overcome me?"

I swallowed, my voice sounding thick. "My lady, what *are* you trying to tell me?"

"Rilla, I . . . I am with child." The whispered confession resonated around the room, louder than a foghorn. "The emperor is not the father."

Obviously not. I was too stunned to do anything but stare at the woman as pressure built up behind my eyes. I rubbed at the tension in my temples. My mouth opened and closed, then opened again. "Who *is* the father then?"

Lady Arlyn closed her eyes and drew a fist to her forehead. "Does it matter?"

She was right. His identity wouldn't change the circumstances. Whoever he was, he would avoid the consequences while she took the punishment for both.

I remembered what Androgy Haming had said during the preliminaries. That if a mentoring faela's sins were discovered, her trinket would be considered an accomplice for not reporting the faela. If I didn't report Lady Arlyn, my family and I would be executed.

Arlyn hugged her arms to her chest. Crystals glinted in her eyes and threatened to spill down her cheeks. "Rilla, help me. I have no one else to turn to."

Now I understood how desperate the faela's previous trifle must have been when she asked Carrick to kill Arlyn's former lover. But this time, the problem couldn't be solved by killing a man.

"My brother made me study the effects of every herb imaginable. I'll put together a concoction for you."

Horror lit upon her face at my suggestion. "No. I don't want to kill my baby. That is the reason I need your help. Please save my baby from those who wish to kill him."

I stared at her. The pounding in my head grew incessant. "You do realize once you can no longer hide your pregnancy, we will be executed before the child is born."

"There must be another way." She folded her arms over her stomach as though attempting to shield her child from a descending blade. "Even if it gets me killed, I *cannot* kill my baby again. Last time, Prince Carrick killed my lover to protect me, and Enlin forced me to murder my own child. She said it was for the best, but I'll always regret it."

She slumped her shoulders. The image brought to mind a little girl caught in the undertow, fingertips reaching for someone to throw her a rope. "I cannot go through that again. I simply *cannot*."

I gritted my teeth, tamping down my frustration, though my anger was no longer directed at Arlyn. I softened my tone for her sake. "Have you tried asking your lover for help?"

"I haven't told him, nor do I wish to," she said, looking away. "I'm afraid."

"Why? Do you believe he'll threaten you as your former lover did?"

She shook her head. "He won't harm me, but he'll wish to get rid of any evidence of our affair. He'll make me give up my child." To my shock, she fell to her knees and kowtowed at my feet.

"My lady, what are you doing?" I urged her up, but she pushed me away.

"Rilla, I beg of you. Don't let any harm come to my child."

"Please, my lady. Get up." She allowed me to help her to her feet, but she stood with her back to me.

"Forgive me," she whispered. "I don't know why I asked this of you. I know there is nothing anyone can do."

If I wanted to save her and keep *my* head, I had to find a solution.

An idea flashed in my mind. Could we convince Terran the baby belonged to him? Perhaps we could trick him into thinking he had slept with Arlyn. But Arlyn needed to catch his attention somehow.

My eyes widened. I had a plan, but to execute it, I'd have to reveal my tin-chai to Arlyn. Did I dare put myself at risk? The more people who knew my secret, the more vulnerable I'd be.

Keep your mouth shut. Mama's warning rang clear in my head.

But a gnashing ache, like teeth grinding against bone, formed in my stomach. My mind placed me back in the Winter Woods. I could still see that pregnant woman and the hopeless despair reflected in her eyes before she strangled herself.

It would be a mercy to Arlyn if she were merely executed for adultery, but Limera would make her suffer as a bauble and beg for death. I could not let that happen.

"I have an idea," I said. "We will trick the emperor into believing he's the father."

"How? He doesn't even remember I live here."

"We'll make him remember you. Do you have a zither, and can you play?"

"Yes, of course. It is essential to every young lady's education." She looked around the cluttered bedroom. "The instrument is somewhere in here, but I haven't tuned it in a while."

"We'd better find it, and then I'll teach you a new song."

She cast me a doubtful glance. "I may know how to play and carry a tune, but I'm far from musically gifted, nor do I have a Shyan tin-chai."

"You don't need one."

There was no turning back now. I inhaled and sang.

"Oh, blossoms of June, sweet blossoms of June,
How the love of our youth e'er did bloom,

'til the fading light of that autumn noon.
And then, oh, those sweet blossoms of June
Died under the light of the Lavender Moon."

Arlyn's skin tightened, and her eyes widened and brightened. I stopped singing before I made her too noticeably young, and I handed her a mirror.

"The emperor will be captured by your beauty now. Combine this with the musical performance I will teach you, and he will be unable to resist you."

She gasped in shock. "Look at my skin. It's so smooth, it's practically glowing." She touched her face before setting the mirror down. "I'm listening. What's your plan?"

"I will act as your voice."

CHAPTER 32

✦ ✦ ✦ ✦ ✦ ✦ ✦ ✦ ✦ ✦

I knocked on Carrick's treehouse door.

He opened it, looking flustered. "Rilla, is everything all right?"

"Yes, it's nothing. I wondered if you have any valelily oil. Lady Arlyn is having trouble sleeping."

He blinked and frowned. "We have spent enough time together by now for me to sense when you are lying. Why do you need valelily oil?"

He met my gaze, looking deep into my eyes. I squirmed and looked away. I couldn't tell him that Lady Arlyn and I were planning to trick Terran into Arlyn's bed. Or that the valelily oil was to drug Terran so Arlyn wouldn't have to face the torture of actually sleeping with him.

"It must have something to do with Lady Arlyn. Is she in trouble again? Has she taken another lover?"

I remained silent, not trusting myself to speak.

"It must be so," he continued. "Don't entangle yourself in her mess. If you're planning to use valelily oil on Father Emperor, it's too dangerous. Mother Empress always throws fits and stirs up drama when another faela becomes pregnant. She'll sniff around, and there is a great chance she'll discover your ploy. I have an easier solution.

Sneak angelica root in Arlyn's food, and you shall get rid of—" He motioned to his abdomen. "—the problem."

I gaped at him. "How did you figure it out?"

"Let's just say I've had to fix a similar situation before," he said. "Lady Arlyn isn't capable of making rational decisions. She isn't completely in her right mind. Even if you successfully dupe Father Emperor into believing he has taken Lady Arlyn to bed, she won't be able to care for a child."

I scowled at him. "It is Arlyn's choice. No one should be able to decide for her."

He gave me a wry look. "We both know that's an idealistic thought. Last time, I had to kill my brother because he threatened to expose her madness. How do you know her new lover will not try to do the same? Who is he? I will take care of that part of it at least."

"I don't know. She refuses to say."

"Do your best to find out. If this man knows about her madness and tells Father Emperor or Mother Empress, Arlyn will be thrown into a bauble cage. In the meantime, I shall get you angelica root. A couple doses, and—"

"I won't do that to her." I thought of how Arlyn's eyes lit up when she spoke of the child. This baby might be the only cure for her broken spirit. If she lost it, I didn't think she'd ever recover. "It's not an option. If you don't have valelily oil, I'll get it myself."

I turned, but he grabbed my hand. "How are you planning to do that? You can't get valelily oil without the doctor's consent, and Doctor Cherrywood dilutes the oil to tea before giving it to patients as a safety precaution. An overdose may cause one to never wake."

"I know. That's why I plan on stealing it."

"Are you crazy? There's a reason valelily oil isn't prescribed so readily, and doctors must report each time they do dispense it. Not only is it dangerous if one takes too much, its vapors will dissolve metal when heated. Enemies of the palace have used it to destroy swords and armory, and it is also why the dungeons and cages here are all made of wooden bars, not iron."

He cast me a stern gaze. "The doctor will notice if a vial is stolen. If you are caught, you'll receive an instant death sentence. I will not risk my own reputation to save you."

"I don't expect you to. But I also don't intend to get caught."

He sighed. "Fine. If you insist on this foolhardy scheme, the best time to sneak into the apothecary is after dusk. Doctor Cherrywood's staff will be done for the day, but the doctor works in his office upstairs late into the night and leaves the front door unlocked in case there is an evening emergency. He locks the door only when he goes to bed."

I nodded. "Thank you."

I waited behind the trees outside the apothecary, Treehouse 168, until dusk. After the last of the staff left for the evening, I tiptoed to the door.

Treehouse 168 smelled musty and earthy, even from the outside. Dim lights shone through the open window panes, small holes that could barely fit an arm. I peeped through a side window. Nobody was there. But upstairs, a candle burned through the window. Must be Doctor Cherrywood's office.

I climbed the grass-carpeted stairs to the door. Red and white polka-dotted truffles grew in clusters on the bannister. Spotting silver bells on the door handle, I took them gently in my palm to dampen the sound, then twisted the doorknob.

Once inside, I closed the door. It squeaked. I held my breath. No sound came from upstairs.

I tiptoed to the wooden cabinets behind the counter. Rows of pull-out drawers lined those cabinets, each drawer labeled with the herb inside, written in ancient Shyan characters. Trained doctors and herbal dispensers were taught to read these characters when they studied medicine, but the average Shyan would not know where to look if they were trying to find an herb here. No one would suspect a trinket of having enough knowledge to steal these ingredients. Thankfully, I'd studied Rell's textbooks inside and out. Though I wasn't fluent in the ancient language, I had enough education to be familiar with the characters. The problem was the hundreds of drawers lining the cabinets, and I had no idea how they were organized.

A sliding ladder was perched against the cabinets. I moved it to the far right and then climbed it to access the top rows. I worked my way to the bottom, scanning the labels for characters I recognized and then opened each drawer to any combination of words that stood out.

I moved to the left and continued from top to bottom until I spotted two familiar words in a series of four characters. The top of the first word looked like a triangular roof, and the bottom depicted a box with rounded edges. The second word meant flower, and the two words placed together meant valelily.

I opened the drawer. Several blue and white vessels lay in a neat row. I popped open the lid of one, and a sugary liquor filled my nostrils. Valelily oil. I pocketed a vial.

A smaller cabinet to the side caught my attention. A few pieces of paper stuck out from one of the drawers, keeping it from closing all the way. I caught some words written in the doctor's scrawl. *Weak pulse, lethargy . . .*

A list of symptoms. Could those be patient medical records?

If Madam Yasmina's file was there, maybe I could find something against her. I slid open the drawer, revealing folder upon folder, papers organized in each one. The folders were labeled with patient names, not many recognizable to me. Faela, princes, and Terran were not among them. But I did see servant names—androgies, trifles, and madams.

I skimmed my finger over the madam names. Yasmina. I pulled out her file. The page on top was dated.

Lunar Month 5, Dynasty Loshi. 9th Year of His Majesty, Terran. Patient has weakened wyis. Evidence of liver damage suggests alcohol poisoning.

A seal stamped the bottom of the report. In big red letters, it said, "Evidence for two year suspension."

Madam Yasmina *did* have a past drinking problem, and she'd already been suspended for it. I flipped through the pages until I came to a different date.

Lunar Month 2, Dynasty Loshi. 28th Year of His Majesty, Terran. This past winter.

Due to history of excessive drinking, patient must be tested for current sobriety as decreed by the Supervisor Madams' code of honor. Wyis does not indicate presence of alcohol abuse. The use of nageel toxin to obscure wyis reading is possible, but unlikely. Patient's quarters and food tested for traces of nageel, but none found.

When Galai had asked why the doctor couldn't use our wyis to test our virgin status, hadn't Yasmina mentioned the doctor's reading could be tampered with?

Nageel toxin. I didn't know much about the toxin, but I recalled learning about nageels, sea creatures indigenous to the waters of the island kingdom, Exentria. Three provinces and an ocean separated Province Senlin from Exentria. It would be difficult for Yasmina to acquire the eel, but she had transformed into a goldfeng and stung Auntie An with its poison. It wouldn't be a stretch to assume she could also turn into a nageel and produce the toxin.

Yet, these were all theories. I couldn't prove anything. The question remained: How could I get the judges to believe she had broken the code of sobriety?

I put the file back where it belonged. I was about to close the drawer but caught sight of another familiar name. Androgy Haming. The same androgy who had interviewed me and who had caught Radi trying to escape. If not for him, she would have succeeded.

Anger burned in my chest. I pulled out his file. If I collected secrets on him, it might come in handy one day.

Only one paper was in the folder.

Patient's wyis is an aberration, like a flood instead of a trickle of water. Cause unknown. Patient has no history of diseases. Possible link to patient's tin-chai though he claims to be koong. Patient has denied further evaluation.

Interesting. I was still relatively new to reading wyis. I'd felt animals' wyis before, and I'd read Auntie An's wyis before healing her, then Lady Arlyn's wyis. But I thought I understood the doctor's notes comparing wyis to a trickle of water. It was an even, continuous stream of energy. Auntie An had been close to dying, and her wyis had faded to a broken trickle, close to evaporating completely.

For Androgy Haming's wyis to be compared to a flood was unusual and alarming. I hadn't tried to read his wyis during my preliminary test, but he seemed like the type of man who carried many secrets. The kind of man who had no allegiances to anyone except himself. I recalled how he'd faced the emperor, unafraid of confronting the man who could order his death.

I didn't know what to make of Haming. But he was the reason Empress Limera had Radi in her clutches now, so as far as I was concerned, he was as much an enemy as the rest of the court.

Bells chimed from the front door. The doorknob twisted.

I shoved the folder back in the drawer and closed it, then scampered down the ladder, but there was no time to hide. The door opened, revealing the visitor.

Carrick. He'd followed me after all.

I glared at him.

"You were taking too long," he whispered. "I thought something happened."

Before I could answer, a man's voice called out from the stairs. "Hello? I heard the door. I shall be right there."

My gaze darted to the door. I wouldn't make it. I dived beneath the counter.

Carrick walked over and stood in front of the counter. He kicked my exposed foot in warning, and I folded my body smaller and tighter. A muscle spasmed in my lower shin. I bit my tongue to keep from crying out. This was all Carrick's fault.

"Ah, Prince Carrick, is there an emergency?" The doctor spoke from the stairway.

"Thank you, Doctor. I apologize for disturbing you so late. I know what I need and will help myself to it."

"Your Highness, please do not apologize. But I do not sense any physical maladies through Your Highness's wyis, so why—" The doctor broke off with a puzzled grunt. His shoes shuffled toward the wooden cabinets. "Forgive me for asking, Prince Carrick, but did you take an *entire* bottle of valelily oil? I could have sworn there were seven vials, but now there are only six."

I winced. I'd been so distracted to see the medical files, I'd left the ingredient drawer open.

"No, I did not," Carrick said. "Perhaps you have miscounted the vials."

"That cannot be," the doctor said. "I do not take my responsibility lightly when guarding such a potent ingredient."

"Are you, a mere servant, accusing a high prince of stealing and lying?" Carrick laced his tone with condescension.

"Of course not, Your Highness. I apologize. I did not mean to come across as insolent. Perhaps I did make a mistake."

"You're forgiven. Now return upstairs. As I said, I will find what I need on my own."

"Yes, Prince Carrick." There was a pause, which I assumed to be the doctor bowing to Carrick. Then footsteps sounded, retreating up the stairs.

Carrick grabbed my hand and pulled me up. We tiptoed out the door.

When we had made it a safe distance from the apothecary, Carrick dropped my hand and turned. "That was a close call. I apologize. I thought you might have been stuck in hiding, so I was going to distract the doctor. Instead, I almost got you caught."

My annoyance softened. "Even so, it was sweet of you to see if I needed saving."

A blush formed on his cheeks. He cleared his throat. "I will continue urging you to use caution. Tell Lady Arlyn that Father Emperor takes tea in the Autumn Court at Moon Lovers' Pond every afternoon. He's in his best mood then. Lady Arlyn will have the best chance of catching his attention. Also, he always has blueberry rice wine before bedtime. She can put a dose of valelily oil in that."

He reached into his pocket and came away with an empty vial. "One more thing. I don't trust Lady Arlyn with a full vessel of oil. Give her only what she needs to dose my father a few nights. I shall take the rest."

I poured a bit of the oil into his vial and closed it tight. "I doubt she'll use it on herself."

He took the original vial from me. "Even so, it's a precaution. Besides, one never knows when one may need the oil to serve a different purpose."

Did he mean placing someone into permanent sleep, or dissolving metal?

Perhaps it was best if I didn't know.

CHAPTER 33

* * * * * * * * * *

I placed the zither in Lady Arlyn's arms, careful not to catch the strings. Lady Arlyn and I needed to act fast. If any more time passed, no one would believe a baby, however premature, belonged to Terran.

"Put two drops of valelily oil in his wine." I handed Arlyn the small vial. "It'll knock him out in seconds. Only two drops. The last thing we need is anyone to suspect you of killing His Majesty."

Although that might not be a bad plan in the future.

"All you need to do is convince him that he shared your bed when he wakes the next morning."

She pocketed the vial into her bodice for safekeeping. "That should be easy enough. His pride would never admit to not remembering a night of passion. I hope I succeed, or I'll have to suffer through a night of boorish intimacy." Slight tremors shook her shoulders.

We waited in the arbor by Moon Lovers' Pond. Autumn leaves covered the ground in a luscious velvet carpet of crimson and gold. The water held still, as though it sensed the importance of this moment and wanted to cover its eyes until it was all over.

I hid behind some foliage while Arlyn sat center stage in the arbor. She settled the zither before her.

We didn't wait long before the emperor ambled down the path. He was distinguishable by his royal attire—an outer robe of the deepest purple, the emblem of a golden kaigon emblazoned upon it.

I sent Arlyn the signal. As we'd rehearsed, she plucked the strings, and the romantic melody flowed from the instrument. Her lips silently formed the words I'd taught her, while my voice rang out, loud and clear.

"My love, he is a golden star.
If only he'd turn toward me.
But the gap between us is too far
So this love is ne'er to be.
No, this love shall ne'er be.

Foolish heart, you still long and pine,
Craving a love that will ne'er be mine.
If only Fate would be so kind
To bless me with a love so divine."

Arlyn stopped mouthing with perfect timing.

Terran stood motionless, captivated. "It has been a long time, my lady. Entirely my fault, I assure you, but I have been busy."

Busy driving women into despair. I bit my lower lip.

He climbed the steps to the arbor and took Arlyn's hands into his. "Tonight, you will allow me into your bedchamber. I want to hear more of your soothing voice."

He motioned to his guards. "Tell Empress Limera to send a dozen of her best trifles to pamper Lady Arlyn for the rest of the afternoon. Also inform General Penweather that I apologize, but I cannot attend his birthday celebration."

Then he patted Arlyn's hands. "I must attend other business at the moment, but I will arrive at your bedchamber at dusk."

He marched away with his guards and androgies. Several other guards bowed to Arlyn before leading her the opposite direction.

I emerged from my hiding place. Tonight, Arlyn needed to slip the valelily oil into his drink, and all would be well. Not only did she not want to have to resort to actually sleeping with Terran, but if he asked her to perform another song, he would discover she was not musically inclined. For her sake and for mine, I prayed for her success.

But I couldn't worry too much about it now. I needed to find Radi. It occurred to me that maybe I should try looking in the Summer Fields this time. Carrick had mentioned that the Summer Fields was a place of entertainment for the men in the palace, and some novelties were meant to entertain guests with their tin-chai. Empress Limera had said Radi wasn't in the Winter Woods, and they must have discovered Radi's tin-chai by now. The emperor would no doubt find her talent for spinning starlight into gold useful. Perhaps he'd already set her up as a novelty to replenish the palace reserves.

I crossed the bridge over Moon Lovers' Pond to the Autumn Courtyard and the Royal House. Trifles hurried down the path carrying red banners. Androgies hung colored lanterns in the trees. Even the guards helped string decorations along the ridges of the arched rooftop.

I glanced at the thick brushstrokes written on the hanging banners. Peace. Happiness. Good fortune. Long life. Wishes for General Penweather's birthday. I stole a sign and scampered across the courtyard, pretending to be a trifle tasked with decorating. No one paid me any mind.

Once past the courtyard, I veered right. Soon, the heat flared up, and the humidity rose, forming a layer of sweat on my skin. I approached a grove of peach trees with fresh fruit, ripe and ready for picking. Birds flocked to eat the juicy flesh of the peaches. They tore the skin with their daggered beaks and chirped with lusty eagerness. A shuroo scampered past me, not wanting to lose his share of pleasure. His bushy tail rustled in the brush, and sharp nails dug into the pulp.

He devoured it until he hit the hard-inner core, and then he pitched the useless seed away.

The gateway to the Summer Fields lay before me. It was time to uncover its horrors.

CHAPTER 34

I crouched low behind the trees. Two guards marched back and forth along the path. Making my way through the grove, I kept cover and waited for an opportunity to steal past them. One guard said something I couldn't quite hear.

"... new pet ... starlight."

Starlight. That had to be Radi.

I moved closer.

"Some higher ranks are already there to see the new girl dance for General Penweather's birthday."

The guards were so absorbed in their conversation, I took the chance to creep past them.

No one came after me. All clear.

I continued walking. Novelty cages scattered the sides of the path, but the curtains were closed, preventing me from seeing the girls inside. The guard had said men were already waiting to see Radi dance, so I needed to look for a crowd. They couldn't watch her forever. Once they left for their supper, I would free Radi. Mama had successfully escaped by hiding in the compost, so that was my plan.

An artificial darkness descended. The stifling heat made my breaths short and shallow. Trees blocked out the sun. Sinister shadows crept in my path like slithering serpents stalking their prey.

More cages appeared on the wayside. These had no curtains. The prisoners were naked. Baubles, not novelties.

The girls lay on the ground of the cages, their gaunt eyes barely open. These were tormented souls wishing for release but still trapped in crumbled casings. Their bones poked out of their skin. Dried blood and flakes of feces caked their thighs and forearms.

A wave of nausea turned my stomach. I gagged. I'd thought all the baubles were contained to the Winter Woods. I shouldn't have been so naïve.

Whereas Empress Limera used the Winter Woods as her torture chamber, the palace men came to the Summer Fields for entertainment. Now I knew what kind of entertainment that implied.

And Lady Arlyn had been forced to watch noblemen rape the baubles. She must have been in the Summer Fields. If Radi was here, what did this mean for her?

My earlier determination threatened to dissolve into fear. Each beat of my heart was like a shovel hitting the core of my gut. Faster and faster, it dug out pieces of my resolve. Streams of perspiration poured down my skin. I clasped the glass globe around my neck.

Baba, Mama, give me courage.

A smidgeon of light shone through the trees. I followed it and came to another clearing. The light came from a lantern.

Raucous laughter called my attention to a pack of men standing in a circle. They whistled and bellowed like animals in heat. My gaze traveled to the pagoda cage at which they leered. No curtains.

"Dance, dance, dance." The men chanted and catcalled.

I forced myself to look at the girl inside. Radi inched in slow increments across the cage as if she had a sword pointed to her back.

I had to bring a fist to my mouth to stifle my cry. The dark sky slowly brightened as the stars came out one by one. They lit up in a rhythmic manner and moved to the beat of a silent song. A shooting star raced across the sky, and a dust of golden sparks fell to the ground.

It must be kept night here so Radi could use her tin-chai.

A guard knelt on the ground and gathered the powder of starlight that fell from the sky. "It's true. This is *real* gold." He tossed the gold above his head and let it rain down on him.

General Penweather stood in the middle of the jeering crowd. He clapped and released a bark of laughter. "To celebrate my birthday and the induction of this new bauble, the emperor has stated that for one week, all men, no matter what rank, are welcome to sample her. But the longest-serving officers get to take her first."

"That means you, General!" someone said. Everyone hooted and howled their encouragement.

The general opened the cage doors. I couldn't breathe, couldn't think. My mind whirled. My vision blurred. An onset of dizziness threatened to pull me down. My legs wobbled and moved on their own, taking a step forward.

I need to help her.

I let go of my necklace and took another step. The clasp at the back of my neck unhooked. The glass globe pendant crashed to the ground and shattered. Tiny glass beads that once formed the beautiful ship inside the globe spilled in every direction.

All the men, including Penweather, stopped.

"Who's there?" The general motioned for someone to investigate. A guard came toward me.

What was I to do? An image of Madam Yasmina's pet shuroo popped into my head.

I grabbed a half-eaten peach and pitched it into the bushes opposite me. Then I mimicked a shuroo's squeak. "*Chit-cha-chit.*"

Footsteps halted. "It is just another pesky shuroo."

The guard backed away. I didn't want to abandon Radi, but I

couldn't get caught, either. I stared at the broken shards of my necklace. I had to leave it, too.

I'm sorry.

I sprinted away. Radi's screams echoed in my ears.

CHAPTER 35

✦ ✦ ✦ ✦ ✦ ✦ ✦ ✦ ✦ ✦

I banged on Carrick's door. When he opened it, I grabbed his hand.

"We need to rescue Radi."

He didn't budge.

Didn't he understand the seriousness of the situation?

"Your father has turned Radi into a bauble." I swallowed the word. The vileness of it closed my throat, cutting off my air. Again, I pulled at Carrick's hand.

He moved, but only to draw me inside and close the door behind me. "I told you I can't help."

"You're a prince," I shouted. "There must be something you can do."

He lowered his head and ran a hand through his disheveled hair. "Rilla, I can't even save my own mother. I've thought about it many times, trust me. I even had a safe house built outside the palace in Senlin Forest, hidden with a remnant of my androgy's shield tin-chai. But if I were ever caught trying to free her, I would be executed. It's not that I don't want to help your friend. I cannot challenge my father. Not yet. Until I find the scepter, I need to remain in his good graces and pretend to be his loyal godog, or he'll kill me."

"Isn't it possible for you to at least ask your father to make her a novelty instead of a bauble? He showed some mercy on your mother."

His expression filled with pity. "He was willing to spare my mother because she bore him a son. Radi was only a trinket who affronted his pride."

I thought of my friend, vulnerable and at the mercy of any man. I couldn't leave her.

"I promise you," Carrick said. "One day, I *shall* take my father's place. My first command will be to free the novelties and baubles and forbid anyone to cage a woman ever again. But one day will never come if I try to stand up to him now."

Those words again. *One day.*

Carrick cast me another warning glance. "Don't interfere. It's for your own good."

He commanded me in a way that reminded me of how Mama, Rell, and Nia always told me to keep my mouth shut and to mind my own business. They all believed they were protecting me, but it was smothering. I wasn't going to let anyone force me back into the shadows again.

"I'm tired of waiting for one day."

"I am serious, Rilla." He huffed out an aggravated breath. "Do you wish to end up like Radi?"

"I'm well aware of the dangers, but it's still my decision."

Carrick pinned me to the wall. I yelped. I was trapped in the cage of his arms.

"That is how easy it would be for a man to catch you off guard." His breath stroked my face. My pulse quickened. "Now are you afraid?"

My throat went dry, but I shook my head. "Not of you. You won't hurt me."

"Someone else will." With one of his hands, he restrained both my arms above my head. I couldn't move. Now he was hurting me, and his dark gaze scared me.

"You've made your point. You can let go of me."

But instead, he angled his head downward.

I gasped. "What are you—" It was all I had time to say before he kissed me.

His lips were hard and bruising, painful and controlling. I turned away in protest, but with his free hand, he grabbed my jaw, forcing my mouth back toward him.

He bit my bottom lip like a punishment. I lifted my knee, but both his legs were positioned between mine, so it did no good.

Panic ripped through my body. His grip on my jaw eased, but only because he had moved to the buttons on my dress. Something ripped.

I tore my mouth away from his. "No, please stop!"

He finally lifted away from me, and we both remained frozen. He still held my shoulders, but his gaze fixed upon the ground. My body trembled. Half the buttons of my dress were undone. A tear was ripped through the right sleeve, and the bodice had fallen open completely. Horrified, I tugged it to my chest and glared at him.

"Have I finally scared some sense into you?" he said. "The difference between my brothers and me is that *they* will not indulge your prudish innocence. And if you were any of my other lovers, I wouldn't have had to stop."

My face heated with humiliation. He treated a kiss with such insignificance, used it as an attempt to control me. Not because he wanted to kiss me, but because he wanted to teach me some perverse lesson. Accuse me of being prudish. As though *I* were at fault.

I raised my hand to slap him. "How dare you?"

"Go ahead, if that will make you feel better."

He lifted his gaze, and something in his eyes made me pause. A dangerous longing dwelled there, but also regret and shame. Vulnerability. Was he ashamed that he *would* have taken it that far with other women before me? Did he believe he was more like Terran and his brothers than he wanted to be?

I dropped my hand. He deserved to be slapped more than once, but I couldn't follow through. He was already so damaged. If I hit him, it might confirm to him his deepest fear that he had been born with his father's cruelty.

"Don't *ever* treat me like that again," I said.

He didn't reply, but he took his cloak and draped it over my shoulders, then averted his gaze. I buttoned up my dress.

"Is it salvageable?" Though he tried to sound nonchalant, there was a breathless quality in his voice.

"It will be fine for now."

Carrick turned back around. He slowly reached one hand to touch my cheek with such tenderness, though he shook. "I understand you want to save your friend. But please also understand I want to protect you. I don't want your innocence to die or the light to fade from your eyes. I'd never be able to bear it."

The vulnerability in his gaze punched me to the core. "As long as your father remains our emperor and Empress Limera is determined to take her frustration out on other women, there's always a chance they'll turn me into a bau—" The word tasted bitter on my tongue. "Bauble. That's the reality of the world in which we live. It's why you have to work to become the new emperor and change things."

The weight of my words jolted him. He wrapped his arms around me with such passionate violence, I fell into his embrace. "No matter what happens, I'll never let you go."

CHAPTER 36

✦ ✦ ✦ ✦ ✦ ✦ ✦ ✦ ✦ ✦

Carrick insisted I stay overnight. "It's General Penweather's birthday celebration tonight. I shall not return until late. Everyone in the palace will be there except Father Emperor. Since the general commands the imperial army, I need to remain on his good side, although he has always favored my brother, Nelan. If we can't find the scepter to establish who has the right to rule, the general has power to command the army to support the prince of his choosing once my father dies. In order to retain his own position in the kingdom, the general will help his chosen prince maintain the pretense of possessing the scepter."

"Have you made any progress in learning if Limera does indeed have the scepter?" I asked.

Carrick shook his head. "But I've been keeping a close eye on Father Emperor. He is now unable to use his tin-chai without suffering excruciating pain. Mother Empress must know. She must not have the scepter, or she would have shown her hand by now." He sighed. "Don't concern yourself with these political matters. Let's take it day by day."

He was right. I had enough to think about. Tonight was the perfect opportunity to help Radi escape. If most aristocrats and officers would be at Penweather's birthday celebration, they wouldn't be visiting the cages.

Carrick patted my shoulder. "You'll be safe here. My bodyguard will remain outside to watch over you."

"What about you?"

"No one will attempt anything at General Penweather's birthday celebration and risk earning his displeasure." He caressed my head. "Don't worry about me. I'm equipped to defend myself."

When I was sure he was gone, I walked out the front door and searched the trees, where I knew Friend hid.

"Friend, I know you're there. We need to talk."

Barely three seconds passed before he emerged from the trees. He jumped from bough to bough before descending to the ground and coming to my side with soundless strides. He bowed, then straightened. His eyes glinted beneath his mask.

"I'm rescuing Radi tonight. I'll smuggle her out in the compost heap."

I've been drawing up a plan, too, he wrote. *But not foolproof yet.*

"There's no time. We must rescue her tonight. Everyone else will be celebrating the general's birthday. I'm going with or without you, but I could use your help."

Friend hesitated, then nodded. *All right.*

He beckoned me forth with both hands. I followed him to a clearing behind Carrick's house. We trudged on. Once in the Winter Woods, the frost curled around my limbs like shackles. I imagined them to be the hands of ghosts begging to be taken away from this miserable place.

At the edge of the Winter Woods, the smell of peaches overcame the pine, and the snow melted into puddles that led to a brook. The cold air quickly turned dense and muggy, making it difficult to breathe. Sweat drenched my sticky skin, and my hair fell limp, soaked as though I had been caught in a sudden downpour.

It was impossible to decide which was worse. Freezing to death in the Winter Woods or baking alive in the Summer Fields.

We passed more bauble cages. Girls with sunken eyes drooped in their prisons like flower bouquets drying out in the sun. One girl lay dead in her cage. A red rash formed on the palms of her hands, and slimy pus broke from white abscesses around her swollen mouth. Bruises covered her flesh in permanent tattoos. I forced myself to continue moving and looked up to the sky. The stars weren't dancing but weeping.

Finally, we reached Radi's cage. The invasive stench of sweat and ammonia, thick and heavy, wafted through the prison bars. I ran toward her and froze.

Nothing prepared me for the sight of Radi's shivering body curled in the corner, where she slumped upon a mound of bristly straw. Shredded rags barely clung to her withered form. Angry red stripes, the remnants of whiplashes, scored the flesh on her back. Blisters ran down her bruised cheeks, giving way to black circles marking the corners of her swollen lips.

A hoarse sound formed low in my throat. My eyes stung, but I fought to retain composure. "Radi," I called.

Her eyes opened, revealing a film glazed over dilated pupils. A knife-like scream ripped from the back of her throat, a sound I hoped never to hear again.

"It's me, Rilla."

She squinted and focused on me. A bit of clarity stole over her when she heard my voice. "Rill-Rilla?"

"Yes. We're going to get you out of here."

I knew of only one way to help her. Despite knowing Friend would discover my tin-chai now, I sang.

"Oh, blossoms of June, sweet blossoms of June,
The innocence of youth e'er did bloom,

'til the day evil drove us to ruin.
And yet, these sweet blossoms of June
Shall still flourish despite our wounds."

The bruising around Radi's mouth retreated. So did the stains of blood. Some color returned into her cheeks, but her eyes remained hollow and dim. My power could heal her physical scars, but even if I sang until I ran out of oxygen, the emotional and mental turmoil she'd suffered could never be undone.

Friend stared at me as I sang, wonder reflected in his eyes. Then he built a flame in his hand and burned through the lock in the door. Radi saw what he was doing. Whatever lucidness she gained disappeared once more. Her expression became wild and blind.

With a ragged voice, she choked out a cry. "No, stay away from me."

"He's here to help," I said, speaking to her as though I were beckoning a wounded bird. "You need to stay quiet. We must not be discovered."

"Don't let him touch me." Her face expanded and contorted into a formless shape.

I motioned Friend, telling him to stop for a moment. I coaxed Radi. "I promise we'll take you far from here. Come with me. You trust me, right?"

She nodded and took a deep, shuddering breath. Her feet moved one step forward. And another.

Behind us, a disturbance sounded. Crescendos of raucous laughter and obscenities.

Two princes approached with their royal protectors. The princes teetered in zig-zagging lines. Their half-naked state told their intentions.

Radi screeched a wail of irrepressible fear. She clawed out, striking me in the face. I fell and hit my head against the pebbled ground. I pushed myself up but immediately fell back down. The world spun.

Someone yelled. "What are you doing? You have no access here."

I finally managed to stand. Radi remained frozen with her arms flung out, protecting herself.

Friend formed several fireballs and aimed them at the group, surrounding them in a wall of flames. The *shiing* of his sword resounded in the air. He pulled it from its sheath, the ugly slice of a blade rending flesh. Shouts of death echoed throughout the forest.

Friend was embroiled in battle with the royal guards. I dragged Radi to the cage door, but the two princes blocked our way. The first tripped over his silk mantle. A solitary ghost-white curl fell from his otherwise tawny-brown ponytail. He pitched forward and stopped advancing. He gagged, retching yellow bile onto the dirt.

His companion tottered forward. He tossed back his long, honey-blonde hair and winked at us. "Two baubles for the taking. Guess I'mma be lucky tonight."

His hands drifted down his body and untied his robes. I stood in front of Radi, preparing for his attack. He lunged. I clawed his face, digging my fingers into his right eye. My fingertips made contact with a mushy, wet mass.

He roared. "You bitch!" He came at me again. He pinned my arms back, picked me up and tossed me to the ground. His heavy weight came down on me. I screamed and fought to kick him, but he sat on my legs. He tore through my clothes like paper.

He froze. The eye I'd poked remained shut, but the other opened wide with what looked like surprise. His bulky mass teetered off me and struck the ground with the thud of a fallen tree.

I pushed at the rest of him and pulled myself away.

A sword was lodged deep into his spine. Blood soaked through his clothes and formed rivulets, collecting in a pool of crimson on the ground.

His killer towered over him. Carrick. His seething eyes glared at me. Without saying a word, he stepped on the dead prince's body and pulled out the sword. Blood dripped from the blade like hot wax from a candlestick, trickling in a steady pulse. Carrick wiped the blade on the dead man's clothes, then sheathed it.

Shouts echoed outside the cage. Two guards remained standing, but Friend was quick, slashing through both bodies. Gore splashed onto the ground as they fell.

No one else stirred. The other prince who had been retching was nowhere to be found.

"He got away." Carrick swore. He pushed me aside, then motioned to Radi. "Come to me."

Radi shrieked. Her fingernails reached for his face with the panic of a feral maocat. He avoided her attack and placed his hands on her arms with gentle firmness. "You're safe now. Shh . . ." His tender tone contradicted the fury shining in his eyes.

For a moment, it seemed he'd gotten through to Radi. She stilled in a faint and slumped over. Carrick caught her.

He didn't meet my gaze. "You lied to me. You said you had no tin-chai, but I saw you heal her wounds. I should have known better than to believe I'd earned your trust."

His words felt like a slap, but I refused to back down. "I'm sorry I lied about my tin-chai, but I thought it for the best. In case—"

"I do not care why you did it. But you shouldn't have gone behind my back to save your friend. You put us all in jeopardy."

Outside the cage, dead bodies strewed the ground. The stench of burnt flesh and fresh blood—raw and metallic—made my eyes water.

Carrick cradled Radi in his arms, treating her as he might a newborn baby. However, his steely eyes glared at Friend. He addressed him through clenched teeth, his tone barely containing his anger. "You knew I would have no choice but to come and help, or we'd all be at the beheading block by sunrise."

Friend stood proud and upright, undaunted by his master.

I placed myself between them. "He did it to help me save her."

"At the risk of all our lives. I told you we could do nothing to help your friend."

I shook my head. "You were wrong. There *was* something we could do. We just did."

His glare silenced me. "The prince who escaped was Nelan."

Nelan? The worst of Carrick's brothers.

Carrick's lips curved into a distasteful scowl. "I hope the blistering bastard was too inebriated to remember anything. You'd better pray he didn't see you heal your friend or that he doesn't recognize you when he becomes sober again."

I swallowed. A thick film coated my throat, and a wave of nausea lurched in my stomach.

Carrick looked so fierce. His eyes narrowed to mere slits, and his fists clenched as tightly as rusted screws. He took two deep breaths, inhaling and exhaling until he regained some of his composure.

"I'll take her to my safe house." He sent Friend a scathing glare. "See that Rilla returns to Lady Arlyn, and make sure Nelan doesn't try anything. I don't wish to see either of you for a long time."

Carrying Radi in his arms, Carrick took long strides away from me. He never looked back once. The chill of his cold shoulder dug deeply, pinching and twisting my heart. I hoped he would forgive me, though I had no regrets. Radi was safe now. And one day, I'd find a way to save more.

CHAPTER 37

✦ ✦ ✦ ✦ ✦ ✦ ✦ ✦ ✦

Three weeks passed. Lady Arlyn had managed to keep the emperor enamored with her for several nights, and when she announced her pregnancy, the palace was overjoyed for the newest royal baby's arrival.

However, this only solved one of my problems. After the night of Radi's rescue, Carrick had avoided me, and Friend had no word from him other than confirmation that Radi was safe. I knew Carrick must still be angry, but I had no time to dwell on him.

Not with the showcase finale looming over me. The finale was next week.

I had spent the last three weeks thinking of a plan to frame Yasmina. I'd tell the judges I suspected Yasmina of breaking the code of sobriety, and I'd seen her drinking. They knew of her past, and my accusation would prompt them to investigate further.

She'd accuse me of lying, of course. She'd tell them she saw me heal Auntie An, but I would tell the judges she had been drinking that day and imagined the entire thing.

This still might not be enough for them to take my word over hers.

I needed to plant evidence on Yasmina. Wine hidden in her

bedchamber. A liquor vial concealed in her cloak.

But acquiring liquor was a difficult task. While faela were given one decanter of blueberry rice wine a week, Lady Arlyn wasn't permitted to have any now that she was pregnant. It had been impossible for me to smuggle any out of the busy kitchen, and I had run out of time.

This was my last morning at Treehouse 4444 before the finale. I, along with all the other trinkets, was required to return to the Apple Barrel for preparations. This week entailed practicing our finale performance and pampering our skin and bodies to ensure we looked our best for His Majesty.

I went upstairs to say goodbye to Lady Arlyn. She lay buried beneath her bedcovers and rolled over to look at me. "Rilla, is it time for you to leave?"

"Yes. But I hope to return officially as your trifle."

"I hope so, too." For the first time, complete clarity shone in Arlyn's eyes, a determination to carry on. "You've never told me of your own troubles, but I've speculated ever since you revealed your tin-chai to me. Your madam must expect you to reveal your gift during the finale. Remember, she cannot make you do anything against your wishes. It's your word against hers. If you choose not to use your tin-chai, she cannot prove that you have one."

She reached behind her pillow and slipped something into my palm. A pocket-sized flask. "I have been saving this for years, but I no longer need it. It is not enough to make you drunk, but perhaps it will give you an added boost of courage. I'm afraid this is the only gift I can offer you."

I stared at the flask. I couldn't believe it. Without knowing it, Lady Arlyn had given me what I needed.

"Thank you, my lady."

She nodded. "We both must remain strong. May Old Grandfather Heaven be with you."

Madam Yasmina stood at the entrance to the Apple Barrel, waiting for me, I assumed from her glower. "It's been far too long since you've come to check in with me. If I hadn't been so busy planning for the finale, I would have gone to see you. I hope you haven't been wasting time—Old Grandfather Heaven! Why have you painted your face?"

I made a show of looking away in shame. "The truth is this is why I was scared to see you. I was careless, and the empress overheard me singing. She doesn't know my tin-chai, but she was jealous of my voice and branded me. Lady Arlyn painted over the burn mark in hopes that the judges would overlook it."

"I wish you'd come to me sooner. I wouldn't have punished you, my favored trinket." Yasmina sighed. "The empress has always been jealous of girls who are musically gifted. You acted wisely under the circumstances. My concern is the judges will wonder why you're the only girl who painted your face and ask you to remove it, but I believe I have an idea. After all, it was a popular trend for rich aristocratic women to paint designs on their faces back in the Ponzo Dynasty."

"What will you do?"

"You shall see." She whistled a tune and continued into the courtyard.

The trinkets gathered around the wide, gnarled tree, all immersed in different conversations, though I guessed they were recounting their experiences with the faela they had shadowed. I followed Madam Yasmina to Treehouse 37. Outside, Galai and Irica chatted with the girls from Treehouse 38 in excited tones, but when Irica glanced up and saw me, she scowled and pointed at my face.

"You cheater." She turned to Yasmina. "Madam, you can't allow her to use face paint. Did she tell you she's trying to hide the—"

"Shush, child." Madam Yasmina clamped a hand over Irica's

mouth and whispered to Irica. I thought I heard her say, "You have secrets, too."

Yasmina straightened and spoke loud enough for the other girls to hear. "I think Rilla is showing her creativity with the face paint, and the judges will be quite taken. It is beautiful, don't you agree, Galai?"

Galai's lips curled down in envy. "If she can paint her face with a pretty design, I want one, too."

"I do, too," another girl said.

Madam Gomi frowned at Madam Yasmina. "It isn't fair for your girl to paint her face."

"It's not against the rules," Yasmina said. "If your girls wish to do the same, nothing is stopping them."

Soon, more girls wanted designs on their faces. They lined up in front of Treehouse 30 to request designs from the makeup artists. Yasmina winked at me.

Later that afternoon, I sat with my feet steeped in water for a pedicure and watched the makeup artists scurrying about to meet the trinkets' demands. The girls were difficult to please, and the artists had to redo their work until each client was satisfied that her design was unique enough from any other trinket's.

At least Yasmina had made sure I didn't have to worry about the judges seeing through to the mark of four on my cheek. I almost felt guilty about betraying her, but if she were in my place, I had no doubt she'd do the same.

The next seven days were the longest in my life. In between facials, mud masks, and massages, the girls were busy sabotaging one another. One trinket ran out of Treehouse 30, screaming and sobbing after her hair was dyed green. The stylist claimed to have no idea how the shampoo contained green pigment. Another trinket had her bed infested with slumber gnats, and she woke covered in itchy, red patches from forehead to pinky toe. Then a dancer had been standing outside her treehouse when a rock mysteriously fell from out of nowhere and smashed her foot.

I had no reason to fear. Madam Yasmina monitored my every move from morning to evening. In secret, we rehearsed her vision for my finale performance.

"I have asked a royal fiddler to accompany you," she said. "I'll stand to your right, and as you sing, the judges will witness the wrinkles and blemishes fade from my face." She laughed. "Don't make me appear too young, or it may be my turn to compete in next year's showcase."

"Don't worry. I know how to control my tin-chai." I sang a line of *Exalted One.* I released enough power to boost her energy but did nothing to alter her physical appearance. "During the actual performance, I'll put in more power to give you flawless skin."

"Purr-fection," she said. "You're proving to be an obedient maocat after all."

Her constant animal references drove me to madness. Temporary relief came when I slept, but even then, Yasmina refused to leave my side. She slept in a cot next to mine to ensure Irica and Galai made no sabotage attempts.

The night before the finale arrived. I couldn't be more relieved and nervous at the same time. Unable to sleep, I lay in bed listening to Galai's snoring, Irica's sleep-talking, and Yasmina's grunts.

I couldn't stop thinking about my plan to frame Yasmina. Could I do this?

I had to succeed. There was no other way. I'd help Arlyn take care of her baby and continue as I had been, with Carrick and Friend as my companions. I'd help Carrick find the scepter, and once he took the throne from Terran, I'd help him eliminate the cages as he returned stability to the kingdom. That was, if Carrick ever forgave me.

It seemed like seconds later when a gong pulled me out of a dreamless sleep.

"Get up, girls," Madam Yasmina said. She struck the gong with relentless determination until my roommates and I sat up in bed. "We must arrive at Treehouse 30 in ten minutes."

Treehouse 30 bustled with activity. The treehouse had been separated into private dressing rooms, one for each madam's group of girls. Madam Yasmina led Irica, Galai, and me into our room, and we sat for our hair and makeup to be done.

The hairdresser looped my hair into a bun and clipped it high on my head. She pulled out a few curls, allowing them to dangle upon my shoulders. As she fixed my hair, the makeup artist powdered my face and spent extra time on my eyes. She managed to remove the baggy evidence of my sleepless night.

I failed to suppress a yawn. Madam Yasmina handed me a cup of elderberry and ginger tea. "Drink this. It will help. Once your makeup is done, I'll help you change into your kipa. I've held it in my private locked wardrobe for weeks. I guarantee you'll be the most fashion-forward trinket at the finale."

Irica and Galai changed into their costumes, and Madam Yasmina helped me into mine. The kipa was indeed the most stylish costume I had ever laid eyes on and likely the most expensive as well.

The silk shimmered in the light, changing from silver to blue and back to silver again, imitating the tint of the sea after sunset. The material clung to my body, showing off every curve of my figure. I also wore anklets and bracelets embellished with bells and charms that clanged like wind chimes.

"You are gorgeous, Rilla," Madam Yasmina said.

"So unfair." In the mirror next to me, Irica's jealous reflection could have burned a hole through the glass.

"All right, my girls, I believe you are ready," Madam Yasmina said. "It's time."

We followed her into the Apple Barrel Courtyard, which had been transformed into a stadium. The stage was made of twined wood. Curtain vines, similar to our bedroom doors, parted upon command.

Yasmina took us backstage. I peered out from behind the curtains. In front of the stage were rows of seats carved from the stumps of chopped trees. Noblemen were seated there. Above them, weeping willow trees intertwined their branches, forming a balcony.

The emperor sat there, surrounded by noblemen and faela. I recognized a few women from the record log Yasmina had given Irica back when we'd selected our top mentor choices for the trinketship.

Lady Poisi sat with two maocats curled in her lap and a shuroo on her head. Next to Poisi, Lady Mika was the most scandalously dressed, her kipa filled with cut-outs designed to exhibit her trim waistline. Unlike the usual twisted bun the faela wore, she styled her hair in a single sleek high ponytail.

More faela filled the rows behind them, but Empress Limera wasn't among them.

Though the empress was banned from the finale, I did not doubt she was elsewhere in the palace, tormenting another victim to take out her frustration for being forbidden to attend.

The other person missing was Androgy Haming. Wasn't he supposed to host with General Penweather? I thought of his impertinence in talking to the emperor. Had he finally gone too far and gotten punished?

Penweather's voice filled the stadium. "Welcome to the showcase Finale. We have all anticipated this day. We shall finally bestow on five lucky trinkets the privilege of becoming His Honorable Majesty's faela, and one winner will be named an elite faela."

Applause broke out from the crowd. Penweather waited for the claps to fade before he continued.

"Honored guests, our first performer is from Peonton. Her dominant channel is Dai, and although she chose to keep the specifics of her tin-chai a surprise until now, she did reveal it is of a musical nature. Please welcome to the stage, Miss Vy Saitoski."

Vy pushed a cart full of musical instruments and marched onto the stage. "I have seven instruments. I am going to play them in a one-woman ensemble. Your Majesty, this is dedicated in your honor."

She stood behind the cart and with quick, graceful movements, used her arms, legs, and mouth to play an instrumental arrangement of *Exalted One*. A flawless performance.

Terran stood and whistled his appreciation. When the applause finally died, Penweather continued.

"Bravo, Miss Saitoski. What a unique tin-chai. Now let us talk to the faela you shadowed." He addressed the audience. "Miss Saitoski was matched with Faela Lady Poisi."

Lady Poisi stood, and the audience clapped.

"Lady Poisi," Penweather said. "How did this trinket perform under your guidance? Do you believe she is ready to take on the duties of a faela?"

"Vy was an excellent trinket. She performed all her duties with grace and punctuality," Poisi said. "But of course, there are always areas for improvement, such as attention to detail. She must remember to make sure the food served by the trifles is always to the emperor's liking, should His Majesty pay her a visit for supper."

"And what is your final evaluation score for Vy, my lady?"

Lady Poisi raised a placard. On it was the number nine. "Nine out of ten."

"A solid score," Penweather said. "Let us give Miss Vy Saitoski one final round of applause."

Vy made her exit, and the next trinket entered the stage, her posture straight and poised. Marguerite Zeng came from Ongol Valley, on the border of Province Yupa and Ailo Kingdom. She wore a fashionable cropped top, revealing a trim stomach and a short skirt, flattering her behind. Her hair was held in a high ponytail, a copycat style of Lady Mika.

Marguerite turned to the audience, but her gaze fell upon Terran as though he were the only one in the stadium. She had an Ailo accent when she spoke. "Your Majesty, I must confess I am only half Shyan, and I do not have a tin-chai. I know I was only brought here to add variety to this group of trinkets, and everyone expected me to become a trifle. However, I have learned so much from the gracious Lady Mika, who is also a koong but did not let this stop her from becoming one of your favorites. She taught me a faela's sole purpose is to please Your Majesty and to be beautiful for you. I will dance for you and only you. I hope you shall see my sincerity and dedication."

Her choreographed movements mimicked a sinuous serpent. Seductive. She might not have magic, but she did have talent. Terran couldn't look away from her. She kept her gaze locked on his as she danced. Even at the end of her performance, his mesmerized stare followed her off the stage.

The next few performances were not nearly as interesting. But I did pay attention when Irica's turn came. She had set up a large tub filled with water on the stage. Not a surprise. I already expected the predictability of her routine.

"Your Majesty, I will now sing *Exalted One*," she said.

I cringed at her window-shattering shrieks. She sang two keys too high. But the water in the tub still danced to the sound of her voice. The audience *oohed* and *ahhed*, focused on the water display instead of her pitchy singing. I had to commend her for that. The water show was delightful.

Irica took a bow. Over in the balcony, Terran seemed intrigued, but there was no standing ovation or overt staring.

"Well done, Miss Tiders," Penweather said. "Now we shall reveal your trinketship score. Unfortunately, Empress Limera could not join us today, but she did provide your score." Penweather opened a sealed envelope and removed the slip of paper inside. "Miss Tiders, you have been given a score of three out of ten."

Irica's face reddened. She stormed off the stage.

"These performances have all been stellar, do you not agree?" Penweather said. Applause and whistles sounded in the crowd. "Now let us take an intermission before the second half of our program."

I walked back to the dressing room. Heated voices came from inside, making me stop at the door. Couldn't be Galai. She was first to perform after intermission. It must be Irica and Madam Yasmina. I cracked the door open and peeped inside.

"She purposely gave me a bad score," Irica said. Her hands curled into fists, and she paced the floor. "I did everything she wanted, endured punishments I never deserved, had my pride bruised, and she still wasn't satisfied. I won't become her permanent trifle. I won't."

"You can't do anything to change your fate now," Yasmina said.

"You must have known how cruel Limera could be, so why did you say she was the best mentor to shadow?"

Yasmina laughed. "Dear child, I may have given you poor advice, but you made the decision to follow it."

Irica stopped pacing and gaped at the madam. "You mean you set me up to fail?"

"I might not be able to eliminate the trinkets the other madams are managing, but I do have power to ensure you and Galai don't shine too brightly. My subordinates discovered you two, and perhaps you are the best among the girls we scouted along the coast, but my Rilla is special. She's *my* discovery, and she has the potential to be the most celebrated faela in the kingdom's history."

"So this was your motive all along," Irica said. "You never cared about my wellbeing. That's why you helped Rilla cover up the mark on her face. I'm going to expose both of you."

Yasmina slapped her. The force sent Irica tumbling to the floor. "Ungrateful girl, you forget, I could have turned you in when I found out you lost your virginity to a bungling village boy. Instead, I injected nageel toxin into you so Doctor Cherrywood wouldn't discover the truth when he read your wyis. Do you think I will continue to keep your secret if you betray me?"

"If you dare tell anyone, I'll take you down with me," Irica said. "I'll tell the empress and emperor you forced me to do it."

"Not if I take you down first." Yasmina muttered odd squeaking noises, and a swarm of rats swept in, surrounding Irica. Several climbed up her legs. Irica screamed and fainted.

Yasmina saw me standing at the door. "Rilla, did you see that? Don't worry. I have everything under control." She pushed past me and shouted out. "Guards, come."

A soldier who had been standing guard backstage approached. "Madam, what is wrong?"

Yasmina pointed into the dressing room at the unconscious Irica. "I have discovered this trinket is guilty of cheating. She is no longer a virgin. Her parents are fishermen from Province Ca. They traveled to the icy waters of Exentria and acquired nageel toxin to tamper with the doctor's reading of her wyis. Inform the empress at once, and let Her Majesty decide on an appropriate punishment."

The guard slung Irica over his shoulder and took her away. A burning sting formed in my chest.

Yasmina turned to me and winked as though I were her co-

conspirator. "One more obstacle out of our way."

Bile rose into my throat. The madam was despicable, and if I harbored any doubt about betraying her during my performance, any residual guilt disappeared the moment she handed Irica over to the empress. The only way to win against a cheater was to become a cheater.

I smiled and reached to hug her. She tensed in surprise. Carefully, I tucked the small flask of wine Lady Arlyn had given me into Yasmina's cloak pocket.

"Rilla, what has brought on such an unusual display of affection?"

"I want to thank you for having my best interest in mind. I am eternally grateful. May Old Grandfather Heaven reward your dedication."

Oh, yes, Yasmina would get her just rewards.

CHAPTER 38

I could barely wait for my turn as the second half of the routines played on stage.

Finally, Penweather called my name.

I took unhurried steps up to the podium. Madam Yasmina already stood center stage, addressing the crowd. "Noblemen and Your Royal Majesty, I know this trinket had a less than stellar start with her audition. She also shadowed Lady Arlyn, who did not provide a final score, probably due to the nausea accompanying her pregnancy. But you must not discount her yet. Hear her sing, and prepare to be amazed."

She gestured to me. "Go ahead, Rilla."

The royal musician drew his bow along the two strings of his spiked fiddle, playing the introduction, my cue to begin.

The song carried a trilling melody, haunting and filled with sorrow. Without using my tin-chai, I sang on key until I came to the highest note, and then I wailed like a vindictive ghost. What a tragedy to butcher such a beautiful tune. Everyone in the audience held their ears and winced.

I returned on pitch, sang to the end, and took a bow.

Madam Yasmina flew toward me. "What are you doing? You're

supposed to make me young again."

I pretended to blink back tears. "I'm so sorry, Madam. I did my best, but I don't know why you insist on making me do the impossible. I told you from the start I have no tin-chai, and you said it was all right. I didn't know you expected me to restore your youth at the finale. There has been a misunderstanding."

Yasmina turned to the judges. "The girl is pretending to misunderstand. I witnessed her using a powerful tin-chai. Her voice heals any ailment, including old age."

The judges looked between me and Yasmina, their expressions filled with uncertainty.

I shook my head. "I swear the miracle Madam Yasmina claims she saw never happened. I do not know why she refuses to believe me. The kind of tin-chai Madam describes is so powerful, I don't believe anyone could possess it."

Penweather fixed a hard stare on Yasmina. "Madam, the girl has a point. Heal any ailment and reverse old age? I have never heard of a Shyan with such a formidable tin-chai. We could all live forever, then. Hard to believe Old Grandfather Heaven and Wise Grandmother Time would even permit this among us mortals."

Facing the judges, I allowed my lower lip to quiver. "I wish I had the tin-chai Madam thinks I have. Then my parents would not be dead. If my voice had the power to heal, I would have saved them."

"But I would never have chosen her to come here if she sounded like a snorting sihai, or if she were a koong," Yasmina said. "I'm not tone deaf. I saw her heal a middle-aged woman and turn her young again."

"Yes, I did save a *young* woman from a hovering goldfeng sting, but I did this based on the medical knowledge I learned from my brother. However, the woman was only in her twenties." I pinned my gaze on the madam. "You were a little inebriated the day you discovered me. Perhaps—"

Her face scrunched with fury. "Liar. I may have made the mistake of overindulging once, but I haven't touched the vile brew since my suspension."

"You're in denial, Madam. I've caught you drinking when you thought no one was looking. You carry alcohol with you." I faced the judges. "Moreover, I heard Madam Yasmina talking with my fellow trinket, Irica. The madam used nageel toxin to tamper with Irica's wyis, so the doctor would not know Irica lost her maidenhood. This means the madam was capable of using toxin on herself when the doctor checked her wyis for the presence of alcohol."

"These are absurd accusations," Yasmina cried.

"Madam Yasmina, given your history, this is concerning," Penweather said. "I have no choice but to test the validity of the trinket's claim. Guards, search the madam's person, and then search her bedchambers."

Yasmina glared and opened her cloak to overturn her pockets. "No need. I have nothing to hide." She reached into the pocket where I had placed the flask, and her eyes widened. "Impossible." The flask fell out of her shaking hand and onto the floor.

With a screech, she flew at me, grabbed my shoulders, and shook me. "How dare you betray me? You planted this."

"Madam, I insist you stop," Penweather said. "It has become clear you have regressed to old sins."

"No, the trinket will sing and prove I am not lying," she shouted.

Her body stretched and twisted. Her skin roughened to scales. The woman transformed into a coiled white serpent. It hissed, fangs threatening to bite. I screamed and jumped back, but its body wound around my torso and squeezed. I couldn't breathe.

"Guards!" Penweather yelled. Two soldiers rushed over and lifted their hands to the trees. Branches extended and curled around Madam Yasmina's body. The boughs pulled and plied her away from me.

I coughed and gasped for air.

Another soldier shoved his hand against her skin. Electric sparks shot into her body. Yasmina jolted and spasmed. Her elongated body shortened. Her spiral form took the shape of a woman once more.

Foam collected at the corners of her mouth, and finally, she passed out.

Terran whispered something into Penweather's ear, and the general said, "Yes, Your Majesty." He turned to address the crowd.

"This sullied woman has broken the code of sobriety and had the audacity to make a full animal transformation on palace grounds as though she were a vulgar shapeshifting Yao instead of a refined and cultured Shyan woman. This is a testimony to her true debased character, and she shall be punished accordingly. The palace will also be investigating her interference with the doctor's wyis readings of herself and one of the trinkets under her charge."

The guards took Yasmina's unconscious body off the stage. I continued to fake sob.

"Do not cry, Miss Marseas," Penweather said, an impatient sigh in his voice. "It is clear this is not your fault."

I pretended to dry my tears and returned backstage. Only one performance remained after mine, and then we were instructed to stand in a line on stage. The spotlight shone on each of us, and we took our bows. But the emperor's attention was diverted. Doctor Cherrywood slipped through the aisles and whispered something into Terran's ear. The emperor stood and walked out of the stadium with hurried strides.

I couldn't believe it. The showcase was done. No one would discover my tin-chai now.

Penweather took the stage. "We have the results. But first, I am afraid there has been an emergency. His Majesty has been called away. Lady Arlyn has suffered a mishap, endangering herself and the child she carries."

A collective gasp sounded from the audience. I froze. How could this be? She had been fine when I left her.

"There is nothing we can do but ask the revered royal ancestors and Old Grandfather Heaven to protect mother and child," Penweather said. "But without further ado, I shall announce the names of our five new faela." He drew out the announcement, but my focus was no longer here.

I'd promised Lady Arlyn that nothing would happen to her or her baby. What was I going to do?

Penweather's voice boomed on stage. "Miss Marguerite Zeng. Miss Vy Saitoski."

The two girls screamed and jumped with excitement, interrupting Penweather from announcing the other names.

I barely paid attention.

What had happened to Arlyn? I'd only been gone a week. She had been nauseated from morning sickness, but nothing had been out of the ordinary. I'd checked her wyis and the baby's. I'd monitored both their heartbeats. They had been fine.

"I understand your enthusiasm, ladies, but please quiet down so I can continue announcing the other winners," Penweather said. The first two girls nodded in agreement, but they still emitted softer, excited squeals.

"Miss Chier Kinsala. Miss Tidinia Whin. And Miss Galai Cresta." Penweather beamed. "May the five of you bring joy and blessings to His Majesty and bear him many sons."

Thank Old Grandfather Heaven. I rushed out of the stadium and ran to the Dark Court.

CHAPTER 39

Treehouse 4444 smelled like musty herbs mixed with the tin odor of blood. A trifle sobbed on the staircase leading to the second floor. Was I too late?

I touched her shoulder. "What happened?"

She turned and blinked at me. "Who are you?"

"I shadowed Lady Arlyn during my trinketship. Tell me, is the faela dead?"

"Not yet, but my friend is about to be. All she did was follow the empress's instruction, but she is being blamed for tainting the tea and inducing a miscarriage."

If Empress Limera was involved, no wonder Arlyn and her baby were in danger.

I spotted the remnants of a dark brew in a bowl on the table. "Is this what was served to Lady Arlyn?"

At her nod, I lifted the bowl to my nose. The overpowering smell was like dried cranberries combined with stale grains.

"This tea contains angelica root and vorinberry," I told the trifle. "Angelica root induces a miscarriage if taken in several doses, but when combined with vorinberry, the effects are instantaneous."

"Yes, Doctor Cherrywood concluded this," the trifle said. "The empress told me to wait here until further instruction. She wants me to tell His Majesty I saw my friend taint the tea. I don't want to betray her. She has been like an older sister, but I'm afraid of what Empress Limera will do to me if I don't comply."

"I cannot tell you what to do, but I hope you'll be brave enough to follow your conscience." But my own words echoed in my ears, making me tremble.

Was I brave enough?

I left the trifle and climbed to the third level, pausing at the landing to take in the situation. Doctor Cherrywood sat on the edge of Arlyn's bed, assessing the pulse at her wrist. Behind the doctor, Emperor Terran stood with his arms crossed. He tapped his foot and scowled across the room to where Empress Limera sat, sipping her cup of tea with languid leisure.

"I told you to wait until after the birth," Terran said to her. "I wanted to know if it was a boy before you got rid of it. Is this your way of retaliating for not being allowed at the finale?"

"I have not a clue of what you are implying," Limera said. "I was trying to do a favor for Lady Arlyn by offering a remedy to cure her morning sickness. It is not my fault my trifle or an herbal dispenser accidentally mixed up an ingredient."

"Well, Doctor?" Terran said. "Can the child be saved?"

"Unfortunately, it is too late," the doctor said. "I might be able to save the mother, but I must act quickly. She has already lost too much blood."

"Do not bother. If the child cannot be saved, then I do not need the woman anymore. I have grown bored with her. Wait for her to die. Then tell the servants to take the body for cremation."

If only I could kill him and Limera. But wishes would do no good for me nor for Arlyn. I couldn't wait for them to leave before healing Arlyn. The doctor said she was already fading. I had to act now.

I closed my eyes, took a deep breath, and stepped forward. "I can save them, Your Majesty."

All eyes turned to me. The unwanted spotlight was bright and blinding. How I desperately wished to hide. But it was too late. I couldn't retreat now.

The empress scowled. "I told you never to appear in front of me again. Leave now, or I will have no choice but to teach you another lesson."

Terran put up a hand, signaling her to be silent. He maintained focus on me. "I remember you. You were the lost trinket near the Summer Fields. I thought you pretty then, but after your abysmal performance today, you are of no use to me if you have no tin-chai. So tell me, how will you save Arlyn and her child when Doctor Cherrywood here cannot?"

"I do have a tin-chai, Your Majesty," I said. "But I chose not to reveal it during the finale to catch Madam Yasmina in her lies."

Terran's expression piqued to one of interest. "Oh?"

"Your Majesty," Limera said and stepped in front of me.

Terran glared at her. "Hold your tongue, woman. Haven't you caused enough trouble?" He shoved her aside. "Was Madam Yasmina telling the truth, then? Can you heal any ailment with your voice?"

"Yes, Your Majesty, I can. I will demonstrate it by healing Arlyn and her unborn child if you will allow me."

He gestured toward the bed, giving his assent. "Cherrywood, since you have proved useless, you are excused."

Doctor Cherrywood bowed and left the room.

I sat by Arlyn, placing my hand over her womb. I'd never tried to save an unborn child before, but I couldn't fail now. I concentrated and felt out the baby's wyis. Then I sensed a slight thud, a heartbeat, faint but still there. A girl. She still clung to a thread of life.

I sang for her life and for Arlyn's.

"My love, she is a summer rain,
Renewing this parched soul.
She marks the end to all my pain;
She's the cure to make me whole.
Only she can make me whole."

The heartbeat thumped once... twice... then steadied with renewed vigor. The blood dripping down Arlyn's leg trickled away. I sensed the baby wriggling inside her mother as she tried to get more comfortable, and then, her heart filled with content, she settled down for a nap.

The sleeping faela's eyes fluttered open, and her gaze flew to mine. "My baby?" she whispered.

"Your baby's fine," I said. At my reassurance, Arlyn nodded and fell back asleep.

I wished I could do the same and avoid what was about to come. Slowly, I turned to face Terran and my fate.

He stared at me, his pupils dilated and mouth agape. "Someone alert Penweather. I am changing the rules of this year's showcase. She is the only one I want. We will be joined as soon as possible."

From her corner, Limera jumped, placing herself between the emperor and me. "You cannot consider her to be a faela, Your Majesty. She has a hideous face, cursed by the mark of four. She hides it with the paint. I shall prove it." Limera shouted toward the staircase. "Elsie, bring water, soap, and a rag."

In a minute, the trifle I'd encountered earlier came with a small bowl of soapy water and a cloth. She flashed me an apologetic glance before proceeding to scrub off the paint from my cheek.

Limera pointed at my scar. "You see, Your Majesty? This trinket tried to fool you and the judges at the showcase by covering that up.

She has the cursed mark of four, and she shall bring disaster upon the kingdom if you take her as a faela."

"If she continues to hide the scar, her looks are tolerable enough. Besides, she serves a greater purpose." He waved a hand toward me. "If you can heal any ailment, then surely that includes aging. Use your voice to restore my youth, and then I shall decide your fate."

I faltered. I didn't wish to be responsible for allowing a tyrant to remain immortal. But at least he didn't have the scepter. Youth would do nothing to stop the eventual exposure of his loss of the Will of Heaven.

Until he was exposed, however, I was vulnerable to his whims.

"You heard His Majesty," Limera said. "Sing, girl." Curiosity reflected in her face, too. No doubt she also wanted to become young again.

I had no choice. I knew this would be the outcome when I'd decided to save Arlyn and her baby. So I sang. Words tumbled out, offbeat. The notes were flat and out of tune.

"Today I dream of glory and fame,
For tomorrow all will exalt my name."

Terran's wyis flooded into my veins. It was the fragile wyis of a dying man. But as I sang, it grew stronger and pulsed back to full vitality.

The silver hairs and roots atop the emperor's head darkened to black, the few lines on his face smoothed out, and the extra fat around his abdomen tightened to muscle. He appeared no older than Carrick now.

"Well, curse the ancestors and Old Grandfather Heaven, this is astounding." Terran walked to the mirror and admired his reflection, flexing his biceps. "Imagine, with her by my side, I shall never die."

"Her voice may appear beneficial, but it also has a potential risk," Limera said. "As the sun must be balanced by the moons, and life is countered by death, there must be more to this girl's tin-chai than meets the eye. Most blessings also come with a curse. I do not want a curse to plague the palace. I forbid you to take her as your faela."

"Forbid?" Terran laughed. "Power has gone to your head. I am the emperor and your master. I may have given you allowances, but I can take them away at any time."

"If she becomes your faela, I—I will expose you. Everyone will know you have lost the Will of Heaven. This girl may have restored your youth, but only the scepter can bring back your tin-chai."

Terran laughed. "Which one of your spies told you that? Well, they did not get my secret entirely correct. My dear Limera, taking the scepter from me did not rob me of my tin-chai. It simply weakened my wyis each time I used my tin-chai. This girl's voice is even more powerful than you believe."

So Limera *had* taken the scepter.

Terran lifted his right hand. Dust gathered in his palm and collected into a ball of red clay.

His gaze connected with Elsie, who tried and failed to blend into the wall. Before I could yell a warning, Terran aimed his hand at the poor trifle. The red clay gathered around her body. She screamed as it covered her skin and solidified. Her mouth remained in a petrified O in the terracotta figurine that replaced her.

Chills coursed through my body. I was responsible for allowing him to use his tin-chai once more. Every life he took from now on would be partly my fault.

"Yes, Limera," Terran said. "You should never have dared to challenge me. I have found one worthy to become my new empress. I can finally be rid of you."

He raised his other hand and thrust it downward, palm to the ground. The floor split, and through the crack, a vine crawled up and encircled Limera. A flash of fear appeared on her face.

"Your Majesty." The words blurted from my mouth before I could think them through. "I cannot marry anyone, or I will become a koong."

He paused, his eyes narrowing. "Explain yourself."

As much as I hated Limera, if she died, there would be a vacancy for empress I had no desire to fill. Better to convince Terran that his current empress was more suited for the position than I was.

I fought to steady my voice. "When I first discovered my tin-chai, my parents sought the holy Lotuses' advice. The sister monks said I must have a strong spiritual connection with Heaven to receive such a powerful tin-chai. But they advised my parents that I must remain chaste to continue using this gift. The connection with Heaven will break if I marry. I know I should have mentioned this to Madam Yasmina, but she was intent on bringing me here to win. She wouldn't have listened anyway."

Limera's wide lips arced into a sneer. "The girl speaks the truth. I can smell it on her."

Never thought I'd find an ally in Limera.

"Of course, *you* would say that," Terran said.

"You have no choice but to believe it," Limera said. "Do you want to take that chance? If you take her to your bed, not only will you forfeit her tin-chai, but also I guarantee I shall never tell you where the scepter is hidden. Not even if you turn me into a bauble."

Terran remained silent. His creased brow indicated he was thinking about his next move. What if he was willing to call my bluff?

"Your Majesty," I said. "You know there are those who believe the old superstitions. They won't be satisfied until they personally see you with the scepter. The empress is the only one who knows where she has hidden it. You cannot afford to divorce or kill her."

"I will create a fake scepter," he said.

"Ha." Limera tilted her chin up and glowered, a spark of rebellion returning to her eyes. "You would have already tried if you believed it would trick anyone. You do not even know who truly remains loyal to you now. Your enemies already infiltrate the palace, spying on your every move, determined to find your weakness. They are not fools. Eventually, they will identify that you hold a counterfeit scepter."

Terran swore and waved his hand in a descending motion. The vines loosened from Limera's body and retreated into the ground.

He turned to address me again. "Since I cannot take the chance of making you my faela, you shall be my cherished novelty. I will show you off to all the palace aristocrats. You will be forbidden to converse with anyone. Your job is to sing to me and the guests who come to your cage."

His voice fazed in and out. My head buzzed. Novelty. I was to become a novelty. It was better than being forced into his bed, but my dream of obtaining freedom was now lost forever.

My shallow breaths interspersed with the steady beat of the clock. *Tick. Ba-dum. Tock. Ba-dum. Tick. Ba-dum. Tock. Ba-dum.*

For the rest of my life, I'd have to serve a man I hated, using my voice to maintain his power and youth.

My legs wobbled and threatened to collapse. I couldn't speak, couldn't breathe. Fear wrapped both hands around my throat and tightened bit by bit.

"My darling," Terran said, looking at Limera. His tone had gentled, removed of any previous anger. "You loved me once. When did your love turn to spite? Do you despise me so much that you would see my enemies take my throne?"

Was he taking a different tactic?

"You believe this is out of spite? Taking the scepter was my only assurance that you would always need me over all your other faela."

A glimmer of vulnerability shone in her eyes, a gleaming of tears. A stray drop trailed down her cheek. Nothing would excuse her abominable acts, but I could understand her a little more. She wished to gain the love of a man who would never love anyone but himself.

Terran walked toward her. His eyes locked on her tears. It was as though his gaze held an invisible magnet that would not allow her to pull away. Not even I could look away. Once again, it chilled me how physically similar he and Carrick were.

He knelt next to Limera and brushed away the streak of tears. "I remember the gossipmongers faulted you for the massacre of our naval officers at the Miyu's hands. They said you convinced me to go to war. You never denied it. You said you would rather have everyone despise you than me. That was how much you loved me. And I also loved you."

Limera sniffed. "You did?"

"Yes, and I will love you again if you will only return the scepter. I know you still love me, and you want to earn back my love and forgiveness."

Could she not see he was manipulating her? I didn't wish to side with Limera for anything, but I couldn't allow Terran to get his hands on the scepter again.

"Empress Limera," I broke in. "Remember, he just tried to replace you with me. You cannot trust him."

"You insolent girl!" Terran directed a burning gaze at me. "Silence."

I'd had enough of keeping silent. "I'm already prepared for a life of silence in a cage, but I will speak now. Empress Limera, you must not give him the scepter. Don't waste your time fighting for a man who doesn't care about—"

"I said, silence!" Terran raised his hand, and a root splintered from the ground. It hit me on the back and whirled around my face, covering my mouth. My teeth jammed against the tough lignin. I tasted the bitter plant on my tongue. I screamed, but my muffled cries went unheard.

Limera hesitated so long I thought she might have fallen for his words. My heart hammered in my chest.

But then she shook her head. Her lips quivered. "I will not give you the scepter. Not yet. But I still wish to make amends and prove my value to you once more."

The emperor's lips pressed together, and his nostrils flared. He forced his words through clenched teeth. "If you will not hand over the scepter, you will never prove your worth to me."

"Your Majesty, I only hesitate because there is an advantage if I keep the scepter for now. The Zhynites are quickly rising in power because whispers that you have lost the Will of Heaven have seeped into the cities and villages. There must be traitors in the palace who are spreading these rumors. If we continue as we were, let them believe I still hold the scepter over you, I can use my tin-chai to sniff out those who are disloyal to the Crown."

Terran considered this. "I believe your plan does have merit, but you will need sufficient evidence that the person you accuse of treason is not simply someone you dislike. I will not wait forever for the scepter. I warn you, Limera. Do not play games with me any longer."

Limera bowed. "Thank you for this second chance, Your Majesty. I will work hard to earn back your favor. I shall return the scepter when we have caught all the traitors. You have my word."

She turned her face to the side, catching my gaze. A calculative glint flashed in her eyes. Did she have a new scheme?

"Your Majesty, I am glad you decided to make this girl a novelty," Limera said. "We shall all benefit from her voice."

"And singing is all she shall be doing in her cage." He scowled in my direction. "Speak out of turn again, and you will regret it."

Cuckoo-koo-koo. Cuckoo-koo-koo. Cuckoo-koo-koo. The crazy bird popped out of the clock. The tree roots slackened and dropped from my mouth. Guards marched up the stairs, came toward me, and grabbed my arms.

All my energy drained from my body. My vision closed in, and they took me away.

CHAPTER 40

My cage lay in the Autumn Court. Golden leaves fell outside my prison.

I saw the plaque nailed to the cage bars. I no longer even had a name. My identity had been reduced to three simple lines.

Emperor Terran's Prized Novelty #658
Dominant Channel: Ha
Cures Disease and Reverses Old Age with Song

The guards draped me in blue silk from head to toe. I took one last look at the sky. Twilight had taken hold of the darkening heavens. Only a sliver of the Turquoise Moon appeared. Clouds veiled the White Moon, and the Lavender Moon had completely vanished.

Then a white curtain closed off the world from my view.

Shoved to one side of the cage was a small straw mattress, covered in pretty, red linens. How ridiculous to cover such an uncomfortable cot with luxurious silk sheets. Terran only cared about the aesthetics.

Two dishes lay on the floor next to the bed, one for food, the other for water. Beside the food bowl was a porcelain pot. At first, I couldn't stomach eating anything next to the foul odors coming from the pot, but by the fifth day, I no longer noticed. A mound of stony pellets—dry, hard, and unpleasant—were heaped in the dinner bowl. I couldn't identify the food, but I was hungry enough to eat whatever it was.

My curtains were drawn open once a day when a trifle brought my food and cleaned the porcelain pot. I treasured that moment each day when a twinkle of sunlight shone on my face before the curtains shut once more. The trifle was the only one allowed to enter my cage. She kept silent as she worked. She was forbidden from speaking to me, and I was forbidden from speaking at all.

At least I'm not a bauble, I consoled myself. At least I'd been spared from becoming Terran's faela. At least I was in the Autumn Court, not sweltering in the Summer Fields.

But loneliness quickly attacked, a taunting creature that grew fatter each day. An ever-growing weight, it gnawed away at my hope and threatened to displace my spirit.

There was no way of telling time. It felt like weeks had passed, yet I still had no visitors. Maybe Terran had forgotten me since I'd already restored his youth. I thought of all my friends. I missed Carrick, Radi, Friend, and Lady Arlyn. I longed to see their faces and pined for their company. Were they safe? Would I ever see them again?

I sang to myself to pass the time. Every ballad and ditty I'd ever learned. I listened to my voice, muffled and garbled under the scarves smothering my face. When darkness descended, I clutched the blankets closer to my body. I sang the lullabies my mother had taught me and tried to chase away the night terrors until I fell asleep. Then I awakened to repeat the process.

I lost count of the days that passed before the curtains parted again.

Carrick stretched a hand to me. I clasped it tightly to confirm he wasn't a figment of my imagination. The warmth of his skin was evidence enough that he was real. Friend stood behind him. He was a welcome sight to see.

"I'm sorry I didn't visit earlier, but there has been chaos in the palace," Carrick said. "The empress has accused numerous officials of associating with the rebel group, the Zhynites. Already, seven lords and their families have been executed. She seems to have stopped for now, though. But be prepared. She and my father will likely come to see you soon. He'll wish to show you off to his friends."

Tears streamed down my face. Carrick wiped them away with his thumbs. His eyes glistened, too. "Please don't cry. I promise I shall find a way to free you."

In one second of desperation, I forgot I wasn't allowed to speak to anyone, and I yanked away the scarf covering my mouth. "But how?"

Several branches moved fast, and I sprawled, facedown, fresh pain throbbing on my back. I shrieked. Each thrash hit with more force than the last. The more I cried, the harder they struck, slashing through my flesh, slicing my skin. My body involuntarily jerked with every lash. Vines curled around my wrists and ankles, holding me in place.

"Stop screaming, Rilla," Carrick hissed. "You need to be quiet for it to stop."

I bit my bottom lip and forced myself to stay silent. Tears trickled down my cheeks. One last hard lash whipped my torn flesh. Then the vines uncoiled from my limbs, and the branches retreated.

I was immobilized like a sculpture petrified in ash, unable to feel anything but the stinging anguish left behind. My entire body pulsed and swelled like I was on fire.

Carrick called to me. "I thought you knew, but I should have reminded you." He sounded wretched and ridden with guilt. "You'll be whipped if you speak to your visitors, or if you continue to sing when your guest orders you to stop."

I finally summoned some energy to turn my head toward him. He knelt and reached through the bars as far as he could. It took every effort to lift myself from the ground, and with straining muscles, I crawled to him, inching my knees forward bit by bit. Every movement I made threatened to tear my skin apart. Blood leaked from my wounds and mingled with sweat and tears, dripping to the earth.

He clasped my hands and assessed my injuries. "It could be worse. Father Emperor needs you to be well enough. He'll allow you to have medicine."

Pain choked my throat. I fell facedown into the dirt. My arms and legs forfeited their strength. I didn't think I'd ever be able to get up again. I didn't try. What was the point?

Carrick tossed measured glances behind both his shoulders. With a covert motion, he slipped some paper, a feather, and a bottle of ink through the bars. "Hide this well. It's fortunate the palace thinks all women are illiterate."

He pushed the offering toward me. It took several attempts before I could lift a hand to take the items.

I forced my shaking hand to form the letters. I didn't recognize my own handwriting, a messy scrawl, but he made sense of it.

Terran using my voice for his tin-chai. Still powerful without scepter. Limera has it.

Carrick placed a hand on my cheek and whispered. "Then I'll find where Limera is hiding the scepter and take it from her. I'll stop them."

Working together to filter out those who oppose him. No one can stop them.

Carrick shook his head. A wild, desperate look overcame him. He recoiled as though I'd slapped him. "Are you saying you don't believe in me anymore?"

He leaned back, unable to meet my gaze. It was my turn to feel like I'd been slapped. His sudden coldness felt like abandonment. "Instead of encouraging me, your negative thoughts place more burden on my shoulders. I can't listen to your doubts right now. I'll come back when you're feeling better."

He walked away. Friend remained a second longer, casting me a worried look. Then he turned and followed his master. The curtain closed, shutting out their retreating figures.

Fresh sobs exploded from my chest. Each spasm, a reminder of my brokenness, jerked and stretched my torn flesh. I didn't know what hurt more—the wounds on my back or my aching heart.

I concluded it was my heart.

The days passed in a blur. I remained in bed. My weak body still felt the sting of my wounds. The trifle who cleaned my cage brought a medicinal balm, but I had to nurse myself, struggling to apply the salve to my back.

Carrick visited twice to make sure I was healing, but he never stayed long. I couldn't be the source of light he expected me to be. It felt as though he had no use for me anymore.

At least Friend remained faithful. He visited once every day, even when Carrick did not. I wasn't sure if Carrick sent him to check on me, or if Friend snuck away and visited of his own will.

No one else came around. I was glad I didn't have to entertain the aristocrats while still in pain.

One night, I rolled out of bed and reached for my dinner. For the first time since I'd been whipped, the flesh on my back didn't stretch and threaten to tear apart again. I tested the scars with my fingers, tracing the thick clots that had formed crisscrossed patterns. The scratchy welts probably looked as horrendous as they felt. A vain part of me lamented that they'd likely never fade.

A pity my tin-chai didn't work on myself.

Coins jingled and dropped into my cage. The curtains parted. Friend stood outside. His presence brought me comfort.

Still covered in a cloak, he sat with me in companionable silence. I sensed his concern behind the mask. I mimed to him, nodding my head and pointing to my wounds to indicate I felt better.

I observed his posture, relaxed and free, though he remained bound to a world of chains. He was so different from Carrick.

His luminescence glowed and seeped into my soul, spreading the way water soaked into the parched earth after a decades-long drought. His wyis burned strong, an inextinguishable candle in a world of perpetual night, and his movements left an amber warmth in their wake. He never sat still, as though he needed to continue moving, to continue casting his radiance, cultivating it to drive away the darkness.

His palms touched the cage bars. The reflection in his eyes sent an unspoken message: *Don't despair. We'll find a way.*

The familiar wave of wonder came over me. After he'd lived most of his life surrounded by darkness, how could he still retain so much brightness?

Are you ever going to tell me your real name? I wrote.

He read the words and drifted away, lost in thought. Then he jotted down something that took longer to write.

You know what my greatest wish is right now? It's that we could be our true selves, free and unrestrained by senseless rules. We would form an instant friendship, talk and laugh for hours, and nothing would prevent us from seeing each other face to face. For now, I can only be known as Friend to you. But one day, when we've escaped this place, the first thing I'll do is properly introduce myself and ask for your name, and it'll be like we're meeting for the first time. I can't wait for when one day becomes now.

The smile in his eyes held a promise. The promise of hope, the promise that the stars would once again be free to dance.

· 279 ·

CHAPTER 41

I woke the next morning to clanking coins. I rubbed my eyes. The curtain parted, and I cringed at the sight of my visitor.

The emperor had come. He still looked to be Carrick's age. This confirmed the effects of my power on his youth must be permanent. Not that the knowledge was of any use to me.

"Hello, my nightingale." Terran cast me a brilliant grin as though we were close friends who happened to bump into each other on an afternoon stroll. In his hand, he carried a staff made of cedar wood. A fake scepter.

The men with him cast wary glances my way and recoiled behind their ruler like scared godog puppies.

"You cowards," Terran said. "There is no curse."

"But sir," one of his men said. "She might sing us to oblivion. There must be a drawback to her power."

Were they scared of me?

He glared at the men. "She will do no such thing. Stay here and receive her healing, or I will behead the lot of you for cowardice." He winked at me. "Be a good girl. Prove to these weak-hearted idiots you're nothing but a harmless little songbird."

I sang the ballads I'd been singing to myself. My gaze traveled over the men. One by one, I felt for their individual wyis and fixed their ailments—a lingering cough, an old ghastly scar, a blood disorder. For those with no physical complaint, I brought back their youth, straightened their wrinkles, and replanted the hair on their receding hairlines. I hated feeling each ounce of my power flow into these men. Monsters who ventured into the Summer Fields to take their pleasure, heartless to the women they defiled.

But what I despised most of all was watching the emperor beam as my healing power entered his body and refueled his wyis. Though his youth had lasted, his wyis had weakened from the last time—but by the end of my song, he was back to his full strength.

The men walked away with shining faces, and I knew it wouldn't be long before they returned.

How could I defy the emperor and aristocrats from within this cage? If I refused to sing, Terran could order my family killed. But if I continued using my power on Terran, he would remain invincible, his right to rule unquestioned.

If only I could sing him and his men to oblivion. If only I could curse them. I didn't want to be Terran's harmless little songbird. I wanted to destroy them and make them pay for their sins.

Never before had I not wanted to be a healer. Never before had I hated my tin-chai. Never before had I hated someone enough to kill.

Never before. Until now.

Days drudged on. Several months passed. Anger and hatred festered, burning a hole in my once naïve heart.

Now that I'd proved I wouldn't sing anyone into oblivion, the palace aristocrats were no longer scared of me. From sunrise to sunset, my curtains never closed. The noblemen fed their addiction, clambering to find me. My voice cured their ailments and restored their youth permanently, but they still needed me to heal recent blemishes, new maladies, or give them an energy boost after a long week of carousing and overindulging in food and spirits.

They paid no attention to my songs, so I learned to eavesdrop on their conversations while I sang. If I had to be stuck here, the least I could do was act as a spy for Carrick and Friend and warn them if I heard someone plotting against them.

No one thought anything of a novelty who would be beaten if she spoke. No one noticed when I lowered my voice to hear them. They believed I was powerless to repeat their conversations. I could probably get away with singing blasphemies about the emperor. While I didn't attempt it, I initiated my own form of rebellion, singing songs featuring strong heroines—a healer who saved a child despite it being illegal for a woman to practice medicine, a woman who dressed as a man to fight a war in her father's place.

One morning, the curtains of my cage parted, revealing the Empress Limera.

It was surprising that I hadn't seen her since I'd exposed my tin-chai. I'd expected her to be first in line to attain newfound youth, which could only mean she had spent all her time building her political power.

"I wish I'd killed you before His Majesty laid his eyes on you," she said. "But since you have such a special voice, I would be foolish not to reap its benefits."

She inserted several coins into my cage, enough to last two hours. "I should have come to receive my beauty treatment long ago, but I have been far too busy."

Busy accusing noblemen she didn't like of being traitors to the Crown. What havoc had she created in the world outside my cage? How many people had she already accused of treason and crimes against the emperor?

Limera bared a wide smile, her polished teeth reminding me of a shatooth fish that smelled blood. "I know you carry secrets. Secrets I shall discover soon enough. His Majesty may not allow me to harm you, but I have other ways of making you regret crossing paths with me."

What did she know about me? What was she planning?

I hated not knowing and not being able to do anything to stop her.

"Sing *Blossoms of June*," she sneered. "And sing it well, little *nightingale*."

Such disdain laced her tone as she used the emperor's pet name for me. She lay on a chaise, her backside facing the sunlight. A trifle handed her a cup of tea, and an androgy boy applied jasmine-scented oils on her back and massaged her shoulders.

I inwardly seethed but forced myself to sing. Limera's eyes widened and gained the doe-like innocence of youth. The bags of fat underneath her eyes retreated. Dark spots and freckles faded away, and her skin tightened, glowing more with each note I sang.

Another man, also an androgy, entered the scene and crept toward the boy. He had a timeless face, which could place him anywhere between his early twenties and late forties.

His ageless features looked painted on like a doll. Long lashes lined piercing, bright blue eyes. His porcelain skin gleamed like white stone under the sun.

By now, it had become in my nature to feel out all my visitors' wyis and sense what they needed to be healed. And what struck me was the strange wyis that emanated from this man.

His spiritual energy was more like an orchestra than a single drumbeat.

He crossed his arms and held his elbows, making his way to Limera.

Placing a finger to his lips, he motioned for the younger androgy to remain quiet. He slipped into the boy's place, then took over massaging Limera's back and shoulders. With a flick of his wrist, he dismissed the boy and the trifle, who both tiptoed away.

Once they were gone, his body shimmered and lengthened. Muscles stretched, and the effeminate facial features hardened. Androgy Haming stood in his place.

Now I remembered Doctor Cherrywood's description of Androgy Haming's wyis. Not a trickle, but a flood of spiritual energy. I knew what he meant now, although I remembered from Doctor Cherrywood's notes that Haming claimed to be koong.

What was Haming doing here?

Haming slathered oils on the empress's skin and kneaded her shoulders. The heady, sensual fragrance of jasmine with a hint of vanilla tickled my nose. Moans of ecstasy broke from Limera's lips. She rolled her body to the side.

"Haming." Limera's tone, far different from usual, sounded sweeter than a honey-coated piece of fruit. "I did not expect you so early."

"My love and my heart, I have missed you and could not stay away."

Limera fell into his arms with a lusty whimper as they kissed.

I stared at the curtain. *Please close, please close.* Luck continued to elude me.

Limera pushed away from the androgy. "Oh Haming, you must leave. We cannot take the chance of being seen. His Majesty believes you are away, taking care of the Zhynite protests. At least close the novelty's curtains."

"The other faela fear you too much to come here," Haming said. "The aristocrats and androgies know not to disturb you, lest they find themselves accused of treason. As for His Majesty, I spied on him minutes ago at the Elite House with Lady Dreama. He is too occupied with her to miss us. And there is no harm in having the novelty see us when she cannot talk. I might as well benefit from her singing while I am here."

He swatted her behind, making her squeal and blush.

"Please Haming, there may still be a trifle or guard walking about."

Haming sighed. "You worry too much. They are too frightened to speak against you. But if it puts you at ease, we shall continue this later." His body altered again, returning to the more effeminate androgy.

Limera's own tin-chai already made her able to discover secrets, but with a body-changing androgy as her spy, she had eyes all over the palace.

"What news do you bring?" Limera asked. "Have you discovered how to destroy the general's reputation yet?"

"The general remains completely loyal. I can find nothing to convince the emperor that his best confidante and friend would turn on him."

The empress folded her arms across her chest and pouted. "That is not the news I wish to hear. Dig further."

Haming's lips pressed together. "How many more people do you intend to ruin before we make our move against Terran?"

"As many as I wish. If you no longer want to do what I ask of you, do not expect me to keep my end of our deal."

"Have I not already proved my loyalty? By the blood of holy Crocuses, we are lovers. I have earned the right to know where you hide the scepter."

Limera scowled. "Perhaps it was presumptuous of me to take you as a lover. If you cannot distinguish between matters of business and pleasure, then I shall have no choice but to break off our affair."

Haming huffed out a sigh. "No, I will be patient. I know it is difficult for you to turn against him, but you are fooling yourself. It has been years since he has visited your bedchamber. That is why you need me to satisfy your needs. He does not love you."

Limera slapped him across the cheek. "How dare you! His Majesty does love me, and I am determined to make him remember he does. Leave at once, and do not expect to enter my bedchamber again."

Haming bowed. "As you wish, my lady. But I shall always be at your service whenever you should need me."

A wistful look glimmered in his eye that made me wonder if his affection for Limera wasn't all an act.

When he was gone, Limera grabbed the curtains on my cage and yanked them closed. I sat in the darkness, silent and alone, but her frustrated screams carried from the other side. And I listened to those screams dissolve into sobs.

CHAPTER 42

When my curtains opened the next morning, my guests were two princes.

The first was Prince Nelan. Bile rose into my throat. His simple burgundy robe fit tighter than what was fashionable, and he'd pulled back his sleeves to show off his bulging biceps. Truffle-brown hair twisted into a slick bun, but one lock, dyed ice-white, fell loose along the side of his head. It gave him a demonic appearance.

I hoped he didn't recognize me, but if he did, he didn't show it.

I'd never seen the second prince before. His long, blonde hair was held in a tight braid that stretched the skin around his eyes until they slanted upward into narrow slits. I studied him.

Again, I felt his wyis. A torrent of energy. This was Haming, of that I had no doubt.

Why was the androgy pretending to be a prince?

The face-changer raised the lower half of his blue-layered cloak, then seated himself on a chaise and pitched his head back against the headrest, revealing a grisly cut below his eye, swollen shut. "Heal me, novelty, and hurry." His whiny voice grated against my nerves. "Oh, the pain. It's killing me."

"Stop your blubbering, Erwan." Nelan sat on the neighboring

lounge chair. He kept a dignified, straight-backed posture and straightened his fine silk garments, inspecting them as though to ensure the clothes were free of crinkles. Then he rolled his neck on his shoulders from side to side. "Give me a boost of energy, but keep your voice down. The recent weather is making me grumpy and lethargic enough. Don't need a woman's screeching to add to my blistering headache."

Why had Haming chosen to become Prince Erwan?

I recalled what little Carrick had told me about the tenth prince. Erwan was dense and slow-witted, a chronic complainer, and exaggerated the severity of his symptoms whenever he fell ill. He had allied himself with Nelan and did whatever his older brother told him.

Perhaps Haming wished to discover Nelan's secrets.

The two men settled back in their chairs. Like all my other guests, they conversed and ignored my singing, allowing me to listen in on their conversation.

"I asked you here to discuss a matter of great importance," Nelan said. "I have been searching for proof that Father Emperor has lost the Will of Heaven and has somehow devised a trick to maintain his tin-chai."

"You've obsessed over this for awhile, Brother. You know we can do nothing without evidence."

Nelan's eyes sparked. "Yes, and I've finally discovered the truth we need. The scepter is not in the palace at all. The one Father Emperor carries is a fake."

Fake Erwan bolted up in his chair. "But if it's not here, then where did it go, and how did it leave? Do you think Old Grandfather Heaven came down himself to take it away from Father Emperor?"

I had to give Haming credit. He certainly knew how to play the part of a dunce.

Nelan rolled his eyes. "Old Grandfather Heaven is only a ridiculous myth we use to gain political support from fools who believe in the Will of Heaven. Mother Empress stole the scepter from Father Emperor, but then someone stole it from her. She confessed this to me herself."

"How did you get her to reveal such a shocking secret? She is so tight-lipped."

"There is one exception. Mother Empress's tongue loosens when she is drunk and lonely in the bedchamber."

"And you know this from experience?" Fake Erwan said with a laugh.

"I admit to nothing, except she has exposed parts of herself I never dreamed she would."

Nelan's teeth gleamed as he grinned. An unpleasant chill crawled up my spine.

"She told me secrets. Particularly of interest was her mistake in asking a former lover to help her steal and hide the scepter two years ago."

Former lover? Then this mysterious lover may have taken the scepter for himself.

Fake Erwan's gaze swished from side to side like he wanted to ask more questions, but he squinted, looking into the distance. "Shh . . . . it seems our conversation has summoned the Mother Empress herself."

Limera approached. "Good morning, my stepsons."

A twinkle shone in Nelan's smirking eyes. "Mother Empress, I trust you had a pleasant evening yesterday."

"Quite pleasant, thank you." A blush rose in the empress's cheeks, which brought a scowl on fake Erwan's face. They all deserved each other.

"I was hoping to have some privacy with the novelty," Limera said.

"Of course, Mother Empress," Erwan said. "We are finished with her services for the moment."

The two princes made their exit, leaving Limera standing in front of me.

She wore a smile drenched in poison. "I have not come here for your singing today. I bear good news. Early this morning, Lady Arlyn delivered a baby girl two months earlier than expected, and I have decided to allow her to visit you. But before I bring her out, I need you to be an obedient girl and promise you shall remain silent. Remember the consequences of disobedience."

She reached through the bars of my cage and stroked my cheek with one taunting finger. "I told you I'd find out your secrets and make you regret crossing paths with me."

My stomach clenched. What had she done to Lady Arlyn?

Limera clapped her hands. Two androgies marched out. They restrained someone dressed in the white linen of a prisoner's uniform, though it was far more red than white. Fresh blood soaked the fabric. They came closer. The prisoner was Lady Arlyn.

Her head had been shaved, and though her arms were bound, both of her hands were missing. Bloodied stumps poked out from the prison uniform's sleeves. Her belly still swelled but no longer held the pointed curve of pregnancy. Her eyes were barely open, and her legs wobbled forward, dragging through the grass as the androgies forced her to walk.

"Kneel to Her Majesty!" An androgy pushed her down. She tumbled over, her entire body crumpling at Limera's feet. Fresh blood spilled from her wounds.

The empress made a sound of disgust and turned from Arlyn to address me. "With the baby arriving so early, it is impossible that His Majesty could be the father, but she refuses to give me the true identity of the father or where she is hiding her bastard. She even had the nerve to burn all the evidence in her house."

I stared at the stumps that should have been Arlyn's hands, the tools she needed to create. All that passion I had witnessed in her, the talent and beauty she possessed. No one would ever know or see it.

I glared at Limera and took a defiant breath.

"Oh, blossoms of June . . ."

Vines whirled from above me and planted two lashes on my back. I shrieked and fell to my knees, but I sang through the pain. My voice shook.

". . . sweet blossoms of June . . ."

The vines coiled around my torso and neck. I choked and gasped for air. They squeezed tighter. Black dots clouded my vision.

The vines retreated.

I wheezed and coughed. My hands tested the raw skin on my neck. My back throbbed from the lashes, and my throat was so sore and bruised, I wondered if I could ever sing again.

I grabbed a hold of a cage bar and pulled myself up.

"Do not dare open your mouth again," Limera said to me. "Remember the rules. As your guest, I control your voice, and I have already commanded you to keep silent."

Before I could attempt to sing again, a vine slithered around the lower of half of my face, sealing my mouth shut. Two more branches curled around my arms and restrained me.

My vision swirled, red with rage. I wanted the next words from my mouth to hurt Limera, not heal her. I wanted to destroy her and take away whatever she held most dear.

A ray of sunlight hit the empress's glossy red lips. They glistened as though covered in a layer of venom. "It is rather fitting. I once made this whore watch what happens to girls who disobey the rules. A pity she did not heed my warning. Now I warn you in the same way. Let us watch your lady bleed to death, and as we do, remember that I have power over you. I may not be able to take your voice, but I can find everyone you love and make you watch them die."

The vines remained tight around my body.

Tears poured down my face and plopped to the ground.

Arlyn opened her mouth, her lips forming words, but no sound emerged. She closed her eyes. Blood streamed from her wounds. Watching her now, I saw my mama bleeding out on the beach. Arlyn had sacrificed herself to protect her child just as Mama had died protecting me. I'd failed to save Mama, and now I'd failed to save Arlyn.

Arlyn's shuddering breaths shook her body until, finally, her chest fell static. She made no further movement.

The vines loosened from my body, and I collapsed to the ground.

Empress Limera turned toward me. "Oh, do not glare at me so."

I wanted to wipe the smug smile off her face. I longed to kill her. I imagined what it would be like if my tin-chai could kill instead of heal. How satisfying it would be if I could make the empress's skin break out in hives. I'd cherish her screams when she saw her reflection portraying the true ugliness of her soul.

A trumpet blared.

"His Honorable Majesty, Emperor Terran and General Penweather have arrived," an androgy announced.

Emotions raged inside of me, a storm that wouldn't be contained much longer.

Terran scowled at Arlyn's dead body. "Someone remove that mess from my presence."

Several trifles scurried to do his bidding. They took Arlyn away, but nothing could erase the image of her dying before me. I replayed the gory stubs of her wrists protruding from her soiled clothes, bleeding out.

"Novelty," Terran said. "You were Arlyn's trinket. Do you know with whom she betrayed her vows to me? You are permitted to speak without consequence if you know the answer."

I glared at him, pursing my lips together. Even if I'd known, I never would've revealed it.

"Do not bother with her," Limera said. "I already asked Arlyn. She claimed she told no one, and I smelled this as the truth when I held the dagger over her wrists. But I have been sniffing around. Doctor Cherrywood tells me Number Eight visited the apothecary awhile back, and he suspects the prince of stealing a vial of valelily oil."

Number Eight? They were going to pin the blame on Carrick. This was my fault. Carrick wouldn't have been at the apothecary if not for me.

"Your Majesty, it is clear Lady Arlyn drugged you each night you spent with her," Limera said. "Perhaps he gave her the valelily oil to cover up their sin, and then he took the child before I could kill it."

"The empress is right," Penweather said. "I have never trusted the eighth prince. Also, I would not be surprised if he were responsible for releasing the gold-producing bauble a few months back." The general sulked as he spoke of Radi. "I know how we can force Carrick to reveal his secrets. He holds a soft spot for his bodyguard. I will torture the bodyguard, and I am certain the prince will confess. With your permission, of course, Your Majesty."

Terran sighed. "I am disappointed if this proves to be true. Do what you must."

Penweather waved his guards over. "Bring Prince Carrick and his bodyguard to me."

My stomach twisted into knots, and my hands shook. They needed to be stopped.

I delved into Penweather's soul as though it were a tangible body sitting before me to be dissected. All that darkness, the evil energy within him, entered my body, a new sensation. I'd never before allowed my rage to attach itself to my wyis, but this time I let it channel through my own soul. I tapped into the darkness of my wyis and gave it permission to enter my heart.

I want them to die.

Unprompted words left my lips and rang into the air, rattling like skeletons against prison bars.

"Do not attempt to control me,
I'm no longer caged in fear;
And if you ever try to stifle my voice,
My song will haunt your ear."

Penweather made a choking sound. He clutched at his chest. His face turned blue.

"What's happening?" Terran shouted. "Someone help him."

I didn't know how I was doing this. But I didn't care how. All I knew was that I wanted him to suffer more. Something inside me shifted—something visceral and base. Red. My mind clouded in an angry crimson fog. I continued drawing my wyis through both my *ha* and *kai* channels.

"When you try to douse my fire
And spit contempt on my dreams,
My light will burn far brighter
For all of Caliwyis to see."

General Penweather's throat swelled. Blood leaked from his eyes and mingled with white discharge. He tipped over and crashed to the ground.

CHAPTER 43

* * * * * * * * * * *

Limera leapt back and screamed. Horror crossed her face. She stared at the general's body and looked back at me. "You. It must be *you*. Shut your mouth at once."

At the empress's words, the vines swept down from the cage bars, trying to whip and restrain me, but I targeted my notes at the creeping plants. My wyis flowed through *ha* and *kai*. I'd had enough of these cursed vines. They needed to die, too.

"You may tear my clothes and skin,
Try to grind my bones to dust."

The branches and leaves shriveled, falling limp like desiccated scallions. I no longer knew what I was doing, or how, only that I needed to release the words. If I didn't, my soul would implode.

"Take His Majesty away before she kills him," Limera cried.

I narrowed my eyes and pinned my attention upon her.

How dare she interfere with my judgment of him. She would have to suffer first. I'd make her pay for all she'd done. Trembling, she fell to her knees and kowtowed to me. "No, please spare me."

Someone laughed, a cackle. It barely registered that it came from me. "Spare you?"

After all the torture she had induced on her victims? The horrible images of the baubles came flooding back. The pregnant woman hanging herself with her own hair. And Lady Arlyn, her broken body missing the parts she used to create her beautiful art. Limera had torn them all apart.

"They will have their justice today." I whispered the words, but Limera trembled as though I spoke louder than an entire orchestra.

"I won't break under your iron fist.
You'll never tame my free spirit.
Your envy is a toxic cyst,
But my soul will remain fearless."

Red boils littered her fair skin, then broke and peeled. Yellow fluid leaked from the open sores. She touched her face. Her hands came away with blood and pus. She ran to the pond, saw her reflection, and shrieked.

I stopped singing, relishing in her screams. I didn't wish to finish her off yet. I wanted her to look into the mirror at her ruined face and know she would never be beautiful again.

Before I ended her life, Terran needed to die. I looked around. Where was he? The coward must be hiding.

I glared at the trifles and androgies who shrank back from me. "Let me out, and bring Terran to me. I will continue to sing until you do."

Nobody moved.

"You can stay alone in your dark cave
While I shine with the stars above."

A trifle lurched violently and vomited up blood. I felt a bit of remorse, but it faded quickly. The trifles had stood by quietly just as I had while other women were tortured. We were every bit as guilty, and if she and the others continued to protect Terran, they all deserved to be punished.

Carrick's voice entered my mind. "Rilla, stop!"

In the distance, two guards held Carrick back. "Let me go," he said, trying to shrug them off. "Let me talk to her."

They were hurting him. Unacceptable. They would die, too.

"Your sins will hold your heart a slave
Until you finally learn to love."

The guards staggered forward, releasing him. Their skin turned yellow, and my pulse leapt. An elated rush filled me to hear their screams.

Victory was close. I could already feel the triumph of crushing Terran's soul. I knew the words I'd sing as I watched his life end. He would be at my mercy.

"Show yourself, Terran," I said.

"You must stop!" Carrick shouted. "If you continue, you will kill innocent people."

Innocent people. I came out of my trance.

I scanned the crowd. Other trifles and androgies writhed and groaned on the ground. Their hands covered their bleeding faces.

My body sank, all my weight collapsing into a boneless heap.

I'd killed Penweather. My entire life, all I'd wanted was to be a healer. But now, I had become a killer. Worse, I had been willing to sacrifice innocent lives to get to Terran.

What had I done? How was this possible? How had my tin-chai turned from a gift of blessing into a destructive weapon?

Carrick came into the cage. He knelt and whispered in my ear. "I must earn back my father's trust. I'm sorry for what I'm about to do." His hand slipped inside my bodice. I jerked away in surprise.

"What are you—"

"Forgive me. You must break out of this cage on your own." His other hand cradled my back, bringing me closer. Then he kissed me. In an instant, my senses were overwhelmed. The kiss deepened, but suddenly, he pushed me.

Two androgies restrained my hands and forced something over my head. A muzzle. I tried to scream but couldn't open my mouth.

Terran emerged. His bevy of guards and androgies surrounded him in a protective circle. "Well done, my son. I did not expect you to demonstrate such bravery and quick thinking."

Carrick kneeled before his father and touched his forehead to the ground. "Thank you, Father Emperor. I hope my actions have demonstrated to you and Mother Empress that I am trustworthy. I would never have betrayed you with Arlyn. Also, I have recently discovered something alarming. My bodyguard acted without my consent in rescuing the bauble who escaped a few months ago. I know how valuable she was to you."

No. What was he doing?

"Oh?" Terran said. "And where is the bauble now?"

"I do not know, and I was also not aware of my guard's treachery until I discovered him smuggling out extra portions of food from the palace kitchens. Unfortunately, he fled before I could confront him, but I swear I will find him and the bauble."

"Good boy." Terran patted his son's head as one would praise a faithful pet. "I was too quick to judge you, but you know your Mother Empress. She is prone to throw blame around without clarifying the circumstances first."

I stared at Carrick. The shock of betrayal shot through me, worse than the pain of the branding iron. How could he? A strange *whoosh* sounded above me. A newly grown vine weaved around my chest and squeezed, compressing my ribcage.

The air left my lungs, and all faded to black.

CHAPTER 44

✦ ✦ ✦ ✦ ✦ ✦ ✦ ✦ ✦ ✦

I awoke in my cage, the muzzle tight and uncomfortable around my mouth and jaw, but my hands were no longer bound. *There must be a way to remove the contraption.* I pulled on it. It didn't budge. It was smooth all around, no keyholes. If not a key, then some kind of magic must've been locking it.

In my cage, the extravagant bedcovers had been taken off the mound of hay acting as my bed. Did this mean I was no longer a novelty but a common prisoner?

The sounds of shuffling cards and wine pouring into cups carried through the cage's curtains.

"It's going to be a long night," a man said. "Waste of time. No question she should be executed for killing the general."

Another man grunted in agreement. "I hope His Majesty eventually sees reason. It isn't wise to keep her. She has a cursed face. Besides, girls with these rare tin-chai are too dangerous to keep alive."

"I'm afraid to even look at her. What if she spreads her curse to us?"

I stopped listening. Instead, I reflected on how I could have used my voice to kill Penweather. Prior to now, I'd only breathed life into others, healed their illnesses. Hadn't I?

Unless . . .

The words of Chief Magistrate Khan played back in my mind.

". . . we did find a pile of Shyan bones left behind. The pirates kept them as souvenirs of those they slaughtered."

What if those bones were not the pirates' souvenirs but the pirates' remains? Had I killed them? Why then had this part of my tin-chai not manifested in the six years since?

Questions poured into my mind. The next time I sang, would I restore life, or would I bring about disease and death? What if I couldn't control the dual nature of my tin-chai? What if I could no longer heal?

A more troubling thought lurked in my mind.

What would happen to my family now? My actions may have sealed their fates. What if they were punished because of me?

I pressed my forehead into my knees. Emotion burst from the back of my throat in the form of silent screams and unheard prayers. Drop by drop, the grief rose in a tidal wave and wracked my body. I screamed until my inaudible voice went numb and my throat became dry. I couldn't swallow. I let the muffled sobs slam my chest until nothing remained but emptiness.

I sat on the ground, back pressed against the bars of my cage, and aimed my hollow stares at the ceiling. Scenes repeated in my head. The death of Penweather. Limera's face bursting into pustules. The servants afflicted with disease.

What haunted me most was Carrick bowing to Terran and betraying us all.

I must earn back my father's trust. I am sorry for what I am about to do.

If I hadn't killed Penweather, he and Terran would have tortured Friend while forcing Carrick to watch, and then they would have been executed. But I had given Carrick a chance to earn back his father's favor, so of course, Carrick would have seized the opportunity. Betraying us was the only way he could survive.

Lose a battle to win the war.

He could choose to lose this round, but that wasn't my choice. I was going to fight to win.

I was going to break out of this cage, and never again would I allow Terran to use my voice to regain his power.

Carrick's voice spoke in the back of my mind.

Forgive me. You need to break out of this cage on your own.

Those were Carrick's parting words before he slipped his hand down my bodice.

I touched the front of my robe. The shape of a tiny box formed through the fabric. A matchbox.

Carrick hadn't betrayed us after all. How could I have doubted him?

I sniffed the matches. Liquor with a hint of cinnamon. These were no ordinary matches. They had been rubbed in valelily oil. The key to removing the iron muzzle. The vapors produced from heated valelily oil dissolved metal.

I struck a match, threw it into the mound of hay, and watched it burn.

The vapors filled the air. The iron muzzle loosened around my mouth. Pieces of it changed to sparkling dust and clung to my skin like paint. Then it lifted off and mingled with the smoke. I was free of the muzzle.

More hay lit up in flames. I jumped away from the heat as it prickled against my skin, and I pressed my back against the cage bars.

Valelily vapor wouldn't dissolve the wooden bars separating me from freedom. And the fire might consume the wooden bars, but not before burning me first. I hadn't thought about that when I threw the match into the hay.

I shouted at the guards, but all I managed was a hoarse whisper. The smoke and all the screaming and singing from earlier had strained my vocal cords. I banged on the bars. Sweat trailed down my scalp and soaked my back.

One of the guards coughed. "Do you smell something?"

A gasp. "Fire!"

"Get the prisoner. The emperor wants her alive."

The curtains opened. Keys jingled. When they unbolted the door, surprise crossed their faces, followed by horror.

The first guard stumbled back. "The muzzle! How did you get it off?"

The second guard blocked my way. He trembled, slowly drawing his sword, though he stared at me as though I were the vindictive ghost of his former lover.

I opened my mouth and inhaled. The guard dropped his sword, and both men plugged their ears, fleeing in the other direction.

I ran after them through the palace gardens. The sun shed its colorful cloak across the horizon until I came to the border of the Autumn Court and the Summer Fields. The sky became an artificial golden, and the overwhelming smell of peaches filled my nostrils. I made out the sound of metal clashing, and something swished through the air.

I searched for a weapon and grabbed a jagged stone. My hands shook as a shadow approached. I tip-toed forward and raised the rock over my head, ready to strike.

A black-cloaked man appeared. I ran at him, full force.

He turned. My feet skidded to a stop. Friend. His sword was drawn, and blood, black as molasses, dripped from the blade and soaked into the earth. Around him were the bodies of several more guards. Their skin was charred and stripped to the bones. The scents of burning flesh and coagulated blood filled the air.

He gestured to the rock, still poised to hit his head. At his knowing glance, I lowered my hand, and he beckoned me to follow.

We fled through the Summer Fields and passed the dozens of bauble cages that lay between rows of peach trees. The sight of the last tree at the end of the grove was a welcome relief.

Ten black-clad soldiers jumped down from the trees, blocking our exit.

Friend formed an orb of fire in his hand and blasted it at them. They fell back at the explosion. Half did not get up. The other half waved their hands through the thick layer of smoke, trying to clear the air.

Friend gestured for me to go on without him.

I shook my head. "I won't leave you." I still couldn't speak above a whisper.

"Rilla!" The sound of my name came from behind us. Carrick signaled. "Over here."

Friend pushed me toward Carrick.

Carrick grabbed my hand. "Hurry. This is our last chance to escape. Soon, my father will figure out I had a hand in rescuing you. My bodyguard can take care of himself. He'll catch up later."

Carrick led me down a dark, unfamiliar path. We came to a cart hidden beneath a pile of branches. The cart contained several wine barrels. Carrick took off the top to one. "Get in."

I fit my body into the cramped space. The cart moved, and I remembered to breathe.

Soon, we came to a halt. Carrick barked at someone. "Who had the audacity to allow this cheap trash into the palace?"

A man replied in a shaky voice. "Prince Carrick, the wine was delivered earlier this morning by the best winemaker in the kingdom."

"You blistering idiot," Carrick said. "Everyone knows my father only drinks blueberry rice wine. This is *cherry* rice wine. Where is this winemaker? He needs to be punished for this egregious error, especially at such a trying time when the palace mourns our great general."

"I will return it at once, Prince Carrick."

"No, I shall personally deliver this back to the imbecile and make sure he never makes such an atrocious mistake again."

To my relief, the cart rolled along once again. After a long while, Carrick stopped to let me out. We were still in the forest, but the trees looked more natural, no longer having the twisted, gnarled appearance of those within Cedar Palace. We'd made it out to Senlin Forest.

Behind Carrick, a black colt waited by a tree. A satchel and some blankets were strapped to the colt.

"Bolting will take you to Fauxhemia Kingdom." Carrick patted the dark beauty, and the horse whinnied. "You must put as much distance between yourself and the palace as possible."

My voice stuck in my throat. I managed to mouth two words. "My family."

"They are safe," he said. "I had my androgy relocate them to Fauxhemia."

My eyes widened. "You did that for me?"

His gaze was soft, and there was a husky note to his voice, a hoarse echo trailing his words. "Do you remember the first walk we took in the gardens? After you told me I was not my father, I knew then how special you'd become to me. I made a promise to protect you always. I told Androgy Solar to find your family and take them to Fauxhemia. In case the day came when you had to escape my father, I wanted them out of danger. I knew you would never be able to leave them behind."

My eyes brimmed with tears. I let them fall. He had rescued my family, and I'd never be able to repay him.

He wiped the tears away from my cheeks. "By now, Mother

Empress and my father will have discovered I helped you escape, and they'll know how much you mean to me. I and all those who are loyal to me will need to go into hiding. Father Emperor won't let go of you or stop searching for Radi. Both your powers are invaluable, especially now that he is in danger of losing his tin-chai without you to heal his wyis."

"If Terran catches me, he'll have to kill me before I use my voice to heal his wyis again."

"That is why you need to leave. My father still has support from those who were loyal to General Penweather. But Nelan is quickly gaining control of many in the imperial army. If he succeeds in overthrowing my father, he will be an even crueler dictator. I must stay and fight them."

How could he manage to defeat Terran and Nelan?

I shook my head. "They'll kill you."

"I have a few loyal men who support my cause, and once I find the real scepter—"

"The scepter is gone." My voice croaked. "I overheard Nelan talking. Limera has been lying. The scepter was stolen from her."

Carrick's face darkened. "Then it is even more imperative that you get far away from here. Don't stop until you cross the border to Fauxhemia. I know my father will personally leave the palace to lead the search party assisting in your capture. He'll bring novelties and androgies with tin-chai to overpower you. With my father away from the palace searching for you, I have some time before he comes after me for my betrayal. This is my chance to kill Nelan and convince more men to follow me."

Our gazes locked. Neither of us wanted to be the first to say goodbye.

But he moved first and drew me into his arms. His body shook. The embrace lingered before he forced himself to pull away. "If I do manage to win the throne, I promise to send for you. But if I do not, then you must promise me you'll live a good life. For now, let us continue to hope that one day things will become better."

Nothing would dissuade him from his chosen path. It was why I admired him so. He touched the side of my face, his fingers grazing my cheek. Then he lowered his hand, and I mounted the horse. It felt like someone had ripped out my heart and drained my blood.

He untied Bolting and whispered, "Knowing you are alive will give me the will to fight. I . . ."

He struck the colt once, and Bolting took off, but not before I caught the end of his sentence.

". . . love you."

CHAPTER 45

✦ ✦ ✦ ✦ ✦ ✦ ✦ ✦ ✦ ✦

I urged Bolting farther into the forest, but an unsettling feeling sank in the pit of my stomach. My conscience jabbed at my heart. As much as I wished to reunite with my family, it felt wrong to leave. I couldn't run away and abandon my friends.

Carrick's words echoed in my mind. *For now, let us continue to hope that one day things will become better.* Sounded a lot like what Baba used to say. *One day, things will get better.*

I was tired of waiting for one day.

I pulled on Bolting's reins, urging him to a sudden stop. He whinnied in protest and nearly threw me off.

"Sorry, Bolting," I murmured, settling him down. "Change of plans." I guided him to a tree by a stream. Taking the satchel Carrick left me, I discovered a loaf of beechnut bread, dried cranberries and two sliced apples, clothes, a small dagger, and a canister of water.

Blood, grime, and smoke covered my clothes. I changed into a dark green day dress, one of two frocks Carrick packed. Then I crumpled the dirty rag I had been wearing, threw it into the river, and watched it float away.

I ate some cranberries and fed Bolting two apple slices. With some of my energy replenished, I leaned against the tree to think.

My escape diverted Terran's attention away from the palace. This was my chance to help Carrick. I needed to make sure Terran never returned. I wouldn't let him hurt anyone else or use my voice for his selfish purposes again.

I probably had a good three-hour headstart, and with it being near nightfall, he would have to stop soon. That bought me some time, at least until morning.

How would I ambush him, though? I needed to strategize. A fog clouded my brain, and my eyes threatened to close. I slapped at my cheeks and shook my head to stay awake, but the more I tried, the heavier my eyelids grew.

The next thing I knew, my eyes opened to a shaft of light. I jolted up and collapsed into a heap. My foot was numb. I winced and pounded at it. How could I have fallen asleep? I scanned my surroundings. Thank goodness, I was still alone.

I knelt on the bank and filled my canteen in the river. Ripples of shadowy shapes materialized in the stream's reflection. The images cleared. Two men edged closer. Not palace guards. Mercenaries, judging by their battered clothing.

Making no sudden movement, I slid my hand from the water to my pocket, where I'd stashed the small dagger Carrick had packed for me. My throat was still sore and raw. I didn't think I could sing.

The men drew closer. When they were within arm's reach, I whirled around and swiped the dagger out.

Several sharp hums zipped through the air. Arrows pierced the men, sticking out of their backs. Their heavy bodies slumped to the ground.

"Up here."

My stunned gaze darted to where a man sat high in a tree above me. Why did his voice sound so familiar?

He waved. From the branch where he perched, he dangled and

swung his legs with casual grace. He held a bow in his hand and quiver at his back.

I took a step back. He was the man who tried to kiss me in the lake that night Radi and I went for a swim.

He hopped to the ground. "I missed one." In a motion faster than a puff dousing a candle, he drew his sword and thrust it behind me.

A man screamed.

I spun to see him drop with a thud at my feet.

The golden-haired man made a tsking noise at the fallen man. "Such poor manners. That is no way to treat a lady. I hope you'll learn your lesson in the next life."

I took three steps back. I recognized his eyes, brighter than a field of daffodils at dusk. Why hadn't I seen it sooner? This man, the same one I'd met swimming at the lake, was *Friend*.

No wonder I hadn't made the association between them earlier. He was so different from the silent, cloaked man I'd come to know at the palace. No longer subdued in the shadows, he had transformed into the charmer who tried to kiss me.

He had good reason to be a flirt. Tousled hair the color of sunlight itself beckoned a girl to run her hands through it. A perfectly sculpted nose, high cheekbones, and a strong jawline spoke of purpose, yet also contained boyish charm. His beautiful eyes were warm as buttercups under the summer sky.

"My lady, I don't believe we've had a proper introduction. May I know your name?"

I cleared my throat and attempted to speak, but a horrible squawk emerged, followed by a fit of coughing. Tears stung my eyes, and my throat burned.

His gentle eyes filled with understanding and concern. He plopped onto a log and patted the spot next to him. I took a seat, and he handed me a canteen of water. "Rest your voice. This should help."

I took a sip. Something sweet in it coated my throat. Carob bark honey. Made from the same ingredient he had used for my burn and my shoulder wound.

"I can talk enough for the two of us in the meantime. But will you do me a favor? Will you spell out your name?"

I located a twig on the ground and wrote my name in the mud.

"Rilla." The way he trilled my name caused a fluttering sensation in my stomach.

I wrote on the ground again. *What is your name?*

He smiled as he read this. "Before I give away that secret, I'd like to share a bit about my life with you, if that's all right."

Do I have a choice?

He laughed. "Not really. I do love the sound of my own voice, and since your voice needs time to recover, we can't track down and kill our least favorite sovereign yet."

Your life story better end with you telling me your name.

Again, he chuckled. "That will depend on you. I believe you already know I was born in Emberwood Kingdom. When I was ten years old, I was kidnapped by slavers and sold to the palace. They intended to make me an androgy." He made a derisive snort. "Thank goodness they didn't succeed. A prince saved me and made me his bodyguard. He treated me more like a brother than a slave."

His wistful eyes contained a faraway look. Then they refocused on me. "Recently, he granted me freedom on the condition that I accompany the girl he loves safely to her destination. She was a trinket, and I became friends with her, too, although she never knew my name. She knew me only as *Friend*. I dreamed of meeting her again one day when we were both free."

I remembered the words he'd written me that night when I'd lost all hope.

One day, when we've escaped this place, the first thing I'll do is properly introduce myself and ask for your name, and it'll be like we're meeting for the first time.

"When we did meet again, I discovered she was going the wrong way," he said. "Instead of leaving the kingdom, she was rushing back in the direction where the emperor was pursuing her. I had to assume she meant to fight him and might need my help." He paused to look at me and broke out of his narrative voice. "Am I correct? Are we marching into battle to kill Terran?"

A smile flitted on my face, and I nodded. I held out my hand. He embraced it.

"Well, Rilla Marseas, it's a pleasure to meet you. My name is Aiden Lang."

Aiden. I finally knew his name.

"Took you long enough, Aiden Lang." The sound of my voice caught me by surprise. I lifted my fingers to my throat. The carob bark honey had worked its magic.

"Just long enough, apparently. I've always had impeccable timing," Aiden said. "So now that your power is restored, let's help our friend kill his father."

CHAPTER 46

✦ ✦ ✦ ✦ ✦ ✦ ✦ ✦ ✦

Aiden sent Bolting off in the direction of the city. "Traveling by foot makes it easier to navigate the narrow paths."

I was sad to see Bolting go, but I hoped he would find a new owner who would treat him well.

Less than an hour passed before we located the emperor's procession marching down the main road. They were coming to find me, as Carrick had said. Aiden and I watched from behind the bushes.

Two men with the legs of stallions carried a golden-canopied chaise. Terran sat upon the velvet cushion. Behind the chaise, two other horsemen balanced a closed palanquin on their broad shoulders. The empress's hongni bird icon was carved on the sides.

"Terran must not know yet that the empress has been lying about having the scepter, or he would have imprisoned her," I said.

At the end of the caravan, regular horses pulled two wheeled palanquins.

"Terran will have brought novelties and androgies with powerful tin-chai to ensure your capture," Aiden said. "They must be in the palanquins."

We followed the procession, and soon, they stopped by the river.

From the carriages, three novelties in emerald robes and three androgies emerged.

Limera exited the palanquin, her face covered in a lavender silk handkerchief. To my surprise, Irica stepped out after her.

I whispered to Aiden. "Madam Yasmina framed Irica and had her taken to Limera for punishment. Why is she here?"

Rather unlikely for Limera to have shown mercy.

Aiden tensed and scanned the trees. "Something's wrong."

Several birds sounded frantic alarms and took flight. Aiden moved in a blur. Gone was his happy-go-lucky charm. His eyes blazed like pure liquid gold, fiery and all-consuming.

The leaves rustled. Half a dozen men dropped from the trees. They were dressed in blue androgy robes, and all of them wore the same face.

"Clones," Aiden said. "No wonder I didn't sense them. It's a trap."

The cloned androgies rushed at us.

A light flared in Aiden's hands. He released fiery arrows from his bowstring. They pierced their targets, and two clones dissipated into the air.

I sang three notes. But the clones remained unaffected, deafened to my voice. One came at me. I grabbed a rock and swung it at him. He evaporated in a dust cloud.

More soldiers emerged. About ten, by a quick estimate. These were palace guards, not clones. Aiden changed his weapon. He ignited his sword, and the metal glowed red. He slashed through another soldier, then another, cutting through them like butter. Screams reverberated in the air. Entrails exploded. Blood splashed onto the trees, the ground, and Aiden's face. He didn't flinch, already focused on his next target.

"*Oh blossoms of June,*" I sang, directing my wyis at the soldiers who surrounded Aiden, but another song rose above me.

*"Today I dream of glory and fame,
For tomorrow all will exalt my name."*

Irica. I spun around. Instead of Irica, a wisp of water floated up from the earth. It curled around Aiden's hands and snuffed out his fire.

Aiden started. "What the—" A soldier attacked from behind and knocked the sword from Aiden's hand, allowing three others to close in. They kicked him to the ground. A soldier grabbed his arms and restrained him.

"Don't hurt him," I shouted.

"What happens to him depends on you, my nightingale." Terran's voice boomed through the forest. "Come quietly, and I may consider sparing his life."

Irica laughed as she approached us. Following behind her were Terran and Limera. The troupe of novelties and androgies flanked them, and the four horsemen and ten palace guards stood in the outermost circle.

Irica was dressed in as fine a silk kipa as those worn by Limera. In fact, it was lavender, and sewn in the center was the hongni bird, the empress's icon.

"Hello, Rilla," Irica said. "I finally have the chance to prove I'm the better singer. I will end you."

Terran cleared his throat. "Irica, my dear. A word of warning. As beautiful and talented as you are, I will not hesitate to take your title of empress away if you hurt my nightingale."

"I apologize, Your Majesty. I got carried away and misspoke."

"Empress?" I said.

"Yes, are you surprised?" Irica twirled her hair with a flick of her wrist. "I have replaced Limera, and I now have these novelties to command. If we succeed in capturing you today, and we will, they become my trifles." She gestured to the empress, who remained uncharacteristically silent. "It's time a new empress ruled. One who is younger, more beautiful, and more talented."

The Limera I knew would never allow Irica to insult her this way. Something was strange. For one thing, I couldn't smell the overpowering scent of jasmine water she usually wore. Instead, I caught a hint of musky amberwood.

I gauged Limera's expression and felt for her wyis. There it was. A familiar powerful wyis overwhelmed my senses.

"Enough crowing, my love," Terran said. "You should not speak so in front of Limera."

Irica shrugged. "She knows I speak the truth. It's why she remains silent."

Finally, Limera spoke. Her voice was soft and defeated, so unlike her. "Say what you wish, Irica. Help us contain the nightingale so she can restore my beauty, and I will do anything, even give up my position as empress."

She beckoned to the soldier who held Aiden captive. "Bring the boy here. In the future, he will become my new pet." Her gaze met mine from behind her scarf. "If you attempt anything, I will gut him."

"Don't listen to them, Rilla," Aiden said. "Sing louder. Sing to kill. Don't be afraid." He grunted as the soldier kneed him in the chest.

"Shut your mouth, and bow before your new mistress," the soldier said. He walked Aiden to Empress Limera and kicked Aiden to his knees.

"Perhaps I should give you the incentive now," the empress said. "Force you to save your friend's life and reap the benefits for myself."

She withdrew a dagger.

"Wait," I said, trying not to let panic overtake me. I needed to remain calm. "Before you do anything, I have a question."

"What is it?"

"Why are you impersonating Empress Limera?"

Terran quaked. Irica gasped.

The impersonator's hand shifted direction and plunged the blade into the throat of the soldier restraining Aiden.

CHAPTER 47

The knife lodged in the soldier's neck. He fell facedown. An ugly croak, and nothing further, escaped him.

"Who are you?" Terran shouted.

The empress's body shimmered, limbs growing longer and muscular. Her nose widened, her eyes narrowed, and her cheekbones spread out and thickened until Androgy Haming emerged.

Terran's face went white. "Haming? You're a shapeshifter?"

Androgy Haming sneered at Terran. "The real Haming is dead. I replaced him long ago."

"Who are you then?" Terran roared. "Reveal your real face at once."

"My real face?" Haming laughed. "You wouldn't recognize me anyway after what you did to me. But I will finally have my revenge. Your enemies are now my temporary allies. Prepare to die."

He picked up the fallen guard's sword and flew at the protective circle surrounding Terran.

In blurred movements, everyone repositioned themselves.

Seven palace guards and four horsemen configured a V-shape in front of Irica and the three novelties. The other palace guards flanked Terran, and they ran into the forest.

Aiden went after them, but one of the androgies blocked his path. The androgy lifted the rocks from the earth, forming a dust cloud aimed to enfold Aiden. A second androgy punched a fist into the earth, making the ground quake. Aiden took off into the trees, in the direction Terran had fled. Both androgies pursued him.

The third androgy murmured a low chant, the vibrations in his chest blurring his body until he split into two copies of himself. Both doubles rushed at Haming and slashed with their swords. Haming thrust his blade and countered. Clones continued to form, driving Haming back into the surrounding forest where Aiden had disappeared.

I chased after them. I had to help. "*Oh, blossoms of June—*"

Irica shrieked, drowning my voice. I whirled around. Irica's cold, bitter eyes reflected another Empress Limera in the making. She and the novelties moved in front of the remaining seven palace guards and four horsemen.

Irica motioned to the three novelties behind her. "Go after His Majesty and protect him." To the horsemen and palace guards, she said, "Don't interfere. This bitch is mine."

She took a deep breath.

"*Today I dream of glory and fame,*
For tomorrow all will exalt my name."

I clenched my teeth and held my eardrums, feeling each of her off-key notes grating against my nerves. The energy of her voice carried toward the river. A stream came up and swirled through the air, then danced around me and wrapped around my body. It tightened, and I could no longer move.

I sang out three notes, but her loud cries were all I heard.

Another tendril of river water rose above me. Then torrents of water poured down. I struggled against the water that bound me, desperate to get away. I couldn't see, couldn't breathe. It was as though someone had forced my head underwater.

The water subsided, and I took a gasping breath, my lungs desperate for reprieve. I wiped the water from my eyes and searched for Irica. She stood to my side.

She came closer and sneered. "You aren't the only one hiding another facet to your tin-chai. His Majesty said I had the loudest voice he'd ever heard, and if I agreed to help him capture you, then he would give me anything. I am going to bring you back with me."

She cleared her throat and wailed.

"All shall admire my beauty and grace
When I enter the palace to claim my rightful place."

Again, the water restrained me and rained down. I choked and swallowed water, falling to my knees. Black dots clouded my vision.

I remembered Carrick's dagger, still in my cloak. My hand inched toward it. If only I could see Irica.

The torture stopped. I gulped the air. Through water-blurred eyes, I located Irica's shoes, planted next to my head. She raised her foot, bringing it to my eye level. "I'll make you a deal. Kiss my shoe, and I may consider sparing you further humiliation when I put you back in your cage."

She waggled her foot in front of my face.

I grabbed the dagger and jabbed it into her foot. She screamed and fell to the ground, cradling the wound.

She glared at me. "I don't care what the emperor says. I'll make sure you never sing again."

I dragged myself upright.

Irica resumed screeching, and though she was loud, I was no

longer afraid. I focused on my own voice. I believed in my power, in my voice. I didn't need to roar over her to be heard. The water danced around me. I sang, bringing more power to my voice than ever before.

"As untainted as a lotus lily growing in muck and mire,
Enduring as the crane flying above the winding water."

I felt my wyis running through my soul, heart, and this time, body—*ha, dai,* and *kai*—three channels working together.

The water crashed to the ground and gathered in a still pool.

Irica sang louder, but the water no longer stirred at her command.

Darkness stirred within me. Why was she still trying to defeat me? I'd never done anything to make her hate me.

Anger took over my consciousness. Memories filled my mind of each time she had taunted me for being a koong, of how I'd forced myself to remain silent. I longed for her to experience what I'd felt, to live a moment in my shoes, unable to use her tin-chai. What would happen if I used all four channels this time? *Ha. Kai. Dai. Ji.* Would I break her the way she had always longed to break me?

"Resilient as bamboo unbreakable in the storm,
Let this song define me as my spirit is reborn."

Higher and higher I sang. My voice soared, producing notes I'd never known I could make.

Irica sank to her knees, holding her ears. Her mouth opened in a silent scream. Her eyes widened, shining with tears. All the water that Irica had summoned now retreated back to the river. She brought her hands to her throat. Her face went white. She stared into the void with unseeing eyes and stayed still.

I snapped out of my angry daze. What had happened? What had I done?

I went to her. Her skin was also as smooth as it had always been, her chest moved in easy breaths, and her wyis still burned strong. It seemed my voice hadn't affected her at all.

Why then did she remain frozen with her hands still on her throat?

But I had stopped her control over the water, and instead, the water had obeyed me. Had I stolen her tin-chai?

Before I had time to reflect further, the thud of heavy footsteps stopped behind me. The ground vibrated, and a man shouted a battle cry.

"The new empress has failed to capture the novelty. Subdue the songbird, but remember, His Majesty wants her alive."

CHAPTER 48

The four shapeshifting horsemen and seven palace guards clad in metal armor were scattered amidst the trees behind me. They rushed forward. The guards drew their swords, and the horsemen charged, their legs galloping at full speed. Channeling more of my wyis through *ha* and *kai* into my voice, I sang, this time aiming to kill.

"These wings may have been broken and torn,
But my dreams will breach those sealed doors."

Pained cries echoed all around. The horsemen fell, legs tripping beneath them. Boils and lesions grew on their faces and bodies, enlarging until the infections exploded and disfigured their skin.

I homed my attention in on the seven guards.

"Singing words to break these chains,
I'll rise again in a glorious blaze."

Skin melted off their bodies. Metal armor and swords tangled with bones, clanking like silverware on fine china.

Silence settled in the forest again.

I turned back to Irica and recoiled at the sight of her motionless body, lying in a crimson pool of blood-soaked clothes.

I rushed to her. Red bubbles gurgled from her slit throat. Evidence of scratches from long fingernails trailed across her face, and the number four had been carved into her right cheek.

The real Empress Limera must be here, too. Had she found out that Haming was impersonating her? I held my dagger in front of me and searched my surroundings. Where was she?

I ran in the direction where Aiden and Haming had taken off in pursuit of Terran. The path went downhill. Still no sign of activity.

I caught a trail of blood and followed it. A pool of emerald fabric soaked in blood shrouded a dead woman, one of the novelties whom Irica had tasked to protect Terran. Her stomach had been sliced through with a sword. A wave of sorrow overcame me. Haming or Aiden must have killed her. These women were tasked to kill us, but they were forced to fight for the emperor. Trapped to use their powers.

I wished I could save them, but in this fight, I had to be ready to kill, or they would kill me. Such was the game Terran forced us to play.

I said a little prayer, hoping this woman found peace in the afterlife, then forced myself to refocus. One novelty was dead. Two remained, along with three androgies and six palace guards. But with one of the androgies having a cloning tin-chai, Haming and Aiden were still outnumbered. I had to find them.

Battle cries echoed to my right. I followed the shouts. A flash of bright fire glowed in the trees. Aiden emerged. He jumped from branch to branch, scaling higher into the tree. Several guards pursued, and the remaining two novelties stood at the base of the trees, waiting for Aiden to misstep.

Aiden no longer had a sword, but flames filled both his hands. He threw the firebombs at the guards. One man lost his footing and screamed, tumbling to the ground. The two novelties darted out of the way. The women glanced at the dead man for a moment and then returned their gazes to Aiden.

One novelty closed her eyes and whispered a chant. Her eyes opened and flickered. Lavender sparks emitted from her pupils and carried upward. Electricity struck the branch where Aiden balanced.

"Watch out!" I shouted.

He fell, but his hand caught another bough. He swung his body around the branch like an acrobat, cleanly landing upon it.

The second novelty hissed. Her voice's vibrations summoned vines to crawl from the earth. They spiraled and coiled like snakes, climbing the tree trunk toward Aiden.

I rushed forward, singing to the beat of my footsteps.

"Do not attempt to control me.
I'm no longer caged in fear."

Soldiers tumbled down from the tree. Their bodies withered and shrank to emaciated proportions, and their skin dissolved into dust. I counted six dead, leaving just the novelties and androgies, one of whom had the cloning tin-chai, to defend Terran.

"If you try to stifle my voice,
My song will haunt your ear."

The novelty with electric eyes howled and bowed over. She rubbed her eyes and came away with blood. With a burbling gasp, she slumped over and moved no more.

The other novelty shrieked and hissed. She faced me. Her climbing plants slithered and lashed out toward me.

I sang.

*"You can try to douse my fire
And spit on all my dreams."*

The vines came within an inch of me. They shortened and withered, breaking down to powder.

*"My light will grow brighter
For the world to see."*

The woman shuddered. Her body crinkled like an autumn leaf and dissolved into pieces, flying into the wind.

Before I could find Aiden again, the rustle of robes echoed in the trees. Two figures somersaulted down from where they had been hiding in the forest canopy and landed in front of me.

Androgies.

One stomped his feet into the soil, and the earth shook, knocking me off-balance. The rumbling wouldn't stop. The second androgy struck the ground with his hand, bringing up a cloud of debris. There was no time to sing. Sand and gravel flew at me, forming a cloud that blocked my vision.

Light appeared in the form of fire. The debris burned to ash, stopping it from devouring me.

Aiden appeared.

"Thank you," I said. "You saved me."

"You saved me first," he replied. "Have to admit, I was getting a little nervous back there." Then he turned, and with a shout, he formed another fire missile and launched it at the androgy who'd caused the earthquake. The man's body lit on fire. With the sounds of his dying shrieks, the shaking subsided.

Aiden faced the other androgy. Another firebomb materialized in his hand. "Haming went after Terran and the last androgy." He nodded to his right, where the woods sloped upward to an overgrowth of bamboo.

The androgy flung another storm of gravel at us. Aiden raised his hand and blasted fire into the air, incinerating the small pebbles.

I hesitated. "Are you sure you'll be all right?"

"Yes, I'll catch up to you after I finish off this last nuisance. Be careful. Haming isn't to be trusted either."

"You be careful, too. The real Empress Limera is here. She killed Irica."

He nodded once, and his focus returned to the androgy.

I took off in the direction he indicated.

The clanking noise of iron against iron echoed in the distance and grew louder. At the edge of the bamboo forest, Haming battled against three clones. He slashed through them as though slicing through soft beancurd. Their bodies ripped apart, limbs hitting the ground, but there was no blood.

A flash of purple. Terran emerged through the curtain of bamboo and sprinted away.

Before Haming or I could give chase, another six men appeared, summoned from the air. Six men became twelve, then two dozen, blocking our path. Where was the original androgy? I scanned the trees.

The androgy perched cross-legged in perfect balance upon the top of a towering stalk. A chant hummed from deep in his throat.

I shouted and pointed. "There."

Haming nodded once. "I'll handle this. Go after Terran. Don't let him escape." He slashed at the clones and bamboo, clearing my path for a second. I rushed through before more doubles could replace them.

Deeper into the thicket I ran. Terran was fast, and I was already winded.

"*Do not attempt to control me,*" I sang.

He turned and threw a flame at me with his hand. I darted to the side, but not before it singed my ankle. I yelped and fell.

Red clay globules flew at me like snowballs. I rolled my body over and dove under the cover of bamboo. The mud hit the stalks and hardened.

I stood but stumbled back down again. A weed had wrapped around my foot, trapping me to the ground. I pulled at it, but another plant sprouted from the ground and wound around my leg. Bamboo shoots came at me, tying my arms back. My body was rooted in place. Clay droplets coagulated on the plants that restrained me, growing closer to my limbs.

He continued to run, out of hearing range to be affected by my voice. If I didn't find a way to free myself, not only would I become part terracotta statue, but also he would get away to find reinforcements.

Red clay continued to pile on, quickly solidifying my restraints. My leg was in danger of petrification.

I thought of my battle with Irica. It seemed I had turned her into a koong and stolen her tin-chai. It was impossible to do the same with Terran from this distance. But had I acquired Irica's tin-chai to command water permanently?

I raised my voice and sang, allowing my wyis to enter first *ha,* then *kai,* and finally, *dai,* as I had when I controlled the water Irica had summoned.

A ribbon of water formed from the stream and came toward me. It soaked into the red clay around my body and softened it. The clay dissolved and crumbled. So did the roots that bound me. I was free.

Losing no time, I pursued Terran. With renewed strength, I picked up my pace.

If I had taken away Irica's tin-chai, I could do the same with

Terran. Then I could use his tin-chai against him. I just had to get close enough to him.

Terran looked behind his shoulder and saw me. He turned his hand upward, building a flame.

My voice tore through the air, my power infused in all channels. Terran slowed and grunted in pain. The spark he'd formed snuffed out.

How I cherished stealing back from him what he had forced me to give.

I continued singing, but this time the music had no lyrics, only intent. I commanded the elements. Terran no longer had power over them. I did.

Obey me. I am your new master.

A bolt of lightning flashed through the sky. It struck close to Terran. In his surprise, he tumbled and fell.

"Having trouble using your tin-chai, Your Majesty?"

He glared. "Limera was right. You are a curse."

I filled my senses with his soul, preparing for the final blow. But the sharpness of a blade pressed against my back. Empress Limera's overpowering perfume flooded my senses. Her warm breath blew against my earlobe.

"Harm a hair on His Majesty's head, and you will regret it."

I raised my hands in surrender. Limera came around to look me in the eye. A scarf covered the bottom half of her face. She held a knife against my throat.

"Limera, where have you been?" Terran said. "I cannot believe you allowed Haming to trick me."

"I am sorry, Your Majesty. It is this stupid girl's fault. If she had not ruined my face, I would not have needed to ask Haming for help. He assured me he had a cure for my skin, but when I went to him, he locked me up."

"There is no time for your excuses," Terran said. "Do not harm the girl. I need her as leverage against the *Zhei* boy and Haming until we return to the palace and figure out a new plan."

He turned his back and headed down the path, expecting us to follow.

Limera pressed the edge of the blade into the middle of my throat and forced me to walk. I took deep breaths. *Keep calm and think.*

"I can heal you if you let me go," I said. "What will His Majesty think if he should ever see your scars? You are already in danger of being replaced as empress."

"Hold your tongue," she said, but her nervous gaze darted to Terran. "I shall be careful never to let him see my face until I find another way to heal, and once we have no further need for you, I will slit your throat."

If she wouldn't take my bait, perhaps Terran would.

The blade stung where it pressed against my throat, but I raised my voice for Terran to hear. "When will you tell His Majesty that you lost the Sacred Cedar Scepter?"

Terran turned. His startled gaze flashed to Limera. "What?"

"The girl lies," Limera said, but her voice faltered. "Do not listen to her."

"I overheard Prince Nelan say so. He seduced you into confess—"

"Quiet, stupid girl."

The pointed edge pressed further into my throat. I inhaled sharply. A prickling sting pulsed, and a trickle of warm liquid oozed down my skin.

Terran's shock turned to anger. "This must be the real reason you refused to return it. I should have suspected this of you. Tell me the truth. What happened to the scepter?"

"It was stolen from the palace. But I believe I know who took it."

"You disgust me. I have wasted enough time believing your lies."

Terran extended his hand, gesturing to me. "Give me the girl, and get out of my sight."

Limera pulled me closer to her. "No, please, Your Majesty. Do not cast me aside. I can still prove my worth."

"Worth?" He laughed. "I have given you many chances, and you continue to manipulate me. Besides, what need would I have for an ugly empress? Do you intend on wearing that scarf in front of my court? Imagine the humiliation you would bring me if the scarf slipped and your hideous scars were exposed for all to see."

Limera loosened her hold on me and reached to secure the scarf higher on her face.

We all had our vulnerabilities, didn't we?

I grabbed the edge of her scarf and yanked.

CHAPTER 49

✦ ✦ ✦ ✦ ✦ ✦ ✦ ✦ ✦ ✦ ✦

The scarf fell from her face. She screamed, dropped the knife, and shielded her marred face with both hands.

Terran lurched forward, fingers poised to grab the discarded weapon.

I stomped on the hilt and kicked away his hand.

"You remain in your dark cave,
But I'll shine with the stars above."

Blood spewed from his mouth. His body spasmed, and his spine curved until the bones of his frame shriveled and threatened to crumble beneath his weight.

"Your sins will hold your heart a slave
Until you finally learn to love."

I sang the final words he'd ever hear, and Terran's gaze passed over me. He extended one frail hand as though he wished to curl it around my throat. His skin thinned, taking on a translucent appearance, then evaporated into dust. Nothing was left but brittle bones.

"No!" Limera screamed. I snatched up the knife and held it in front of me, ready to attack. But her knees wobbled, and she collapsed into a sobbing heap on the ground. Her shoulders shook. Though it didn't seem like she'd retaliate, I remained wary. *Should I kill her?* She had committed so much evil. But only she knew who had stolen the scepter.

Footsteps sounded. Aiden and Haming ran down the path toward me. Haming knelt by Limera, and Aiden came to my side.

His eyes widened for a second at the sight of Terran's skeleton. Then he breathed out a sigh and whistled. "Damn. I can't believe I missed out on the fun." His attention turned to me, and he sobered. "Are you all right?"

I threw him a glare. "I could have used some help."

"I'm sorry. That last androgy was a bigger nuisance than expected." He lowered his voice to a whisper and nudged his chin toward Haming. "Don't let your guard down just yet. I'm still unsure how I feel about that one."

Haming stooped low, his gentle gaze falling on Limera. He whispered comforting words to her. "Do not worry. I will provide for you."

I didn't know what to make of him either. Was he an ally or a foe? He seemed to detest Terran, and he had fought on our side today.

"I know one of your former lovers stole the scepter. Who was it?" Haming asked.

Definitely a foe, power hungry as the rest.

"We only need to find him and take it back. Then we will finally rule together."

She gazed sadly at him and shook her head. "That is your dream, not mine. All I wanted was for him to love and need me. Perhaps he will in the next life."

She grabbed her needle-shaped hairpin and plunged it deep into the vein at the side of her neck. Black blood oozed from her flesh, splashing onto Haming and gushing into a pool upon the earth.

Horror crossed Haming's features. "No!" He caught Limera in his arms and pressed the scarf to her neck. Her body twitched.

A last burbling exhale rippled through her. Limera's head slumped to the side. The hair ornament still skewered her throat. Her eyes remained open and haunted, her neck covered in shining crimson sheets.

Haming closed her eyes, then rose, cradling Limera's body in his arms. He dripped with her blood. "I will bury her. We should all leave before the palace sends more guards and they find their emperor dead."

Aiden blocked Haming's path. "Wait. Who are you? Is Haming your true name? You'll have to forgive me. I never forget a name or a face, but since you can change both, it's been hard to keep track."

"As far as you're concerned, I am the next emperor."

Aiden raised one eyebrow. "Oh? What makes you believe you have earned the Will of Heaven?"

"Because I will be the one to find the scepter and prove it." Haming turned his back on us. "We were allies today because it fit my needs, but should you decide to aid Carrick in his quest for the throne, we become enemies. Take my advice. Leave the kingdom and do not return. If we cross paths again, I shall be forced to kill you."

Why didn't he kill us now?

He marched away.

"In that case, safe travels to you until we meet again." Aiden kept his tone friendly and light as he waved goodbye to the androgy's back. He looked at me and rolled his eyes. "Such a pleasant fellow."

CHAPTER 50

◆　◆　◆　◆　◆　◆　◆　◆　◆

I felt compelled to give Irica some kind of burial. Aiden and I gathered branches for a pyre. We had no incense to burn or paper spirit money to send with her into the afterlife, but at least wild animals wouldn't desecrate her body.

Aiden set the body upon a mound of brushwood. Irica's bloodless face made me shiver. She had been my bully, but I saw only fear in her eyes when she could no longer use her tin-chai, that same haunted expression I'd seen in the other novelties and baubles. All the fight in her gone. Powerless. And I was the one who had made her so.

I said a silent prayer to Old Grandfather Heaven. Perhaps one day, Irica and I would be reborn and meet again in another life. And I hoped we wouldn't make the same mistakes. I hoped we could be friends.

Aiden formed a flame in his hand and lit the pyre. I looked away, unable to watch Irica's body turn to ash.

Aiden squeezed my arm. "We haven't really had a chance to talk about what happened. Are you all right?"

"Other than some bruises and scratches, I'm fine."

"That's not what I meant." He cast me a concerned look. "I'm used to seeing death and destruction, and I've had to kill so many times that it doesn't bother me so much anymore. But I remember the first time I killed someone. You never really get over it. I don't mean to force you to talk about it, but I'm here if you need me."

So much had happened that I hadn't been able to think much about what I'd done. How I'd turned from a healer into a killer. I hadn't allowed myself to think about how the darkness inside of me had turned my voice into a weapon of destruction.

I didn't know if I wanted to talk about it, but Aiden's gaze felt so welcoming that I spoke my thoughts aloud anyway. "I'm glad Terran and Limera are dead. What bothers me isn't exactly that I had to kill, but *how* I killed. I've always wanted to help others with my voice, to sustain life, not destroy it."

Aiden's golden eyes reflected nothing but kindness. "It may not be much comfort, but by killing Penweather and those novelties, you did save my life."

"And I will kill again to protect the people I care about," I said. "But what scares me is that I didn't know I was capable of using my voice for anything other than healing until it happened. Right before I killed Penweather, my emotions took over and changed my tin-chai. My anger and hatred felt so strong. I wanted Terran, Limera, and Penweather to die, and I wanted to be the one to execute their punishment."

Aiden didn't say anything, didn't try to talk me out of my feelings. He just nodded, urging me to continue. So I did.

"Causing disease and killing isn't the only other facet of my tin-chai I discovered. When I fought Irica, I wanted her to know what it felt like to be powerless just like I'd felt when she bullied me. The next thing I knew, she had lost her voice, and I had acquired her tin-chai. I did the same to Terran. I stole their gifts."

Somehow, that seemed worse than killing someone. To people like Irica and me, our tin-chai was part of our identity, a part of our very existence. To lose it would be like having no name. No purpose. I didn't regret stripping Terran of his power, but I didn't mean to take away Irica's voice.

"I could have stopped Irica another way." I whispered the admission, but once spoken aloud, more confessions toppled from my tongue like a snowball gaining momentum. "I had already stabbed her foot. She was down. I could have tried to use the dagger to prevent her from singing. Instead, my rage overcame reason. I ripped her voice out of her throat forever. My brother said his only job is to heal, no matter who the patient is. A healer isn't supposed to want to kill or administer justice to those who have committed wrongs. But I did. And I probably will want to again. What if that dark desire has permanently driven away my healing tin-chai? What if instead of bringing life and healing to the sick and the hurt, I've become someone who can only rob them of their existence?"

Aiden regarded me for a moment. "You haven't tried to heal anyone since your tin-chai revealed its other facets. You don't know for sure that you can't."

"No, but I feel like something has changed inside of me." My gaze shifted to the burning pyre. Despite the warmth of the flame, a chill crawled on my skin. "I can't explain it, but my wyis feels clouded with this shadow that wasn't there before. It's different, and I don't think I can ever change back. I don't think I can remove the shadows."

"No one can change back to who they were before," he said. "Besides, it's the presence of shadows that make us appreciate the light." He paused and placed a hand on my shoulder, turning me to face him. "You will never be someone who only robs people of their existence. You have always been and will always be a healer."

How did he always know exactly what to say? My heart fluttered, not completely unburdened, but a little lighter than before.

We watched the fire burn for a little while longer. Then Aiden sighed. "I know we just finished one battle and have barely recuperated, but we need to return to the capital and find Carrick. Then we can figure out where to start searching for the scepter."

He was right. We needed to move quickly. Many would be searching for the scepter, and until it was found, the kingdom would be in chaos as multiple contenders battled for power.

Aiden stilled. "Shh, don't move." His gaze went on alert.

A crash sounded through the trees. Aiden moved in a blur, and then stood in a defensive pose in front of me.

A man staggered toward us. His clothes were soaked in blood. His nose hung at an odd angle, and the tip of his right ear had been chopped off. The man tottered, but Aiden caught him before he collapsed to the ground.

"Solar!" Aiden cushioned the man's head in his arms. "What happened?"

Androgy Solar? Carrick's androgy, the man with a shield tin-chai whom Carrick had charged to take my family to Fauxhemia Kingdom. I'd never met him in person, but I owed so much to him.

Androgy Solar gasped. "Nelan's men ambushed me. I was weak from using my tin-chai to secure the safe house with a permanent shield, so my shield failed me on my way to find you. I barely managed to escape."

I knelt and placed my hands over the older man. I said a little prayer. *Old Grandfather Heaven, let my tin-chai work. Let me save him.* Then I sang.

"Oh, blossoms of June, sweet blossoms of June,
The innocence of youth e'er did bloom,
'til the day evil drove us to ruin . . ."

Nothing happened. Blood still dripped from his wounds, and his wyis grew weaker by the second.

No, please no.

I tried again, singing louder.

Nothing.

It was true, then. My healing powers were gone for good.

Tears blurred my eyes. "I'm sorry. I'm sorry." It was all I could say.

His kind eyes gazed upon me. "It's all right. Wise Grandmother Time has decided I must journey into the next life." He gripped Aiden's hand. "I need to deliver Carrick's message. He suffered minor injuries but managed to go into hiding. Safe for now." Solar wheezed. His voice was fading. "But you must not return. Nelan controls . . . palace. Go to Emberwood. Carrick's . . . only chance."

"Emberwood?" Aiden said. "Why Emberwood?"

Solar's voice was barely a whisper. "Find wielder . . . scepter . . . in Emberwood."

Aiden gasped. "The scepter? Are you saying the wielder of the scepter is in Emberwood? Do you know who he is?"

"Wielder . . . Emberwood."

"Yes, but who wields the scepter now?" Aiden asked. "What's his name?"

But Solar's eyes closed, and his head fell to the side. The last of his trickling wyis shriveled and vanished.

Aiden stared at the man's body in disbelief. He wiped a stray tear from his eye and turned to me. "You should continue to Fauxhemia as Carrick instructed. It will be safe for you there."

"What about you?" I asked.

"I don't know who I'm supposed to look for, but if Solar thinks the scepter is in Emberwood, that is where I must go. I'll find the scepter and figure out a way to steal it back for Carrick."

I shivered at the thought of facing those who wished to control me. Terran would not be the last to wish to use me as a weapon. Now that I no longer carried a healing tin-chai, whoever tried to capture me next would force me to kill for them.

But Mama's words echoed in my head once more. *Your voice is powerful, and that makes it dangerous, Rilla.*

No one could force me to do anything. I wasn't going to allow anyone to use me.

I looked Aiden in the eye, and I made a promise. "Don't think I'll abandon Carrick or you now. I don't care how dangerous the journey becomes. I will never live in a cage again."

GLOSSARY

CHARACTERS

RILLA MARSEAS—(RILL-ah MAR-see-aahs)

RELL MARSEAS—(RELL MAR-see-aahs) *Protagonist's older brother*

NIA MARSEAS—(NEE-ah MAR-see-aahs) *Protagonist's sister-in-law*

AUNTIE AN—(AHN) *Protagonist's family friend*

EMPEROR TERRAN—(TEER-ehn) *Emperor of Seracedar Kingdom*

RADI YING—(REY-dee YEENG) *Protagonist's best friend*

PRINCE CARRICK—(KEER-ick) *Emperor's son and protagonist's love interest*

AIDEN LANG—(EY-den LAHNG) *Prince Carrick's loyal bodyguard*

EMPRESS LIMERA—(lye-MEER-ah) *Empress of Seracedar Kingdom*

LADY ARLYN—(AR-lyn) *Emperor's concubine and protagonist's mentor*

MADAM YASMINA—(yass-MEE-nah) *Palace madam in charge of protagonist during the showcase*

MADAM GOMI—(GOH-mee) *Palace madam*

IRICA—(AIR-ee-kah) *Protagonist's neighbor and bully, also competing in the showcase*

GALAI—(gah-LYE) *Another girl from the protagonist's village, also competing in the showcase*

ANDROGY HAMING—(AN-dro-gee HAH-meeng) *Emperor's advisor*

ANDROGY UNTHER—(AN-dro-gee UHN-ter) *Showcase judge*

✦ ✦ ✦

SEVEN KINGDOMS OF CALIWYIS
(CAL-uh-WEES)

SERACEDAR—(SEER-ah-SEE-der) *Kingdom of Shyan people, a race born with tin-chai, unique magical abilities controlled through four channels*

EMBERWOOD—(EHM-ber-WUD) *Kingdom of Embers, also of the Shyan race who rebelled and started their own kingdom two hundred years ago*

FAUXHEMIA—(fo-HEE-mee-ah) *Kingdom of Fauxhemian race, artists and storytellers with blood magic*

AILO—(EYE-low) *Kingdom of Ailo, a race of rock dwellers conquered by Seracedar and became a tribute kingdom*

YAO—(YOW) *Kingdom of Yao, a race of animal spirit shapeshifters conquered by Seracedar and became a tribute kingdom*

MIYU (MEE-yoo) ISLANDS—*Sea nation of fish shapeshifting women warriors said to have descended from the sea goddess Mi (MEE)*

EXENTRIA—(ex-EHN-tree-ah) *Kingdom of the Exentriks, technologically advanced people who can banish ghosts and demons with their magic*

◆　◆　◆

PLACES IN SERACEDAR

PROVINCE CA—(KAH) *Province where fishing is main industry*

PROVINCE YUPA—(YOO-pah) *Province where textiles is main industry*

PROVINCE PEON—(PEE-AHN) *Province where agriculture is main industry*

PROVINCE SEN—(SEHN) *Province that is the kingdom's main trading hub and home of Imperial Palace (Cedar Palace)*

CASCASEA VILLAGE—(KASS-kah-SEE-ah) *Protagonist's hometown. A fishing village in Province Ca*

JAILONG VILLAGE—(JHAI-loong) *Village in Province Yupa*

SENLIN CITY—(SEHN-leen) *Imperial City*

◆　◆　◆

OTHER SHYAN TERMS

TIN-CHAI—(TIN-chhye) *A Shyan's magical ability*

KOONG—(KOHNG) *A Shyan born with no magic*

KIPA—(KEE-pah) *The formal dress of Shyan women*

WYIS—(WEES) *Spiritual energy*

DAI CHANNEL—(DYE) *Body channel. Magic through this channel controls physical elements.*

JI CHANNEL—(JEE) *Mind Channel. Magic through this channel controls telekinetic abilities.*

KAI CHANNEL—(KYE) *Heart Channel. Magic through this channel controls emotions, desire, and passion.*

HA CHANNEL—(HAA) *Soul Channel. Magic through this channel controls health, wellness, and healing.*

FAELA—(FAY-lah) *Term for a concubine of the emperor*

SIHAI—(SEE-HYE) *A sea creature with a sleek body and whiskers*

GUITLE—(GWAY-tul) *A sea creature with a hard, protective shell known to hide in the sand*

GODOG—(GOH-dawg) *A furry land creature that can be a faithful pet to its master*

MAOCAT—(MAOH-kat) *A land creature often kept as a pet, though more finicky and disobedient than a godog*

SHUROO—(SHOO-roo) *A forest creature with a bushy tail*

SHATOOTH—(SHAH-tooth) *A sharp-toothed fish that preys on weak and bleeding animals*

DOFEI—(DOH-FAY) *A playful sea creature with an arched body and fins*

SEAZHI—(SEE-JHI) *A slow-moving, poisonous sea creature with eight tentacles*

NAGEEL—(NAHG-ee-ul) *A snake-like creature. Produces electricity and a toxin that can tamper with one's wyis reading*

HUMOTH—(WHO-mawth) *A gray-bodied, two-winged insect*

GOLDFENG—(GOLD-fung) *A gold and black flying insect with a poisonous sting*

KAIGON—(KYE-gahn) *The emperor's icon. A heavenly creature with a slender, scaly body, four legs, and talon-like claws*

HONGNI—(HOONG-nee) *The empress's icon. A heavenly creature with colorful feathers and the appearance of a composite of birds*

ACKNOWLEDGEMENTS

As a shy, introverted girl growing up, I always had a dream of becoming a writer and sharing my stories with other people. Unfortunately, I was scared that I wasn't good enough. Insignificant. Why would anyone want to read anything I wrote?

Back in 2011, I dreamed of girls called trinkets who were locked in cages and used for their magical gifts. I wrote the first draft of Rilla's story in a month. I went on to revise it for nine years. Rilla's growth in discovering her voice paralleled my own journey of self-discovery. In developing Rilla's character and her voice, I was finally able to gain enough confidence to share my voice as well. But of course, this wouldn't have happened had I not had a number of people in my life who continued to encourage, challenge, and build me up.

First and foremost, I'm thankful to my parents, David and Lily Fong, for putting up with my wild imagination since I was a kid and for supporting me. Not only did you encourage my dreams, you taught me that dreams are nothing without action. I'm also inspired every day by my brother, Daniel. Watching your determination to grow and be better makes me want to be better.

I'm so grateful to have a close group of friends whom I've known since those awkward tween years of prepubescent acne and thick-rimmed nerdy glasses. A shout-out to Wing Ning Yung Taketa, Cindy Shao, Jean Tseng, and Judy

Liang for always loving and supporting me. A gigadruple portion of thank yous to Tiffany Wong, Esther Kim, and Christina Colorina for your encouragement and willingness to read my drafts. Spiffy Tiffy, your feedback is always so brutally honest but also encouraging, and I need every word of it. And Christina, I don't know if you remember, but you were the one who suggested that I go to a conference when I broke down crying after another rejection. Basically, you told me in a nice way to stop feeling sorry for myself and get back up. You've all been on this journey with me since the beginning, and I know you'll always have my back.

Sonya Stephens, I am so grateful to have met you. Thank you for giving me the boost of confidence I needed to pursue my dreams. You were the first person besides my mother to read and compliment my writing, and it meant everything to me.

Jordan Duncan, my travel buddy. Thanks for your support and encouragement.

I also owe a million times a million hearts of gratitude to my dear friend, Rie Takata, the amazing artist who helped draw the map of my fantasy world. I knew since we met in middle school that we'd make an unstoppable force.

Thanks to all the writer friends I've met along the way. I've learned so much from you, not only about writing, but about life. I don't believe in coincidences, and I know you were put in my life because I needed you at that moment.

Stephanie Braun, you were the first friendly face I saw at my first writers conference. I cherish your friendship and deep conversations.

To the person I call Summer Guy, I'm appreciative for the life experience and inspiration that helped me figure out Prince Carrick's character and provided some of Carrick's lines.

Melanie Hooks and Laura Perkins, the dynamic duo. To both of you, I'm so grateful you were there to welcome me at my first SCWC. The past self-deprecating me never expected you both—whom I deem high in the hierarchy—would have wanted to befriend me. Melanie, it still amazes me that you think I'm interesting. And Laura, you understood my voice from the start. You have helped me shape this story into something I can truly be proud of. Thank you both for your friendship. There's no one else I'd rather have coffee with while sharing real life dating horror stories in between fantasy horror stories.

I also hold so much gratitude and respect for Janis Thomas and Ara Grigorian. I have learned so much about storytelling from you, and your encouragement means the world to me. You've always believed in me more than I believed in myself. Thank you for treating me as an equal and a friend when I lacked the confidence to see myself as having that worth.

Marla Miller, thank you so much for being an amazing workshop leader. I was able to read my work out loud for the first time ever because of your encouragement and support.

Huge thanks to Holly Kammier and Jessica Therrien for taking a chance on me and Rilla's story.

Thank you to Molly Lewis, my editor. Because of you, this book has become better than it ever was.

To all the key figures at both the Santa Barbara Writers Conference and Southern California Writers Conference, you may not know me because I'm super shy, but you all have played such a huge part not only in my growth as a writer, but also in my growth as a person. These conferences changed my life. I have made so many friends and expanded my tight, introverted circle beyond anything I could have imagined. For brevity's sake, I can't name everyone who has had an impact on my writing and my personal growth, but know that if I interact with you on social media or say hi in the halls at conferences, I appreciate you. Being around other writers with similar struggles, I finally feel seen. And instead of trying to be the person I thought society expected me to be, I'm finally able to accept myself as I am.

ABOUT THE AUTHOR

After graduating from UC San Diego, Christina Fong built her career as a food scientist, but she never gave up on her true calling, writing poems and YA fantasy novels based in Asian American culture. She especially loves reading and writing about underestimated good girls who are pushed too far and must embrace their dark side to kick some butt. When Christina isn't writing, she's probably stuck in LA traffic, jamming out to her girl crush, Taylor Swift.